This Passing World

Journey From a Greek Prison

by

Don Cauble

Bloomington, IN Milton Keynes, UK

authorHOUSE

AuthorHouse™
1663 Liberty Drive, Suite 200
Bloomington, IN 47403
www.authorhouse.com
Phone: 1-800-839-8640

AuthorHouse™ UK Ltd.
500 Avebury Boulevard
Central Milton Keynes, MK9 2BE
www.authorhouse.co.uk
Phone: 08001974150

First published by AuthorHouse 8/7/2006

ISBN: 1-4259-2541-3 (sc)
ISBN: 1-4259-2542-1 (dj)

Library of Congress Control Number: 2006903133

Printed in the United States of America
Bloomington, Indiana

This book is printed on acid-free paper.

Also by Don Cauble

early morning death fragments
Inside Out
Three on Fire
I am the one who walks the road
*A selection of poems by Tom Kryss, Douglas Blazek & Don Cauble,
with poem-drawings by Linda Neufer*

Author's Note

THIS PASSING WORLD tells the story of a light being, much like you and me, who incarnates on this planet but soon gets tangled up in the web of lies and illusions and dust of this world. Through his own willful actions he finds himself in prison in a strange country. He must then undertake the transformative journey of remembering who he is (before he was born), the reasons for coming here, and the true source of his being. I began writing this story more than thirty years ago in Greece. THIS PASSING WORLD is my story. Is it fiction or a true story? Real or imagined? *All stories are fiction; even true ones.* Be you a traveler in some foreign country or a wanderer in your own back yard, this book is my gift to all those passing through this world, who long for the lights of home. I salute you. May you always be true to yourself. May you always be kind to one another.

Acknowledgments

Grateful acknowledgment is made for permission to print the following:

"A Few Years Later In Madrid" by Paula Atwell © Paula Atwell

"THE QUEST" by Douglas Blazek © by Douglas Blazek; "A snapshot of the fever" by Douglas Blazek © by Douglas Blazek; "Edible fire" by Douglas Blazek © by Douglas Blazek

"My Angels" by Audy Davison © Audy Davison; "Asha's Poems" by Audy Davison © Audy Davison

"To Think That None of These Things I Heard in Traveling Were True" by Tom Kryss © Tom Kryss; "What Is It They Think Might Dance Like The Sun" by Tom Kryss © Tom Kryss

Beyond Dreaming and the Stream of Time, Linda Neufer © Linda Neufer; **Transformation**, Linda Neufer © Linda Neufer

"Just Outside of Centerville" by Michael Earle Ruby © by Michael Ruby

Letter excerpts from Tom Kryss & Willie Bloomfield

"Everyday is a good day," first appeared in the Spring 2001 edition of **The MacGuffin**, edited by Arthur Lindenberg & published under the auspices of Schoolcraft College, Livonia, MI.

"A bone for the dogs," first appeared in **thee tight lung split roar hum**, Spring 2004, Slow Toe Publications, edited & published by Matthew Wasovich, Cleveland, OH. "Beyond walls", "On the work farm", "Chopping corn", & a singular version of "Aspirations of a poet" appeared in THEE FLAT BIKE #1, 2004, Slow Toe Publications, Matthew Wasovich, editor.

For Jessica, who showed me a dream
in the curl of the sea;
& for Poul and Thea, who befriended me.

Special thanks to:
Douglas Blazek, Tom Kryss, Linda Neufer, Audy Davison,
Tony Ogle, Polinski the Peanut Butter Witch,
Lo Caudle, Jim Caudle,
Arthur Lindenberg & Larry Setnosky, for their help &
encouragement;
Shanti & Michael Marshall, for listening, hour after hour;
Ramas, for his love & wisdom;
& to Jane, who loves both truth & mystery.

"Each of us live in both Light and Dark in our shared life.
Ancient spiritual teachers taught this Light in Self is the Light
of God.
But there is darkness also.
The darkness in everyone fears God because God is unknown,
uncontrollable and not material."
Harriet Douthitt,
Undoing the Darkness, Sincere in Portland, 1989
Teacher, friend, spiritual warrior
2/20/54—10/26/89

CONTENTS

THE TRIAL

AWAKENING FROM A DREAM

THIS PASSING WORLD

THE DAYS COME AND GO

FREE

"It is difficult to admit to admit your journeying ghost into this extensive personal cave of myth and lore.... In truth I am uneducated and uninnovative in most geographical matters, but, ah, hell, what, I suppose, does it matter. We go down through the years on a train and the years are like caves I once dreamed of, darker than dead candles, deeper than cold hell, lit there and there by small shivering fires. And you are riding shotgun on this strange conveyance shooting at rusty stalagmites that seem to move ominously in the shadows. And there are stations, isolated platforms sitting in drab yellow light, and refugees, children with faces covered by their mother's skirts, and you take the children on the continuing train, leaving the rest behind, speechless, almost motionless, certainly hopeless. End of dream."

> Tom Kryss, in a letter
> December 1972
> Cleveland, Ohio

∞

A rock is what we find.
We sit down on it
and it is not there.

Now the quest begins in earnest.

Douglas Blazek
"THE QUEST"

August 1972

Prologue

The wedding

A
single
flame
lights
the
universe.

A flock of wild canaries fluttered from the dry grasses into the air. Earlier, the man had watched dark clouds gather in the south, like a gathering of armies; but in the glow of the late afternoon sun, the dark forces had suddenly vanished, leaving an empty sky. In the tangle of golden grasses the man worked hurriedly with a sling blade to clear a circle in the meadow for tomorrow's wedding. He stopped for a moment and gazed across the meadow toward the August sun sinking below the tall fir trees. He watched a hawk soar across the sky. His heart felt light and happy. He thought of Angelina.

His Angelina. His very own Angel.

She had changed her name not long after they met. Actually, the man had given her this new name. And, once again, he mused how well the name suited her. Even his friend Anya, the astrologer, had told them their coming together was no accident or chance meeting but a true spiritual marriage. A marriage made in heaven? Indeed, he never doubted it. But he knew this long before Anya had looked into the mathematics of their astrological charts. He would celebrate his thirty-first birthday this coming November; and, for the first time in his life, David Pendarus did not feel as if he had one foot in the bedroom and one foot on the street. He felt secure in his love for Angelina. He felt at home with her soul's intentions. He felt free in the circle of her arms. Angelina, like an uncorrupted child, delighted in the stepping-stones of this world and it was not her nature to worship these stones or to carry them around in her pockets or to turn them into stumbling blocks. Heart's enthusiasm danced like streamers in her grayish blue eyes. Heart's playfulness nudged David's own heart's stubborn door. Her spirit boldly sang to his: **"Don't be so serious, come out and play!"**

"A shooting star" his friend Eden had once called her. Meaning here today and gone tomorrow. But Eden Maldek saw Angelina not through the daring new heart's awakening but through the mind's ancient protective veils. Her flower essence evaded him. Her vibrancy, her sudden appearance in David's world, the directness of her truth, her openness, all these left Eden feeling a little uneasy, a little mystified. What does this all mean? He wondered, as he watched the happy lovers walk out of the shadowy woods and make their way along the grassy bridal path. Does Pendarus really know what he's doing? Eden shook his head in amazement. A sudden breeze of fear touched his heart.

Holding hands the two lovers pass a small struggling garden and follow the thin ribbon path that David cleared through the tall grasses of the meadow. In the distance they hear their friend Michael O'Dell on his guitar, accompanied by a flute player, gently playing "Here Comes the Sun". They come to the altar with the flowers arranged to represent the seven centers of human consciousness; to the decanter of symbolic red wine and the cup they will share; to the small bamboo cage that's holding a pair of mated white doves; to the two rainbow candles that they will light separately and then merge with a white candle into a single flame. They kneel beside the altar and face their friends and guests who have gathered to witness this great coming together of purpose and dreams.

"Listen!
Today in Heaven the angels are singing!
Can you not hear their sweet song within your own souls?
Heaven rejoices for Angelina and I have chosen to love.
We have chosen to laugh and celebrate.
We have chosen to become husband and wife,
and yet to honor within each other the need for sovereignty.
We have chosen to be free.
Free to choose each moment this wondrous love.
Free to be together; free to dream this happy dream; our souls
two flames that merge in the vastness of all that we are,
to burn as a single shining light."

A jet plane flies low overhead, drowning out part of David's speech. He doesn't even notice the plane. Nor does Angelina. They bring the two rainbow candles together into a single flame. They share the cup of wine. She squeezes his hand tightly. Then she speaks.

"It isn't possible to speak a thought;
nor is it possible to speak a feeling.
But we can give a thought,
and the easiest way to do this is through love.
A friend of ours once lived in Nepal and she told us the people
greet each other with the word Namaste.
It is a greeting to the God within the other person.
A way of saying I recognize the God-ness within you
and I honor you.
I honor the place of light, the place of peace,
the place of truth within you.
May this marriage, however it may change,
however it may grow, whatever form it may delight in,

have forever as its purpose the highest expression of our selves,
the reflection to each other in all situations
the Godself in each of us.
David and I honor each other for who we are,
and, in so doing, we honor each of you and the whole universe.
Thank you for celebrating this moment with us.
Thank you for being who you are.
We love you!"

Giggling like children, David and Angelina release the two white doves. Immediately the birds take flight and vanish into the tall fir trees. Then comes the feasting. Everyone shares in the preparations. The moment glows with happiness.

Quickly, David and Angelina disappear from the others.

They go to find a hidden place in the tall meadow grasses, to celebrate in another way, this day, this love.

THE PROUD SOUL

"Before I visited Greece nature was to me something apart. Only here have I understood the meaning of nature. Perhaps because not until I saw Greece did I come to a full realization of what I am. Now I feel both less and more than I thought myself to be. Less in the sense of personality, more in the sense of manhood. Here all conflicts are resolved in a fusion between spirit and nature. It is the great truce one has to make in order to achieve individuation. I would urge no one to come to Greece unless he is prepared to meet himself face to face."

> Henry Miller, in a letter to Anaïs Nin
> Delphi, 21 December 1939
> *Henry Miller Letters to Anaïs Nin*
> Edited by Gunther Stuhlmann
> G. P. Putnam's Sons, Boston, 1965

Everyday is a good day

Last night, Christ, what a mess! I was on my way to pick up a bottle of retsina at Artemis' restaurant, on the main street of Monemvasia, just around the corner from the old sea captain's house, when a wild gust of wind nearly blew me off the sidewalk right into the street. It was all I could do to stand up. Once inside the restaurant I was immediately stopped by a bunch of Greeks. They offered me a glass of retsina and some delicious fried sausages seasoned with fresh squeezed lemon juice. More wine. One man spoke a little English. Another gustily repeated in French *"Comme si, comme sa!"* His friend beside him shouted *"O-kay!"* with a big warm earthy grin.

There was an old fellow sitting at the table. At first I didn't recognize him. Then I realized that he was Tassos' father. (We had helped Tassos and his family pick olives a few weeks ago, on the old man's farm, way up in the hills. Angelina and I often spend our days in Tassos' cafe, playing cards with Tassos and sipping cognac and learning the Greek language.) There was one woman at the table. They were all joking with old Popadakis about him going to California, dancing and loving it up with young girls. The old man grinned toothlessly and pulled a pint bottle from his coat. The Greek next to him turned to me and whispered, "Whiskee!"

Artemis appeared from the kitchen, bringing with him a huge raw cabbage. The men quickly sliced up the cabbage and squeezed a lemon over it. By this time I was beginning to feel the wine and getting a little nervous about Angelina, wishing that she were here to join us. "I'll be back in a sec," I had told her, as I stepped out the door.

Artemis returned to our table, this time bringing six large grilled steaks on serving platters. The big Greek who liked to shout *"O-kay!"* took a knife and sliced the savory steaks into small pieces. He squeezed a lemon generously over the meat. We each took a fork and another glass of wine.

I finally broke away from the celebration and headed home with my bottle of retsina. Oh, Jesus, did Angie look pissed.

Immediately I tried to explain but she wouldn't wait. "He tried to grab my boobs!" she blurted out.

"Huh?" What's she talking about?

"The sea captain," she said and her eyes flashed with anger.

"Oh, come on, Angel! You gotta be kidding. Why, he's seventy years old if he's a day!"

But NO. Angelina broke into tears as she described precisely what happened. Before I left the house to buy retsina our land lady and wife of the retired sea captain had asked to use the petro stove in the upstairs kitchen to cook spanakopita. The sea captain and his wife rent us the upper flat of their house for fifty dollars a month. They live downstairs in a smaller apartment. At nights our Divine Mother (as we call the sea captain's wife) sleeps in a tiny passage room between our bedroom and a tile roofed veranda that connects to the kitchen. And she knows how much we like her spanakopita. Traditionally, the Greeks make this dish with spinach and feta cheese encrusted between two layers of pita bread and baked in a large pizza-type pan. Instead of spinach, however, our Divine Mother goes into the fields around Monemvasia and gathers certain wild growing plants for her greens.

So the sea captain brought up a plate of his wife's spanakopita. Then the old fart tried to get cute with Angie. Christ, he's wheezing every time he climbs the dozen or so steps to our tiny kitchen. He crouches down to show us how to light the little kerosene heater and needs a lift crane just to straighten up again. Maybe I should go down and whack him over the head with my retsina? Nah, better to give Angie a big hug.

"Everyday is a good day in Monemvasia!"

That's how one little Greek widow who's always dressed in black greets us whenever we pass each other on the street. But we haven't seen her for days. I wonder where she could be now?

We're watching Tassos play a popular dice game. The December sun warms my back through the cafe windows and I'm dreaming of birds flying South. Already it's snowing in Istanbul. Down by the docks three men are making repairs on a fishing boat. Tassos sends them each a glass of cognac. He gives me a free drink for making the delivery.

Winter has come for sure. Yesterday, Tassos hauled his big old clunky oil heater out of the closet. As soon as we saw smoke pouring into the morning sky Angelina and I abandoned our blankets and Henry Miller's *Tropic of Cancer* and our tiny, not-so-warm kitchen and headed for the cafe. Tassos sees us and quickly fills three glasses with cognac. He dips his hands into a large U. S. CARE gunny sack that's filled with raw peanuts and spreads a double handful on top the hot stove. I've mentioned our little kerosene heater already, but we were low on fuel and saving it for the evening. A liter of kerosene costs five drachmas and lasts maybe two days. A drachma is worth about three U. S. cents. Not much money, true. But we want to stretch our savings in order to stay in Greece as long as possible. We had not expected to pay so much for rent. Fifty dollars a month seems quite a bit, even though our Divine Mother does include the laundry—a chore she does every week. (A good deal, I suppose, since there is no public laundry in Monemvasia.) A liter of the town's best retsina costs only eight drachmas. We actually found some retsina we don't mind drinking. Actually, we've simply forgotten how good wine tastes. Actually, we're desperate.

It's nearly noon and four Canadians are in town. They've just rented a house for the holidays with the help of our friend the Old Prospector. Years ago he went looking for gold in California. "Three years," he tells us. Then he moved to Canada and bought a farm. Later, he lived in West Palm Beach, Florida.

I ask him if he ever found any gold.

"Hell," he says, laughing, "I don't even know what gold looks like!"

The Old Prospector shows us a Greek Orthodox newspaper that comes to him through the mail. He claims he has no use for the priest and his long beard. "I'll pay a lawyer to get me into Paradise!" he scowls.

We ask him about caves near Monemvasia.

"Greece is full of caves," he tells us. "Not far from Monemvasia are some of the best limestone caves in southern Europe."

The Old Prospector chuckles.

"Hell, if we have a war we'll just hide in the caves!"

It's the day before Christmas. I slip out of the house early to find Angelina "a little something, I know not what." Ah, I'll surprise her with decorations for our tree. The only "real" Christmas tree in Monemvasia. But then Monemvasia doesn't have any trees to speak of. A few small pines. Some fig and olive trees, of course; and a small grove of orange and lemon trees that belong to George's father. The lemons you can eat right off the tree they taste so sweet and the oranges are as big as large grapefruits and the best I've ever eaten. George lives in Australia but he's back in Greece to find himself a wife. His father owns a little grocery store in Monemvasia, and every time Angie and I go in the store his eyes light up and he immediately pours us each a glass of cognac. Then there's a grove of tall cypresses at the far end of town. So the people of Monemvasia use make-believe plastic trees for Christmas.

Yesterday we stole our tree from a small cluster of scrubby pines near the cemetery. We bought two strings of blue and red "worry beads," unstrung the beads and hung them like balls on the branches.

Worry beads.... You see wrinkles on the little women. But the little men, the men in business suits, the farmers and fishermen, the butcher, the baker, all carry their worry beads and they're playing with these beads continually, swinging them absentmindedly around their hands, counting them with their fingers. The beads are strung on leather, long enough for the wrist but sometimes longer, and as fancy as you please. Big as golf balls, too, some of them. For tourists of the absurd I suppose. Sisyphus and his giant worry bead....

Angelina has been after a string of these beads ever since we came to Greece. I keep telling her she'll worry ME to death, playing with those blasted things.

I assume it must be morning. For the first time ever I notice that the ceiling over our bed looks crooked. The whole damn room looks crooked. Or is it my eyes? "No," Angie assures me. The room really is crooked. It feels funny to be walking. Angie won't even budge from the bed. The door to the kitchen is ajar and on the table I see a strange cat, sniffing the plate of holiday cookies left for us by our Divine Mother. I yell at the cat. The cat scrambles out the kitchen and down the cement steps. These damn kerosene fumes! Oh, God, the little sea captain shuffles up the steps and he's trying to tell me when Christmas dinner will be served. I smile and agree several times. *"Endoxi, endoxi!"* But I don't understand what he's saying. Maybe Angelina can translate. If I can just get this coffee going....

How do we explain to our Divine Mother that we're hung over? Believe me, there's NOTHING you can hide from her. Accidentally break one of her dishes (as I did two days ago) and that's the very morning, before I can finish my breakfast and hide the broken pieces, that she sends up the captain to empty the garbage sack. I plug in the little hot plate that we bought when we first arrived in Monemvasia, which our Divine Mother frowns upon because of the high cost of electricity, and damn if I don't hear her footsteps on the veranda. Naturally I'm in a panic, shoving the hot plate back into the cabinet and burning hell out of my fingers. It's uncanny, I tell you.

"Who paid for the meal?"

"The Frenchman," says Angelina.

Actually, Chrysanthos is just half French. His father was French but his mother Greek. We met him for the first time last night. He and his German friend Bubu came over and asked if they could join us for dinner. We were sitting at their favorite table, next to the warm wood stove. Bubu's been living in Monemvasia for three months now. Later, we talked to a man "saturated with hatred for the Americano." One of the Canadians. The one who told us seventy million people travel through Spain in a single summer. "You go for days and never see a Spaniard!" he says. The Canadian belongs to the Socialist Party and wants to save the world. One of his companions, in a proud boast, tells us: "The fellow at the hotel bar couldn't believe a WHOLE bottle of cognac! We Canadians can drink!" But he's barely able to stand. He's all gushy and homesick (he's only nineteen) and Angie gives him a warm sisterly hug. It's way past midnight but Artemis doesn't seem to mind. He dozes off in a chair beside our table. He brings us more wine. The next thing I remember the world is spinning madly at the top of the stairs to the restroom. I'm sitting on the top step, trying to get my balance. Artemis is pouring hot coffee into me. Hot instant coffee, I might add. In Monemvasia you can get either Greek coffee in the tiny cups or the instant stuff imported from France, and the instant stuff they'll serve cold if you don't remember to say hot. That's why, the last trip to Athens, we bought a little Italian coffee maker and some dark roast ground beans.

"Artemis was really concerned about you," Angie tells me.

Probably about her too. I remember her getting sick down by the harbor on the way home and joking about feeding the fish. Then I remember quiet-as-a-mouse stumbling to our bed past the sleeping room of our Divine Mother.

Oh, Lord, I think I'm dying this very moment.

But today is not so cold. If I can just swallow this cup of coffee....

A single entrance

A woman
made an ethereal motion, as if she were buttoning her
    dress
with the voice of a bird. And it astonished me
that I entered so easily into my own voice. Higher up
a single dark green leaf dominates the landscape,
and my heart fits into the world as easily
as my key fits into the door of my house. I shall
open—

> Yannis Ritsos
> —from "Inwards or Outwards?"
> Rae Dalven, translator
> *The Fourth Dimension, Selected Poems of Yannis Ritsos,*
> David R. Godine, Boston, 1977

Monemvasia means "single entrance." A single entrance to the ancient town on the rock. Actually you have two towns: Yephra, or "Bridge," an unpretentious little fishing village on the southeastern tip of the Peloponnesus, and the ancient town of Monemvasia. Angelina and I live in Yephra, which is connected to the ancient town by a slender, paved causeway. Even the old town goes by another name—the Kastro, or upper fortress—called the "fortress of the clouds" by the invading Turks who sailed their ships into this harbor centuries ago, when there were thousands of Greek families living on the rock and this region was famous for its wine. The Greeks still hold Easter services each year in the eighth century Byzantine Church of Aghia Sophia. But the proud fortress—the "Gibraltar of Greece" as Nikos Kazantzakis called Monemvasia—is mostly rock and scrub and decaying remnants of a medieval acropolis: a graveyard that glitters in the morning sun and howls in the night whenever a strong wind blows in a storm off the sea.

9

Yannis Ritsos, one of Greece's best loved poets, was born in Monemvasia in 1909. He was arrested by the junta 21 April 1967 and sent to the prison yard at Yarios. They banned all his books.

Below, protected by an ancient fortress wall, lies the town of Monemvasia. Only a handful of Greeks live in the town today. There's a hotel. The one Bubu lives in. Most of the time he's the only occupant. There's a popular restaurant owned and operated by a widow named Matula. Matula, as everyone knows, once had her culinary skills highly praised in a book on Monemvasia by a British writer. Matula always dresses in black. She makes her own pasta noodles from scratch. Each day at the back of her restaurant she feeds scraps of food to the starving cats that overrun the alleyways of Monemvasia. These cats, left to fend for themselves by homeowners who come to stay only in summertime or during religious holidays, are the scruffiest, scroungiest, most paranoid creatures I've ever seen. As Bubu succinctly puts it, these cats are "too nervous." And it's no wonder. One warm afternoon we're eating lunch at an outside table. We watch Panayotis, a Greek fisherman, twist pieces of his paper napkin into tight wads and sop up the olive oil left on his plate from a meal of fried fish. As a joke, he tosses the oily pieces to the cats. So hungry are these poor creatures that they grab and devour these bits of paper and fight each other viciously for the least scrap.

There's a taverna of course.

Every night but Sunday you can find the old Greek who owns the taverna sitting in the same wooden chair and the only time he moves is to get you a glass of ouzo or a glass for himself. He wears the same dark rumpled suit without a tie. His hearing is not so keen anymore and his creased, timeworn face looks as if it, too, like an ancient olive tree, grew out of the sparse and impoverished earth of the southern Peloponnesus. You never see his wife, though they tell us he does have a wife. He sings aloud to himself in the night. You can hear him as you pass by on the street.

Monemvasia has no automobiles. Cars can not physically pass through the narrow stone gateway. And no electric lights. Each evening the woman who owns and runs the hotel will light a few kerosene lanterns placed along the thin cobblestone streets.

On the main street near Matula's restaurant there's a tiny library. Inside the library there's a sign posted saying that it's forbidden to take the books. (I'm not sure what that means. We only saw the library open once.)

You can find forty-odd churches and shrines in Monemvasia. Or so they say. I know that every which way Angelina and I turn we find a candle and a holy picture. Some of the churches and shrines still have original frescoes and icons. Each Sunday the people of Yephra walk over to the old town and hold services in a large, lovely, whitewashed church that has a dome and traditional red tile roof and an enclosed courtyard. A bell hangs from a big tree growing in the yard.

An architect's delight, the ruins in the lower town are being reconstructed into expensive summer homes and holiday retreats. Reconstruction is strictly controlled by the Greek National Architectural Society in Athens, to preserve the integrity and authenticity of the original architecture. A French baron owns one of these houses. So does an industrialist from Boston. A retired German architect and his wife live here. And, each Christmas, an American-Greek professor of anthropology at Princeton University returns with his mother to their house. They tell us of an earlier time, a joyful time in the '50s, when you could find dancing and singing at night in the tavernas and streets of Monemvasia.

The proud soul

We open our eyes and awaken from a dream. In Athens and on the roads through out this ancient and harsh and lovely land we see signs of a new myth: the military junta. Even on the mountain sides with whitewashed rocks: 21 APRIL 1967. (Like a dog that leaves his mark I'm thinking.) In the cafes and on the walls of the tavernas now hangs an image of a new idol, a little higher than Jesus Christ and just above the exiled King and Queen. Around his sinister-looking face with its thin, sharply arched eyebrows and balding head they've painted a soft pastel aura. Last night, in Tassos' café, we saw him on TV. A snake in a dark tailored suit, flanked by olive green puff toads and Father Orthodox with his cross and long beard, Popodauphlis was on Crete, speaking to a huge open-air crowd. The people cheered. They clapped. They waved their arms in the air. "It's enough to gag a maggot," as my mother-in-law would say.

Crete, ancient and joyous land of the Minoans, island birthplace of the supreme god Zeus, I call out to you from my heart's love of freedom. Have you forgotten so soon your proud and heroic Kazantzakis and the words he wrote and witnessed to? "No power in heaven and earth is so great as the human soul." Will you cheer these filthy Colonels that mock the greatness of your Grecian soul, even as this luminous spirit—your beloved son Kazantzakis—cries out to you from the earth you trod upon, and whispers to you through the sea winds you breathe, and sings your praises through the beloved almond tree that each spring delights your senses in a dazzling white resurrection?

∞

I hear children singing Christmas carols outside in the street. They knock on our kitchen door but I don't answer. Why not? I ask myself. How could their glad tidings interrupt this scribbling of words about a petty tyrant who would be king? What am I afraid of losing? Perhaps those proud, jeweled images that would dazzle us like pearls in dreams of half-remembered worlds?

Well, Chrysanthos is not dazzling us.

Chrysanthos is drunk and his songs are forbidden songs of Theodrakis. At another table sits the harbor master of Monemvasia, looking as handsome and affable as Randolph Scott in his early cavalry movies. Labés, sitting at our table, belongs to the home guard. (The Secret Police as Bubu calls them.) Labés and Chrysanthos are best friends. Labés and the harbor master must look the other way or be forced to act against Chrysanthos.

Chrysanthos hurls a dinner plate crashing to the floor. Then another one. And another one. Rachael and I dodge for cover as food and shattered plates go flying past us. In a panic we grab the unbroken dishes as fast as we can. (It's forbidden by law to break plates. Popodauphlis thinks breaking plates a barbaric custom and uneconomical.)

Without a word Artemis calmly walks out of the kitchen, gathers the plates and disappears. Labés explodes in anger and abruptly leaves our table. He goes to sit alone with his back to us but in a moment he returns, shouting at his friend. Chrysanthos ignores him and continues to sing. Rachael moves down the table toward Chrysanthos. She's crying with her head against his shoulder. But Chrysanthos won't stop singing. Now Bubu is beside him. And beside himself with anxiety.

Bubu first came to Greece at the beginning of summer. He stopped in a taverna one night and took his guitar in with him. He played a few songs and drank more than a little retsina. As his affections for the Greek people warmed with the wine and the hot summer night he played some banned political songs of Theodrakis. Bubu had his back to the door and didn't see the police come in. The police threw him in jail for three days and smashed his guitar to pieces.

Damn lucky his head wasn't too.

His real name is Burmeister. (Bubu is a childhood nickname that translates into Latin as "Big Owl.") Before coming to

Greece he worked in Bonn as a private secretary to one of the German political ministers. Besides German, Bubu speaks French. He graduated from the Sorbonne with a degree in Law and married a French woman. A doctor, I believe he said. They were married for five years. He also speaks English, Russian and a little Greek. With Chrysanthos he speaks French. Chrysanthos calls himself a communist but he's really a socialist Bubu tells us. And he's the only mechanic in town.

A few weeks ago the automobile that Chrysanthos had been driving for years finally quit and gave up the ghost. Chrysanthos took off for Athens with three thousand drachmas (or some such amount) and the intention of buying himself another car. Bubu went to Athens with him. It seems that Chrysanthos enjoys singing and drinking in the cafes and tavernas so much, and he's such a generous soul with his money, that, before long, he had spent the whole three thousand drachmas.

Chrysanthos returned home empty-handed and his wife got so angry she wouldn't speak to him. So Chrysanthos went to work on his dead car. Soon he had the car up and running again. Now he drives everywhere in the old green clunker. And often, I might add, in the middle of the road.

Bubu lives in the hotel in the Kastro. In fact, he's the only person living in the hotel. He likes to swim and in warm weather he explores the Aegean Sea with a fin and snorkel, looking for treasures and sunken cities. He's about my own age. He has blond hair and blue eyes, a broad forehead (a sign of superior intellect I'm sure he'd say) and a receding hairline. I have a thin body, longish hair (blond hair that's turned dark over the years), and a full, dark beard. Bubu is clean shaven and much sturdier built than me, but not as tall. Most of the time he runs around in just a flannel shirt and a leather, fleece-lined vest. When he first came to Greece he camped out in the hills and took baths in cold mountain streams. In fact, the shower in his hotel has only cold water. I mean really cold. From deep underground. Sometimes Angie and I sneak into the hotel to use the shower. We dash into the water, howling all the time. Then we step back and soap up. Then dash back in to rinse off. It's a little easier to enjoy the shower they've rigged up on the outside of the fortress wall, facing the sea. The small pipe runs straight out of boulder sized rocks, so the water must be coming from deep within the earth. It's certainly cold; but you can jump in and out and there's sunshine and the sea all around you. It's a lovely place to sunbathe on the large rocks, with the waves lapping right beside you.

Bubu really loves the sea. A true Pisces. But when he goes exploring, looking for treasures and sunken cities, always he's closely watched.

"We don't talk about this government!" whispers an old timer, a Greek we met in a cafe in Sparta, who once lived in Chicago. He zips his thumb and forefinger dramatically across tightened lips. "Too many ears!"

Bubu has a Greek friend, Maria. Maria's an archaeologist. Often she guides Bubu to caves and ruins not mentioned in the books. On one trip they visited some old graves not officially opened. The next day the Monemvasia police summoned Bubu to the station to answer some questions. They searched his VW and hotel room for relics.

To earn money Bubu writes free-lance articles about his travels in Greece and sends them back to a German newspaper. (More tourists come to Greece from Germany than from any other country.) Bubu remembers events with rich and precise detail and crafts his stories with both drama and humor. He's convinced, he tells us, and with reason, too, that the Greek police have opened and examined his mail.

The harbor master has quietly vanished.

As if on cue, suddenly everyone at our table is leaving. There were ten of us altogether. Who's going to pay the bill? I'm wondering. We must have ordered the whole restaurant. Platters of roasted young lamb and pork and sautéed livers. Sausages, feta cheese. Tomato salads and black olives and never-ending baskets of bread and fried potatoes and kilo after kilo of retsina.

Angelina and I step out into the night air. Rachael comes rushing past us in the dark. She's weeping hysterically and running towards the harbor. We dash in pursuit. We catch up with her down by the docks and Angie wraps her in her arms. When Bubu sees what's happening he abandons Chrysanthos to his car and rushes over to comfort Rachael. Rachael seems caught up in her own personal drama. Perhaps it's too much wine mixed with the events of the night. Or perhaps her romanticism of Greece. Perhaps Bubu has something to do with it.

She and Bubu met only a few days ago. But there exists a certain vibrancy in this place. An energy that creates a sense of immediacy, and even urgency, between people. A feeling of instant relationship as if we'd known each other a long time ago and suddenly we've found each other again. It's difficult to explain. Perhaps it's only us and this time. And when we go this too shall pass. Perhaps there's so much sky and sea that we've allowed ourselves a new kind of openness, a new kind of freedom. It's certainly different from the intense city energy that I felt in Paris. And different from London and Rome. Though I really liked Rome. Especially in the early mornings. But Monemvasia feels different from any other place in our travels. I can feel a special aliveness in the energy here. Even when I'm simply just sitting on a rock and enjoying the sun and the sea.

One day, not long after we first arrived in Monemvasia, Angelina and I walked to the far side of the old town past the fortress wall and followed a simple goat path around the curve of the Rock. It was a beautiful day, light and sunny and warm. Out on the sea in the distance we could barely discern two tiny fishing boats. A few birds floated high above the blue water. We found a clean, soft spot of grass, hidden by large grayish colored rocks. We took off our clothes and embraced each other. The sun beamed down on us as if the light were entering our very cells into the secret loving thoughts of our arms and our entwined almost motionless bodies. For a moment Angelina became Gaea in all her magnificence and all her sacred, sentient forms and the blue infinite sky and sea around us and the yellow flowers dancing in the scented air. And I, with the vastness of skies far beyond this single planetary dome and with the might of the creator sun and the memory of other star systems streaming through me like glimpses of crystalline ships, I tenderly surrounded her womanness from above and below and entered the darkness and the light in her body like a god come home, proud and radiant with spirit's unfathomable love.

Rachael comes from Boston or maybe Philadelphia. She's a graduate student in architecture at a university in Athens and she's only visiting Monemvasia for the holidays. A thoughtful, caring woman. Nice looking too. Long reddish hair. Tall, slim body with soft, full breasts. A warm flashing smile. A quick sense of humor. She's a sweetheart for sure. A high-spirited romantic. But she says to me, "You can't be a romantic in America!" Later, Rachael will share with me Gabriel Garcia Marquez's book *One Hundred Years of Solitude*. She loaned me this amazing book when Angelina and I went to Athens for a short visit. We stayed a couple of nights in her apartment, sleeping on the floor in our sleeping bags. She loved this book *One Hundred Years of Solitude* but to finish the book I had to take it with me. I never saw Rachael again. I mention this to suggest, if only in a small way, how Rachael gives from the heart. And Bubu hits on her pretty hard with his exaggerated ego and his heartless references to the past. His father was a bigwig in the Nazi Party during the War. Rachael, of course, is Jewish.

Meanwhile, I'm still concerned about the bill.

"How can you be thinking of money at a time like this?" Angelina demands to know. "The Greeks don't worry over such matters!"

She stalks away in anger.

And I walk home with the nervous steps of a fool.

Bottoms up!

Now, it's barely light outside. I'm in the kitchen with a warm blanket wrapped around me. Our little kerosene heater helps but not much. I woke up early and couldn't get back to sleep. I kept thinking of how every culture has created a myth to explain the origin of the world. The Greeks certainly had their turn at it. The Hindus, the Egyptians, the Chaldeans. The Semitic tribes, the Mayans, the Toltecs. None that I knew, however, satisfied me. The teller of the tale could explain the elephant holding up the world but could never explain the tortoise holding up the elephant. None could explain Before the beginning. Like the scientific Big Bang, they all began and ended in a lot of noise. The Great Cosmic Mother, the Father Warrior Creator: both cosmologies had failed us. Now the time had come to heal this fracture and move on. Time for a new vision, a new language. A language that once more would capture the essence, the heartbeat, the mystery. A process that we could participate in, that would bring balance and wholeness into our lives, and not a creation of distance and control and domination. But who am I to tell the tale of how the world came into being? I come from a cultural tradition that's mostly interested in the origin of money and power and how to keep score with it—not in the origin of self. If the "self" exists. Perhaps the self, too, is just another myth. Just our values at the moment; just our fluid, ever-changing—or rigid—beliefs; our likes and dislikes that come and go like buddhas on the cosmic sea. Somewhat like scientific truths. Science shackles itself to the edge of this planetary ship with self-measuring lines of timid consistency, afraid of falling over the edge. Most of the time anyway. And am I not like this myself? Longing to know the truth but sticking like a barnacle to the familiar and comfortable and to what I can see and hear and smell? Lazy as a summer day I am. Narcissistic as a full moon. Pompous, arrogant, full of pride. Ready at the drop of a hat to defend the rightness of my beliefs, the back of my neck bristling like a junk yard dog. As a lovely friend of mine (and a spiritual healer/teacher) once said to me, in a fit of laughter and exasperation: "David, you're the most prideful motherfucker I've ever known!" And I've been known to betray myself in a moment for something greater, someone more perfect, more intelligent, more beautiful, more anything, than I am. All these grand flaws I admit to. So who am I to receive this vision? This new language? Again I ask the darkness. But Spirit will not be put off. The answer comes quickly. Who am I *not* to respond to this vision? Who am *I* to deny the calling of Spirit? The words and images keep coming like sparks suddenly released from a burning log. They persist like the hum of a jews'-harp in a master's hand. But, before I share with you my masterpiece, let me share with you another shiny pearl from the necklace of my lovely friend and spiritual healer—a necklace that you can bet charmed me, even disarmed me, so that she could work her healing energy through my thick skin down into the marrow of my bones. This one I even put on a sign and taped to my small oak desk.

DO WHAT SCARES YOU THE MOST.

Something Henry David Thoreau had once said to her I believe.

Being honest with myself and others scared me the most. To express my innermost feelings, without the distance of philosophy as a buffer, terrified me. You might think that truthfulness would be a burning ambition for a poet. Or at least my best intention. But truth can live behind so many veils and in so many hidden places. There are many doors to the truth within us but the digging shovel or the battering ram will not open these doors. I have learned that most often the very doors that look and feel like devouring monsters, that once opened, these doors reveal the most exquisite and gentle truths about ourselves. Whereas the doors that seem to offer us the greatest escape, these doors contain the very monsters that we fearfully and continually seek to avoid. Life is strange that way. You have to desire truth with your whole heart. Then you must court truth as a lover. With vulnerability and honor. With fearlessness and purity and quietness. With a tight-rope balance of boldness and sensitivity. With deep trust and intimacy and commitment and hard work and perseverance. And certainly not with hands like dissecting shears. Or with a heart sticky and possessive as flypaper. Or with a mind like a steel trap. Or a mind like my own that yakky yaks all the time. Especially when it's cold out there and I'm in a warm bed and putting off the inevitable. Angelina stirs and smiles in her dreams. She sleeps in the nude. I sneak my head beneath the covers to kiss her a few lingering times. She moans softly. Half-awake now she cradles my head to her heart. Ah, such womanness, such playfulness. I want to stay longer. I want to enter her. As if to find the origin of the world in the solid fact of her body. But the urgent call of Spirit will not abate. I slip from our warm bed and the circle of Angelina's arms. I tiptoe past our Divine Mother and into the kitchen. I make a cup of coffee and sit down at the kitchen table. I start to write. Images flicker alive in my hands like tiny candles. They seem to have a life of their own.

Suddenly I stop.

I hear the muffled voices of some fishermen passing by outside beneath my kitchen window. Then quietness. I hear the Aegean Sea. Always I hear the sea! Like an ancient lullaby at times. At times like an angry tyrant. At times like a lover knowing my innermost thoughts. And at times like a good friend, steadfast and true.

Speaking of good friends, Eden Maldek should be here. Eden likes a good story and tells even a better one, if you know what I mean. Like Bubu, he enhances the details with a keen sense of drama and emotional exuberance. He lies a little too, I suppose. Anything to give the tale more power. Eden looks so serious and intense and philosophical most of the time. Like a man with a great mission to accomplish. Like Moses in the Old Testament. Or a fourteenth century alchemist, dabbling in the Secret Arts. And he's secretive, like a pirate. Eden has this great curiosity and fascination with the dark energies. He likes to live in the shadows, to observe and to draw power from the darkness. Living on the edge this way seems to give him the illusion that he's able to go beyond his own limitations. He thinks that he can draw specialness from the darkness, and in this way he can create an image that's larger than life, in the same way that you can make huge frightening shadows on the walls with your hands and fingers. This allows him to maintain a certain aloofness and a feeling of invulnerability. Even his physical appearance supports this larger than life image—his long dark hair, sometimes wound in a single braid behind his back; his barrel chest; the intense, almost Mongolian look in his eyes; the coiled energy around his body. For a moment I saw him the other day down by the harbor. He came ashore from the passenger boat that stops by once a week from Athens. I'm seeing things of course. How could Eden Maldek be in Monemvasia? But for that brief moment, I swear....

Then, early the next morning, up came the sea captain and he had "Eden" with him. Jesus, he even talked like Eden. A slow, soft voice with strength, like the voice of movie actor Burt Lancaster. But this Greek "Eden" is a university student home for the holidays. His mother lives here. He seemed a bit bewildered, or amused, maybe even mystified, by the whole situation. And how like Eden!

The captain warned me the sea was dangerous that day. He said that I shouldn't venture out. The day before, Angie and I had gone with Bubu and Labés to a little village up the coast. Bubu has a friend back in Germany who keeps a sailing yacht moored for winter in the harbor of this village. Bubu wanted to make sure everything on the boat was in good order. He hired Labés and his fishing boat to take him to the village and asked us to go along. Bubu wanted to show us the ruins of a Mycenaean temple in the hills overlooking the sea near the village, and the nearby ruins of an ancient wall and doorway that had been built long before human beings understood the concept of an arch. But to go out that morning never entered my mind. And why of all people should the captain have chosen "Eden" as our interpreter? I'm sure he had a perfectly natural reason. And yet—and yet—.

Bottoms up! It's a mystery to me!

How the world came into being

Once there were three Divine beings. One called Man, one Called Woman, and the other called Child. Man went out to put on airs. First he built a fire. He forged an arrow to penetrate the mysteries of time and overcome space. He analyzed a tree and invented the wheel. Man traveled in grand circles and wrote a book on *Chance & Circumstance* and called his designs to control the world "The Great Purpose." (Man feared death, he feared to be alone; but most of all Man feared the unknown.) He imagined his destiny among the stars and played very serious games with names that Child could never remember and which bored Woman to tears. Man suffered with great pride and would not give up his arrogant ways.

Soon, Woman grew weary of breathing dust and stirring the coals. After all, Woman could envision a totally different world. A world of feelings and relationships and ever-changing forms and colors. The color red she envisioned for the awakening of desire and green to herald the Earth and the coming of Child. Yellow she gave to the intense summer sun and to the flowers that loved her gladness, and blue she gave to the sea and to the reflection in Man's eyes whenever he looked upon the world without lust or impatience or greed for power. (To edge Man onward she called her vision of a new consciousness NO MORE WAR.) Woman needed orange for balance and for the autumn leaves that delighted Child when they fell from the trees and whirled about upon the garden path; and pink she created so the mind would not freeze in abstractions. Purple she placed on the inner rim of the rainbow, in the amethyst she wore over her heart, and in the bedroom curtains near the fireplace. (Woman was never quite sure of purple.) Then, without batting an eye, Woman appeared in radiant white.

This mystified Child, who stared in wonder.

Child longed to be like Man in all his marvelous adventures, but Man would not speak of the great mysteries, but only repeat what he had been told with great authority. Child turned to Woman for comfort but Woman looked too busy putting spring flowers in her hair and wishing Man would come to his senses.

Child felt utterly alone.

"I will not play these games!" cried Child. "I will not memorize names and ancient causes and I will not be deceived by appearances."

Child vowed this intention with such clarity and with such boldness that, like a dream that awakens the dreamer, or like a bird of pure light, the desire within Child's heart instantly cut through Man's circular reasoning and startled Woman from her enchanting arts.

Deep within consciousness a leaf trembled.

The wheel burst into flame and the flame into a human heart.

This is how Man and Woman saw each other for the first time.

And this is how the world came into being.

Everyone you meet is your mirror

We see the old man near the fire. He speaks to us in a wheezing voice and smiles with only one tooth. He wants to buy us wine and wakes the cook with a clanging coin on the table. The cook, Artemis' wife, looks as big as all Greece and twice as lazy but she's the best cook in town. (And a real fox Bubu tells us.) The old man walks with a wooden cane and a bowed leg. He has one tooth and a tiny squared mustache and a flat brim hat which he wears indoors or out. Over his tie-pin shirt he wears a sweater and a coat and then an overcoat, even by the fire. He sits alone in the restaurant each night, nursing his red wine, always with a slice of apple in his glass. He's sixty-five and his wife—he points upward with his index finger—his wife is in Heaven. We soon find out he's the father of Labés. The old man drinks wine, laughs and falls asleep, he tells us; and he tells us—with a dramatic gesture of his hands—that he doesn't break dishes on the floor! The old man orders more wine. He insists on paying. Today is festival day. The first day of a new year. Perhaps he thinks I'm strange, scribbling these words down on a scrap of paper. But no stranger than he, surely. We're all on God's stage and only the devil has cold feet.

Panayotis, "the big-nosed fisherman," (as the book on Monemvasia described him; the same book that praised Matula's culinary skills), orders us all veal and side dishes of black olives and potatoes and more wine. Labés joins us at our table. Papa sits alone tonight, nursing his glass of wine and slice of apple. At another table a group of men drink wine and sing songs. Chrysanthos joins the singers but tonight he drinks only beer. He glances cautiously toward us, for the memory of last night has created a painful silence between he and his friend Labés.

Suddenly, Papa steps to the stage and dances.

"Bravo! Bravo!"

Papa has a bowed leg and too much wine. He's ready for sleep and certainly he'll need his cane to get home tonight. Yet, how marvelously he dances!

There's something in the air, a feeling of anticipation, as if we're expecting someone...and where's Bubu? We haven't seen him all evening. Ah, speak of the devil, up he drives at this very moment. Rachael's in the car with him and they have five liters of a special white wine they picked up earlier in the day at another village. Bubu quickly explains that we're all going with Chrysanthos to his home to celebrate his oldest son's name-day. In Greece they celebrate name-days rather than birthdays. For example, if you've been named after St. George of the Dragon or Mary the Mother of Jesus then you would celebrate your name-day on the day set aside to honor this famous person. I'm thinking of the meal that we've just eaten with Panayotis and of the name-day feast that will soon surely appear before our wondrous eyes. Oh, Lord, I groan happily, how long must we endure the pains and pleasures of the body?

But tonight it's more than the body I see.

Tonight I see The Madonna.

I look upon Her and Vishnu turns to stone; Han Shan to a Cold Mountain ghost. Nowhere in this land of light and rock have I seen one so lovely and fetching as this girl. She's the daughter of Chrysanthos and she's barely sixteen years old. Her name is Maria Thesponia. Thesponia...Maria Thesponia... The Madonna.

My soul burns with longing. I want to look upon Her, to touch Her, to adore Her eternally. I will die for lack of Her love. She means everything and I am nothing, nothing.

But all this is history.

A memory, a fable.

A road I once traveled.

A dream. (And I,

the dreamer of dreams.)

Thesponia brushes my hand and her slender fingers feel cold to the touch. She's still a child, this lovely girl, her dark innocent eyes ever-glowing with anticipation and excitement and wonder. A child admiring and caressing Angelina's long tumbling shiny hair. Angie's beaming and hugging everyone. She's in love with this whole family. She's also getting intoxicated on this delicious white wine. Labés and Chrysanthos are back on speaking terms again. Labés shows us a large framed photograph of himself in a soldier's uniform, cradling a machine gun. He looks very serious and proud but like a little boy playing soldier. Across the room, Rachael looks really angry with Bubu. No doubt Bubu has made some insensitive or stupid remark. Deliberately, of course. Bubu turns sorrowfully to his friend Chrysanthos. All this heaviness in Bubu. All this secret hostility. You see, Bubu's heart and head play war games with each other. Bubu's logic may be superb—even when he's falling-down drunk—but he doesn't know how to feel the world with his heart.

I step outside to relieve himself. The night is cold, clear. I can feel the nightness with my whole body and in that moment I feel connected to the whole universe. For a moment, anyway. I gaze with wonder into the heavens and breathe a spontaneous prayer to the twinkling stars. Feeling the world means to touch all this energy with your heart. You're not trying to do anything or prove anything or be anything. You're not trying to save yourself or understand yourself or explain yourself. You're not even trying to see. It's like e.e. cumming's delightful poem in praise of singing—singing as opposed to mere talking—which he ends suddenly with the words "singing is silence." Feeling the world comes through this inner dynamics of being and blood; it comes through the heart. Bubu doesn't understand this. He understands with the intellect.

I pour Angelina another glass of wine. She's certainly having a good time tonight. Now she's chattering in part-Greek, part-American, to Chrysanthos's son. He seems like an intelligent, sensitive young man. Good-looking too. You can bet Angie's in love with him more than the others. She certainly had a crush on Bubu when we first met him. Bubu doesn't have any scruples when it comes to chasing women. On our trip to the Mycenaean ruins, right in front of me on the boat, he started hitting on Angie. But what the hell, who am I to throw stones? Faint heart never won fair lady and I believe a woman will let you know soon enough how things stand with her. Maybe not so much in what she says, (we all lie to each other, intentionally or unintentionally, when it comes to sex and romance), but in the subtle energy currents around her body, and how she responds to your voice, your smell and touch. Bubu seems so insensitive to such delicate messages. He puts up such a protective screen that he doesn't catch the signals telling him to fuck off. Unless, of course, he does. And he just ignores them. Love must really scare Bubu. For to love would mean to be vulnerable, to be open and real. His ego won't allow this and Bubu identifies with his ego. Eye to eye with true love, his ego—this hero with a thousand and one faces—goes into stone-dead reaction. Like a hunter of prey he zeros in on Rachael, with his talk of Nazis and the Holocaust. Kind of like knocking on Heaven's door with a pistol in your hand. So, really, he zeroes in on his own shadow, becoming his own prey and dancing to his own death.

The Chinese have an ancient saying. "Everyone you meet is your mirror." So, I wonder, how does Bubu see me? What I know about him—what I know about my perceptions of him—I've learned from my own painful experiences. In him I recognize the ghost of my own past self. A specter that still loves to hang around the closets and corners and turn up at the most unexpected moments.

Angelina likes Bubu but she doesn't miss a thing when it comes to second glances, old hats, and false longings. Most of the time anyway. It certainly didn't take her long to lose her romantic interest in Bubu. Sometimes I think she travels with the speed of light. No; with the simultaneous *thereness* of consciousness. Or is it *hereness*? She's like the new physics. She simply *knows* what's going through my mind and heart. She knows spontaneously; instantaneously.

How does she do this?

Who are you, Angelina?

As if she had anticipated this question, or the peculiar conspiratorial way I would someday ask this question, Angelina wrote me a letter soon after she left her husband and moved in with me. I worked as a printer for a community college. That's how we met. She and her husband, who had just returned from Viet Nam, wanted to buy a house. Angie worked nights for a bank and she came up with this wonderful idea of getting a second job for extra income. She had taken graphic arts courses in college and had some press experience. She was only twenty-one; her husband a year younger. Her husband went to Viet Nam just after they got married. Whenever she smoked grass these strange, wonderful ideas and visions kept coming into her mind and she didn't know what to do or where to go with them. Her husband and their friends certainly showed no interest in her visions. They just wanted to drink beer and pig out on junk food and have a mindless good time listening to rock music.

Anyway, the letter.

"Allow me to introduce myself. I am the last of a rare generation, known as the Hidden Answer to All. Now if that isn't enough to contemplate on, here is just a few more mind games. I am several thousand centuries young and still using my present body for my mode of materialization and travel. All parts herewithin are original. Also there is but one change, that being the language I speak. No, I didn't always communicate with other beings verbally; I used a method that is generally known as Thought Transference Control. For sometime I have been testing you and the results have proven that within a short span of time we will be communicating through this method. There are several other members of the Hidden Answer. I have recently been in contact with them, although I haven't had a chance to converse and re-occur with them. You probably have known them as they were the ones who arranged our meeting. Perhaps sometime in the very near future we will all be meeting, I believe the chosen place is located in Europe. I do not have the details as of yet; but I am allowed to say that you are going to be a milestone to us. When the works of outlying members and I have been completed there will be a surprisingly better change in the evolution of your mind. Your mind will be the central chamber containing the total PAST, PRESENT AND FUTURE of us."

Crossing the Great Waters

"Quick, more Vitamin C!
I think this may be a long journey."
Angelina

The moment that Angie made the decision to leave her husband, the very next moment she told me that she had always wanted to go to Europe. She wanted to travel and she didn't want to wait until the house was paid for and the kids were grown and they had money in the bank. About three months later, one crisp night in early October, we stayed over at a friend's house in the country. Patrick was an amateur astronomer, and for this occasion—a partial eclipse of the Earth's moon—he had positioned his telescope in the middle of a cow pasture next to his land. There were no clouds in the sky and we could see the rings of Saturn and the moons of Jupiter. To see the eclipse of the Earth's moon we had to wait until three o'clock in the morning. Too excited to sleep, Angelina and I snuggled near the fireplace to keep warm. As we waited for the eclipse I read to her from Henry Miller's *The Colossus Of Maroussi*. That night we decided to go to Greece. So we saved our money and a year later we arrived in Monemvasia.

The first few weeks in Monemvasia I nearly went stir crazy. We had maintained such a non-stop, adrenalized pace at home and on the road that I actually went through withdrawal symptoms. I kept pulling out the map and staring at North Africa and wondering if Julia and her two young daughters had made it to Morocco. (We met them briefly in Athens; they were on their way to Marrakech.) But not Angelina. Angelina stretches catlike in the warm winterish sun, shuts her eyes and becomes one with the endless lulling of the sea.

∞

There's a Sufi saying: "He who sleeps on the road will lose either his hat or his head." Before leaving America I came down with a severe head cold. The plane would go up and the plane would go down and each time I thought my head would just about split open. After a few days in London I felt better. We went to London to visit our poet and rock musician friend D. R. Wagner and his wife Karen. D. R. and his rock group had a gig at some night club in the city. In fact, the inspiration for our outdoor wedding had come from an early summer trip Angelina and I made to Sacramento, California, to see D.R and Karen's Tibetan style wedding ceremony. D. R. had talked to the poet Gary Synder and Synder had given D. R. instructions on the proper rituals for such a wedding. Douglas Blazek, another poet and friend of mine, also lived in Sacramento. Blazek and D. R. Wagner were close friends. So Angie and I drove down from Portland, Oregon, for the wedding. Melina Foster, a close friend and an artist, came with us.

The Tibetan ceremony, which took place outdoors in a garden with a white gazebo, had been a grand and colorful affair. A wedding with a sense of integrity. D. R. and Karen had created an exotic and spacious experience yet without losing a sense of intimacy with their wedding guests. This lyrical and thoughtful pageantry captured everyone's imagination. Wow, A fun wedding. What a wonderful idea! Angie thought. Only we wouldn't call our marriage a ceremony. We would call our marriage a celebration. A celebration of what already had taken place between us on a soul level. We would write our own vows and create our own rituals. And Melina would design our wedding clothes. Angelina would wear a soft sky blue wedding dress, with a sleeveless gold velvet mantle and an orange sash at her waist, and a full-length front skirt of lavender velvet. In the center of this shining golden vestment Melina would stitch an appliqué of Angelina's "tree of life"—a tree of white branches with leaves turning into embroidery of red flames. Inside the branches she would create a circle and inside the circle a mountain and around the peak of the mountain a shining aura of white light, with yellow beams extending to the boundary of the circle and a purplish ray going upward into the light blue sky.

After seeing a bit of London—particularly the William Blake paintings at the Tate Museum—Angie and I hitched a ride to the city of Cardiff on the coast of south Wales. I wanted to visit Peter Finch, who published a small poetry magazine, and go to a pub with some of his poet friends. We had corresponded and exchanged books in the past.

"HURRY UP PLEASE IT'S TIME."

In my university days nine o'clock at night had always been about the time I closed my studies and went out seeking adventure and companionship. In Wales, the pubs close at nine.

"HURRY UP PLEASE ITS TIME."

To think I came half-way around the world to hear T.S. Eliot's familiar high-brow poetry in such a seedy, provincial little tavern as this. ...

Angelina and I decided to cross the English Channel by hovercraft and arrive in France at Calais. We hitched a ride without any problems to the hovercraft port but we arrived too late in the day to make the crossing. We were sitting in the waiting area wondering what to do when an elderly gentleman with a kind face came up to us. Before he retired he used to work for the hovercrafts he explained. We discussed our situation and he invited us for a small fee to stay for the night with him and his wife. The price was right but Angie and I both felt a bit suspicious at first. As it turned out, he and his wife were lovely, generous people. They lived in a small cozy house not far from the hovercraft station. They fed us tea and scones and strawberry jam and provided us with a nice fresh bed for the night. Travelers, particularly backpackers, they explained, would often arrive too late in the day to cross. As a way of earning extra money, and as a way to be of service to others, they decided to offer their home as lodging for the night. They also explained to us how we could cut our fare in half by hitching a ride onto the hovercraft. Cars were charged a flat rate to cross. We could offer to split the fare with a driver if he would take us aboard the hovercraft in his car. The next morning we found that this worked quite nicely.

Three days it took us to hitchhike to Paris from Calais. A distance of one hundred fifty kilometers. About a hundred miles. All along the road on signposts and rocks and bridges we passed these hand scrawled messages, their authors telling us in no uncertain terms what they thought of French drivers. The first day, we crossed the English Channel at dawn and then stood till dark on the side of the road in Calais. Out of boredom we finally walked to the edge of the town. I went into a little grocery store, came back out with cheese and fruit and I found Angelina in tears. A bunch of school kids had come by yelling and throwing stones at her. Oh, great. Here we are traveling with everything on our backs, we're hungry, it looks like rain, and now they're throwing stones at us. An old man walked by. He asked us in French where we were going and we answered in English. A sudden light shone in his weary eyes. He smiled. "La Paree!" he sang, bringing the tips of his cupped fingers to his lips in a kiss, and then walked on.

A few drops of rain began to fall.

Two young Frenchmen in an old van rescued us. We crawled into their van over a pile of antique brass tea kettles, lamps and pots. They had been driving around the countryside buying all the antique brass kettles they could find. Eventually, they explained, they would transport them to a dealer somewhere on the southern coast of France. The dealer, they told us, would then repair and shine the kettles up and pass them off to tourists as antiques from Morocco. Angie dug into her leather purse, came up with a French-English dictionary and with mercurial charm interpreted all this. We talked excitedly. Their names were Jean and Pierre. Ordinary French names but they sounded marvelous to us. The two men were warm, unpretentious, down-to-earth folk. In their late twenties. They mentioned Viet Nam and President Nixon and made faces. They had smoked hashish, tried LSD. They knew the songs of Bob Dylan. It didn't matter that they understood little or nothing of his lyrics. Dylan's intensity, the urgency in his voice, his evolutionary being, his deep caring, these came through his words and music like a blue planetary flame, catching their hearts like an American Fourth of July fireworks; like the mathematics of a crazy, free wind.

We stopped for the night in a village on the coast. They found us a room in a small hotel over a bistro with the harbor just outside our window. We ate dinner with them and then we picked up several bottles of cheap wine. We sat around in their van on top of all those copper kettles, laughing and talking till the wine ran out and most of the night too.

The boys love Angelina.

Must be her smile. So direct and real, she disarms you. Or maybe her sense of burlesque. Back home, a friend one day suddenly discovered the delightful spray of freckles across her face and blurted out: "Hey, you have freckles!" Angie looked incredulous and without missing a heartbeat she gasped, "I do?" In Pompeii a tour guide caught our attention. Or should I say Angie caught his attention? Just like that the man offered to take the two of us on a personal tour of the ruined city. He showed us the brothels and other places of interest that I gather normal tours sometimes by-pass.

Angelina has an intensity about her, a vibrancy like millions of tiny mischievous springs dancing in every direction, spiraling. A loving heart bursting to love. She's strong-willed too; but double-minded. A Gemini, you see. Impish, playful;

tomboyish at times even. A bit of the missionary, too. She's generous—and greedy—but no fool. Even in the clouds she's down-to-earth. Most of the time. She moves through different roles as eagerly as she enjoys wearing hand-me-down clothes and sometimes she seems to lose sight of herself. But not for long. *"This is not me!"* she cries. The old clothes quickly vanish. Springtime comes once again and the angel of my heart doesn't look back.

With all these sudden changes, though, and with my own restless and sometimes satyric nature, and perhaps for darker, subterranean reasons which I do not fathom, Angelina seems deeply insecure, as if she's afraid of being abandoned, afraid of being alone. She certainly keeps a sharp eye on me around other women. And when she gets angry because of some careless remark I've made, some insensitivity upon my part, I swear her glance cuts right through to my soul. Makes my teeth chatter. Keeps me on my toes. I couldn't ask for a better traveling companion.

Some of my friends believe I've turned her into a myth. I've even changed her name. What can I say? For that matter, who really knows anyone, be they husband, wife, mother, father, sister or friend? We don't see others as they are but as we see them. As they reflect back certain truths about ourselves. Or fantasies. Those Chinese mirrors again. Others see Angelina differently. They see other versions, other choices. They see other distortions of her soul. They see not the intimate Angelina I know. "The eye is blind to what the mind can not see," as the proverb goes. Her purity, her winged sandals, her ethereal, Rembrandt hands; she sparkles like a diamond. She shines according to the light which you bring to her. And she gives you back the radiance of your own mind. It's within you and within her and within the heartbeat of all that is. As for me, I shall claim next of kin to Swami Yogananda's wonderful little ant. I'll take the sugar and leave the rest.

Beginning the journey

by jumping up
& down
I tried to make a mountain
in the air

over 20 years now

I don't walk
normally
anymore

Douglas Blazek
"A snapshot of the fever"

"You'll be wanderers for three years," Nadine told us last spring. Nadine's a professional psychic, a reader of palms. She's a close friend of Anya the astrologer that we know. "You'll live in Paris for a while," she predicted, "and something will happen." She looked at me with steady, compassionate eyes. "Something that will change your life."

What the devil could it be?

I could be hit by a truck. Now that might change my life.

Or I could meet my Guru.

I do have Pluto in the Ninth House. Which means, I'm told, inner transformation through long journeys. Angie's staring into the map of my hands and pondering each and every line. What could it be?

We go to Shakespeare & Company and ask for George.

Shakespeare & Company is located on the Left Bank, across from the Notre Dame Cathedral. This is not the original bookstore of course. The original Shakespeare & Company was owned by Sylvia Beach and was a favorite gathering place for Hemingway and Pound and Gertrude Stein and all the literary people in Paris in the 1920s. The one original we found in Paris was Notre-Dame. Those windows! Like the dazzling *yantras* or power images in Tantra art, those wonderful stained-glass windows convey the secretive, creative force of the Female—the Mother/Goddess energy—the sacred dream of Nature. St. Peter's in Rome, on the other hand, impressed us as a monstrous jewel box, a supreme ego trip. The Sistine Chapel, ahh. We wander for an eternity through Ancient Greece, Rome, Egypt, room after room, not knowing where we are; and what about Michelangelo? At last we find the long stairway down to the Chapel. By this time, however, I'm feeling half-disgusted, and more than impatient, and Angie hasn't eaten all morning though it's nearly closing time. But never mind, we'll see Michelangelo even if it kills us. "The Creation Of Man" unfolds on the ceiling. There's so much creative fire in this Renaissance man, the whole room might well go up in flames. (Enough dead wood here for sure I'm thinking. Lord, seventy million people in one summer.) So out we go, speaking of Michelangelo. And just across the street the waiters are waiting for us. They charge us more for the white linen table cloth than for the spaghetti. All because of a few stains of red wine. But what can you expect? First the Pope, then the maitre-d.

George is swamped at his desk. He's a little man with a gray goatee who looks like the ninth ghost of Trotsky and claims to be the illegitimate grandson of Walt Whitman. He insists we call each other "comrades." He's very brusque and says that he has no time to prepare us a meal. He demands to know who gave us his name. We have a hotel and we've already eaten, I tell George. We only want to show him three of our small press poetry books. My intention is to show him these books in hopes that he will place an order from our distributor in Berkeley, California. Angie and I printed and published the books and we did all the binding by hand. The person who gave us George's name and told us that we might get a free place to stay out of him is an underground small press publisher who, at the time, was being sought by the French police for printing "Universal Citizens" passports. The man told us that he actually used one of these passports in crossing the borders between France and the Netherlands. But I don't mention this to George.

I place three books on his desk.

George glances through our books. *I Am the One Who Walks the Road*, a limited edition of selected poems by Douglas Blazek and several other underground poets, measures 9 x 12 and opens from top to bottom rather than left to right. Angie and I used different colored inks for each poem, matching the ink color with what we thought to be the color of the poet's essential energy. In designing this book we had been inspired by the Loujon Press publications of poet Charles Bukowski. The second book, a collection of poems by Tom Kryss entitled *Sunflower River*, Angelina herself printed on a small offset press, with black ink on gray paper, and she used a binding technique of double-folding the pages back into the spine. The last book is a book of my own poetry called *A Bone for the Dogs*. This book I hand printed on an old letterpress in our garage, using colored inks and heavy deckle-edged paper. Angie and I were really proud of these books. We had spent more than a good year printing and putting them together and they were indeed labors of love.

George insists that these books must be too expensive for Shakespeare & Company. I tell him our prices. Immediately he wants to buy all three books. These are our personal copies I explain. I tell George how he can order copies from our distributor in the U. S. He scowls and shakes his head and doubts any future orders. And well we could see why. Indeed, his store must be the most jumbled collection of new and used books in all Europe. George then suggests that perhaps we really don't want our books in Shakespeare & Company. There's no time to analyze his madness; I must act. So for seventy francs I sell him the books. George then relaxes. He smiles warmly and invites us to stay in his "Writer's Guest

Room" for the rest of our visit in Paris. We accept his invitation and the next day we move into Shakespeare & Company.

We don't have a toilet at Shakespeare & Company, but we do have a small sink downstairs, hidden within a closet of books, and at night a tin can disguised as a bouquet of dried flowers. We have a kitchen sink that keeps clogging, and a gas stove for cooking meals, but we can only cook before twelve noon, when the bookstore opens, and after twelve midnight, when it closes. Already living in the bookstore—in various odd places among the books—is a French cockroach, although George claims he's a poet; a young, attractive English woman named Elizabeth Scott, who writes poetry; and Roy Watkins, an English writer and traveler about my own age. Angie and I have the upstairs "Guest Room" to ourselves. And the bed bugs. But at least we had the good sense to put our sleeping bags on top of the sagging bed.

Across the street is the Notre-Dame Cafe. Here we spend our late mornings drinking cappuccino and using their "crash-pit" toilet—the floor kind with no seat. And waiting. Waiting in the cafes with a sense of humor and impending destiny. Like Robert Tabbs, a black American poet. Bob says he's stuck in Paris. When money comes he'll go to either Morocco or the States. Bob grew up in Alabama. He's also lived in New York City but he prefers Alabama and he loves Southern food. Bob seems really warm and genuine. He speaks softly and laughs a lot. Innocence abroad, like ourselves. But deep within him I sense an intense feeling of unease and bitterness. A silent, nagging rage toward the world. But he's young and in Paris, and we're from home, and it's good to see each other, to talk and share stories. For a moment we can let go of any racism and fears that we have of each other.

Jean and Pierre—our two friends on the road with the vanful of copper kettles—had given us the name of a friend of theirs in Paris. "She speaks good English," Pierre said. "And she loves American jazz. Call her. Perhaps you can stay at her apartment for the night, until you find a hotel." This we did, much to the surprise of Emmanuelle. She and Pierre had not seen each other for awhile and we gathered that at one time they had been lovers. Emmanuelle welcomed us into her life and even took us on a driving tour of the city to show us the historical landmarks, like Victor Hugo's tomb. (Or was it his birthplace?) Then she took us to a wonderful little restaurant. "A typical Parisian restaurant," Emmanuelle told us. Angie and I were the only foreigners in the restaurant.

Henry Miller—May he live a thousand years!—Henry Miller called Paris a whore. But nowhere in Paris did I see a ghost of Henry Miller. Or the incredibly lovely Anaïs Nin. I stop for a moment in my travels to remember them, and to honor their intense love for this city, and for each other, and for this sensual and sacred mystery called life. Thinking of Henry and Anaïs in Paris—those secret, feverish nights and days of lying in each other's arms; her tender, wise and elusive heart embracing and surrounding the tough and brilliant and excessive mind of this great American writer—it's like going inside my own heart to find an old faded love letter that I had long ago safely hidden away; and to re-read once more the bittersweet words; and to allow once again the flowing of tears to heal the pain so deeply vaulted within my consciousness. No, it's not Victor Hugo's tomb or the Eiffel tower or the grand historical landmarks that give the city of Paris such special charm and romance and danger. It's the everyday streets of Paris. The narrow, intimate, cobblestone streets. The little cafes. The spacious boulevards. The sinfully delicious bakeries. The open sidewalk markets with their colorful fruits and vegetables. The antique shops around every corner. The Middle-Eastern flavors and politics and the many faces of Africa. The under-and-overground commuter trains. The jammed-together apartments. The wine stores fat with bottles of French wines. The painters selling their art on the Left Bank. That wonderful park near the Louvre. The magnificent Louvre, however, I found a bit cold; and certainly way too much for a single day, as we crazily tried to do. The Mona Lisa we glimpsed through a crowd of eyes as thick as bees swarming. The van Gogh paintings we couldn't even find.

Roy Watkins came up from Spain after living for a year inside the country. He's translating a selection of poems by the French poet Henri Michaux. Michaux has seen some of Roy's translations. The poet lives in recluse outside the city and wants to see Roy when he arrives in Paris. Roy's conversational French, however, needs a good brushing up and, so, like Angelina and myself, he's hanging out in the cafes.

Roy's a tall and lean man, an intense looking man, and handsome in a rugged way. Most of the time he wears a leather cowboy hat, high Spanish boots and a brown fringed suede coat. I really enjoyed hanging out with him in Paris. I liked his warmth and spontaneity and the clarity in his eyes; and I admired his ability to cut through literary pretensions and rules and ideas that limited the mind and imagination. We knew each other for only a brief time, of course; but I instantly recognized him as a kindred soul. We were like alternate versions of each other. We both were born under the zodiac sign whose symbol is the centaur: half-beast and half-man; in Greek mythology the offspring of Ixion, a Thessalian king, who was bound to a constantly revolving wheel because he desired Hera, the wife of Zeus, queen of the gods.

Before we left Paris, a teaching possibility came to Roy from the Sorbonne. Roy has a degree from Columbia University and the city of New York left its mark on him. The German poet Rilke, with his *Letters to a Young Poet*, inspired Roy and gave him courage and some comfort, but Roy still carries this American city around within him and translates his remembrances—like the time he was robbed at knife point in the subway—through stories with a dramatic sense of terror and humor. Especially in the early hours of the morning, when we're sitting around in Shakespeare & Company, surrounded by volumes of literature, and we've just smoked a gram of Turkish hashish.

A Bone for the Dogs

Today,
I just want to sit,
like the poet Neruda would sit,
deep in his thoughts of Chile
and the ocean and shoes.
I want to feel the breath of solitude,
like Castaneda in the desert at night,
listening to the heartbeat
of a moth.
I want to remember the Aegean Sea,
this ancient sea,
before it was invaded
by a surf of oil
and makeshift huts upon the shore;
and I want to walk
along the Great Coral Reef
and ponder a new world,
in reality.
I want to drink strong, black coffee,
the way Gurdjieff did,
(so they say),
and sit with Henry Miller
in Paris, in a cafe
before the War,
before he went to Greece.
I want to sit like Chief Joseph,
who traveled freely among his people
—when this land was free.
I want to sit like Bodhidharma,
alone for 20 years,
without eating or shitting or masturbating.
(No one even knew Bodhidharma was there
under the tree. They saw only the tree
and the shadow of the tree.)
I want to sit quiet as a tear

on the cheek of Christ.
I want to drink this bitter cup;
I want to feel my aloneness,
without thoughts of bare bosoms
and the burning bushes of youth
and tomorrow; pleasure
and pain, we are constant worlds
entwined with nature's vines,
roots; flowers that fly away
in remote jungles; dinosaurs
that rule the world with profit
and greed and patriotism on their lips.
I want to sit, to know my aloneness,
to ask questions one must answer alone
to oneself, awakening
from the years of false pretenses;
the sham beliefs I have been taught,
the limitations I have chosen.
***
Desires come and go,
I do not detain them.
But I will sit here, quietly
listening to this passing world:
the noise of a car going by;
a dog barking angrily; a boy
playing on the sidewalk;
the rain dripping off the gutters;
the slow Oregon rain that falls
like a soft funeral train,
like the tenderness of a sweet friend
who died long ago.
I will sit here,
calm in this moment of solitude;
my individuality a bone for the dogs
that would devour us,
for those who would feast upon the earth
and perish of famine in their souls,

for those who would tear out my
heart, (if they could),
in the name of brotherhood,
Mother, Father, God.
I will sit here, lofty
in my heart as the redwoods,
unobtrusive as a scrub or
an ancient, gnarled olive tree,
invisible as truth,
mysterious as life, unknown,
lyrical.

Other than the Bible, I had no early contact with Great Writing.
My mother had loved the Bible; and because she treasured this
book, I too treasured it. My father had dropped out of school
in the eight grade and went to work on the family farm in
North Carolina. John Pendarus was a physically strong and
handsome but hard, stiff-necked man with a selfish side and a
slight mean streak in him. Once, on the farm in Arkansas, after
I was just born, Dad encouraged my brother Stephen to poke
a large wasp nest with a stick. Stephen and our dog Boozer
had to run for their lives. Many times as I was growing up I
had been scornfully warned by my father to "Get your nose
out of that book!" and get outside to do some chore or another.
Usually this meant that I had to hoe weeds around the corn
or the sweet potatoes or the fruit trees. We had a wonderful
orchard: all kinds of peaches and apples and plums and pears
and muscadines and concord grapes. My brother Jack and
I would sneak into Dad's batch of homemade wine or peach
brandy whenever we could and one of my favorite memories
was swinging in the one-seater rope swing tied to a high
branch in the big oak tree in the front yard, a swing my father
had made for my younger sister Jenny, as I waited patiently
for my grandmother's sweet potato pies to cool on the outside
kitchen window sill. Or it meant that I had to cut okra for that
night's supper. I hated cutting okra. On a hot summer day it
would always sting and itch my hands. But I loved the flower

of the okra plant. And it didn't get any better than fried okra with Mom's biscuits and mashed potatoes and gravy and fried chicken and sweet corn on the cob and maybe watermelon for desert. We raised our own melons and one summer day for some reason the passenger train that every day ran on the railroad track only a few hundred yards from our house came to a long stop and the train was full of soldiers and my father told the soldier in charge that the men could pick all the watermelons they wanted and the soldiers ran into the field with big grins and helped themselves to these huge melons and my dad looked real happy that day as he watched the soldiers. Or sometimes it meant that I had to pick green beans and tomatoes from the garden; or blackberries or strawberries or something. My two brothers and I, we were afraid to eat the strawberries that we picked. We swore to each other that probably every berry in the field had already been counted. As for blackberry picking that usually meant an exciting trip into the woods with Dad. I loved Mom's cobblers and the jams and jellies she made that lasted us through the winter. Sometimes our whole family would go blackberry picking together, and huckleberry picking too, and I would always return from the woods with my bucket full of berries but the chiggers would get me too and in the most tender places like the back of my knees and under my arms and that I didn't like.

Sometimes Dad wanted me to gather caterpillars from the Catalpa trees or dig for red wigglers in the worm beds, to sell to the fishermen that would stop by on their way to Sweetwater Creek or to the big lake off Highway 78. Dad raised and sold Catalpa caterpillars and red wigglers and it was always an adventure to pick the big fat black fuzzy caterpillars off the large heart-shaped Catalpa leaves but you had to be careful or the caterpillars would spit dark tobacco-like juice on you; and digging for red wigglers in their raised boarded beds, turning the soil over with a pitch fork to uncover hundreds of squiggling, wiggling, squirming worms, and catching them before they could disappear once again into the ground, this was exciting and fun too. Some days, Mom would ask me to go to the chicken yard and gather eggs for her and sometimes I even had to feed the chickens. Barefooted, and stepping very gingerly with eyes wide-open through the weeds and grass of the chicken yard, I reached for eggs with one hand and in the other hand I waved a big stick for the red rooster that never failed to stalk and instantly attack me if ever I turned my back and sometimes even when I didn't turn my back the rooster would try to spur me, and I figured that's when I really had to whack the rooster as hard as I could. Poor rooster goes to show what getting up so early in the morning and boasting about it and then chasing hens around all day can do to a rooster's brain. One time the rooster hurt himself and I watched with amazement as the old rooster's favorite hens jumped on him in no time, viciously pecking him.

Going to the barn to feed the mule was a different story. I had a great fondness for our old, blind, grayish-white mule. Unlike at plowing time with Dad the mule never acted mean or bad-tempered or ornery with me when I would go for a little ride on her in the grassy field across the dirt road next to the woods that belonged to Old Lady Harper (as everyone called her because she looked so ancient), or the times I would ride up and down the dirt road when the honeysuckles were in full bloom or when the small, wild cherries turned ripe on the tall trees and the only way I could reach them was by standing on the back of the mule and grabbing a low branch. With me the mule always behaved slow and gentle.

One Saturday Jack and I worked all morning for Mrs. Harper. We raked and gathered the leaves, dug the weeds out of her flower gardens and picked up broken limbs that had fallen from the huge oak trees around her yard. Mrs. Harper gave us each a quarter and each a pear off the ground beneath her pear tree. We felt so disappointed, all our high hopes of earning big money. But we were just kids and didn't know what to do but say "Thank you". And when we came down the hill and got home and Mom heard about it, I had never seen Mom so angry. Except maybe the time she and Dad locked horns over selling the house and moving back to California.

She wasn't even that angry the Sunday afternoon my friend Marcus and I accidentally set fire to the field across the road and had the fire department and all the neighbors rushing around to save Old Lady Harper's woods; which they were able to do okay; as Marcus and I hid by the bed in my room. Setting the woods on fire I figured couldn't be any worse than the "unpardonable sin." Whatever the unpardonable sin was. As a boy I never figured that one out. But whatever it was, I lived in the terror that somehow, some way, I had committed this sin from which there could be no pardon. I lived for years with this nameless guilt and terror inside me; never daring to ask my mother or the preacher or anyone else if in fact I had or had not committed this sin against God.

If it ain't one thing, child, it's another. One thing after the other. Always. There ain't no rest for the weary, I tell you. No rest for the weary. We're all sinners, child. Every last one of us. Born into failure and to live in fear. And Jesus our only salvation. Our only hope. It says so in the Good Book. And don't forget your prayers, child. "I lay me down to sleep, I pray thee Lord my soul to keep…" Child, I just don't understand your father. Always tryin' to start a fight. Every night at the supper table, always pickin' a fight. I'm sick and tired of it. I don't know why I put up with him. Lord, can't you do anything right, child? You're always in the way. Always under my feet. Now git out of here. Git, before I knock your head off! One thing after the other. I tell you, we're all gonna wind up in the poor house. Or in Milledgeville with the rest of the crazy folks. Working nights in the cotton mill and John sneakin' around borrowin' money, not sayin' a word to me. I'm so tired, child. Go outside and play, will you? I'm fixin' to lay down. And for cryin' out loud shut the screen door! One thing after the other. There just ain't no rest for the weary. It says so in the Bible, we're all sinners. I tell you in the eyes of God we're all sinners. Sinners….

It was October a year ago. Coming back from a trip to the American Southwest, Angelina and I stayed overnight in a small hotel in Sausalito, just across from San Francisco's Golden Gate Bridge. We had taken the coastal route through California and had stopped at many different wineries to taste the wine—to select the perfect wine for our wedding—and to watch the grapes being harvested. While visiting my friend Larry Czenkoszy in Venice Beach we had picked up some mescaline. That night in Sausalito we decided to take the mescaline. At first we had the weirdest experience. We watched the people in this little harbor village running around in masks and costumes. Is this normal for Sausalito? Surely we weren't hallucinating all this! Indeed not. In our travels we had simply forgotten that it was Halloween.

So back to the hotel we went. A lovely, intimate little hotel it was; styled in late 18th century French furnishings. Only now we noticed an odd energy about the place. We soon realized that the desk clerk and most—if not all—the male occupants were gay. This didn't bother me, but, nevertheless, Angie kept a watchful eye whenever I went to the bathroom down the hall. "Just in case," she assured me. She didn't trust that blond guy in the room across the hall.

Angelina, unlike me, had no inhibitions about her sensuality and she saw no reason that the hallucinogenic experience should be limited to the mind. I watched her as she carefully removed her earrings and laid them beside the small ornate lamp on the vanity. Such a simple act and yet accomplished with such grace and certainty that it seemed to capture the very essence of the feminine mystique. Angie had found the earrings in a little shop in Arizona. Three silver feathers dangled below a single turquoise stone that was held in a delicate silver setting. She placed her copper bracelet beside the earrings. Her long hair shone in the soft light of the lamp.

As I poured us a glass of cabernet sauvignon, Angelina slipped out of her simple dress. I liked that dress. It came down to just above her knees and was almost the color of her new turquoise stones but the dress had all these big daubs of maroon and darker blue like scattered clouds or leaves or flowers. And it had wonderfully big puffy sleeves and a low neckline that revealed the full sensuousness of her throat.

The wine tasted funny and we both made faces.

"Probably the mescaline," we agreed.

I placed my glasses on the vanity. Lying on the bed with her womanness tenderly opening up to me, I allowed myself to slowly explore Angelina's beauty and all her yumminess, as if for the first time: her crinkly toes, the warm golden butterflies of her belly and the full, moist softness of her lips; her healing fingers that touched my body with the essence of crocus flowers and her ethereal fragrance that seemed to anoint me with an aura of sweet forgiveness.

That night, wrapped in Angelina's arms, I realized that I had begun a journey back to the natural world: a journey back to re-establishing an intimate connection with my body and with my heart and feelings. I had no idea, though, that our coming together would be the start of a journey that would eventually take me face to face with all the terrors and denials and self-doubts that I had ever created in my travels through this passing world.

An American back-packer shows up at Shakespeare & Company. He's hitchhiked from Switzerland through Yugoslavia and he's dead tired and needs a place to crash for the night. The next day, to help George out, Scott mops the floor with an old rag. But he has a cut on his finger that hasn't been treated. Three days later Scott telephones the bookstore and tells us that he's in a hospital near Notre-Dame. The doctors have whacked a good chunk off his finger and he's pretty worried. (Next to him in the hospital ward there's a man whose hand was taken off by an electrical paper cutter.) Scott wants us to bring him a medical book from his pack and some writing paper. He tells us the French are very careless. They drip the needle across the floor. Or they even forget to take the needle out. To cheer him up Angie and I take him a sack of fruit and cheese and a pint of vodka. But we have a ride to Athens waiting for us at the American Express and we're pushed for time. All we can do is wish him good luck.

Douglas Blazek wants to know if I have a fear of dying in a foreign land. "The fear of dying because of people with cruder technological convenience & less knowledgeable scientific devices?" He wonders about the confidence man—"the man saturated with hatred for the Americano." And he feels skeptical and discouraged about approaching a large publisher for *I Am the One Who Walks the Road*. "My success with these publishers has been so depressingly poor that I feel it might be something about my image or my tact that turns them off, that I might jinx the book's reprint possibility by approaching such publishers... Everyone hustles so much better than I do & the scene is so polluted with poets all claiming to be the next Blake or Pound or somebody--."

All directions come together in me

All directions come together in me. All directions come together in me. All directions come together in me. I could chant these words like a spiritual mantra till doomsday but would it make the next few days and my encounter with Christine Isbell any more or less painful? Any more or less real? Would the reason behind the reason we met in this precise time and geography ever be revealed? Meeting Christine Isbell felt like the straight and narrow inside me suddenly coming to a screeching split in the middle of the road and the only signpost the ancient riddle WHO AM I?

The Divine plays in mysterious ways. But now what?

Like the strange, very strange, encounter I had with Anna Sylvan. Anna came by to visit one afternoon, not long after the wedding. We were in the middle of preparations for our journey, packing boxes to store and those sorts of things. That afternoon, Angelina happened not to be home. I was surprised to see Anna alone. She had never come to visit by herself but always with Eden. Yet why should I act surprised? Had not I harbored this desire in my heart, to be alone with her before leaving America?

I had never felt at ease around Anna. Her brooding sensuality unnerved me. I felt exposed. I couldn't look into her soft earth-burning eyes and not give myself away. Being near her felt like entering a quiet, mysterious forest, and I babbled like a running brook. Anna could have been a Native American princess: the high cheek bones; the full, vulnerable mouth, and her low, whispery voice, as mesmeric to my soul as a Celtic harp or an ancient Egyptian lullaby; long flowing dark hair, sometimes braided and sometimes bound by a red bandanna; her lean body and her soft voluptuous breasts and the long lovely dresses she wore so gracefully; her slender fingers like soothing homespun touches of eternity; and, oh, those incredibly soft eyes. If I were an artist in another time I would paint her image on the wall of a temple in some exotic land like Nepal or Ceylon, like the ancient Sinhalese goddesses on the cliff ruins of the palace of Kasyapa at Sigiriya that I once cut out and stole from a *National Geographic* magazine. I would paint her bathing on the warm banks of the Nile River. Or dancing to the sensuous flute of Krishna. Or smelling a flower in a sunny court in Pompeii. I would paint her voluptuous body in flowing lines and luminous earth tones and then sit before this sacred shrine without moving for a hundred years. That's the kind of crazy energy I felt when thinking of Anna. That's what I sensed beneath her casual, guarded aloofness, her shadowy beauty, her elusive silences. A nurturing earth woman with the seed of fire and anger in her slender fingers. A sad-eyed Madonna in the wrong century. A vibrant rose aching to bloom with her own man, but her man, my friend Eden, was like a candle in a shifting wind, continually dancing to the tune of a thousand jigs.

At times she lived with Eden, and at times with her parents, and at times alone or with some man. She worked for a while as a waitress in a tavern on the north side of Portland. I remember how this image of her working in a bar jolted me. I suppose the "Good Father" in me wanted to protect her. But she seemed quite able to take care of herself and her little girl Monica, Eden's daughter.

We talked for a while, God knows about what.

As we talked, all the time I wanted to reach out and touch her, but instead of listening to my heart, or telling her how I felt, instead of being real, I distrusted my own feelings. So we evaded each other and the truth of the moment. How could I desire her and yet be so much in love with Angelina? My devotion to Angelina I never doubted; nor did I wish to betray her. Our marriage had been revealed in the divinatory stars and in the lines of our hands. I felt wholly at ease with the forces connecting us and with my own awakening heart and the immense journey that lay before us.

As we talked I could feel a great sorrow in Anna.

Like the sadness and exquisite beauty of Heifetz's violin solo "Ave Maria."

Something between Anna and me, something subtle, intense, primal, needed acknowledgment. Something that had nothing to do with Angelina or with Eden. I trembled inside uncontrollably. I longed to taste and smell the ancient sea fragrance of her body. I wanted to abandon myself to her incredible softness. I adored her mythical dimensions, her timelessness.

And I wanted to heal her pain.

But she could be a bear to live with. Or so she claims. For sure she could drive Eden up a wall. She would disappear for days and he wouldn't know where she had gone or when she was coming back or what. But Eden's no saint. I've seen how he treats Anna. Always taking off with another woman. Or thumbing across the country to visit old friends back in West Virginia and leaving Anna with the kid. Or going to some spiritual retreat in Colorado to hear the Dali Lama. And getting high on basement acid too many times and seeing demons. You know, the kind that appear out of nowhere. The man could be a real ass hole. But, hey, "a beautiful ass hole," as someone once tagged him.

Before Eden, Anna had a sweetheart who wrote her passionate, romantic poems. He would carefully print these sensual lyrics in calligraphy on handmade Japanese paper. As a gift, he bound them in a book and gave them to Anna just before they split up. Eden knew she kept the book of poems tucked away in her personal belongings. One night, probably after Anna had vanished for several days, Eden stole the book from her. She watched in humiliation as he burned the poems to ashes in the fireplace. All the time his clenched fist and the glare in his eyes dared her to say one word of protest. So Eden's about as stable as the San Andreas fault. Together, they seem as crazy as a Brazilian song and dance.

Those Chinese mirrors.

I rolled some grass. Anna likes to smoke and I've been known to push the river now and then, to give the flow a little nudge.

(What's this I hear? A thunderous roar just around the bend?)

I sensed Anna was waiting. But what to do?

Keep moving with your own juices, with the spontaneous impulses, and the poetry in your blood. This I've learned. Socrates didn't beat his head on the walls when they condemned him. (If our reports are true.) He didn't reproach himself. Or blame the gods or fate or circumstances. Socrates used even his death to keep moving.

Worse than playing the fool is not taking that essential risk.

But how?

Perhaps Anna understood no more than I the energy between us. What was she thinking? What did her eyes say? Her eyes like liquid summers rounded with the soft dark intimations of autumn. I looked into her eyes and wanted to surrender. I wanted to die a thousand times over. For a moment the world seemed to stop. And I tumbled over the edge. Breathlessly I traveled through a remembrance of deserts, immense stars and something I had no words for. Something like a flight of golden birds, singing. I reached for her body. She embraced me, our mouths kissing, exploding. My hands fumbling with the buttons on her white blouse. Her long Biblical hair tangled in my fingers. She collapsed into a chair and I went down on my knees, clinging to her. Quietly she held my head to her bare bosom. I could feel the warm, pulsing heart of the Mother essence.

Just as suddenly we pulled apart. The madness gone.

It was just too crazy for Anna and me.

The dance of energy

"....every sat. night they got acid dances
at the avalon or fillmore auditorium, 300
 mics & the dance of energy dont stop till
weds or thurs w/me...& the prettiest girls
in the world...they even come home w/you...

if you get out there & show them that you
got more electricity than their old man..."

Crazy Willie in a letter, 1/17/66

Christine talks about living for two years near the desert outside Los Angles. Here on the edge of the desert she first read Carlos Castaneda's *The Teachings of Don Juan*. As she talks she reveals her enthusiasm for the weird, incomprehensible acts of don Juan's sorcery. She turns to me, starts to say something, stops, changes her mind, then looks away. Time passes in silence. Now she's telling me about some incident in the desert but I can't make any sense out of what she's saying, too many gaps, allusions that she never follows up on, secrets and private thoughts. But it doesn't matter. I'm totally absorbed by her voice. She speaks with a slight English accent. She lived in London several years and went to school there. One moment light and airy, her voice weaves like a subtle wind through sensuous beach grasses, twisting and turning. The next moment her voice like a warm wave of the sea is washing up on the softened expanses of my mind, bringing me exotic spiral shells and small, magical, ancient stones. Then she stops speaking and gazes into my face with such an intense longing that I'm stunned. Just as quickly she relaxes and takes me by the arm and smiles. She's wearing a simple black dress with a modest but sensual V neck and it's all that I can do to keep my eyes off the whiteness of her throat and the curve of her breasts. Illusive as the moonlight through these ancient Greek ruins, she enchants me effortlessly, and I want to abandon myself to the slender whiteness of her throat and the elusive chemistry of her body.

Christine Isbell was on holiday with her lover. She was Swedish and summery blond and twenty-four years of age. Her lover was a quiet, contemplative man a couple of years older. (Like myself, as I remember, an astrological brother to the Greek centaur.) They were staying in the old town in a partially reconstructed house that belonged to a friend back in

Sweden. Angie and I liked them immediately. We drank wine and made dinners together and prowled the pitch-black streets of the old town at night, holding hands tightly so as not to lose one another in the darkness. The nights were chilly and the wind would sometimes come blowing and howling through the rocks. But on a clear, cloudless night, to look out over the ancient ruins and see the moonlight dancing and playing on the sea, one could not help but enter into a spontaneous silence; the mind hushed momentarily by this natural, miraculous beauty.

We were standing in the shadows, the pale light from a kerosene lantern flickering across her face and Northern blond hair. I wanted to say something, but she smiled as if knowing my innermost thoughts and we stood there in feverish silence.

"What are you waiting for?" she asked.

"I don't know." I could barely speak.

"Is it Angelina?"

"Yes. No. No, not really." I shook my head.

I could hear the wind blowing against the window.

Angelina was in the kitchen making a salad. But she must know what's going on. How could she not? This was too crazy.

My body trembled. I couldn't stop trembling.

"Are you afraid?"

Christine touched me lightly on the arm.

"Shit! Of course I'm afraid. But it's not fear that's stopping me. It never has before. I don't know."

Her curious eyes glanced into mine and she waited.

"What then?"

I felt trapped.

Later, for some reason, I thought of Castaneda's almost disastrous encounter with the sorceress la Catalina. On the pretense that la Catalina was out to kill him and that he needed help, don Juan tricked Castaneda into attacking the sorceress.

As she walked by him on the road one day Carlos attempted to pierce her in the belly with the foreleg of a wild boar. Naturally he could not come close to touching this powerful sorceress. Don Juan had devised this ploy in order to trap his apprentice. La Catalina would be out for revenge and Castaneda would have no choice but to learn how to defend himself as a warrior. A warrior, don Juan told Castaneda, could never afford to abandon himself to anything. But, I protested to the universe, I never wanted to be a warrior! Better to be a lover like Rumi. Better the flute of Krishna than the sword of Arjuna.

But what to do?

The Zen masters say to take every situation as a personal test, and, yet, at the same time, never to have the arrogance to assume that this universe has set the stage up for your private drama.

If I went to her...what?

An explosion, devastation, loss.

Christine wanted power, not awareness; electricity, not transformation. To become entangled in the luminous but fragmented intentions of her dreaming self would have been crazy and self-destructive for I would have perished and she would have abandoned me. For I would have abandoned the light within myself. A light that I unswervingly trust. A light that Angelina so clearly reflects.

Still, I wanted to go to her.

The intensity, the risk, the power, in her touch and kiss. The moment poised in my mind like a thunderbolt in the hands of Zeus. One kiss. A single kiss and my arms holding her in the shadows of the lantern light, forever.

New Year's Eve we all went to a party given by the Greek-American professor of anthropology. To get even with me, to hurt me for hurting her, Christine went after the professor, dancing and flirting with him at the party. "You'll die a lonely old man!" she flung at me, as if putting a curse on me, anger and pain flashing in her celery green eyes.

Christine's lover silently watched the drama. I couldn't tell about him. I didn't know what he was thinking or feeling. Perhaps he'd seen the show before. Angelina wouldn't let me out of her sight. "I finally trust you," she cries, "and look what happens!"

The day Christine and her companion left Greece, we drank wine together at Artemis', the four of us. Then we waved good-bye to each other in the street. Christine knew something had been lost. She could not hide the sadness from her eyes. Her beautiful mouth trembled.

These enchanted eyes

Our Divine Mother screams. The priest has arrived to bless the house and Angelina and I are still in bed. Today is Epiphany and the priest will bless each room with holy water. A choir of little boys, surrounded by smoky clouds of incense, ceremoniously announces his arrival. Quickly, Angie and I scramble into our clothes and head for Tassos' cafe. Later, near the Castle, the priest throws a large cross into the sea and three men dive into the cold water to retrieve the cross. Angie and I arrive too late however and we miss the ceremony. Already the people are returning to their homes with little bottles of holy water clutched in their hands. Labés was one of the divers and he came up with the cross. He visits the homes during the day and people give him money. That night he's drunk and happy and singing in the cafes.

We step out into a warm, bright winter sun. The sea sparkles the sky is so clear and for the first time I notice the tiny purple and yellow flowers growing on the side of the road to the ancient Castle. We wave hello to the American-Greek professor and his mother who are hiking into Yephra for a late breakfast at Artemis'. And speaking of breakfast, what a wonderful smell: fresh eggs pan-frying in virgin olive oil. (Or eggs swimming in oil as the case may be). It's a smell that I know shall always bring back memories of this land and this time. At first, Angelina and I were appalled by the amount of olive oil they use for such a simple dish. But they can cook the eggs without turning them over in the pan and olive oil is so plentiful. The morning that we went up into the hills with Tassos to help him and his family pick olives, before we left he invited us to have a late breakfast with him. He served us fresh baked bread with a huge bowl of delicious green beans. The green beans had been cooked with tomatoes, chopped potatoes and onions, oregano and lots of olive oil. Tassos then dipped a ladle into a barrel of oil and poured another ladle into each of our bowls. Angie looked at me in horror. Now, THAT, I thought is carrying one's love of olive oil a little too far.

Angie wants to see the graveyard. Bubu told her that after three years the bones are dug up and washed in sea water. Then the bones are placed in a little box beside the grave. Angie wants to see the little boxes of bones. She's poking here and there, lifting lids, peering in this box and that vase. At last she finds a box of bones. Then another box with a skull. The bones don't really interest me but I am fascinated by their custom of placing photographs of those who have died on their gravestones. Outside the cemetery walls Angie finds a few scattered bones. Someone who didn't make it. But WHO? Perhaps it's the bones of a washed-up sailor. Or the bones of a saint.

"It looks like Demetrious!" Angie jokes.

With light hearts and enchanted eyes we walk through the ancient town and out the far gateway. We pass a small herd of goats tended by a woman dressed in black. As we pass the sacred spot where once we made love Angie and I smile at each other secretly, holding hands.

We come to the light house and then around to the far side of the rock. Here this massive rock juts straight up into the clouds. A long time ago this almost sheer vertical wall acted as a natural defense against enemies from the sea. We both can feel the power and beauty and purity of this place, uncorrupted by the rage of assaults.

We tread carefully over a thin path. The steep wall is cracked with fissures, their crystallized edges like tiny marbled daggers. A large opening in the wall catches my eye. I pause. Perhaps it's a cave. I venture a little closer. An eerie feeling seizes me. It's a vagina! A yoni perfectly formed in gray rock and pink marble and wet, glistening moss.

I once read about a famous temple in India, at Kamakhya, in Assam, I believe. The temple is dedicated to yoni-worship. Something to do originally—or mythically—with Sati, the beloved wife of Siva. Inside the temple at Kamakhya there's a cleft in the rocks shaped like a yoni, like this one, I suppose, (but probably not as pretty), and, like this one, the temple cave has a natural spring inside that keeps Her yoni moist.

Do I dare go closer? Do I dare honor this Greek goddess with a kiss?

Crazy Willie the poet, a friend of mine, says that it's all sex. That I'm only mystifying it. If it's all sex, so be it. Old age and death too. And what comes before and what comes after. (Think, can you remember when you ever were *not*? Can you imagine when you ever will be *not*?)

But I see no mysticism here. And no ZEN!

Zen you'll find in a monastery. Or in Max's tavern before they cleaned the place up. Would you like a poem in seventeen syllables?

"A Wise Man never eats sweets.

A Wise Man never eats meat.

A Wise Man never sleeps."

(Give or take one or two.)

I catch up with Angelina down by the sea and we trace our steps back to the ancient town. We take a wrong turn, a dead-end. And in the middle of the road—actually, it's not really what you'd call a road, more like an alley—someone has taken a huge dump.

Now why didn't they go just a few steps to the side of the path? If this were India or Nepal or Afghanistan…. But this is Greece, home of the gods. And in the middle of the road, before our enchanted eyes….

REMEMBRANCE OF YOU

Before the breath,
there is you.
Before the 99 names
of the Essence,
before the Divine Mother,
before birth and death,
there is you.

Before time and space,
before earth, fire, air and water;
before the cosmos,
there is you.
Before you is the sea,
within you the road.
Before both sea and road,
there is you.

Monemvasia / November 1972

We just make it up as we go,
the whole movie!

Panayotis, "the big-nosed fisherman," lives in the ancient town. He owns a large citrus grove and has his own fishing boat. One day Angelina and I take a ride with him to see his orchard, a few miles from Yephra on the way towards Sparta. We come back to Yephra with bags full of sweet, juicy oranges and tangerines. Panayotis works as a fisherman most of the time. When he isn't fishing he's usually drinking. This winter has been especially bad for fishing. Almost everyday the three of us go drinking retsina together, usually by early afternoon. Then Bubu joins us and we drink until Artemis closes for the night.

Angie wants to go fishing with Panayotis and his crew. So one morning, way before daybreak, Panayotis comes by to pick her up and they go out into the darkness of the sea, looking for fish. I decline the invitation; too early in the morning and too cold for me.

Panayotis is married but not happily it seems. He's also a man after the ladies. Tourist ladies, I mean. Naturally, he has his eye on my lovely lady but Panayotis isn't pushy and Angie feels okay with the situation. Anyway, one afternoon the three of us are drinking together at the hotel—the one just across the street from Artemis' restaurant—and Angelina mentions to Panayotis that we need to find a cheaper place to live.

"Do you want a free house?" Panayotis asks us.

A FREE house? My mouth nearly falls open. It never occurred to us to ask for a free place to stay.

"Nai, nai!" we answer in our best Greek. Meaning "Yes, yes!"

A few days later Artemis hands us the key to his house in the ancient town. Artemis was born in the house (we find his wooden cradle stashed away in the dusty root cellar) but no one has lived in the house for twenty-one years. The house has no electricity, no running water, no toilet. But the kitchen has a big fireplace built into the wall and the upstairs has a nice view of the sea.

In mid-January we move into the house, much to the dismay of the old sea captain and his wife. For a whole day we sweep and shovel fallen plaster and debris out through the upstairs broken windows and wash the floors by running a hose into the house from a neighbor's outside connection. There's a covered well in the back room. Bubu has heard that the Greeks often put an eel in their well to keep the water clean. So he and Angelina are shining a flashlight down into the well, looking for the eel.

The first night in the house we built a roaring fire in the kitchen fireplace. That wasn't a good idea. The fire caught in the chimney, charring the ends of the second floor beams. Two nights later we discovered the bamboo under the tile roof was still smoldering. Believe me, it's not such a pleasant thing to wake up in the middle of a winter's night with your roof on fire. Tonight, a capricious wind is whirling gusts of smoke down the chimney into our faces and blowing the walls away piece by piece. We hear a strange noise upstairs. Probably the third wall going but I'm not about to look. Ah, but I will go outside and steal a few pieces of wood for the fire and stare at the wondrous golden moon.

"Everything is all right!" swears the Prophet.
"Everything is getting better and better!"
The Prophet pulls out the best Afghan hashish we've ever smoked. It doesn't do away with the walls like the wind does but they certainly warp and bend like crazy. Barney comes from Canada and works as a seaman when he works. Now he's having fun, traveling around this part of the world in an old VW van with his lovely lady friend from Belgium, smoking Afghan hashish and espousing the message and psychedelic vision of Timothy Leary. We invite him and Lieve to stay in our house and sleep in the downstairs room next to the kitchen.

"It's wonderful!" Barney says and laughs gleefully. "Can you imagine? Here we are living in the ruins of a castle. We just make it up as we go, the whole movie!"

Davina gazes into my hand and tells me I'm a Thinker.
I think she's drunk.
Johan's drunk. Eva's drunk.
The whole house weaves into the warm spring night.
Barney rolls some hashish into a cigarette. The tobacco nearly kills me. Thank God it only takes two hits. The Prophet watches the movie with a boyish grin, while the pretty young thing from Norway giggles as he tries to explain *"Everything is all right."* Then there's Caroline from Scotland. Caroline's very serious and uptight and feeling outraged over what she perceives as our lack of social responsibility, and she wants the stage to air her grievances. She's convinced that we're all escaping in our tumbledown house by the sea and our circle of passing smoke. Bubu brought her to the party by accident. Bubu wishes she had stayed home and turns to me with a saddened heart.
He's an idealist, a heavy dancer, Bubu.
He reads complicated German philosophy and writes poetry. But, in his heart, he says, he has no hope. He sees no way to save the world or the future. "You can only save yourself," he confides in me. He keeps a shotgun in his VW for just that purpose he says: "a way out."
Around midnight we take a stroll out to the fortress wall. The wind has died down. The night sky is clear. Everywhere above us the stars twinkle, and, looking towards Yephra, we can see a tiny nest of home lights and way in the distance in the hills a few scattered glows.
In the churchyard grows a tree with a bell hanging from a large limb. Bubu wants to test the bell. He wants to determine if the bell is Italian or Greek. The difference, he explains to us, can be heard in the subtle and precise variations of tone. After a few loud gongs—loud enough, I think, to wake the Tibetan dead—Bubu decides it must be an Italian bell.

The Prophet and his lovely lady stay with us for a month; then they leave for India on a shoestring and the Prophet's convictions. (Gadzooks, there goes another version of myself. And born under the same sign too.) Davina and her husband continue north. They were traveling by van from South Africa. Bubu leaves the hotel and moves in with us. Clever Bubu is here. *"Everything is gonna be all right!"*

The delicate ribbons of light
that we are

"In the beginning
there was you.
Then there was light
and I saw you."

We weave in and out of lives and what we need just appears.
We need a free house and fall we do is ask. We need a ride
to Athens and a ride shows up, just like that. One night, not
long after moving to the ancient town, we're laughing and
joking and drinking wine with Bubu in Artemis' when in
come Johan and Eva. We've seen them in Monemvasia, and on
the road in their van, but we've never had a chance or reason
to meet. Bubu has an album of Theodrakis music that he
hasn't heard and he knows that Johan has a player and a house
with electricity. Bubu goes over to their table and introduces
himself. He explains the situation and Johan invites him to
their house the next evening. Bubu then motions for us to join
them. Johan's a big guy in his mid-forties, with a full beard
and coal black wavy hair, and you immediately feel a rich gold
mine of humor and vitality in his energy. He's wearing blue
denim jeans and a denim jacket and a leather cowboy hat that
he bought in the Flea Market in Athens. Eva reminds me of a
dove. She's gentle and soft looking with pale blonde hair to her
shoulders. She smiles a sweet, sweet smile, and speaks only a
little English. We talk for a while and Johan and Eva invite us
all to come out for dinner. Johan seems to be really taking us
in, his clear blue eyes twinkling with secret, inner electricity.
  Wow, civilization!
  We enter Johan's house and we're back in Europe. A stereo.
An inside toilet. A refrigerator. Books. The living room is huge.
A nine foot long wooden table, which Johan built himself, fits
perfectly into the room. The large fireplace, with side vents, he
copied from a Swedish design, and it can hold a fire that'll run
you out of the house in no time. Once you get the green olive

wood burning, that is. The Greeks like to sell you green wood, Johan explains to me, because it weighs more. (Well, I think to myself, that makes sense.) Anything to keep down the cabin fever, they seem to have. A dark room, a stone polisher, power tools. A rainy day's stash of booze. A sewing machine and a loom for Eva. A television, a typewriter, jigsaw puzzles.

Johan generates his own electricity. For plumbing, he has a small motor outside the house that pumps water from the cistern beneath his patio into a large metal drum on the roof, and then gravity takes over. He and a Danish friend built the house five years ago. At the time Johan was living with another lady, but it turns out that she preferred the society of Copenhagen to the peasant ways of Greece. There were other things going on too. (But isn't that always true?) Something about her and the German architect who lives in the old town. But I never got the full story behind that.

Johan works in Copenhagen during the summers. Then, in late September, he and Eva return to Greece to live until the next April. They're not married but it's obvious they care a great deal for each other. Eva certainly seems to enjoy the slow casual pace of Greece, although just as certainly she does not adopt the subservient role that most Greek women pretend to play. Not knowing the language, she ignores the unspoken customs too. Johan, of course, speaks good Greek. He hears about the little sly scandals and private dramas and the dramas that aren't so private that go on in Monemvasia.

That night, we enjoy an incredible Danish feast. As soon as we've had a tour of their house, Eva serves us fresh squeezed orange juice with vodka. Actually, it's not vodka but straight distilled alcohol. A Greek pharmacist friend supplies it to Johan. Some kind of covert arrangement they have. After dinner, Bubu drives back into town to pick up more wine. While in town he also picks up two Greek university girls from Athens that have come to Monemvasia for a two-week holiday. Meanwhile, we're having a wonderful time swapping stories. Johan was once stationed in Greenland and that's where he learned his version of the American language. He learned it from the American servicemen there. The subject of schnapps comes up. Johan opens an antique wooden cabinet and takes out a selection of different flavored schnapps. Angelina sips a tiny glass of peppermint but it's way too sweet for me. But, inside a discreet little box, what should appear before our wondrous eyes but a special little pipe and a chunk of hashish. A Canadian friend smuggled the hashish in his shoe across the Greek-Turkish border, Johan tells us.

We haven't smoked any hashish since Paris. Johan offers us a smoke and we graciously accept. The energy in the room feels nice and safe and warm. Exciting and electrical too. Once again we tell Johan how much we like his house. Then out of the bluest skies in the world, Johan offers us his house for the summer—*for free.* "If you want," he says. "For free!"

Just like that.

In Copenhagen's Tivoli Gardens, where Johan works each summer, his job is to keep the electrical juice flowing and serious little old ladies from assaulting broken-down slot machines with their canes and black heels. All this he must accomplish with a straight face. In Greece, people bring him their broken radios. He never charges for his work. The Greeks give him baskets of eggs, fruit, vegetables, and kilos of olive oil and wine. One Sunday morning his best Greek friend, Christos, the town carpenter, drags us all out to a bucolic little village in the hills to repair a juke box. The juke box belongs to his sister. She owns a cafe in the village. But let me back up a bit. It was almost a week ago when Angie and I walked the six kilometers out to Johan's house, just for a visit. The four of us were having so much fun together, running around the countryside doing good deeds in the day and drinking wine in the night, cooking special dinners and sharing our histories and going on adventures, that Angie and I just never went home. In a village not far away the church bell had stopped ringing. The pulling wire to the bell had been wound too tight. So the priest of the village sends for Johan. Johan and I climb up into the bell tower, and in no time he has the bell ringing again. This makes the priest very happy and he gives Johan five kilos of olive oil. Then the priest leads the four of us to a local taverna and the taverna owner gives us five liters of wine. That evening we drive into Yephra to have dinner and we take the five liters of wine into the restaurant with us. But Artemis doesn't mind. It's a custom in Greece, at least in the villages. Bubu soon joins us. Then two strangers drive up in a van with Dutch plates. They come inside to eat and soon we're exchanging names and greetings, and the next thing we're all going out to Johan's house to have a party. And that's how we met Barney and Lieve. Then, last night, Bubu came by to visit and we stayed up most of the night talking and drinking wine. Now Christos wants us to go somewhere in the middle of nowhere so that Johan can repair a juke box. (Never mind that Johan has never repaired a juke box before.) Johan groans happily in his misery and crawls into the back seat of his van. I climb in back with him. Eva smiles sweetly and Angelina does the driving. Christos will not ride in the van but insists on going with Bubu in his Volkswagen. "Because a woman is driving!" he explains.

"One time," Johan tells us with a chuckle, "I actually kept an olive oil factory running on just the G string from my guitar."

Johan's heart overflows with love. His eyes dance with light. A good story or a show is all he asks. One evening the three of us smoke a little of his Turkish hashish and Johan puts on a tape of gentle and mellow American country western music. We blow up a few balloons and Johan gives us a most wonderful show with the floating balloons, capturing in an almost ethereal performance the quintessence of what Tivoli Gardens means to him. He loves American country and western music, and his dreams come true when he loses himself in the slow, sentimental currents of "Red River Valley".

Johan's a big man with a big appetite for life. But, because of a dysfunctional thyroid, alcohol stays in his system for a long time. Like the Sunday morning we went to repair the juke box. The rest of us just felt groggy from lack of sleep but Johan was still flying high because of his thyroid. To make matters even more comical the instructions on the inside back of the juke box were printed in Japanese. I don't know what Johan did, or how he managed it, but he got the juke box to playing again.

In early April, on their way back to Copenhagen, he and Eva smuggled fifteen bottles of Polish champagne into Denmark. He sent a cassette tape telling us about the episode. "It's so cheap!" he cried. Then, in one good evening, with the help of three friends and some sad, Swedish ballads, they wiped out eleven bottles.

"And it was worth it!" he vowed.

In the merry spirit of comradeship Johan will over-eat and fall jokingly onto the wooly rug. There, lying on the floor, he'll contemplate sawing the legs off his giant table so that, like the Romans, we can feast, roll over and throw up, and begin again.

Johan is not a man to put on airs. He just likes to fly.

But there's more to Johan than his exuberant appetites. One evening we're drinking a little wine together at his house and he seems to get really drunk. Extraordinarily so for the amount of wine that he's drank. Myself, I feel quite clear and sober. Angelina too. Eva's just quietly being there. A nice fire's burning in the fireplace. Standing near the fire, Johan and I are talking about light. The other day he took some photographs of Davina, to try and capture the quality of light around her. I mention the earlier pictures he took of Angie.

"Ah!" he says. "But Angie *is* the light! She *is* the light!"

"In the beginning there was light," I venture to say.

"No, no!" he says. "In the beginning there was you." He pauses dramatically. "Then there was light and I saw you."

Suddenly I feel the room change. The whole room feels charged with a new, vibrant energy. It feels as if we're surrounded by this fountain of incredibly warm, clear light. How could Johan express such profound truth in such simple, intimate words? As if the words were coming through a dream. Or from some place of great knowingness. Had Johan stepped into some altered state? Had he drawn this energy to us in some extraordinary way? After all, we're in the ancient homeland of the Delphic Oracle. But he didn't seem to be in a trance. I thought about the day that I took a long, thoughtful look at the sea and at the one road going in and out of Monemvasia and wrote the poem "Before." We had been in Monemvasia only a week. Did those words perhaps come in the same way as the words Johan had just spoken to me? Why not, if consciousness is a unified field of energy? Inwards or outwards, how do we tell the difference? Most of us have so many voices inside our heads anyway. All those voices of authority telling us what to do or not to do and what's right and what's wrong. We walk around all the time thinking other people's thoughts and don't even know it. How absurd not to recognize our own thoughts! No wonder we get so confused. It's a wonder we even know how to put one foot in front of the other. Or one thought I should say. Where do thoughts come from anyway? Do they just hang around in the elements, like movable islands in a vast ocean, waiting for us to discover them? I thought about the first time I read the Upanishads. My mind opened like a lotus blossom. Certainly each of us contains moments of great clarity and enlightenment; moments when we resonate with some grand truth and we remember the heartfelt truth of our own beingness.

"A drunk man will tell you the truth," Johan says to me, suddenly, and as deliberately as if handing me a tiny bird's egg; as if he had been carefully following my oh-so serious inner dialogue.

I laugh at this thought.

Johan motions Angie to join the conversation. In the future, he tells us, our language will change. In the future we will communicate to each other not through words but through a kind of vibrational energy. We'll be able to share our thoughts and directly communicate our feelings. Soon, he says, many changes will be coming into our lives. The whole planet will be undergoing "a shifting in frequency". And there will be great numbers, he warns us, who will refuse to accept or to recognize what is taking place on the planet. This is not our concern. The planet will slough off these beings that are not in harmony with this new energy, the way the body sloughs off dead cells. The human story as we know it on this planet is coming to a close. "Like the closing of a book," he dramatically calls it. We'll be stepping into another dimension. We'll be looking at the planet and experiencing the world from this new dimension; not from within the world, as we have in the past.

"But do not turn your back on the world!" Johan says with much emotion. "Love the world! Love this planet! Do not turn your back on it. Or revile it. Or spit on it. Or call it a lie and dismiss it as illusion. For it is one of our creations. Love it. For the world is like a terrified child crying in the dark."

Johan pauses for a moment as if to gather his thoughts. Then he continues his story. In this new dimension death and decay will be a thing of the past; the birth process as we know it will change and eventually cease. We'll have bodies of light. These new vibrational bodies will not be so dense. They'll have a lighter, higher frequency and contain a great deal less water and physical matter. We'll be able to re-vitalize them. We won't need to protect ourselves as we do now with such—Johan smiles, pointing to the walls around us and the wood burning in the fireplace. We'll be able to move with great freedom, and travel great distances, and not need cars and boats and trains and planes; or even metal space ships unless we so choose. We'll have time to experience our lives in a more open, sensitive way. "In your terms," he says, looking directly at me, a hint of conspiracy appearing in his blue eyes, "a more poetic way."

"It is time now to make ready for these changes," he emphasizes several times. "It is time we begin to attune ourselves to this new language. It is time we begin to honor our own energies."

Like "delicate ribbons" he says are the energy currents of our bodies. He encourages us to begin to become aware of the subtle fluctuations of these currents of energy, and to ask what color they would be if we could see them, and what flavor if we could taste them, and how they might sound if we could hear this unique vibrational energy of our beings. Johan urges us to love these delicate ribbons of energy and to carry them as gifts and as wondrous things to be shown to the world. "Carry them with love," he says, and protect them from onslaught by others through these changes that will soon be upon us.

I thought about the strange letter Angelina had written me, about coming to Europe and meeting someone who would help change the evolution of my thinking.

Angie looks at me and smiles knowingly.

I breathe deeply. This is strange business indeed. Johan Rasmussen doesn't sound like any drunk I've ever known, that's for sure. So what kind of crazy talk is this? Is he the one who will bring everything together? Who is this man really, beneath his twinkling blue eyes, his dysfunctional thyroid, his electrical wizardry, his outrageous prophecies? And, more to the point, how will I ever remember all this in order to put it in my book?

Another time, we're sitting around the dinner table, just the four of us. Johan speaks about how wonderful it is that we're together, and that we're all connected through love. His face beams and his heart radiates such warmth and sweetness. Such a gentle man, such a tender man. To be safe and surrounded by loving friends: that's what he wants in life.

Most of the time with Johan, everything is a joke.

One nice day in early April we take a trip to the caves of Dios. With us is Yrsa, an artist and Danish friend of Eva's. Yrsa came down from Copenhagen to visit and to sketch the ruins of Monemvasia. Yrsa doesn't approve of hashish and he isn't aware that we smoke. So Johan and Eva pack a picnic basket of Danish treats and load some apple cakes with hashish. Elizabeth and her boyfriend Peter come with us. Elizabeth has been living in Ghana for six months and Peter's been traveling in Europe. Now they're on their way back to the States through Greece. On the way to Dios we keep a bottle of wine in Yrsa's hands (an easy thing to do), and we dig into the innocent looking apple cakes. Later, in the parking lot, after the long boat ride in silence beneath the dripping limestone and the colorful subterranean lights, Johan opens a bottle of orange liqueur and sets up his portable gas stove. In the parking space next to us two American tourists are eating peanut butter sandwiches. And here we are, laughing, gasping, loaded to the gills and going up in flaming crepes suzette.

Everything is a joke

"Don't believe anything!" Johan tells us right from the beginning. "From now on," he says, "everything is a joke!" To Johan, the "babies," as he called our tiny cannabis plants, were a joke. For me, they were a secret spice, a delicious bit of wickedness that would turn our everyday, ordinary vegetable garden into a "Garden of Earthly Delights." The seeds came from the cannabis that Johan's Canadian friend had smuggled across the Turkish-Greek border. Johan and I started the plants in small plastic pots inside the house on the window sills. In mid-April, shortly after Johan and Eva left for Denmark, I decided to transplant ten of the little ones outside.

But where to put the "babies"?

We decided to build a rock-walled garden on the south side of the house. Here the plants could catch the sun all day. The garden wall would make an attractive architectural extension to the house and give Eva a nice enclosed border to plant roses or spring flowers. The garden would also serve as a way for us to express our gratitude to them for the house. We wanted to surprise Johan and Eva with the garden when they returned in the fall.

Angie and I plundered Johan's land for large rocks—an easy task since the fields around Johan's house and the whole of Greece are forever generous with such stones. Each day we hauled several wheelbarrow loads to the house. At first we made the mistake of putting up a single row of stones. No, that doesn't work. The stones fall over. So we gathered more rocks and built a second row to support the first.

In the backyard of Johan's house grows a giant carob tree. The Greeks don't know how to process the carob fruit, I'm told, and so they export it to Germany. The Germans then turn the fruit into a commercial product. Anyway, beneath the shade of this giant carob tree we dug up wheelbarrow loads of dark loamy topsoil and transported it to the garden bed. Then we mixed in loads of sand that had been abandoned by the construction workers five years ago when Johan built the house. To that I added countless buckets of donkey droppings.

Each day I would take my little plastic bucket and go out into the fields surrounding the house, following the donkeys and the goats. That's another thing, the goats. "The devils of Greece," they call them. The goat herders run their goats over the land and the hungry goats will eat your grass, your trees, your shrubs. Your grapevines, too, as we found out. Johan finally put up a barbed wire fence around his place. But the fence is down on one side, and, yesterday, after a goat herder had stopped by, asking for Johan and for a drink of water, here came a herd of goats.

Angie had spotted the goat herder peeking through the kitchen window before he knocked at the door. Since she walks around the house barefooted and often bare breasted and sometimes bare all over, we were thinking of our privacy, and it didn't enter our minds that perhaps the goat herder was checking to see if the coast was clear to bring his goats on the land. Thick green grasses and weeds grow in the fields around Johan's house but he allows only one farmer, Andonai, to feed his animals on the grass from these fields.

The road that runs by Johan and Eva's house is the main highway between Monemvasia and Sparta and the rest of Greece. Everyday the workers blast the road with dynamite in order to widen it. They need explosives because the ground contains mostly rock. Rock and red clayish soil. (Just like the red old hills of Georgia that I grew up with.) And it may take five years, at the pace they work. One thing about the Greeks, they don't rush themselves to death. Between one and three in the afternoon they stop work altogether. They eat lunch and sleep or whatever. They tell us that soon the heat will become unbearable for mid-day work. In the early part of the morning, and when the workers leave for the day, I hurry out to the road with my wheelbarrow to gather fill dirt from the heaps of red earth that have been bulldozed up. So the old road to Monemvasia becomes part of our garden.

One for the road

Once there lived an elephant called Truth. This elephant belonged to a Traveling Metaphysical Circus renowned throughout the world for its spiritual materialism and other strange and unbelievable acts. One day the Circus came to town. The people had never seen an elephant before. Five curious townsmen were determined to witness this mythical creature and bring back a report on its appearance. They arrived late at night. There was no light in the elephant's tent but the townsmen were too impatient to wait for morning. The first man, a promising poet, grasped the elephant's trunk, and, in the darkness of the tent, imagined that this mysterious creature must be like a fierce and powerful dragon and decided to steal its fire. Another man, the town drunk, stumbled against the elephant's ear and he swore that the creature was very much like a tavern door. The third man, a famous scientist, examined the elephant's tail and logically deduced, that, according to all known laws of the universe, the elephant, if, in fact, such a creature existed, was unscientific, (if not a downright hoax), and, bumblebee or no bumblebee, didn't have a leg to stand on. The fourth man, an evangelistic preacher who feared that the Circus would lead the good people of his community astray, cautiously ran his hands up the elephant's hind legs and immediately became obsessed with thoughts of his neighbor's wife. The last man, a highly respected mortician, who, at one time, had been grand mayor of the town, climbed upon the elephant's backside, and, in a loud and pompous voice, cried out that, by god, the elephant stank to high heaven and was nothing more than a pile of dung.

(The moral of this story is left up to you.)

We raise our glasses high, one for the road. But no one smiles. Bubu looks darkly sad, and, at times, angry, surly. He's driving to Athens, to see a lawyer friend of someone he knows. The police will not allow him to stay in Greece. They refuse to grant him an extension on his visa and they offer him no reason for the denial. (Little do we know at the time—we only find this out much later from Johan—that the police suspect Bubu's archaeological friend Maria to be in with a gang of thieves. These thieves have been stealing relics and smuggling them out of the country. Because Bubu has been seen many times with Maria the police want him out of Greece.) Bubu feels confused, resentful. But what can he do? No doubt his friends in Germany will be glad to see him return. Now they can relax and feel safe again. Now they won't have to doubt, if only for a moment, the sanity of their rigorous, predictable lives. They could not understand Bubu quitting his job with the government. He had such a good job, even had a Mercedes with chauffeur. They could not understand Bubu going off to Greece to play his guitar. He even let his hair grow long. (Well, it wasn't *that* long). They could not understand Bubu simply going on adventures.

Good-bye, Bubu. We'll miss you!

Remembrance of you

They say you were born when the earth & mountains
turned green and bright yellow,
& bees swarmed the hills to gather flowers
for their Queen,
& goats with singing throats
roamed the rocks.
The blue morning sea and sky
were one
in the moment of your awakening.
You saw the oneness of life,
& you saw the oneness
dissolve
before your eyes
into so many streams,
& the streams into an unwavering light
within you

I stopped, not knowing how to end the poem. I was sitting alone at Johan's big table, using his old manual typewriter with the Danish alphabet. It was late April and the hills on the road between Sparta and Monemvasia had turned bright yellow with tall flowering shrubs. These fragrant, bright yellow flowers reminded me of the Scotch broom growing along the freeways in Oregon. The singing goats came from that incredible evening as the sun was going down and a goat herder with his dog was herding more than a hundred goats into a canyon corral for the night. The sound of the goats in the wind at dusk in the shadows quickly darkening into night, and a starry sky with a crescent moon, held us motionless, enchanted. In the near distance the lights of Yephra twinkled and we could hear the sea lapping the land with soft, dark, unending waves.

One morning, late in February, I had looked out over the old fortress walls of Monemvasia and gazed into the bluest sea and sky that I had ever seen. For a moment I stood still and quiet, becoming a part of the blue oneness that I gazed upon. I decided that this sparkling azure sea could, indeed, have been the birthplace of Venus. Like the Venus that I had seen in a painting by Alexander Cabanel. The Goddess, in all her soft and sensuous beauty, lies sleeping (or perhaps she dreams?) on the ocean froth. Frolicking above her in the air little winged cherubs are blowing conch shells. I could well imagine that she must have been the most gorgeous woman Alexander Cabanel had ever painted. Probably he fell in love with her and that was the death of the artist as a normal man. For a moment I amused myself with this thought. Then it dawned on me how much this blue Aegean sea and sky reminded me of the gem stone that we had found in a shop in Athens.

It was a small shop on one of the winding streets that eventually leads one up to the Acropolis. Angelina and I walked into the small shop by chance; or so we thought. We were looking for a fire opal to have set in silver as a wedding ring for Angie. She had combed the little jewelry shops in the Flea Market area of London but had seen none that she really liked. Here in this little shop in the Plaka we found what she wanted: a lovely and brilliant Australian fire opal in a simple silver setting. It was a beautiful ring, and, no doubt, symbolic in some way of our marriage. As for myself, I seldom wore jewelry. Not even a watch. I didn't care for metal things on my hands. So I was just curiously looking at the rings inside the glass case when a blue sky stone, set in a man's silver ring, caught my eye. I had never seen a stone like this before. The blue was as blue as the Aegean Sea but with a hint of white clouds. Like the earth seen from outer space. I asked to see the ring and it was a perfect fit. As perfect as my large knuckles allowed. The proprietor of the store—a man who looked more Turkish or Middle Eastern than he did Greek—motioned for his daughter, who spoke good English, to answer our questions about the ring. She called the stone Larimar and said that it came from only one place in the world. She said it came from a mine that had recently been discovered on an island in the Dominican Republic.

She looked at me curiously, or so I imagined.

The woman was about my own age and had coal black hair and luminous eyes and an earthly, sensual beauty in her face. "It is a stone of free will and free joy," she said, articulating her words slowly and precisely. Her eyes glowed with an inner light, as if she were seeing into the heart of the stone. "I see this to be the Child's Stone. A stone of being who you wish to be—and doing what you wish to do—with the freedom of the child. A stone of knowing how you feel and what you want—as a child knows—instinctively."

I slipped the stone on the ring finger of my right hand and imagined myself wearing it. For me this blue stone was the stone of the warm shallow seas and the white cloud sky. The stone of the wanderer who finds joy and never loses his way.

The woman, still looking at the ring with warm, dreamy eyes, raised one hand to her neck and pulled a thin silver chain from beneath her black wool sweater. On the chain, set in a delicate silver loop, was another blue sky stone.

"I love this stone," she said to us, almost in a whisper. "I keep it with me all the time. It is the stone of a Dreamer."

A quiver of excitement showed in her voice. Angelina squeezed my hand. We both felt honored that this woman had shown us her personal power stone. Glancing at the ring still on my finger, the woman said, "These are Dreaming stones. They carry a new message to the world."

What did she mean by that? I was afraid to ask, afraid that the question would break the magical spell. Looking at the stone on my finger in that strangely warm and dreamingly way the woman said, "I feel that this is your stone. Yes. The Child's Stone is your personal stone."

Perhaps she was just saying this to sell me the ring, quibbled the doubter in me. But I don't think so. She was not a woman to lie about such things. Besides, I had made up my mind to take the ring right from the beginning. I felt that the energy of the blue sky stone was closely connected to my heart. I bought the ring and Angelina took the fire opal and we walked back down the hill, both in a slightly astonished dream.

But the inspiration for the poem?

The elusive chemistry, the subtle indivisibility of this remembrance, felt to me like a fleeting dream in the early morning light; like a moonbeam in the grasses or the shadow of a hand against a tree limb; like the dancing flitter of light among trees or the pattern of reflections in water or the movement of a young girl passing by a window: all these things that come and go, that you see and do not know if your really saw or not.

I wanted a good ending to my poem. Something solid, final, unshakable. To be the few notes of a melody heard faraway and not the complete song, this felt most unsettling to my mind. I was used to thinking in terms of tight, defined structures, and the routines of daily life, and concrete forms that seemed to defy the changes of time and the tides. In my belief system I judged things right or wrong; real or not real. The undefined: all those things that you couldn't touch, and that have no continuity, belonged to the world of illusion and fantasy and to the dangerous and watery realm of Neptune. But not to the planet Earth. I could not imagine that the essence of the life force might happen randomly from day to day, here today, somewhere else tomorrow, a bit of this, a pinch of that, a little piece of sunray, a little rainbow, a dewdrop, a flower, a butterfly's wings traced against the sun. I could not believe that these things might contain any real meaning, expressed in a way that only the peripheral of my mind, the edges of my sight, the inner ear, the half-beat between my heart beats, could understand. Nor could I see that these elusory impressions and fleeting images and memories that could not be made tangible, or stuck into some rigid category, or confined in a system, or explained by a theory, or controlled by the laws of this or that: all these things that come and go, that slip past the corner of your eye, that you see and do not know if you really saw or not, contain the essence of magic and beauty and playfulness and are just as real and meaningful and alive as the life animals live or plants live or human beings live; that these things are more than just frosting and adornment and ornaments solicited by a none-too-real imagination,—or temptations that would lead me astray into sloth and indolence and false longings; but they are living strands of energy and power and essence that help to keep the mind from turning rigid and cold and going dead; and through these things that come and go, that you see and do not know if your really saw or not; that through these flights of fantasy, these delicate ribbons of light, these rainbow colors, these fleeting dreams, I might cease this ancient war within myself and bring a great opening to my heart and to my mind and to the other energy centers of my body, and create within and around myself a kind of healing spaciousness and a gentle passage that would bring me home to the truth of my being, to the wholeness of personality and self, and to my unremembered identity.

Now that we've seen each other

A tour of the solar system reveals not
even one white horse standing still
under a willow tree,
not even one man who remembers me
and perhaps it is time I fell
with the leaves that are not of any tree.
From where I stand on the soft cliffs
of this night
I see a fire on a wall
and a man singing onto it;
there will I go and assume a name
in the world of illusions,
buckling the ribs like a sword
around my soul.
I will be seen again
loved, hated, and forgotten
again.
All these years past I have drifted,
awakening several children sleeping in
far places, yet I have not found
the hand into which
all rivers run their course;
and what is there to say
that the grassless night does not
say better, and longer?
Now, perhaps
it will all count for something.

Tom Kryss
"To Think That None Of These Things
I Heard In Traveling Were True"

We first met Bob Messina and Eric Savier on one of our trips to
Athens. Bob rented a house in the city and he taught English

lessons to the kids living on the American air force base. Eric immediately felt a strong attraction to Angelina and Angelina to him. Originally from a small town in Florida, Eric had recently lived in India under the guidance of a spiritual guru and had taken a vow of silence upon his return to Greece. Eric communicated with others through emotional and psychic vibes and through physical gestures and notes. He wrote notes constantly and one of the first notes he wrote to A'lina, as he called her, at the dinner table that first night they met, said simply: YOU FEEL BEAUTIFUL. I admired the man's boldness, his directness, his openness, his humor, and the ways he expressed his metaphysical ideals. While in India, Eric, or "Omeric", as we sometimes called him, had lived in a cave and taught himself ancient Greek by translating Homer. He meditated and chanted OM; he wore a gold earring in one ear and walked barefooted on the streets. He pulled his long reddish hair into a pony's tail behind his head. He collected all the seeds from the fruit he ate and gave the seeds to anyone who would plant them in a garden. He took A'lina on a motorcycle ride to the sea and they didn't return until noon the next day. That night—the night after her motorcycle trip—Angelina announced to me that she had found her "spiritual teacher" in Eric. I said nothing. For the first time in our relationship I felt the taloned fears of jealousy plunge into my heart. Perhaps my pride kept me silent. My pride had certainly tripped me up before. I had a "high ass," as Eric joked. Or perhaps I still had Christine Isbell on my mind. Above all else, though, I considered Angelina a free spirit. Free to follow her heart. Free to honor her feelings. To me, that came as a given. I never had any other rule. I prized freedom and I gave to others what I asked for himself.

Still, I felt caught in the cross-fires. I had wanted a marriage of true minds. I had wanted a monogamous relationship; for I did have a great desire for constancy, loyalty, and faithfulness. I could hope that Angelina would not want to make love with another man but I knew all too well the pangs, the impulses, and the wild, curious desires of the heart. I knew the premature heaven that in a heartbeat can plunge into its opposite. I knew lust on a spit, the fevered heat, the twisting and the turning. I knew the arrow poised and drawn, quivering for flight. I knew the expense of self-denial: the hatred, the loathing, the betrayal, the resentment, the hypocrisy. I knew the sudden reverses, the flip-flops, the flickering energies, the ambivalence. And I knew how untrustworthy I might seem to others. As Melina Foster had once warned Angie: "David can make a 180 degree turn without even so much as a signal."

That night I couldn't sleep. What had happened on their motorcycle ride to the beach? What was really going on between Eric and A'lina? Between myself and Angie? Between the three of us? I had no idea what to do with jealously and anger. They felt to me like a dense cloud around my heart.

The night passed in painful solitude.

Toward morning I fell asleep and in my sleep I had a dream. In the dream my friend Dusty Atman kept taking her dress off and then putting the dress back on, but in an odd, funny way, and I could still see her body naked through the dress. All the time she kept touching herself intimately and talking to me casually about the death of Ishtar, a bright colorful song bird, that, she said, had once belonged to her. I just stood there staring at Dusty through her clothes. Only, suddenly, she turned into Christine Isbell. She had on a pale white dress and her Swedish blond hair glowed like streams of sunlight around her face. I felt absolutely stunned by her beauty. She stood silent as if waiting for me to speak.

"I'm so sorry," I blurted out, my heart tearing inside me—a flower ripped by a careless child. "I never knew what to say to you."

She touched my mouth with her finger tips. "David, my love, for I did love you, why are you so unhappy?"

I blinked my eyes and could not answer.

"Take my hand," she said.

Suddenly we stood in some desert canyon land on a high bluff beneath a full moon. Through the shadows made by the scattered clouds we followed a delicate moonlight path. On the edge of the abyss I looked down. I could see the tiny lights of cars like memories or past lives or civilizations whizzing by on the thin ribbon road that lay far below us and below the slow graceful flight of a hawk in the hot morning sun. "I'll come to see you in the form of a butterfly." I remembered my promise to Christine. At the time we had been teasing each other and just having fun. Now I closed my eyes and softly landed on a tiny red ribbon in her hair. Ever so lightly with dark butterfly wings that had bright yellow eyes I touched her lips. She laughed gaily as she recognized me. My dark wings brushed the milky whiteness of her breasts, and tickled her on the belly, then circled to nestle on the pale yellow flower below, a flower as delicate and beautiful as the prickly-pear blossoms that dotted the high desert bluff. Then, in a burst of brightness, she vanished. I stood alone on a high mesa overlooking the sea on some planet that wasn't the Earth. Luminous butterflies fluttered all around me. Two shiny moons brightened the night sky. I felt a flood of tears come to my eyes and great sobs shaking my body. Then I woke up.

A continuous dream

If we could meet
At a touch
Over 10,000 miles—
It wouldn't be enough,
It wouldn't mean
That we were real.
Even if naked
In yoga position
We could sit
For years
Without changing—
Ourselves—
Thru time
And situations
I couldn't see enough

To convince me
Or fill me—
Not your hand
On my breast
But a cannibalistic journey
Thru the cells
Of your body,
Your mind—
You
Like sperm
In my belly.
But this would be a touch
Too real—
Our mutual gift
Would destroy us.

Paula Atwell
"A Few Years Later In Madrid"

I hadn't seen Dusty Atman in a long time. For years she had been like a continuous dream that I couldn't wake up from. In the second summer after the Summer of Love in San Francisco I caught a glimpse of her on Market Street and I followed her for blocks, trying to catch her, but she was still traveling in Spain or the South of France or somewhere. Dusty had left a most painful memory in my heart, a wound that had never really healed and would not heal for many years to come, when at last our lives would once again momentarily converge and diverge, just before she left Seattle for Hollywood to become a famous screen writer, and I already had gray hairs in my beard. She would invite me into her room, and I would kiss her as I had always dreamed of kissing her, as we lay together in the dark amidst the sweet, delicate scent of orchids. But for us it was too late. Time had already passed us by.

I first met Dusty when we were students in college. An intelligent, pretty girl of eighteen, she had been born, like me, on the cutting edge of winter. Dusty seemed so intense and sensitive and quick of spirit. She had tinted blonde hair and grayish-green eyes and a slim, athletic body; and she could laugh and cry and get outraged, and sling her coat down onto the sidewalk, and stalk away like a child who abandons her toy, but she never stayed angry for long. She had a real directness about her that I liked, even when this directness caused me pain. At times, Dusty could be as vulnerable as a leaf on an oak tree in November; and, yet, in a heartbeat, she could double her fists and go to battle for me against the jocks—"those strong trees with shallow roots," as she called them, and the campus Greeks who made cruel jokes about me, out of jealously over the attention and respect that she showed me. Yet she persisted in going out with these same athletic toads, expecting a prince, perhaps.

Delicate at times, coarse at times; sensuous, creative; Dusty identified with Apollo and I with Dionysus. She sought the masculine ideal of beauty and grace in her lovers and she could not reciprocate my intense, wounded longing for her. Yet she never meant to be unkind, this I knew. She never intended to hurt me. Perhaps she was a bit selfish, as my friend Lisa claimed, but she never lied to me. She never acted under false pretenses. She simply chose to follow the rhythms of her own heartbeat and heed the integrity of her own path. For this I would always honor her. It would take years for me to see that, for all her courage and honesty, her intuitive wisdom, and her sunny, cheerful spirit, Dusty lacked the willingness to enter a certain depth of heart and through this lack she denied herself an authentic connection to the truly rich, deeply creative powers within her. Be that as it may, at the tender age of eighteen Dusty became for me a viable symbol of the female energy that I felt so disconnected to within myself. It was this lack of connection to the female within myself—the female as nurturing, creative, supportive energy; as the space that allows action to take place; as the encompassing nutrient out of which specifics emerge—and not my unrequited love for Dusty—that had created such a feeling of polarization within myself; such a feeling of grief, of loss and separation.

One Sunday afternoon, when we were walking together in the orange groves on campus, Dusty taught me to kiss slowly, without rushing and overwhelming her with ambition, but with softness and playful affection, and with a kind of sweet friendship that allowed the kiss to go on and on like an endless summer day. She taught me a new meaning to William Blake's song "Tyger Tyger burning bright in the forests of the night." Later, when we did play on the grass together by the shore of the lake and kiss, the night quickened by spring and forbidden vodka, Dusty did not protest when I unbuttoned her blouse and touched her breasts. My whole body trembled with wanting for her and yet she could not return my desire. The night she came to the campus theater to see me in a performance, I wrote a message to her on a piece of paper. I gave the note to her as we walked back to the dorm. It was a line from *Winnie the Pooh*: "Now they we've seen each other, I'll believe in you if you'll believe in me."

Lisa accused me of seeing in Dusty what wasn't there. Perhaps I had turned her into a fantasy; I couldn't tell for sure. I found myself spontaneously acting out her odd, little behaviors, like the way she would rub her finger tips nervously together whenever she heard the sound of a plane overhead. Dusty couldn't explain her anxiety over the sound of planes and I couldn't explain how she seemed to enter my mind and body and take over my sense of identity. I didn't understand at the time how little I really inhabited my own body and how deeply my soul dreamed of wholeness and connection to the earth and to the feminine. I felt so sexually alone and incomplete, and so exaggerated with unacted desire, that I once confessed to Dusty that I wanted to lie naked on the warm green grass by the lake and embrace the earth, as a man would a woman. She didn't laugh at me, and had I realized the truth of my own inner disconnectedness this notion perhaps would not have felt so ludicrous as I imagined it to be at the time.

One in a million

I first met Dusty Atman in the middle of sunny Florida at a small liberal arts college; a good dropping-off place for rich kids with sport cars and folk guitars. Religious morality served as the official rule and conformity, social identity and hypocrisy as the everyday, guiding principles. In this environment I had the singular reputation of being the only "intellectual" on campus. This, no doubt, said more about the college than it did about me. Even then I would have flunked my language requirements for sure, if it hadn't been for a kindly, middle-aged, alcoholic, second-year French teacher who admired my poetry. (A poet? I could barely articulate my native tongue. Always mumbling, like James Dean in the movies.) To protest the racial policy of the church-supported school, two of my friends and I, with the conspiratorial assistance of a faculty member from the English Department, decided to publish a small mimeo magazine, confronting the school's position.

We printed the first issue of *the barbaric yawp* in the winter of '64. Immediately we were all called up before the Administration's newly-formed Student Conduct Committee. That day I got an education I would long remember. It all came down to money. If the college pursued an aggressive policy of racial integration, we were told, the college would lose alumni support, and parents would pull their kids out of school, and so on.

Everything runs on money.

But, hell, I had no money. To get through college I took a part-time job and a student loan from the government. I remember reading in some book that the word money came from the Roman word *Moneta*, another name for Juno, queen of the gods, wife of Jupiter. Well, I suppose, if you're going to worship something, you might as well worship a goddess. But money has its limitations. Money doesn't create the cells in our bodies or the light in our eyes. How is it then that we allow something that we make-up, something that has no soul of its own, something so limited, to enslave our lives with such ferocity and such fearful intimidation?

I felt trapped in this school in the middle of Florida. After reading Donald Allen's *New American Poetry* anthology I played with the idea of transferring to Black Mountain College in North Carolina. I wrote the college an inquiry only to find out that Black Mountain had been defunct for several years. I went to see the campus shrink about my feelings of isolation. I got to the door, started to knock, then changed my mind. I refused to give my power over to some authority that I didn't respect.

Actually, the college had good teachers, even excellent ones. Like Dr. Raymond Lott, who taught creative writing classes and served as faculty advisor for the school's literary magazine, which I co-edited with Harvey Dexter. Like the English language instructor who had helped my friends and I print *the barbaric yawp,* whose favorite novel had to be *Tom Jones,* and, who, with humor and infectious passion, urged everyone of his students to see the movie. Like the head of the English Department, a man who loved the writings of Thomas Wolfe and was writing a book on him. Like the drama instructor who talked me into trying my hand at acting; and the professor who taught art history and showed me how to really look at a painting; and the young philosophy teacher from Scotland, who encouraged me to balance my analytical processes with my natural tendency toward synthesis and harmony. Like Jean Smith, who belonged to Mensa and taught English grammar and sometimes gave public lectures on Zen Buddhism.

A warm, egalitarian relationship developed between Jean and me. Jean treated me with kindness and affection and intellectual kinship. Married to an Englishman, they had a son in high school, an unruly, whiny kid that they had raised using the "no discipline" method. Toward the end of my senior year, however, Jean's marriage fell apart. A brief, sexual affair took place between us at this time. But most of the time, during these undergraduate years, I went through a chaste, sweetly tortuous, best buddy romance with Lisa Friedman, a Jewish girl from New York.

It was a disastrous affair, this romance.

Or so it seemed at the time.

When I first met Lisa all she talked about was New York City and F. Scott Fitzgerald and Picasso and how much she hated Florida. She smoked one cigarette after another and told me about her parents who lived in continual frustration and absolute American emptiness and who actually thought, she said, that if you didn't send a Hallmark card you didn't care enough to send the best. Lisa stuttered when she talked. Except when she swore and Lisa swore constantly. She colored her expressions with goddamn and fuck and shit, and she wore miniskirts that showed her nice slender legs all the way up to her snatch when she sat cross-legged, which she mostly would as often as she could, and, she said, if the idiots wanted to gawk, fuck 'em! But beneath Lisa's abundant bosom, which she proudly enhanced with soft, tight fitting sweaters, beat a gentle, vulnerable heart. Sometimes she reminded me of a photograph that I had seen in a book called *The Family Of Man*—a black-and-white picture of a moody, sensitive teenage girl with the caption: "I am alone with the beating of my heart."

Lisa Friedman was one in a million, though she swore that there were a million like her in New York City. Lisa wanted to be a writer, an artist. She wanted to be famous, desirable, profound. She wanted to be honest, direct, none of that philosophical blah blah. "What's he mumbling about now???" Lisa would ask impatiently whenever I tried to explain the universe or some other wave-like particle zipping through my mind. To tell the truth, I felt more than a little intimidated by her frankness, her vulgarity, her Big Apple sophistication, but I loved her boundless energy, her outrageous good humor, her practical wisdom, her short skirts and leather sandals.

When Lisa sang songs she didn't stutter. So she bought a guitar and learned to play folk songs in the style of Joan Baez. Lisa had long brownish hair, which she loved dearly, and a real slender waist, and grayish-blue eyes and a thin, waifish like face with full lips that could pout and scream and moan and swear and, to my delight, speak French very well.

Lisa would never forget the day of finals in the fall/winter semester of our first year French class. All the test questions came written in French, naturally. For some reason I had not expected this. I just sat dumbfounded, staring at the exam. I had diligently memorized my daily assignments by listening to recorded tapes of the lessons. I could read the lessons aloud in class. I could please Mrs. Goldberg, our teacher, but I never clearly understood the meanings of the words I read. Now came the moment of truth. I didn't have the vaguest notion what the questions meant. I felt lost, absolutely lost. Or in the words of my beloved Thomas Wolfe: "O lost, and by the wind grieved...." When Lisa glanced over and witnessed the look of total incomprehension on my face—I kept waiting for the hallucination to make sense or maybe to go away—she broke into a fit of smothered laughter. Even I had to grin at the disaster that lay before me. Gathering courage from the words of poet Dylan Thomas—"Do not go gentle into that good night", I plunged into the exam.

The first time we went to bed, even the French disaster seemed pale in comparison. She wanted to rent a motel room in town, which I did. It was the only way we could be alone. We talked most of the time, before Lisa had to leave at eleven to check back in at the dorm. What exactly Lisa wanted from me that night I never clearly understood. She was still a virgin and I had made love only once. We kissed and played and wrestled and took off our clothes but Lisa cried when I wanted to enter her, and she felt so tight, and there was no way I could make love to her without her absolute spoken willingness. *Yes she sang to him yes yes oh yes yes as she opened her heart her arms her legs her sweet oh god yes yes yes.*

Only Lisa could not sing this Joycian song to me, and I could not force, even if it were a game we played, even if she wanted me to. Later, it did happen to her this way. By some redneck who worked in the nearby phosphate mines. Lisa went to his place and got to drinking Scotch with him. Lisa was crazy about Scotch. When she wanted to leave the guy forced her into bed and raped her. Had she set herself up? I couldn't tell.

Dear David,

I really don't know what to write to you about; friendship or love or roses or children playing--I only know I share with you a special kind of friendship which I will never give up. Maybe it's like a child playing--but children never stop playing and yet, time goes on. Life--

When you read "The Hollow Men" think of me, for I really believe that my outlook on life will never completely change. I would lose myself if it did.

On page 221 of this dear book, the second paragraph, the last two lines is my meaning of what friendship is--the deep friendship that I have tried to explain. Will anyone understand--

You will be a great poet someday; and just maybe you will pass a bookstore in New York and see the name Lisa Beth Freidman across the cover; just maybe. We will meet again someday, as all writers do, if only in books.

HAPPY BIRTHDAY, DEAR FRIEND
Nov. 30, '63
With love and friendship,
Lisa

Lisa invited me to visit her in New York City during the summer of '64. She wanted to show me her beloved crazy city, the Metropolitan Museum of Art, the New York Public Library, the Village, Central Park, Broadway and Fifth Avenue, the subway, the Jewish delis; and she wanted to take me to a Yankee's game—she loved the Yankees and she loved Mickey Mantle. She had arranged for us to stay overnight at a girlfriend's house in Westchester, whose folks were vacationing in Europe for a month. Our tryst might have been a perfect ShangriLa. Or so I thought. But in bed, wrapped in each other's arms, once again I got her maddening yes-nos, and once again I pulled back.

That fall I met Dusty Atman and Lisa started going out with Harvey Dexter. Dexter was intelligent, smart, intense, a good writer, an excellent editor, a game player, stout, boisterous, arrogant, coarse, controlling, an emotional bully, and, from what I saw, he acted like an animal toward women. I worked with "Harve" as co-editor of the school's literary magazine. I admired his knowledge of literature and his rapid-fire intelligence, and sometimes even his loud-mouth defiance of authority and good taste, and I dismissed his moon shots out the dorm windows and his jeans that hung so low they revealed the crack of his ass; but I couldn't overlook his attitude toward women.

Dexter drew Lisa to him like a magnet. They fucked and fought and split up and got back together, and fucked and fought and split up and got back together again, and I was the most trustworthy, loyal, Good Friend she could have, without suggesting that she should do this or she should do that; and, yet, it pained me and wounded my male pride to see the sexual and emotional abuse that Lisa put up with, when, with all the love and affection between the two of us, we couldn't even once—not ONE TIME—make love.

Everything between us seemed to get mixed up, confused, and entwined like a sticky ball of string. Maybe Lisa really needed this craziness—the advances, the retreats—and maybe I did too; but to learn what? I kept hoping things would change. Always I felt like I had to play by her unspoken rules. To openly acknowledge or challenge these rules would have seemed like breaking some covert agreement, some conspiratorial pact that we had secretly made. Whenever I tried to sidestep her dreaming, anytime I tried to make things real and solid on my terms, she would pull some off-the-wall stunt that would totally baffle and frustrate me. It seemed as if she guarded the door to some secret, walled garden and I would never have the key that would allow me to enter. Yet she loved me, she wanted me to enter, she invited me to enter, but just as I got to the threshold she would go into this inexplicable panic. And I would step back.

Were we simply wrong for each other and somehow Lisa sensed this? Would we lose each other forever and never know the reason why? Or perchance, would we meet again in the autumn of our lives, (if only in books), to share the wisdom and knowledge that we each had gleaned from our different experiences? I pondered these questions in my heart and I kept coming back to Lisa's dreaming. As far as I could see she had woven this dream out of her wounded childhood, and out of adolescent needs and desires, and out of movies (*David and Lisa* we saw three times together) and paintings and poetry, and bits and pieces of books that mostly came out of the literature of the Lost Generation. Like the doomed-from-the-beginning affair between Jake Barns and Brett Ashley in Hemingway's *The Sun Also Rises*. In the end of the book Brett turns to Jake and says something like, "We could have had such a damn good time together." And Jake answers: "Yes, isn't it pretty to think so?"

But I nurtured a different dream. I wanted to write my own book. I wanted to imprint my very heart and breath onto each and every page and word of this great and wondrous book: my voice and the voice of all those who flowed and tangled and merged and gathered with mine, like living streams flowing into a single, shining river, singing to the sea. I wondered if the power of my destiny—the need to experience and endure and create and manifest my own vision—would someday, if not already and perhaps even from the beginning, clash and struggle with the great need within Lisa to find her voice, her power and creativity.

Going back to Florida for the summer, after my first year of graduate work at the University of Oregon, this had been Lisa's idea. Her parents had arranged for her to attend summer school and she thought that I could get a job near campus and we could set up house together. But it didn't work out that way. The very day I arrived on campus Lisa had already made a date for that night with some fraternity guy. I lived alone that summer in a rented house near campus. I got a job working for the college, brush painting the women's dorm rooms white on white. As the hot, breezeless summer months passed, never going to bed with Lisa, I slowly realized that never would we share power together as lovers, not ever. Yet I wanted to be absolutely sure. I wanted every iota of illusion and false hope knocked out of me—if that's what it took to be real, if that's how love had to be. And that's more or less how one night at a small party our romance ended, with Lisa in the kitchen talking to another man, and me in the street, drunk and crying my heart out. Even then, even after this, in her deep caring, Lisa wanted to end my holy quest for truth and beauty and romance with a touch of grace. The day before I left Florida she came to the house to make love to me, to say good-bye.

Good-bye Zelda.

Good-bye T. S. Eliot.

Good-bye New York City.

Good-bye Holden Caufield.

Good-bye "Hide and Seek."

Good-bye Lady Brett Ashley.

Good-bye *Splendor in the Grass.*

Good-bye Lisa.

The tide always comes back in

A friend gave to me a message about a man who's building a gate next door. The man doesn't have a yard or fence, but he's building a gate. This man, he doesn't even have a dog or kids but he's building a gate right next door. This man, is he me? No, can't be.

But who?

I'm here, far away from there and this man who watches, he's there and not here. Ah yes, a master he must be, I see.

There's a gate next door painted in light and a touch of green, but this gate is not a gate, but a path. Let the gate speak then if it must,— but can it truly speak? For this man it can.

My good friend gave to me a message about a man and his gate, a fine looking gate indeed, but now I'll not build a gate anymore, but an open door.

I don't know, I just don't know...Angelina thought.

She sat staring at the enigmatic message—or whatever it was—a Zen parable, maybe?—that she had just typed out on Johan's typewriter. She sipped at her morning coffee, glad to be alone in the house. David had gone out into the fields early to gather rocks for the garden wall. Carefully she put a clean piece of paper into the old machine.

I just wish I could talk to David about so many things. I just wish I could talk—we could talk—there's so much silence between us now—so much avoidance and distance. I just don't know what's real. What can I say? I know I love him. I know I like traveling with him. I like the adventure. I like the way he sees connections so quickly and the way he's always ready to do the transformational things. The way he asks and looks for truth. One day he'll find the Holy Grail. I know he will. He's that special. Even if he does remind me sometimes of a man hobbling with a wooden crutch under one arm—Captain Ahab?—and banging his other leg, the good one, you know, with the crutch and yelling, "Faster, faster!"

But I don't know....

Sometimes when I want to talk he acts so abrupt with me. Sometimes, you know, I just want to tell him about all the feelings and thoughts that bubble up in me. As separate from him. Like with Bubu. I wanted to talk to him about all the things that came up with Bubu. Oh, lord, did that feel strange. And now I need to talk to him about Eric.

Yet I don't say one word.

It'd be nice to let all these thoughts wander out of my mouth and GET A RESPONSE FROM DAVID other than shut down, go away. God, sometimes I feel like I'm doing it all by myself. I mean, sometimes I just get NOTHING back from David except the spiritual stuff and physical hugs and night closeness...which is wonderful. I need that. But then again his nervous system is so strung out that sometimes I just can't dream and really sleep, with him tossing around and getting up and coming back to bed. And lately there's this feeling that I can't get what I want. That I can't just talk and say things and be whatever. That I always have to stop AND HOLD EVERYTHING IN. Men. They really can be a trial. They're always shutting down and being so serious. If they aren't serious then they're crazy, drunk or angry or loud or bumping into things and being generally out of control. Women can be so much more fun. They laugh, they talk, they listen, they understand emotions, they play, they bend and are flexible and negotiable, and soft and sweet and nurturing. Sometimes I think, God, here I am married to another man and why? Yeah, I know, SEX and romance and that spark and passion and the tenderness. The kisses—maya, I DO LIKE his kisses—and the interplay of male/female and being able to talk—TALK—WHO CAN TALK?—about different points of view—his view, my view, all God's children got the views—and to create a bigger whole, you know, than a couple of women can. It always starts out so wonderful. But almost all of that is shit right now between David and me. And I would like to talk to David about that. But all he talks about are abstractions, or HIS adventures, old friends, past experiences.

Angelina walked down to the sea and sat on the warm white sand. Patiently she waited for the waves to clear her mind, just as the sea had done for thousands of years. Sometimes she felt like a beautiful picture that David had framed inside a slender golden frame. He had seen into the heart of her and recognized her, and for that she would always be grateful, and she dearly loved this man and his imagination. The image in the golden frame was true and yet it wasn't. All that was missing she mused were the chubby little cherubs hovering around her head. But it felt like such a tight fit, this golden frame. Like he had narrowed her down to a single band of light—like one of those abstract painters—and entitled his vision "THIS IS IT". But what about all her thoughts and feelings that did not fit so easily into this beatific image? All the thoughts she kept back from him for fear that he would disapprove.

Little things, like roller skating.

She loved to roller skate. She had never even mentioned this to David. Roller skating would seem too frivolous to him. Like playing cards. Here in Greece she finally got him to play cards. Simply because they had nothing better to do. Playing cards served as a great way to pass the time with Tassos and the tourist police, since the Greeks had such a passion for games. More important, she could watch the thinking of the Greeks. She could pick up on their habits and ways of looking at the world. She could learn their language, in other words.

She smiled, remembering the first times she and David had smoked grass together. His head had seemed so large. So much bigger than his body. She knew from the beginning that she had much to learn from him—they had much to learn together—but now things were bubbling up inside her so fast, spilling over like champagne bubbles uncorked after many years. I know he sees all this, she thought. He certainly knew about Bubu. And Yannis. She had such fun riding around Monemvasia in Yannis' big construction dump truck. He had been a fun guy to joke with in her broken Greek. David had been aware of the sexual attraction between them but he had just not said anything. Just like with Bubu. David gave her so much room and now she wanted more. As if she were swimming in the ocean, yet crying out for water.

She loved to sail. Another thing that David had never done. Wow, to sail the Mediterranean Sea. She and David had been invited by the German architect and his wife to go sailing with them this summer for three months in their boat. Three months sailing around the Mediterranean. But they had decided against it. Sailing the Mediterranean would have been fun with Johan and Eva. But not with the German architect. He wanted to play Captain too much.

Checking to make sure no globs of oil had washed up near her, Angelina stretched out on the white sand and closed her eyes. The warm breeze felt so sensuous to her skin. She was wearing a skimpy, bright orange bikini that Johan's ex-lady friend had left at the house. The suit fit her perfectly. She knew that David had a hard time getting use to the idea of sunning. Perhaps because he grew up in the South, who knows? But she grew up in Vancouver, Washington. In the summers of the Pacific Northwest—whenever they had a summer—you coveted every bit of sunlight on your skin. Otherwise you just might turn to rust and mildew. To David this seemed so decadent, lying in the sun and doing nothing. Not even reading a book. He seemed so hung-up on "doing". Unless he smoked. Then his "doing" was smoking and he could allow himself to "not-do". Is that strange or what?

In Portland, on hot sunny days, she would sunbathe nude in the tiny strip of back yard beneath their bedroom window. A lilac tree and some golden bearded irises that David had planted—she had never known a man who loved flowers so much; wherever he went he planted flowers—and a three-foot wire fence, overrun with clinging vines that were choking out the briery rose bushes, separated their yard from the parking lot next door. The parking lot belonged to the musical repair shop. She felt well hidden in their back yard. She could easily dart into the bedroom through the open window. David would sometimes hang his head out the window and talk to her, if he were home.

Strange, in body size David appeared a mere slip of a man, yet up close she could feel such strength and intensity and such heat. His sexual energy was like a light or like a stream pouring into her. He's like a star she thought. The distant stars seem so cool and unchanging and peaceful. You think you can depend on them. And up close? All this fiery energy. All this restlessness. Did some stars have cold feet like she had? Or freckles? Yes, spots they do have. Everyone should have their own spots. They say you can put your hand into the center of a star and you won't get burned. But you could never get that close, could you? David had a tightness within him too. She could feel this and she wanted to ease him into her and teach him to let go and float on the sea of his feelings, the way her body loved to lay on the water and float and the way her mind sailed so effortlessly on the currents of the wind. She enjoyed her body. She enjoyed the physical world and physical pleasure. So did Eric. Eric had such a strong, healthy body. He had such a catlike grace. That excited her. She admired his fluidity and his physical daringness and that shock of red hair. An image flashed in her mind of them flying over the road toward the sea on his motorcycle. She could feel the power of the bike under her legs and the power of Eric's heart in her arms as she held on to him tightly as they floated over the landscape. For a moment she allowed herself to imagine making love to him. His bare-chested body rolled against her on the sand. One moment they were smiling, teasing each other; the next, his arms went around her, hugging her to him. How gentle and cool his hands felt against her skin, stroking her back, her neck. His green eyes searched hers. *Oh, yes,* her eyes whispered back. And then he kissed her, and the words he had never spoken, because of his vow of silence, now pressed into her mouth, creating tiny waves pulsing through her. Her heart beat wildly. She closed her eyes, her face against his neck, as he unbuttoned her loose shirt. She stretched out on the sand, pleased by his urgency. His mouth and curly red beard nuzzled her breasts, his silent tongue dancing a light dance around her nipples. She didn't have large breasts and his gentle sighs reassured her. A fire stirred in her womb. She lifted her hips and he stripped the rest of her clothes off. She unzipped his jeans and he quickly stripped naked. *Not yet, not yet.* She moistened her fingers with salvia, touching her yoni. Eric quickly took over for her, first with his wet fingers and then with his tongue. Gently he probed, circling, questioning. *Is this okay? Does this feel good? More...*her heart whispered back...*more.* He raised his body slightly above her and she squirmed down between his thighs. She lay still as he gently nudged the tip of his swollen penis inside her. He quivered. *Now, yes. Now.* He rocked slowly back and forth inside her, barely moving, her legs and back and butt pressing into the hot sand, her toes curling and sweat running down her breasts and belly. A long, delicious wave rolled through her body. She heard herself moan as she felt a tremor of reddish energy flowing into her, penetrating her.

Suddenly, Angelina became aware of the noonday sun burning into her skin. She opened her eyes reluctantly and wondered if she had been dreaming. Looking around, she saw David coming down the path toward the sea. In one hand he carried a child's red plastic bucket, to gather the marble stones that each day the sea washed up to the shore. She watched him as he collected the stones that caught his eye. He seemed so happy and at peace with himself, like a happy child, and the tightness in his body disappeared whenever he wandered aimlessly up and down the beach, gathering his tiny colorful treasures.

Angelina knew that someday she would want to have children. This was not so easy for her to imagine with David. He would agree and go along with her but intuitively she knew that his heart would not be there. She could see in moments of clarity that he had a great fear of children. For the child inside him that had never been allowed to be was afraid of himself as a man. This child had no way to reach out and ask for what he needed. Angie could see this great vulnerability of his and she knew that he had a great tenderness here that he covered with a harsh brilliant surface. It amazed her that she could see this. For in this seeing she recognized the child within herself that had gone without recognition, and gone without real support, and that had not been taken seriously, and listened to and loved, and honored by others just for her own individuality. She remembered her teenage pregnancy and the baby she had given up for adoption. It had been so easy for her to get pregnant. One time she had sex. *Oh why not?* Then another and then she was pregnant. Only now, these years later sitting on a beach in Greece, could she begin to make the connection between the child that she had given up and her own childhood fears of loss and shame and abandonment.

Suddenly she began to cry.

In the words of a friend of mine

Just a few miles from Centerville
I got caught out in the rain
I knew I was on the right road
I couldn't understand the pain
I watched the people passin' by
Both ways in the night
Neither one could tell me
Who was wrong or who was right

Michael Earle Ruby
"Just Outside of Centerville"

Angelina and I soon left Athens and returned to Monemvasia by boat. I still didn't know how things stood between us. I took care not to make any sexual demands upon her. Nights passed slowly as I lay awake, wanting to reach over and touch her and to be touched, but I made no move. Traveling, rather than bringing us closer together in our love making, as I had imagined that it would, had actually diminished our sexual intimacy. I noticed this as early as London. In Paris, Shakespeare & Company did not offer us any privacy. In Rome we did find a little time for romance—three nights in a hotel away from our VW van traveling companions; but in Monemvasia, sleeping in a room next to the retired sea captain's wife certainly didn't encourage love making in the middle of the night or day, nor, later on, sleeping in separate mummy-style bags in the cold upstairs room of Artemis' house.

(I noticed, however, that the two weeks Barney and Lieve stayed in our downstairs room that they didn't seem to suffer any deprivation. In fact, some days they stayed almost the whole day in bed. We could hear them laughing and talking to each other.)

Even when spring came and then summer and we slept in the big bed at Johan's house, Angie's attention seemed to be elsewhere. She didn't seem that interested in sex at all. She had always felt so passive in love making anyway. Sometimes I wished she would just show a little more fire and roll around in her sweet baby's arms and moan and yell or something. I worried, too, about the tiny hairline crack in her wedding ring. Somehow, some way, the fire opal in her ring had cracked. The crack ran through the center across the face of the stone. Could this be some kind of dark omen? I couldn't shake the thought from my mind.

Now, Angelina seemed all caught up in a book that Eric had loaned us the first time we met: Paramahansa Yogananada's *Autobiography Of A Yogi*. She even wanted me to write a letter to get information on joining the Self-Realization Fellowship in California that Yogananada had established before his death. So I kept my feelings and thoughts to myself. I said nothing to her about the pain and uneasiness that I felt between us. Nor did I ask her about Eric and the confusion and restlessness that she seemed to be going through.

Back from Athens, I spent my days alone, sitting in the dry grasses of the field around Johan's house, pondering the source of my pain, pondering Angelina's pain, and pondering what to do. I knew that it wasn't sexual passion that bonded us as lovers and companions; I had recognized that from the beginning. We played with the energy between us. Our thoughts and desires danced and pranced and ran together and bounced into one another and tumbled and laughed like idyllic peasant lovers in the hay. Angelina gave to me (and to the world) the gifts of lightness, playfulness, childlike joy. She delighted the senses like a spring meadow come to life in a burst of wildflowers.

I realized that it wasn't sexual jealously that frightened me the most about Eric, but jealously of the other man's power to draw Angelina's soul to his. With Angelina I had found myself playing the teacher, the guide,—a role by no means unfamiliar to me, and, yet, from the very beginning, I had been wary of setting a trap for myself. For I knew that sooner or later Angie would step outside the teacher's shadow. I knew that she had set her mind to "catch up" with me. For, like myself, the need for spiritual identity, affirmation, self-discovery; the need for experience and adventure; the need to heal the hurts of the past and re-establish a fundamental trust in life; the need for love and security and wholeness, kept Angelina in restless motion.

I had been struggling with a short poem, not long after we first got together.

> Why do you cling to your thoughts?
> Welcome the void where you belong.
> Let go the past and your limited visions:
> Those joyless tricks you seized for magic.
> No fire rises from ashes.
> Consider the earth, always turning.
> Why do you cling to your thoughts?

"What title would you give this poem?" I casually asked.

Instantly she answered: "There are no doors, there are no walls."

So that became the title of my poem.

Everything exists in relationship, it seems to me; and to cut oneself off from others, and to isolate oneself in pride, or in marriage, or in some special artistic or spiritual belief, or in some religious cult or some glorious past life, or in some hidden valley where only the silence of the universe can be felt, is to try the same separation from the world that man has tried to create from nature; and in this process of separation there can be no wholeness, no compassion, no tenderness, no integration and no eventual renewal. I'm not saying that a desire to be alone with oneself isn't wise and natural and nurturing. Each of us is different, and separate, and unique, and we can't always be who we are when we travel with others. We often find the deepest parts of ourselves when alone. We often reach the highest into the sky and the clouds and the stars when alone. In our fears, and in our desire to idealize, we too often forget this wisdom, and so we must learn this wisdom over and over again in all of the inter-human connections that we form. We need to have the greatest respect for each other's freedom on the levels of feeling, expansion, reaching, understanding, sensing, intuition, loving, holding, reaching out and returning. The more that we can allow each other space and freedom the greater will be our strength and power together and alone.

This need for time alone hasn't been easy for either Angie or me. We both have tendencies to idealize relationships and to see our marriage as a security and as a hedge against the chaos of the world around us. In my experiences of the world to be alone means loss and pain and separation and abandonment. But Angelina and I are both basically travelers; and it seems to me that the more we could feel at ease with aloneness, the more we could free ourselves from the fears of loss and abandonment, the greater would be our enjoyment and delight in each other.

Plus, we had another problem.

Or I had a problem.

Drinking wine had become such a happy pastime for me. Bubu had left Greece. Johan was gone. But every evening when the sun went down, when I thought of doing something, I thought of drinking wine. And it was so cheap. (As Johan might say.) One afternoon Angie and I walked into Monemvasia and bought a bottle of cognac. It was a popular Greek cognac and cost only thirty drachmas, about one U. S. dollar. Evening came before we walked the six kilometers back to Johan's house. But evening time meant drinking time. We walked slowly, laughing and joking, enchanted by the starry night sky and the distant soft rush of the sea onto the land. By time we got home half the bottle was gone. I drank most of it. What bothered me most was not the amount I drank so offhandedly but the confusion and alienation that my drinking seemed to create between us. Angie and I both treasured clear communication. In the normal course of events, whenever we wandered off in each our individual ways and became momentarily lost to one another, it was this desire and willingness and intention to communicate that would bring us together again. What's going on with you? What are you thinking? What are you feeling? What do you want? I saw that the energy between us had become like a camera out of focus. And now my drinking was no longer fun. So I quit. I quit about a week after we got back from Athens. Just like that, I no longer had a desire to drink. No regrets. No sacrifices. No looking back. Whenever my Greek friends offered me wine now I would just point to my stomach and make a whirling motion. Or I would discreetly pour the wine into Angie's glass. Or anywhere convenient.

As for smoking grass, the two seemed like inseparable mates. Whenever I smoked I wanted wine. This had been my experience and my preference. So I simply quit both. The truth is, though, that I didn't have a real desire to stop smoking. I had always.... Well, not always...but most of the time...I had treated my participation in psychedelics, not as a casual affair, but as a sacred journey. I remember the time that Marcus Holmes and I had stayed up all night taking drugs. First we took acid. That didn't seem to do much. Several hours later we took some mescaline. At least it was suppose to be mescaline. But hallucinations didn't interest us. We were seeking a vision of greater consciousness. As we talked, seeking to find a single image that would represent reality in its most concrete form and that couldn't be divided, and couldn't be reduced, the simplest image that came to our minds was that of a ball of light. Try as we may, however, we couldn't manifest this ball of light. We couldn't create this light around ourselves, visible to our all-too-eager straining eyes. And we couldn't step inside this ball of light to travel wherever we might have desired.

Dawn came and we were still sitting on the sofa with no signs of a vision. No signs of another world. No signs of extraordinary power. Nothing out of the ordinary. Naomi woke up around six and put on coffee and made a Southern breakfast with biscuits, eggs, bacon, grits. For a while I watched Naomi as she moved barefooted around the kitchen. She looked so pretty, so down-to-earth, in her faded jeans and worn plaid shirt, her warm brown almond-shaped eyes still blinking back sleep. I loved her eyes. They looked Asian. Chinese with a dash of American spice and sparkle. Naomi Aspen-Holmes was not an early riser and she needed several cups of coffee and a cigarette before coming into the room. Marcus, too, would sit and drink a whole thermos of coffee and smoke cigarette after cigarette, whatever the time; as if time with his eyes closed meant time lost forever. As much as I enjoyed coffee, however, that morning I only sipped at my drink. Determined that the whole night wouldn't be a waste, I rolled a joint. "Might as well get high," I said to Marcus, with a grin. I had known Marcus since childhood. Marcus laughed. "Why not?" Which was Marcus' attitude mostly to life: Full speed ahead and count the dead later. We were half-way into the joint when a shiny, brass candleholder sitting on the dining table captured my eye. Suddenly I was caught in a rush of light that seemed to come from everywhere. Like in the flying dream I once had. In this dream I was soaring over the greenness of the earth beneath me. Then suddenly I soared into pure light. All around me nothing but wondrous light. This frightened me so much, however, that I immediately woke up. If only I could have gone beyond my fear and soared into the light...or so I thought, whenever I pondered the significance of this dream.

As I sat quietly at the breakfast table my mind's eye was filled with streaming, radiating light. Somehow I knew that if I asked I would be shown the contents of my deep consciousness. I asked to see the images that I carried in my mind of Woman. Immediately I saw a theater of changing, archetypal images: one image becoming another image becoming another, like I had seen in the *Stephenwolf* movie. Certainly I was seeing into my own personal dreaming consciousness and into the dreaming consciousness of the world. I sat enthralled by the show; as my friend Marcus watched me in puzzlement and Naomi busied herself with the breakfast dishes. I assumed that the grass had triggered this release of light. Or was it perhaps an act of Grace? I wasn't sure. I considered the psychedelic a tool of knowledge, not something to get loaded on and dance to rock music in strobe lights. In my exploratory and often happy-go-lucky mood, however, I was reluctant to see the inevitable: that as I came to depend upon the smoke to expand and sensitize my perceptions, that this transference of power would gradually erode and undermine any trust in my own natural intuitive and creative abilities. As I concentrated upon the enlargement of my mind I intensified my emotional denials even more.

Sitting in my uneasy silence, in the dry grasses of the field around Johan's house, thinking on these things, the words to a song kept running through my head. The song was about pain and not knowing what to do and about being stranded on the road at night somewhere in the universe—Idaho—or maybe Colorado—in the middle of nowhere.

> There were no stars the sky was black
> But the mornin's gotta be soon
> In the silence of that stormy night
> I finally glimpsed the moon
> Then in the words of an old friend
> I finally saw the light
> If yr headin' into Centerville
> It's just on through the night

I first met Michael Ruby in the summer of '67 and he was singing his songs on the street corners of Portland, Oregon. Immediately we became friends for life. Flakey Joe from Florida and I were sharing a big 1920's two-story house near 21st and S. E. Ankeny Street with Marcus and Naomi. One afternoon Flakey Joe came back to the house, bringing Michael and Evening Fire with him. Michael had been living in San Francisco and on the spur of the moment decided to grab a bus up to Portland. He met Evening Fire on the bus. She got the name Evening Fire while taking an acid trip. Until then her name had been Jennifer and she had been a political activist and college student. Now she ran around in hardly nothing at all, which was the first thing I noticed, and, at the same time, tried not to notice. She smoked grass like eating candy and she danced in clubs as a nude dancer when she worked, and, with her tireless Leo energy and lean good looks and sensual, sexy body, she could certainly set the night on fire night after night. She had one lover she said who fucked her seventeen times in one night. This happened before she got on the Pill and he was using condoms for birth control. The next morning they counted seventeen condoms. But this guy, she said, was just too weird even for her.

Coming to Portland, every time the bus made a station stop she and Michael would hop off (more or less) and smoke a joint. And that's how they arrived in the City of Roses. Flakey Joe, who fancied himself a guitar player, saw them playing songs on a street corner downtown. Since they needed a place to stay he invited them to come live with us in the house on Ankeny Street. By this time Michael and Evening Fire had become lovers. Like a cat, though, Evening Fire came and went as she pleased. As Michael soon found out. Early one morning, after making love, Evening Fire crawled out of their zipped-together sleeping bags to go to the bathroom. Twenty minutes later she still had not returned. Aroused and wanting seconds, Michael went to find her. The door to the bathroom stood open but he could see no Evening Fire. Strolling down the hall he passed Flakey Joe's room. Through the open doorway he saw Evening Fire on top of Joe, the two of them balling like crazy. Michael, who grew up on a family farm in Idaho, didn't quite know what to do with all this uninhibited sexual freedom.

Then he met Uma. Uma was a beautiful dark-haired woman who read tarot cards. Michael rescued her from a bad situation and he fell in love with her as much as any man could love a woman. They got married. Then one day....but that's a story Michael himself will have to tell. Right now he's traveling his own chosen path homeward, and for the next twenty years he'll be traveling through the darkness and the pain and the crosscurrents of his mind.

> So Angel of the sunrise
> With your breath as sweet as wine
> Wontcha come   to my rescue
> Ah show me the way   wontcha show me the way

T' get on home
Father of all directions within your eyes so fine
won't you help me to find the right way

One morning I woke up from a dream. In the dream I was back in rural Georgia in the house that I grew up in. Only my mother wasn't living in the house. Living in the house now was a man I recognized to be a spiritual master. The whole house felt different to me. I felt beauty and order and meaning in the house. I paused to admire an Oriental carpet in the hallway. I liked the rich, sensual maroon coloring and the simple, abstract design woven into the carpet. (It reminded me of the burgundy in the Oriental prayer rug that I had borrowed to use as a cover for the wedding altar when Angelina and I got married.) I entered the master's room and the teacher spoke to me urgently, as if time were short, about the untruth of the roles we play in our lives. Then, over the doorway going into the master's room, these words appeared in large bold letters: **EVERYTHING IS A GIFT.**

I pondered this dream for three days.

Finally, I just couldn't take it any more. The pain inside me felt like—well, I imagined it felt like a wolf's foot caught in a trap. Better to lose the foot, I thought, than to die like this. So I went to Angelina. I took her by the hand and we walked dramatically out to the open fields. We sat together, facing each other. "What's going on, Angel?" My voice was tender and my heart trembling, but my intentions felt firm and strong and unwavering. I had prepared myself to hear what I must hear, even if she wanted to leave me. As Angelina opened up her thoughts to me, not about Eric, but about the turmoil within herself, her restlessness, her conflicting feelings, the battle between her heart and head, she could see and feel me really listening to her, as if for the first time, and a wondrous healing began to take place between us. Much, much more needed to be said, and it would take years in the saying, but this day seemed like a fine beginning.

A single flame lights the universe

It is night;
a single flame lights the universe;
and my love lies sleeping in the quietness of our room.
It is an immense room
in a timeless land by the sea,
and the air is warm and still, and only the light,
only the light softly covers her beauty.
I gaze into the night and milky-white galaxy.
I see a star dying in the vast calmness,
and my heart returns home,
without hesitation, but with joy,
and comes to rest in my love's moonlit arms
and in her gentle breathing.
My eyes gaze upon her beauty.
I look and look and am not filled.
(Her beauty is elusive, unborn; never will it be exhausted.)
I am breathless with her beauty.
I look and look and am not filled.
I see her playful treasures hidden in dreams
and gifts washed from the sea.
My love, she dreams as a child dreams
of green trees shining and shining
and of golden summers gathered in her hair.
The blue, jewel sky universe embraces my love,
rosy dawns awaken her,
and purple rim rainbows come to rest at her feet.
My eyes gaze upon her beauty.
I look and look and am not filled.

I fight a losing battle

It's May and already the field grasses and thistle bushes have turned green to dryish brown. In two months we've seen only one sign of rain. That day, dark, ominous clouds had filled the noon sky. A few drops of rain fell upon the parched earth. We cheered and silently praised the heavens. Then the clouds blew over...just like that. In desperation, the insects invaded our garden. In delight, I should say. We didn't stand a chance. Overnight they wiped out the zucchini, devoured our three potato vines, chomped thirty onions into the ground, ate all the radishes, ate the egg plants, and then settled in on the corn. We hastily covered our carrots and lettuce with mosquito netting; but we had planted the lettuce too late, and soon the hot spring sun bolted the plants. The carrots, which we had planted near the carob tree, could barely break through the clayish soil.

To stop the invaders we poured garlic juice on the plants. Still the little chain saw monsters kept coming. (Of course. This is Greece. They probably love garlic.) They're everywhere, these marauders. They're on the road, in the fields, on the beach; even in the kitchen, feasting on red ripe tomatoes given to us by Johan's friend Andonai. Aw, damnit. Leaf hoppers have cut down our favorite little tomato plant. These small, brownish insects chew through the stalk—I suppose for its juices—but only in one place. Then they abandon the plant. The way blue jays peck a single bite out of a ripe fig, then fly to another. It seems a bit like humans killing an elephant or a rhino just for its tusk. Or like harvesting a certain kind of ocean fish just to make soup out of its fins. When very small, this tomato plant had been badly damaged by grasshoppers. We nursed the plant for several weeks and its little green arms seemed to be lifting upward in a gesture of joy and thanks. Then came the leaf hoppers. Later, two of our "babies" were cut down by these bastards. So now we're down to a more primitive method: the strong arm of the law. That's me with a stick in my hands.

Can we live without killing?

Where do we draw the line?

As I ponder this question, (all the while thinking of the sacrificial spring lambs and baby goats that we saw the other day bleating in the back of a truck on its way to help the orthodox celebrate the Resurrection), I think of abandoning our vegetable garden altogether. I look at the rock wall border that holds our tomato plants and the "babies". In the corner next to the patio I can envision a crimson-spot rockrose. This plant is drought-resistant and native to the Mediterranean region. I love their papery thin flowers. I can see it now: tall and bushy and in full bloom, enhanced by a border of silver thyme, heather and lavender, and maybe some Oriental poppies and carnations. At the other end of the border, I see an *Acanthus mollis*; I think it's native to this country. Or a giant Matilija Poppy, a native of Baja, California. The Matilija Poppy with it's large, knock-out white flowers could withstand the drought and summer heat of Monemvasia. Somewhere I would squeeze in a Coreposis "Sunburst", maybe next to a rose, an Alba, say (in praise of Eva) "Queen of Denmark". Or the Hybrid Tea "Dainty Bess". Or a lovely Floribunda. Maybe "Iceberg". For late winter and early spring blooming, I could plant Grecian windflowers and (in honor of Oregon) "Mt. Hood" narcissus and a few wild irises. To greet Johan and Eva with a scent of heaven when they return to Monemvasia in September, I would add *Nicotiana affinis.*

Yeah, well, dream on.

So how about a rock and sand garden?

We'll arrange the garden close to Johan's banana tree. We'll plant dates and pomegranates and mangos with the seeds that Eric brought back from India. We can gather rocks from down by the sea, and at the same time search the shore for colorful marble treasures that get washed up every day. Such wonderful stones! They're like polished little pieces of a painted desert. Some look like red and yellow colored road maps with thin colored lines running all over. Others remind me of a bloodshot Cyclops' eye the morning after the night before. The Greeks have a law against skinny dipping but Angie and

I sometimes venture out into the clear blue water, slip off our swim suits and frolic in the gentle waves. We keep an eye out for sheepherders and righteous farmers. Every now and then we see a farmer ride by on a horse or mule or donkey, usually with a transistor radio blaring out popular bouzouki music. It's a long stretch of sandy beach that turns northward into a rocky coast. At one spot on the sandy beach you can enter a delta of lush bamboo, which quickly changes into a small fertile valley that's cultivated by farmers. Most of the time we share the beach with only two or three other people and some days with none but the old invisible gods. Soon, we're told, the beach will be mobbed with Greek tourists and gypsies and thatched huts. The beach has no facilities and it'll stink of garbage and human excrement. Already they're staking out house claims with poles and name tags.

The only water at Johan's house comes from the early spring rains collected in his cistern. The cistern holds about eighteen hundred liters. That provides plenty of water for the house but not enough to water the garden as we would like. In the valley the farmers pump water from a deep subterranean spring. In the valley all looks green. On Johan's land, above the valley, we tread a thin path through dry grasses and prickly weeds. As we descend into the valley the scent of wild thyme and oregano fills the air. A breeze rushes through the bamboo. Mama turtle and her four little ones see us approaching. They paddle for dear life. At the deep end of the pool a frog goes "plop!"

The farmers work from early morning into the night, continuously pumping water or fighting new bamboo shoots, and cultivating and harvesting their vegetables, fruits and melons. Fortunately we have a friend in the valley. Andonai brings us vegetables and gives us tomato and egg plant starters. Before Johan and Eva left for Denmark, Andonai invited us all to his house and to his little village for a holiday and name-day celebration. Later, he and his wife came by to prune Johan's grape vines. Through awkward translations we found out how to turn our store-bought grain into bread. Actually,

Angie speaks pretty good everyday Greek. She makes herself understood and she can pick up on what's going on. I'm still working on "Good morning, how are you?"

In May we offer to help Andonai and his family tie and prune their tomato plants. Then we help them pull, top, and sack their onion crop for shipment to Athens. Each day that we venture into the valley we return loaded with tomatoes, onions, egg plants, potatoes, apricots. Soon we'll have melons, and, later, lemons and even bananas.

The invaders descend. The bananas disappear.

Except for wild thyme and the toughest quill bushes the grasshoppers will eat anything. Onions, bread, whatever its pinchers can pierce. The grasshopper—this grasshopper— behaves like a cannibal. His own left leg will do should it rip off; which it easily does, as an escape mechanism, I suppose. Or the grasshopper will disembowel a dead kinsman should he find him (or her) before the hungry wasps do. These are desperate times and I must slaughter by day and night. I clip their wings; I rip legs; I smash heads. There's no end to the killing.

O thinking mind, give me another measure!

I'll germinate more seeds. I'll grow more plants. I'll cover the "babies" with protective netting. Never mind that I've stopped smoking. Never mind that on our Easter trip to Athens the *I Ching* warned me of impending danger. I'm determined to have my way. I'll harvest the "babies" for Johan. But it's late. I must act quickly. Even as I plot and scheme, flies mercilessly attack my arms and legs. Swat the bastards! The ants have invaded the honey and sunflower seeds. Drown 'em! Scatter seeds in front of their holes to keep the workers at home. Quickly, light the mosquito coils: King Kong, Double Elephant, Moon Tiger. We'll hide behind screens. We'll leave their rotting corpses in the sun. We'll drop their mangled bodies into the jaws of innocuous spiders. And should the spiders turn into giants…. Believe me, it happens. There we stood, face to face with the BIGGEST spider we'd ever seen in our lives. I grabbed for the straw broom.

One night, after I had given Angelina a slow, sensual head-to-toe massage, we were sitting without any clothes on in front of a small fire in the fire place. I had my eyes closed, listening to the geckos on the ceiling sing to each other. I felt something run across my leg. I opened my eyes and saw a horrid, giant, orange centipede. Holy shit. Quickly I scooped it into the fire. Checking carefully, we found two more in our bed sheets. Johan and Eva had warned us of these creatures. Immediately we stuck the ends of the four bedposts into cans of water. Earlier in the spring, while building the rock-wall garden, almost every time I turned over a stone I would find one of these huge orange centipedes. These centipedes look so scary and dangerous that Angie and I call them scorpions.

Even the grape vines are being devoured by runaway goats.

Is there no mercy in this land of devils?

They arrest me

On the second day of July five policemen come to the house with an interpreter. "What it this?" they want to know, pointing to our "babies." "It's tea!" I answer. "No, no! This is hashish!" they insist. They confiscate our ten plants and take me to the police station in Monemvasia. The Greek police never really say that I'm under arrest. They politely ask me to come down to the station with them to answer "a few questions." The interpreter, a young Greek, apologizes to me. He says the police did not tell him why they wanted his services. In the evening, Angelina brings me something to eat from Artemis' restaurant; and that night I sleep on the floor in a make-shift cell with mosquitoes relentlessly after my blood. The next morning, after signing some arrest papers, I have to wait in front of the police station with Yanni, a young policeman who often played cards with Angie and me in Tassos' cafe. I try to find out from him how serious this may or may not be. Yanni shrugs his shoulders and tells me not to worry. He doesn't seem to know; or else he doesn't want me to know. Tassos walks by on the sidewalk. He pretends not to see us. An older policeman—a very serious, fatherly type—the one who asked all the questions yesterday at the house—takes me by public bus to the courthouse in Sparta, a three hour ride, where I must appear before a hearing.

Angelina goes to Sparta with us. Dark clouds gather in the sky and a light rain begins to fall. Not a good omen...I'm thinking. Angelina looks frightened. She begins to cry. In a sudden panic I realize that these clowns with their guns are serious actors indeed; and THEY CAN PUT ME IN PRISON.

I ask for a lawyer. A young lawyer comes to the rescue, bringing an interpreter with him. From the interpreter I find out that the lawyer does not agree with their harsh hashish laws. He feels sympathy for me. The lawyer tries his best to get me out on bail but the judge denies his plea. The judge is afraid that I'll leave the country. (Now, would I do that?) They take me to jail. I never see the lawyer again. I never even have a chance to pay him his fee.

Angelina returns to Monemvasia.

The police fingerprint me and I spend the next three days by myself in a smelly, cement cell, the walls cluttered with scratched-in Greek names. Above the door, using the edge of a coin, some prisoner has scratched a single English word—the word LOVE.

Every morning, before dawn, I hear a rooster crowing outside my window.

He crows and crows.

I think about Socrates. But mostly I think about Angelina.

On the third day, at the bus station, I wait in an empty bus, as two escort policemen wait outside for the driver. They're transferring me to the prison at Nafplion to await trial. Out of the blue, Chrysanthos bounces into the bus. He reaches for my hand and presses a bunch of folded drachmas into it. I thank him in Greek but have no other words I can say. For a moment we look into each other's eyes—his eyes so dark and shining and open. In our souls we embrace each other. He wishes me luck. Then he turns and vanishes out the door.

THE TRIAL

The man was mad and some said, a genius
they found him out on the street one night
counting the stars
and writing them on a piece of paper
and he just smiled out of half of his mouth and
said he had a long way to go

Tom Kryss
—from "What Is It They Think
Might Dance Like The Sun"

The big iron gate

I see a man in pain and a man who wants death,
and a man who asks *"Why?"*

He turns to me in anger;
and I hear an old man talking to the stars.
"What do the stars tell you, Old Man?"

The old man mumbles under a great moustache,
"Tonight the stars are joking with me!"

And I hear the guards closing the big iron gate.

Beyond walls

To see you for just moments—
my heart turns to rage.

I'm in prison, guards at every turn.

I see you through an iron screen.
I love you beyond walls,
beyond rage and the guards.

Remember, they shot Garcia Lorca.
They tried Blake for treason.
Who escapes?

To be free

The greatest wonder in life,
and on earth, is this:
to see, to love, to be free.

Anger, greed, selfishness, pride:
all are prisons.
They limit my spirit.

Only love does not limit my spirit.

The cry

Love- being an essential word-
Begin this song, envelop it all.
—Carlos Drummond De Andrade

Love!
The very stones cry out,
as poets make old hats
& twist sur-
realism
into a mathematical
landscape.

Bravo,
worn out history
& women in dreams.
Bravo, the everlasting sonnet
—a corpse
on rue Saint-Lazare
where the River Seine
overflows black oil,
misery
& initiation into death.

Love!
The very stones cry out
in so many languages,
surely the stones
have retreated into the desert

or sank into the poisonous sea,
as work horses transform
our dreams into a cellular fog,
& love turns the other way,
seeking the heart
clear of smoke and relics.

Melancholia: over-indulgence;
anger & bitterness.
Some mornings, I swear,
my soul will not bear
another day in this prison cell.

Ten times worse

Look, here I am in a Greek prison,
& workers are hammering yet
another roof over my head,
high above the walls.
I find distraction in symbols,
while my neighbor groans in his sleep.
One man worships a cross;
another man kills his mother.

Each moment is a replaceable part
in this prison;
each act a play for mercy.
We walk from one cell to the other;
we pace the concrete yard
& with nervous steps we wear out infinity.

The world bitches without pause.
There's no end to misery!
We're prisoners of the past, the future,
of everything we know
& of all that we do not know.
We're prisoners of thought.

To the impatient heart

What is it you desire? Is it power you desire?
They tell me (as a child) the streets of Heaven
are paved with gold.
Is it childhood dreams you covet?

Is it ecstasy? Are you greedy for love?
Will you be God or his next of kin?

Always there comes the One who will lord it
over us.
What is all this?
Am I superior to you? Are you superior to me?

What better place than prison (surely there are
better places)
to reveal this mystery to my impatient heart.

In stillness comes the fire

The Farm...Will I ever see the Farm?
Evergreens and Oregon rains...homemade peach ice
cream...peppermint tea and Naomi and yellow
wildflowers by the stream....
     Day and night in this prison
     I dream.
       Enough!
     Be still and flow.
     I am here,
     and truth is just *this*.

The trial

It's the day before my trial. I'm at a holding station in Kalamata, a city on the Ionian coast of the Peloponessus. The famous Kalamata olive comes from this region. But I'm not thinking about olives. I pretend that I'm walking to Monemvasia. I count each step. But this cell is so small, and so crowded with other prisoners, that I take five steps and make a circle. Where's Angelina? Is she all right? A month ago she left for Denmark, hitching a ride with a friend. She wanted to catch Johan and Eva before they came back to Greece. I've heard nothing. What if she doesn't show for the trial? Why doesn't she come? Where is she? Those bastards! If anything happens to her…. I need a tie, a new pair of pants. I'll look like a clown and I want to look like one of *them*. There's even a growing doubt that my lawyers will show. I have two lawyers. One lives in Nafplion and the other in Kalamata. They're working together on my defense. Last night the attorney in Kalamata came by. He's the best lawyer in Kalamata the police assure me. The lawyer speaks no English, however, and arrives without an interpreter. He stays long enough to establish that it's my wife—and not me—who has the money. "And where is your wife...?" Then, early this morning, I get a call from the son of my Nafplion lawyer. His son goes to the university in Athens and speaks good English. "Is everything okay?" he wants to know. "Have you settled the fees with my father? How is your wife? Where is she...?"

He thinks...he believes...he's sure I'll go free at the trial. But will he wait on the money until it comes from America? "EnDOXi, enDOXi!" he replies. He dismisses the problem with an emphatic shrug, as if to say: "We are men. Freedom—not money—is our first concern." His heart seems to be in the right place. Nick, a Greek prisoner at Nafplion, has already spoken to him about the money and warned him not to overcharge, that I'm not a "rich American." The lawyer's an old family friend and Nick's personal attorney at the moment. He's head of the

131

Lawyer's Association in Nafplion. He's a financial advisor to the Government. He's qualified to go before the Supreme Court in Athens. But seven hundred dollars! I was thinking three hundred at the most. Still, if he's sure I'll go free.... "In meeting danger thoroughness is all that counts, and in going forward so as not to tarry in the danger." That's my counsel from the *I Ching*. As for his courtroom partner in Kalamata, he wants only two hundred and fifty dollars. In fact, if I wish, I may choose to work with just the attorney in Kalamata. But I don't like that idea. He'll probably treat me as just another case and I can't afford to take that chance. I want out.

The other prisoners have gone to court. I'm sitting outside the holding cell, in the waiting area near the guard station. The guard on duty orders us two Greek coffees. I thank him for the coffee. He stares into his newspaper, and I continue to gaze out the window at the blessed sight of the sun and clear blue sky. I'm thinking about the last three months, and thinking about tomorrow, and about the handful of poems that I've written since jail. So far the guards haven't questioned my writings. But I'm not sure what to expect. I remember the letter in my shirt pocket and I take the letter out to read again. The letter arrived a few days ago, from a woman that I don't know.

Hi David,

I haven't met you, I only know you as a friend of Melina's and from the poems that I've enjoyed so much in *A Bone for the Dogs*, and from the letters. But the emotional place you describe sounds like places I've been and I just feel like writing a few things too.

Sometimes we just need a reminder of things we already know, but that we forget when life gets painful.

Remember to love yourself. To love all of yourself; don't divide yourself against yourself. Don't love this and hate that. Love all of yourself. Love the part of yourself that goes into rage and wants to do battle with the whole Greek government. Love the child in you that got scared and forgot how to go home. Don't be afraid to cry. Tears wash away years of crud and frustration. Love the misery, love the anger, love the anguish, love being exactly who you are right now, as you are being it. There is something you want to learn from these feelings. Don't turn against yourself. Let yourself have your despair and melancholy, if that is what you want. But also let yourself have everything you want. Everything is allowed. We can have anything we want, whether it be outrageously wonderful or self-destructive. Life doesn't judge. But we do. We are always giving ourselves (by wanting, imaging, projecting) what we think we should have. What others expect us to be and do and become. We limit our options to a trickle, to a meager ration. Let yourself know what you really want! All of it. Know what you really want. If you want understanding, if you want wisdom, if you want to be free, ask the universe for what you really want, and then ask for more.

Remember the *I Ching*. When the Yang energy builds to the greatest peak, that is exactly when the Yin energy rushes in. When Melina read your letter to me I thought, here is a man at a turning point. Know what you have completed; know what you no longer need or want to experience. Love even this prison adventure you have created, to show you what you want to know. You are a great soul at a turning point.

Love your great and beautiful self; love all that you are; love all the experiences that have brought you to this moment. Love all the possibilities that you can create out of what you are, what you have become. Good luck. And I hope to see you, when you and Angelina return to America. We'll take a few long walks in the rain and sit around the wood stove and talk about life.

 With love,
 Alora

It's October 2nd, exactly three months since my arrest. The day they arrested me, I left with only the clothes that I had on at the time. I had no shoes on my feet, only beach thongs. I had no money, blankets, nothing. In holding jails you have to buy your own food and bring your own bedding. In the prison at Nafplion we lived barracks style, about twenty men. Only one other prisoner spoke English. Nick had lived in the United States for a few years, in Bowling Green, Kentucky. Then, for ten days, two Yugoslavian university students got thrown in prison with us. They were caught with their girl friends skinny dipping in the sea. Some peasant had seen them and called the police. The two women had a cell in another complex on the other side of the wall.

For some reason I expected Yugoslavians to have dark complexions, like Turks or gypsies. These two men had fair-skin and blond hair. They spoke excellent English; and this created a strange situation. Strange for me, at least. Suddenly, Bobby, a Greek friend, wouldn't speak to me. He acted jealous and huffy. Bobby's about ten years older than me, a family man, and a real physical dynamo. He got thrown in jail for fighting. The police came to arrest his brother for something. His brother got in a fist scuffle with them and Bobby jumped in. The court gave Bobby nine months. If there was any man at Nafplion who didn't belong in jail, who could tolerate constriction even less than me, it had to be Bobby. We became fast friends. He taught me to speak and write Greek. I taught him to speak a little English. Bobby managed to get hold of a Greek grammar textbook; probably from his son. For having a stubborn, volatile personality, Bobby showed real patience in teaching me the phonetic sounds of the Greek alphabet and sentence structures of the language.

I even wrote Angelina a letter in Greek. This letter surprised and impressed the prison warden. Whenever I wrote Angelina, because my letters were in English, they had to go through the Justice Department in Athens. My Greek letter went straight to Monemvasia. Writing in a foreign language—not Greek but my own native tongue—this concept startled me. Just as I had been surprised when we first came to this country and realized that the Greeks don't call their land Greece but Hellas. Assumptions that I had made for years about the world suddenly began to lose their meaning in our travels. I discovered that travelers from other countries, like Denmark and Germany and Yugoslavia, could make naive and dumb cultural mistakes too. No doubt cosmic travelers from deep space and other dimensions will make dumb mistakes, too, when they come here to visit. If they haven't already.

That night, a lady from the American Embassy calls. She's in Kalamata for the trial. It's unusual, she tells me, that we're even allowed to speak over the phone. "I've made friends with the police," I joke. Actually, I have. One policeman even offered to go out and buy me a tie for the trial. "Have I settled the lawyer's fee?" she wants to know. "Well..." and I explain the situation. "These lawyers don't like to work without money, you know, Mr. Pendarus. Have you heard from your wife? Where is she?"

I don't know, I don't know!

An hour later the woman calls back. She's contacted the lawyer in Nafplion and he'll be down early in the morning. Angie has already talked to him from Monemvasia.

I arrive at court in borrowed shoes and dress coat and a brand-new tie. I see Angelina with Johan and Eva, waiting. Big, beautiful Johan, grinning, but looking worried. Already he's hitting the wine. Eva, lovely Eva, she seems confused, as if she's trying to recognize me with a tie but no bushy beard. In a briefcase Johan's carrying a thousand dollars for the lawyers.

Angie arrived in Copenhagen the day after Johan and Eva left for Greece. (Why didn't she send them a telegram? I don't even ask. And what about the post cards she promised me?) Immediately she takes the "Magical Touring Bus" out of Amsterdam, back to Athens. (Later I meet the driver of this bus. He's arrested in Athens for hashish and takes five years.) The bus keeps breaking down, losing time. At the Greek border Angie flags down two longhair Germans in a truck. She explains the situation and they rush her to Thessaloniki. Here she grabs a night flight to Athens. The next morning she races in a taxi to catch the bus to Monemvasia. The bus to Monemvasia means an all-day trip. Already it's the day before the trial. On the bus Angie discovers she hasn't enough money for the fare. Some Greek men quickly come to the rescue. In Monemvasia, everyone tries to tell her the trial was yesterday... and where was she?

As Angelina stood to testify before the court, I could see the horrific strain these last few weeks had been upon her, and I could feel the strength of her spirit. When she wept, tears blurred my own eyes. I could feel her love, and her beauty, and her aliveness, burning, radiant, purifying, and so utterly real. In that moment I felt my life, my world, shifting.

Suddenly I knew what I wanted.

The other prisoners had warned me about Kalamata. To make matters worse, they said the area around Kalamata is where most of the Greek hashish is grown. I remind the court that I've been in jail for three months already and that I was denied bail. The judge smiles down on me: That's-the-way-it-is-in-Greece. We're not saying you're guilty, Mr. Pendarus. Not yet. He asks only a few questions. Where was I born? When? My Father's name and birthplace? My Mother's? What work do I do? What education do I have? Am I legally married? The arresting officer tries to say that Angelina and I aren't married. I jump to my feet. "That's a lie!" I shout. The bastards, can't they see that our passports have the same last name? Do they think I'm traveling with my sister? Well, the lawyers had urged me to show emotion. When the court found out that Johan and Eva weren't married, I'm sure that their testimony in my favor went flying out the window.

"I do not smoke, not even cigarettes.

I did not know those trees were hashish!"

(Trees? What trees? You mean those scrawny weeds?)

Truthfully, I never suspected the plants were "hashish." It was their choice of words and I'm not one to quibble over detail. I soon find out that to the Greeks it's all hashish: the "black smoke."

Before taking off to Denmark, Angelina came to Nafplion and brought me a few good books, including a tattered copy of Walt Whitman's *Leaves of Grass,* and a TIME magazine, and, unexpectedly, the prison officials allowed me to have the books, without sending them first to the Justice Department. They had Nick look the books over. President Nixon and the Watergate scandal was in the news and TIME magazine contained an analysis of John Dean's testimony. A very dry testimony, I gathered, but filled with exacting details. This barrage of details impressed everyone and gave credence to Dean's testimony. That inspired me. What did I have to lose? So I sat down and created a ten page defense, with very exacting details, part truth and part fabrication. All in a grand strategy to convince the court that I wasn't intentionally growing "hashish" and to obscure the origin of the seeds. I gave this testimony to my Nafplion lawyer, who may or may not have believed anything I said, and he had this grand document translated into Greek for the court.

I cultivated and protected the "tea" along with other vegetables in my garden, in plain sight from the road, and only a few steps from the donkey path traveled each day by farmers and tourists on their way to the beach. Does that sound like I was growing hashish?

My mistake, true. (Between you and me.) In Greece you can't hide anything, anyway. Not for long. I just figured the plants were marijuana. The Greeks won't recognize the stuff. (It never occurred to me that Greek peasants had been growing this psychedelic weed for centuries.) If they do catch me, they'll just throw us out of the country.

Who gave me the seeds?

Obviously I'd been growing the plants. But I had to keep Johan out of this mess. After all, I alone am responsible for my decisions. I was bound and determined to grow those plants, even if it meant going out in the night with a flashlight to battle a never-ending siege of grasshoppers. An old Greek in prison for one plant swears a bird must have flown over his yard and dropped the seed. Who knows? These seeds were surely the seeds of my doing. Or un-doing. I was careless; I acted stupid. I ignored the signs. I even ignored the *I Ching's* earlier warning of repeated dangers: K'an / The Abyss.

An American traveler that I met in Athens gave me the seeds, I wrote in my document. He brought them back from India along with lots of other seeds. All of which I planted and cultivated in my garden.

(With apologies to Eric.)

My lawyers put on a good show. I thought for sure we'd win. As a final twist, an extra measure, the lawyers dramatically reveal how a legal mistake has been made against me. One legal paper identifies the plants simply as "hashish," which includes even the harmless, "non-narcotic" bird seed variety they sell in Greek shops. Another legal paper calls the plants "India hashish." India hashish is the narcotic, so the book says. It's this kind of hashish that the prosecuting attorney has charged me with cultivating.

The prosecutor isn't one to split hairs, either.

They find me guilty.

The court sentences me to two years in prison with loss of all civil rights. Immediately after my release I must leave the country. Hashish is a felony and there's no appeal court. If a legal mistake has been made against me, however, I'm entitled to apply for a new trial, with new judges and a different prosecutor, through the Supreme Court.

"Patience!" cries my Nafplion lawyer in English, as they're taking me away.

The tears fill my eyes. I can barely see.

My arrogance, my pride; these mean nothing. I love. That's all. It's that simple. Tomorrow the police will take me back to Nafplion. The thief will come too. A small, thin Greek, he coughs and trembles. He looks scared. He says nothing as I weep with my hands over my face. He turns his back so as not to interfere. Thank God he does not speak or try to console. He smokes a cigarette. I hear him coughing but I don't look. He asks the guard for a drink of water.

Thinking of Angelina tears me in half.

I might never see her again. I could die in this damn prison.

My body feels so strange. Gone. As if a fire has swept through every nerve. I feel only the agony of my heart. It lodges in the back of my neck and eyes and casts an acid-like glow throughout this shabby cell with its damnable, eternal control light. It's the burning anguish of the soul I feel; caged in my breast, a dark clot, utter misery. I can't think it away with the future. "In two years"…No!

I hear the church bells tolling. It's eight o'clock in the morning.

Even the bells seem to toll the air with agony, agony, agony.

AWAKENING FROM A DREAM

"Remember,
in this world
*things are never what
they seem.*"

A friend of a friend

In a bad cycle

I watch a Greek prisoner carefully roll hashish into a cigarette, and I'm thinking about the letter that came yesterday. The letter came from Melina Foster. In her letter Melina writes that I'm in a bad cycle. (I suspected that already.) She says the peak will run from October twelfth through November. Yesterday was October twelfth. She writes: "Haole told me that he looked in on you the day of your trial, with the thought of insuring that your vibrations be high. He said that he saw around you eight bright lights and that his attempts to influence you were unsuccessful because of all the energy around you already in force...." Haole, who seems to understand these things, says that my higher self is putting my lower or egoic self through a purification process—a trial by fire. Like frying an egg while it's still in the shell, I suppose. As I'm pondering this new information Nick rushes in and tells me to gather up my things, that I'm leaving tonight. "Orders from the D. A.," he says. They're transferring me to the prison on Corfu. Damn, tomorrow Angelina's suppose to bring my clothes, shoes, sleeping bag. Nick makes out a telegram to Angelina while I'm stuffing my things into a brown paper sack. It's evening lock-up time, and, through the haste and confusion of the prison, I hear the Beatles singing over the loud-speaker in the yard. They're singing "Let it be, O let it be...." I smile to myself. Surely, this song at this precise moment must be a divine omen!

As I go out the main door Nikos the cook slips me two loaves of fresh-baked bread and a big hunk of cheese. A light rain begins to fall. Two guards whisk me away in the back of an old transport truck that keeps breaking down. They take me to a crowded, filthy little police station in Athens, known as "Met-a-go-go." That night two Spanish sailors share their blankets with me. It's their first time on a ship to Greece, the sailors tell me. While ashore they made friends with a young Greek. "The friendliest people in the world, you know," they say. The three men went back to the ship. They shared a little food, a little whiskey. The sailors offered the Greek a smoke. "It was the natural thing to do!" the sailors wail. "We've always smoked with the people. We've never had any trouble with the police. Until this fucking country!" Clothes, money, everything's back on the ship. *"Dhembirazi, dhembirazi!"* the police say. *"Never mind! It doesn't matter!"*

Next morning, the police take me to a large holding station at Piraeus. I have to wait here for three days before the next transfer truck leaves for Corfu. I glance around. Jeez, what a pigsty.

"Well, whatta y'know, a foreigner!"

I hear loud, friendly guffaws. I turn around and see two grinning Americans. They introduce themselves as Jim and Steve. Jim points to their cell and invites me to stash my things. They're in a large cell with a young French guy named Francois and a Belgian named Jacques. They soon tell me the latest news: "Oregon has legalized grass!" (As it turns out, this news, like most prison gossip, like the death of God, is more than slightly exaggerated.) But the REALLY BIG NEWS is that the U. S. Government is paying the Greek Government five dollars a day for every day a foreigner's in jail convicted on a drug charge. (The amount of money may vary but every foreigner I meet in jail swears this rumor is true. It seems the information originally came from a German TV program.)

Jim, Steve, Francois and Jacques have been in jail for seven months, along with two underage Arab twin brothers, and an Israeli guy, whom I later meet. They've come to Piraeus for trial. I double with laughter as I listen to these guys squabble and scheme among themselves, rearrange and shift the blame, to come up with one plausible story to tell the court. They were all staying in the same hotel in Athens, which is how they first met. The Arab twins had smuggled a kilo of hashish across the border into Greece. They hid the hashish inside their hollowed-out boot soles. Jim sold some of the hashish to an informer. The next day everyone got busted. Francois doesn't smoke or deal but the police found him sleeping in the Israeli's bed. The Israeli was in Francois' bed with Francois' sister. Underneath the Israeli's bed the police found scales and a liter of pharmaceutical opium. The opium belonged to an Israeli girl. To keep the girl out of jail, Francois admitted that the opium belonged to him, though not the scales. The scales actually belonged to the Arab brothers. In Steve's mattress the police uncovered some hashish and more opium. Steve told the police that he stole the dope from Francois. Jim had a few hits of acid on him, and then there was some extra hashish that no one wanted to claim. Jacques had just flown up from Crete with his new girl friend. With his long hair and beard and crazy energy he must have looked like a super freak to the police. So they grabbed him too. He had a few grams of hashish on him. They beat him, and to keep his new girl friend out of jail he confessed to a selling charge. I notice slash marks on his wrists. The others tell me this happened after a letter came to prison saying his girl friend had been killed in a car accident. Jacques cut his wrists and they rushed him to the hospital. As it turned out, his girl friend had made the whole story up. The truth was that she had found a new lover.

That night, all the mattresses have been taken by other prisoners and we have to sleep on the bare floor. Steve unzips his sleeping bag so that I can share a side. Steve comes from Virginia. He raps about the past, rock festivals and dope. He's excited about Malaysia. Malaysia is his future Paradise. In quiet moments, though, I can see that his talk of the past and future serves only as a thin distraction to hide his fear. The Greek newspapers have turned their bust into an international dope ring. Tomorrow morning Steve and his friends will go on trial. Who'll be screwed the most? That's the question running through all their minds.

In the next cell are three Greeks. They invite me over. "No need to be alone," they say. One's an old farmer and he's in for growing hashish. The youngest man seems about my own age. He comes from Athens, and, like myself, he's waiting on the truck to Corfu. The third man claims he doesn't know why he's in jail. He works on a ship, he tells me in broken English, and when he came home the police arrested him on entry. He's been inside eight days and says he still doesn't know why he's in jail.

Then he tells me his story. He's in Piraeus, he says, ready to ship out, when a man comes dashing along the docks. The man's carrying a box. The man hastily stashes the box out of sight, with the police hot on his heels, and then leaps into the water. The man escapes. After the police go, the sailor pulls the box from its hiding place. It's packed with hashish. He's not a smoker but who's to turn his back on a gift from Heaven? The box disappears with him to America. Months later, while in the Panama Canal, he has an accident that injuries his hand and forces him to stay over for two weeks in a hospital. His young son works on ship with him. The son stays over, too, and they both fly back to Greece. The police arrest him at the Athens air port. Meanwhile, he says, some really weird things have been going on at home. His wife has received threats through the mail. Someone has even tried to set fire to his house. He suspects the man who owned the box is behind these strange events. Whatever, the police refuse to give him a word of explanation. They just take him to the pokey. *"Meta, meta,"* they say. *"Later, later."*

By lock-up time I've scored a mattress. I move into the cell with the three Greeks. I mention food. When it comes to food the Greek understands his prison. The three men set out a full course meal brought in by their families. Cheese, shrimp, meat loaf casserole stuffed with hard-boiled eggs, a sauce, greens with meat, tender boiled okra, bread, olives, grapes and apples. They joke about wine. (Actually, in most holding stations, getting a bottle of wine or ouzo doesn't seem to be a problem for the Greeks, as long as they behave discreetly.) The younger Greek, the one on his way to Corfu, has a coarse, degenerate aura about him that immediately puts me on guard. He speaks to me in a mixture of English and his own language. Soon he's telling me that two years without a woman is a long time. In prison, he shrugs, what can you do? He slyly grins. Holy shit, just my luck. They'll probably put me in a cell with this creep. This bad cycle....

The next day a friend of his arrives. His friend is even worse. His friend wants to mess with my hair and he keeps assuring me how nice it feels to be screwed by another man. When they see that I'm getting uptight with their silliness, this just eggs them on. That night, the first Greek gathers his belongings and disappears with his friend into another cell. I sigh with relief. They pick the cell farthest from the main door and settle into a dark corner where they can't be easily seen by the guards.

What can you do?

"The battle is real.
Only the gods are not!"
Lord of the Initiates,
The Man Who Crossed The Great Sea

Back in Oregon I knew this guy named Jude. I shared a house with him for a few weeks. In school, Jude was a bordering mathematical genius. One day, without warning, Jude dropped out of his college honors program and started experimenting with mind altering drugs. He left the East Coast, hitchhiking to Oregon with a married woman. He bought himself a second-hand guitar and started going into country and western taverns. He wore old hats and baggy Goodwill clothing. He met Michael Ruby and the two of them would sometimes play songs together on the street corners of Portland. That's how I came to know Jude. Jude's father worked for the CIA. One thing his father told him, which stuck in his mind like hardened gum, and which he passed on to me one rainy day, as we were walking back from Kienow's with a bottle of wine, was this: *"Remember, son, in this world things are never what they seem."*

Thanasis was imprisoned because his neighbor accused him of growing hashish. Thanasis knew nothing about this hashish. He's married with a family and has a large farm near Kalamata. He doesn't need money from selling the "black smoke." He's really a gentle person, a good man. I believe civilizations are built upon the kind of quiet, down-to-earth strength, patience and endurance that make up this man called Thanasis. The police caught his neighbor growing hashish. The police beat the man. They wanted names of other growers. The man panicked and accused Thanasis. The hashish plants were not growing on land that belonged to Thanasis nor had anyone seen him attending the plants. (Excepting his neighbor of course.) *Dhembirazi, dhembirazi!* Thanasis was imprisoned in Nafplion for six months before he finally went to court. By then his neighbor had changed his tune and the case was thrown out because the police couldn't positively identify the plants as "narcotic." But what about the six months in prison, the separation from his family, the thousand dollars he paid in lawyer fees? Thanasis shrugs his shoulders with pained resignation. *What can you do?*

Dedee, a young Frenchman, and his girl friend are living together on Crete. (Already you can hear the whispers flying... the Papas lifting his eyes...the police looking for reasons.) They get busted for growing hashish plants in their garden. Dedee had purchased the seeds from a pet shop in Athens. They were bird seeds—bogus weed. *Dhembirazi!* Dedee and his girl friend both get two years in prison. The judge warns them: "We could give you ten!"

They call hashish the "black death."

"Every gram is the life of a child," says a district prosecutor.

Andrea, another Frenchman, gets six years and a sixty thousand drachma fine for less than eight grams. It's not even his shit. *Dhembirazi!* Here's the dope and someone must go to jail. Andrea doesn't help matters, of course, when he shows up at court wearing a big beard and hair past his shoulders and plays the mute. "It's not mine!" is all he would tell the judge.

Barry forgets his jacket in a restaurant. When he reports his loss to the police they have the jacket already in their possession. "Is this your passport?" they ask. "Yes, yes." "Is this your wallet?" "Yes." Then they place a small piece of hashish on the desk, which Barry had completely forgotten. "And is this your hashish?" The police can't prove the hashish belongs to Barry but he's naive enough to tell the court that he once smoked in England "to see what it was like." You once smoked in England? Well, here's sixteen months for you!

They know you're guilty. It's only a matter of how many years.

If they bust a man and his wife perhaps the woman will go free; or perhaps, like one German couple, the man will take fifteen years and his wife three. They'll imprison your wife and baby; and, if you're lucky and not charged with conspiracy, your wife and child may go free at the trial. Greek law defines "conspiracy" as a gang of two or more persons and sentences start with a minimum of ten years for each charge. Like the three Arabs who took sixteen years for three hundred grams.

Germans, Arabs, Turks: these people take the stiffest sentences. They're often heavy dealers, true; but the explanation is not so easy. With Arabs it's religion, politics, color. An Arab with two kilos may easily take five to twelve years. The Turk represents a sacred memory, a persistent threat. The Greeks want their revenge. With Germans, the Greeks remember the War all too well. One German I know took eighteen years. But, then, he had eighty kilos hidden in his van.

A mechanical engineer by profession, Joseph, an Egyptian, had lived in Athens for several years. A Greek friend informed on him. His "friend", he tells me, now lives with his woman. Joseph tells me this with a dark, menacing look. He swears that he'll get even with his friend once he's out of prison. Joseph was sitting handcuffed in the police station. "Where's the hashish? Where's the hashish?" "What hashish? What hashish?" Suddenly, without any warning, the police hit on the back of the head. Joseph, a past Golden Gloves champion, whirled in a rage and half a dozen cops scattered. He held them off until they smashed him to the floor with a chair, kicked and broke several of his ribs, and he had to be hospitalized. The police never found any hashish but Joseph had a lot of money, a new Cadillac, and a diamond ring. The court added two and two and came up with seven years.

The police like to beat you on the legs and feet where it doesn't show. They use electric shocks, yank you around by the hair and beard, or threaten to beat your woman and imprison her. (Halfass tortures, perhaps; but this is Greece.) The British consul warned Alan that if he didn't confess the police would beat him for sure. Are the judges simply looking the other way or do they even care? Whatever, you're going to jail.

"Here's your confession. Sign!"

If you demand to see your Embassy or a lawyer the police can always out wait you. "First sign this confession. Then call your Embassy."

You never know for sure what you're signing. You can bet, though, it's probably up to here with lies. Unnecessary lies, even. For instance, the police grab Mike and Dominque on the street in Athens. Dominque has a kilo of hashish and he's on his way to make a deal with someone. Mike goes along for the ride. In court Dominque takes all the blame. *Dhembirazi.* The police charge Mike not only with possession, which would have been a reasonable charge, but with "storing." Mike gets two years six months. Dominque gets four years.

In Greece you must prove you're innocent.

Being guilty, this is most difficult.

In the courtroom you don't argue what "should be" and what "shouldn't be." (Prison, I found out, is full of lawyers.) You lie like crazy to save your ass. You don't know HOW those forty-two kilos got in your car. You explain that newspapers claim hashish and other weird dreams ARE AGAINST THE LAW. You wouldn't touch THAT SHIT with a ten foot pole. Or, to grab a little mercy, you go the other way and play up to their worst fears. I'M A HASHISH SLAVE! A VICTIM OF THE BLACK SMOKE! I CAN'T HELP MYSELF! Lie for lie, tooth for tooth. And let the next man fend for himself, as the myths pile higher and higher.

Awakening from a dream

It's four in the morning and two policemen have Keith Guellow suspended upside down in the air with the straps of their rifles wrapped around the calves of his legs, so that a third man can beat his feet. The man uses a device that looks like an old riding crop. A loose wire poking through the leather cuts one of his toes. (Even their torture instruments are halfassed.) They make Keith stand in a puddle of cold water on the cement floor and dance his feet rapidly up and down. This keeps his feet from swelling and showing the beating. Keith won't admit to anything. "I was ready to sing like a bird the moment they messed with my balls or brought out the electricity," he tells me. "At first I thought, nah, this can't be real. They're not really gonna beat me. Actually, my feet soon went numb and I couldn't feel any pain. Then the bastards threatened to beat Paula." Keith feels sure they won't, but he can't take the chance. Even then he only makes a part confession. *Dhembirazi*, the police fill in the rest. They even put in a bunch of crap that incriminates Paula. Keith doesn't know this when he signs the statement. They persuade Keith that only he's going to jail, that Paula's okay. After he signs THEN the police tell him that she must go to jail too..."for a few days."

A Greek gift is a wooden horse with a string on it.

The police busted Keith for ten plants and some grass they found in the spice rack. At the time Keith didn't know about the grass in the cupboard. The grass had been left there by his friends who own the house. His friends were back in L. A. for a visit and he and Paula were staying in the house while buying land of their own. With money borrowed from Paula's folks, they bought seven acres that included two hundred olive trees. They had a horse and donkey and were already working the land. Naturally Keith decided to grow his own.

A few days before the bust, Keith suddenly got paranoid about the plants. He pulled the plants up, but he was in a hurry, and just tossed them in a field not far from the house. To the police obviously Keith was harvesting the marijuana.

152

At first Keith decided to take one of the local lawyers on the island. The lawyer assured Keith that ten thousand drachmas would release Paula on bail. The next time they see the lawyer it's four months later at the trial, Paula's still in jail, and the ten thousand drachmas they never see again.

By now Keith's friends have returned to Greece. They feel so badly about his arrest that they're taking care of all expenses. Patty's even willing to say the grass in the cupboard belongs to her. Keith says "NO!" There are enough people in jail as it is.

They bring in two lawyers from Athens. After an intense plea from the lawyers Paula goes free. Keith sighs with relief. Ah, he thinks, the most I'll get is two-and-a-half years. He faces three charges: cultivation, harvesting, and possession. The prosecutor pictures Keith as the villain. He has led this poor girl astray. Because Keith comes from a good family, however, and because this is his first offense, the prosecutor asks for only two-and-a-half years for each charge: seven-and-a-half years.

Keith almost shits. Seven-and-a-half years.

This can't be real!

He flashes on suicide...escape!

Seven-and-a-half years!

The judges go out; they come back in. They give him three years and fine him one thousand drachmas for each plant. After his release from prison he must immediately leave the country.

(As Keith tells me this I remember the words and Mona Lisa smile of the fortuneteller in Portland: "You don't know how lucky you are.")

And the farm?

Before his trial Keith had quickly put the land under Paula's name. Like all hashish prisoners Keith has been banished for life from Greece. His lawyers will try for a pardon but that's one helleva big MAYBE. Meanwhile the police transfer him to Corfu. Paula comes to see him but the law requires that an interpreter be present. The Embassy sends her to Immigrations.

Head of Immigrations doesn't want to be bothered. With the help of a young tourist policeman who speaks English, Paula arranges four half-hour visits.

When she returns a second time to Corfu, Immigrations has discovered that she and Keith aren't legally married. So Head of Immigrations puts a stop to the visits. Paula gets desperate to see Keith about the land. By taking food parcels she manages three five-minute visits but these desperate minutes flow with tears. Paula goes to the prison director. He agrees to a half-hour visit if she has an interpreter. Back to Immigrations she goes to plead. Head of Immigrations says Yes, if she'll go to bed with him. Paula can't take it anymore. In tears she leaves Greece to live in another country.   And the relationship between her and Keith soon changes.

Now Keith is on his own.

He laughs to himself and says to me: "All I wanted to do was bounce my ball on the beach!"

We kiss good-bye

The lawyers took all the money in Johan's briefcase: a thousand dollars. That's fifty dollars more than our original agreement. I find this out when Angelina unexpectedly shows up at Piraeus, the night before they transport me to Corfu. I also find out about her wrecking Johan's van, on the way to Nafplion. She rolled the van just outside Sparta but came through without a scratch. "Drunks, I remembered, never get hurt. I just pretended to be drunk and rolled with the van." The frame got smashed as well as my specially-delivered-all-the-way-from-Denmark-peanut-butter. Johan pretends it's a joke, this peanut butter. But I suspect he really believes Americans take their peanut butter as seriously as the Danish their schnapps. (Which, of course, we do.) Back in Monemvasia, Johan's holding my telegram—the one Nick sent from Nafplion—in his hands. The weird thing is that both he and Angie had a premonition that she was going to have an accident.

After the accident, Angelina went back to Monemvasia and then took the boat to Athens. From Athens she wired Marcus and Naomi. They emptied our bank savings and sent a thousand dollars to her and enough money to repair Johan's van. Through the Embassy Angie learns that I'm at Piraeus and she rushes over to see me.

It doesn't look good for a second trial she tells me.

Two years is the minimum for growing hashish. Suppose a new court gives me more than two years? Tom and Eric know a lawyer in Athens. The lawyer's a good friend; he smokes; and he's willing to help us for nothing. Angie doesn't trust the Nafplion lawyer. She thinks he's only after more money.

Angelina wants to leave Greece. Bubu has written and promised her work in Germany and she's excited about living in their castle. *(Keep centered, Pendarus. Keep centered.)* Eric has broken his silence and after five years he's returning to the United States. He sends me a heavy, black, Greek wool sweater and a pair of brand-new athletic shoes and socks, all which fit me perfectly. (The next night these clothes really save my life when we stop over in an ice box of a holding station, before taking a boat to Corfu the next day.) Tom has quit his teaching job and he's packing to go to India. I've never met Dale but she's back from the East and she has Angelina excited about the Tibetan yab-yum way of making love...and so how soon will I be free???

Radiant, flushed with excitement, Angelina tells me of a vision that she had. She saw herself looking down upon the world. She saw the sufferings of the world, and she wanted to help, but she had glimpsed her own death and there was so little time.

So little time....

The guard shuffles his feet.

I have a book of Rumi's poems—an earlier gift from Dale. On the back pages I've written a poem for Angelina. I pass the book out to the guard through the space in the door used for passing in food. The guard does his control and hands the book to Angie. He smiles. *"Endoxi, endoxi!"* he says. Quickly, before he can protest, we kiss good-bye through the prison door.

THIS PASSING WORLD

"There must be a way without language or thought.
A way through action. And this action is love."

Tom Sawyer,
American prisoner

When souls love,
governments do not exist

11/11/73

Love of my soul,

There has been no mail from you for about three weeks. What can I say, other than it worries me. Sounds simple, yes. Actually, no. It must be cold as hell up there. Why did they send you to one of the farthest points of Greece?

I've been sewing little things now with colored threads, bits and pieces of material. Making funny things, a little doll. I said earlier that Johan made a doll dress. Well, now, I made the doll to fit it. Chuckles and concealed thoughts. How shall the head be made? Marbles, rocks from the sea, olive pits. Dolls must have heads. I should think so. Or, no-head, no-thought. The sublime doll: headless, mindless. What's left to get in its way? No thing. Arms and legs only fill sleeves and skirts? Practical, yes. Useful, no. Every child deserves favor. A head must come; or heads will roll. Surely nature will bring fourth completeness. The power of the world works in circles, says Black Elk. Ah, ha! It must be round. It. How did It get involved? Come now, Angelina, It is in everything and everything is in It. Now back to the crown charka. One eye, leave the sense organs off! Simplicity must rule. Rule you say, THERE WILL BE NO RULERS IN MY HEAD. Yes, yes, sorry, mind. No teachers, no gurus, no leaders; what's left? Left is only created, existing when there is a right; and this duality duet could go on forever. But time is short and we need a head. All things come to those who wait. Om love ah hum on that. Yab Yum is THE position. David, did I tell you about our special gift from Dale? It is bath salts used by the Indians (East) for marriage ceremonies. Twenty-four hours before the wed of souls the male-female bathe and cover their bodies with this divine powder. And, bingo! Twenty-four hours later your prana is directed to all your charka centers simultaneously and "A single flame explodes in the universe."

Gifts of the Magi. Treasures from the East.

Om hummmmm.

As if there will be a need for it.

Marriage is performed with every uniting of male, female. Governments and ignorance do not exist when souls LOVE.

The truth shall be known when fear has departed.

Bless all beings every place.

Mars peeking in through the window has discovered the warm heat of passion rising from its hidden cave, my heart. DARE you look at this sacred jewel I have forcefully concealed! I KNOW THE USELESSNESS OF PASSION. Accuse ME of passion and my soul shall flare up and devour you in the fire. "THERE IS NO PASSION." Aphrodite and I scream to be let off this tumultuous sea. We are sisters, endlessly riding the crimson shell, tossed by the wind-flicked foamy waves. "Dare you to accuse us of passion?" again and again we cry, until the storm has carried our voices to distant space, merely to be rebounded from cloud to star then sea once more. At rest now on Winter's shore, we embrace. Sister divine, sleep. Winter is long, love will warm our flesh. The eyes of the Universe close, night of the soul hovers over the body of the sisters. Cloaked in gentle moonfilled darkness; the voice sings softly the spiritual timeless lullaby. "Sleeping child I will never leave your side."

Our egg plants have finally yielded fruit. One baby about three inches long, and, actually, it is all grown up now. Who shall taste this gift? Should there not be a Closing of the Earth harvest festival? The animals of the field and air shall come. The wind; its melody will sing of life and death. The sea and brother sky, balance and peace. Hills and valleys cradle sweet love. And Sun shall penetrate all with iridescent oneness. Milk and honey shall flow. And Moon, lovely lady of the eve. Her promise is woven with the finest beams and silken thread. A rainbow to span time with eternity's colors. The people of the earth, laughter overflows. They come in colors from everywhere. The Autumn is now, work near done. The breeze blows cool. Together my love and I watch the changes. Home is you, home is with you. I love you so completely.

Soon,
Angelina

Return to the source

The Greek government has fallen once again and tanks are in the streets. On Corfu, we're waiting for amnesty. We're always waiting for amnesty. It's Christmas 1973. Over the radio we hear that in Turkey, in Yugoslavia, in countries all around us, they're opening the big iron gates. Surely the Greek Government will do the same. I hear an Arab singing softly a Bob Dylan song: "Any day now, any day now, I shall be released...."

> Christmas comes and goes,
> & now it's Easter time.
>
> Look, here comes the priest!
> Aw, he's old and fat,
> he looks like death warmed over.
> Around him, candles burning,
> chant a dozen prisoners.
>
> The seven locked gates
> he sprinkles with holy water.
> Inside, we quietly celebrate
> our beer and cakes,
> & the sacrificial entrails
> we throw to the cats.
>
> The wind whirls ashes before my eyes,
> clouds gather in the sky.
> The night falls in rain.
> And only the earth—
> this earth that catches
> & transforms my spirit—
> only the earth is my resurrection.

While we're waiting for amnesty I'll make a pot of tea.

We drink a helleva lot of tea in this prison. If there's no room in the kitchen we'll build a small fire in the exercise yard with yesterday's newspapers and empty soap boxes. It's not so much the tea or sugar but the routine, the ritual: Oh, what shall we do? As Louis says, in a soft Brazilian accent, and a roll of toilet paper in his hands, "Even shitting in prison is a pastime."

Shall we play war games or Scrabble?

Pass beads? Read a book? Tell stories?

Meditate on enlightenment and other exercises in measuring the void?

Zero is Arabic for the universe, so I discovered in Paris. Later, Henry Miller tells me: "Zero is Greek for pure vision." Or, altogether now: The goggle-eyed monsters that once terrorized the seas have now moved into outer space....

The truth is, I never did too well in mathematics.

I open my eyes and am seen. I open my heart and am loved.

My part in this divine play, this passing world, contains no special art or disguise or knowledge of time. I claim no new physics or advancements on reality. I follow no path but the unnamed one under my own feet. Like Whitman I choose the Open Road. Like Rumi I enter the God Fire. Like the Navajos I walk the Night Way. Hand-in-hand I journey with my great-grandmother; we walk a trail of tears to a place called Oklahoma. In a prison yard in Greece I walk shoulder-to-shoulder with thieves, murderers, and outlaws. I am the lamb that is slaughtered and the one who devours the slaughtered lamb. The light within the darkness I am; and the darkness that holds the light I am. Only in complete surrender to the cosmic fire within you will you know who I am. There's only one universe: *you.* You alone are responsible for the love within you and the world in which you live. Return to the source (of all things). *Remember who you are.*

Waiting for Houdini,
Or,
If you can see me I can see you

"This is a train station!" says Terry. "You're always waiting for the train!" Terry comes from London and he's a thief by trade. He and his wife both, birds of a feather. They worked as a team. In Greece, they were busted at the border with two kilos of hashish. A tall, lanky guy with short flat hair and deep-set eyes, Terry has a cunning mind that's always on guard, always ready to defend and rationalize. If provoked, he'll physically attack without warning. At the trial they let his wife and baby go free. After the trial his wife went to Poland to visit her family. Now, Terry gets a letter from her saying that the Polish authorities have confiscated her passport and they're refusing to let her return to England. Terry glances at his watch and at three prisoners pacing the yard. "First," he says, "you're waiting for trial. Then you're waiting for a transfer to Corfu. And then, when your one-third is up, you're waiting for the work farm. Maybe..." He pauses. "Maybe you'll be lucky and the Ministry will approve your work farm application the first time. But even that takes two or three months. Then once you're on the work farm you're waiting for anostoli." ("Anostoli" is the suspension, or probation, of your last one-third.) "That is," he continues, "if all your court fees have been paid...and your fines...and if the District Prosecutor doesn't have a fight with his wife the night before the committee meets and he decides that "you're not ready for the future.'"

Or you're waiting for a second trial.

The mythical Second Chance.

Like Douglas. Douglas comes from Belgium and this was his first experience with smuggling hashish. He had sixty-two kilos in his car. At the trial Interpol supplied the Greek police with erroneous information. They gave the court information on another guy—a man with a similar name—a criminal, who, Douglas later discovered, was incarcerated in a Kansas penitentiary, even at the time of Douglas' trial. When Douglas' lawyer heard the Interpol report he trembled and went to pieces.

"But this is not possible!" Douglas protested. "I am not this man!"

Dhembirazi. The court gave him fifteen years.

Or you're waiting for a letter. (Letters take forever.)

Or for a package of German chocolates.

Or for a book like *Houdini's Great Secrets Revealed.*

Your letters must be approved by the Ministry of Justice in Athens. Your packages will be ripped apart by a guard and then overtaxed by Customs.

"I have a family!" cries the tax man.

Technically, hashish prisoners aren't even allowed packages. It seems, however, that the enforcement of this rule is left up to the individual prison directors.

Max, an Italian prisoner, mailed a post card (post cards sometimes bypass the long journey into Athens) with a message that went something like this: DEAR GRANDMA, HAPPY BIRTHDAY! I LOVE YOU. MAX. Between the lines Max had decorated his card with twenty-two kisses, or X marks. Three weeks later the Ministry of Justice returned his card with an official letter. His card contained "too many words."

One day at Nafplion the director called me into his office. He wanted to see me about a four page letter that I had written to Angelina. Nick acted as translator. The director explained that I was allowed only two pages, that if he allowed me four pages he might be penalized by the Ministry. By law, Nick explained, foreigners are allowed four letters a month, two pages in length. The law even states the exact number of words a prisoner may write. At Corfu, this law gets blatantly ignored. Even if you write ten or twelve letters a month chances are the director won't say anything. But he can. Anyway, at Nafplion the director randomly pulled out pages one and two. Then he handed me pages three and four and told me: "Now you can send your letter."

"No, no!" I cried. "I'll rewrite the letter!"

At Corfu they once called me in to see the head guard. The Ministry had returned a letter that I had written six weeks ago to Melina Foster. I had said some bad things against the Greek people. What?! Nothing that I hadn't said before in other letters. Only this time I had mentioned their ignorance about marijuana.

"It's not my fault you're in jail!" wailed the head guard.

When Dietrich was transferred to Corfu he arrived with several bundles of stalk tea, popularly known in Greece as "tea of the mountains." "What's this?" the control guards wanted to know. Dietrich explained that it was tea and that he had bought it at the other prison. The guards wouldn't accept his answer. Exasperated, Dietrich told them that it was marijuana.

"Ah, marijuana!" they cried. And they confiscated his tea.

They're lazy, these guards; and they have to be a little stupid, crouched in their tiny whitewashed guardhouses just outside the inner gates, with the rain pouring down, locking and unlocking the gates each time a prisoner wants to go for coffee, or to the kitchen, or to see the director. What other prison in the world can you over boil your tea water and put out the kitchen fire? Or sleep all day? Or yell at the guards? When the guards pull their monthly search the new ones will even apologize for waking you. They seem embarrassed about poking through your belongings. Looking for what? Hashish? A knife? A pack of cards? Homemade raisin wine? The guards make a mess out of your bed. They turn things upside-down and rip a few pictures off the wall. They flip through a magazine or two. Or they peek inside a guitar. Or they tear down your light shade. Light shades are forbidden, you see. But most of us put some kind of shade over the ceiling light. Maybe the guards will tear down the shade in the next cell and won't even bother looking at yours. If they do tear it down, *dhembirazi*. The next day you just put up another one.

One night the guards rushed into cell 18 and ripped down the light shade. Then the guards took a guitar from another room, for reasons we never did understand. Next they rushed into cell 2. This time for sure the guards must have seen the tiny wires connecting Ewen's cassette tape machine to the overhead light. But the guards retreated in confusion—or deliberation—when Schultz and Ewen began shouting at them.

At night, after lock-up, they allow us transistor radios and cassettes but we have to turn the machines in each morning. In our section someone's forever hooking a radio up to the ceiling light—to save on batteries—and blowing a fuse. One time Schultz borrowed a tape machine from another prisoner and made the wrong connection. He blew out all the lights in our section and melted the transistors in the tape machine.

The guards must be waiting. It's another trick. But what?

About the only thing they leave untouched is your plastic piss pot. The more elaborate your decorations the more destructive their search. But out of carelessness, not through malicious intent. They're so harsh with things.

Once, I received a fountain pen and bottle of ink through the mail. The pen came from George, a lawyer in Athens. George and his wife knew Angelina. They met her through Tom and Eric and she did some baby sitting for them. George had written me a nice letter asking if he could help in anyway. I wrote and thanked him and suggested that he might send in a work farm application for me. (I thought the application would be approved quicker if handled by a lawyer). I told him that I would appreciate a fountain pen and ink. Two weeks later an application arrived for me to sign, along with the pen and ink. The control guard, before he completed his search, had ink stains on his uniform, his hands, the floor. I shook my head incredulously. Then I took a deeper look. When I'm impatient and careless and bent on having my own way: Am I not this guard? Is not this myself I see?

In January, Angelina left for Denmark.

Before leaving she mailed me her sleeping bag, my clothes, some Tiger Balm, sea shells, and a well-worn Krishnamurti paper-back book, carefully wrapped in a silk scarf from India to hold the loose pages together.

I swear it rains more on Corfu than in Portland. These thin, gray prison blankets—woven from the wool of dead sheep I've been told—feel just about worthless against the prison's cold damp stone walls. I pile the bed higher and higher and still wake up shivering. Twice I see the director about my sleeping bag. "No, it's forbidden!" he explains, without lifting his eyes from the very important papers on his desk. More than half the guys in my section have sleeping bags. Well, I reason, trying to see his side, my sleeping bag *is* a mummy style bag and it can't be disguised as a comforter. I could hang myself with the draw strings. Or, better yet, I could hang one of the guards. Still, it's absurd! In fact, the very next day, Mike, the Australian who got busted with Dominque, transfers in and brings a sleeping bag with him. The guards give him no hassle whatsoever.

Oliver, a Swede, went through the same rigmarole over a silver flute. When Oliver wanted his flute the director told him: "No, it's forbidden." Perhaps the director thought Oliver might hit a guard over the head and escape. We have iron bed ends. We have heavy boards, stones, guitars. But who knows? On Oliver's fourth visit the director handed him the flute without a word.

The fool, the miser, and the man who saw the White Light

"I AM FREE AS LONG AS
I AM ONE WITH THE BUDDHA."
Graffiti scratched on the wall at Piraeus.
Beneath this graffiti,
another prisoner has added:
"WHAT ARE YOU GONNA DO
WHEN THE FIX RUNS OUT?"

In this prison we live in dreams and illusions about the past, and in the future that will pick up where we left off, with little changed but our daily routines and the guards. One man plays the fool. Another the miser. Another has seen the White Light. The fool seems clever, a fox. He's quick. The game he plays will shift at any moment. Ali is from Sudan, the son of a tribal chief, and he hates the British for what they've done to his country. As for the Greeks..."Inside or out," says Ali, "the Greek is a prick and a coward. All he wants is cock. So I give him cock!" "I know myself," he boasts. "Believe me, I know myself well!" he laughs mockingly.

"King of the monkeys—that's ME!"

But why is the Greek afraid? What makes him lie?

Even the fool doesn't know.

Worse than the fool is the miser. The miser hoards sugar, tea, cigarettes, books. He keeps his stash hidden under the bed and counts it every week. Mike comes from Santa Barbara, California. When a yogurt gets stolen from his cell, (deliberately by Paul, to teach Mike a lesson), Mike plants another yogurt by his door, with soap on the inside, hoping the thief will return to steal it. Each week new books arrive from his family: books on science fiction but mostly books on spiritual enlightenment.

He and the Enlightened One swap books.

Worse than the miser is the one who has seen the White Light. Gunther left Germany with a friend and a batch of counterfeit money to buy hashish in Morocco. They were traveling on his friend's boat. The two men got into a quarrel over a woman who had come with them. When his friend tried to smash down Gunther's cabin door, Gunther shot him with a pistol. Then he dumped his friend's body into the sea.

Inside, Gunther took one acid trip and saw the White Light. Now he's very particular about his diet. (Except for the cat that he and another man killed to cook and eat, just to see what it would taste like.) He's very particular about all his things. You can't play with his volley ball until the rain stops, but he'll play with *your* ball. He packs a cardboard box full of good books and sends them home to Germany. A few old ones on yoga and astrology he generously donates to our little prison library.

Is this a mountain in my eye or a speck of dust?

From darkness we come and into darkness we go.

Escaping nowhere.

BANG! BANG! BANG!

Each evening the guards hammer their long wooden-handled mallets against the window bars, checking for loose ones.

BANG! BANG! BANG!

Steve, a big blond German, and Francoise, a crazyass Dutchman, escaped from the island hospital. But where to go? They had plans to steal a boat but ended up on the wrong end of the island, wandering around on the beach, until they were captured three days later.

Escape without violence usually means another two months, and there's a chance you won't get to the work farm. For hitting the guard, Steve and Francoise each took another two years. Steve tried once more. This time he tried digging a tunnel out through the floor in the shower room. For this attempt the guards gave him a beating and threw him in the cooler for a month.

Paul, an American with nine years, (the same Paul who took the miser's yogurt to teach him a lesson), broke loose on his way to court. He roamed the Greek countryside for a week, and, for all his courage and daring, got an assful of buckshot from a keen-eyed, bounty-hunting farmer.

Whitmore, a Viet Nam veteran from Ohio, made a dramatic escape in a mad dash through the streets of Piraeus. Russ had planned his escape so that his sister would be waiting for him in a car. But his timing was off and a policeman in relentless pursuit nabbed him. Back at the station the boys gave him a beating. One cop got so frustrated, when he saw that their rain of blows hadn't really hurt Whitmore, that the cop threw a bucket of whitewash in his face.

An Egyptian did make it free so I hear.

(Only to wind up later in a Turkish jail.)

Like Paul, the Egyptian escaped on his way to court. Later the police went to Aegena where he had been imprisoned and asked the foreigners for his address. The police wanted their handcuffs back.

Everything runs on money, everything but the universe

Everyday they feed us macaroni or white rice or potatoes. For variety they feed us fat noodles one day, thin noodles the next, and the day after that we get noodles that look like large swollen grains of rice (or maggots, as one prisoner has delicately observed). The cooks prepare everything with tomato sauce and tons of olive oil. Except for the rice pudding. But sometimes that comes without the rice. On meat days—about three days a week—first the cooks boil the lamb to defrost it. Then they broil the meat in large aluminum trays, with potatoes, or white rice, or noodles. In spite of all the sheep that I've seen in Greece, the lamb they serve comes from New Zealand. And, this year, Greece exported so much of their olive oil that they had to turn around and import cooking oil from Italy.

On some meat days we're served small fried fish, probably smelt; a popular, inexpensive dish that I learned to enjoy at Artemis'. Mostly you eat everything, heads and all, depending on your courage and the size of the fish. (Man, how I long for a bowl of Artemis' delicious avgolemono soup, and his tender kalamaria, and domas, and feta cheese and red, ripe tomatoes still warm from the sun....) Vegetables, or "horta," the prison cooks boil like laundry or soap or a witch's brew. Then they drain all the juices, vitamins, and life-giving minerals into the sewer for the rats. Big rats, too. Every now and then I hear loud, excited shouts in the yard, and dash out to find some prisoner chasing after a huge rat.

The food may get monotonous but we have plenty to eat. I've been told that it's far worse for prisoners in Morocco and places further East, where you'll literally eat crumbs if you don't have money, and you won't sell you ass. One thing for sure, this Greek prison is no day in the life of Ivan Denisovich. Everyday we get half a kilo of whole wheat bread, hot from the prison ovens. Three times a week they give us cheese and yogurt, and eggs once a week. We may cook the eggs as we like. On Sundays they serve little cakes and on holidays a beer. (Before inflation, I'm told, they even gave us wine on Sundays and ice cream during the summer.) Once a week from an outside store we may purchase fruits and vegetables, meat, canned goods, shampoo, toilet tissue, Nescafé and black tea.

Every morning at Corfu the guards bring us tea and a cup of hot sugared milk. The hot milk I often drink with a spoonful of Nescafé. The tea comes so thin, even that can be used for making instant coffee. At Nafplion, each morning the coffee runner would come to the window bars and we enjoyed our kafes—our Greek coffee—in bed. On the work farm at Kassandra they serve either tea or milk, but not both. And no coffee. (They won't allow hashish prisoners to buy coffee from the outside store either.) On meat days at Kassandra they serve tea rather than milk, to offset the price of meat.

"Everything runs on money!" bemoans a prisoner.

Now where have I heard that before?

In winter, on Corfu, we must even pay for our own heat: "parena," a charcoal-like substance finely ground from olive pits. Parena will take the dampness from the walls and stop my shivering. We can make a cup of tea and fry an egg. (Once, Ewen and I even tried our hands at making crepes.) In return, parena fumes can really give you a terrific headache. And should your hand ever slip as you're lifting a tin of hot water from your makeshift stove—and believe me, it happens—the whole room turns to smoke and ashes.

On weekends at Corfu I like to avoid the kitchen. The store comes on Saturday, and this means all Saturday afternoon and Sunday the kitchen gets jammed, especially with Greeks and Germans. Generally speaking, the Germans seem elaborate and well-organized. They have everything down pat. The Greeks, well, I've never seen so many boiling tempers and bad stomachs. Old hens couldn't squabble more. A real salad, as they say. But to the Greek everything falls in place. Or so it seems.

Chasing the butterfly on Chuang Tzu's nose

"We are so anxious!" Pedro says to me and smiles cunningly. Pedro comes from Brazil and has lived most of his years on the street. In England they arrested him for vagrancy and for carrying an over-sized knife. In Holland they deported him. In France they busted him for selling hashish and he spent two years in jail. In Greece he took nine-and-a-half years for dealing two hundred grams of hash. (And for his arrogant manners in court I hear.) The day before his trial, even then he was planning to consult the *I Ching* about robbing a bank.

I don't say anything. I just listen.

Pedro refuses to eat the Greek prison food and cooks his own macrobiotic diet. He looks anemic and he gets thinner and more gaunt each day. But he's determined. Fanatically so. Pedro has a shrewd mind and he prides himself on his shrewdness and his insights into the Greek mentality.

"But," he confides to me, lowering his voice, "there's no pattern!"

In other countries Pedro could quickly pick up on the people's habits and their basic assumptions about reality. But not with the Greeks. The Greeks baffle him.

Pedro gestures toward a cluster of wild mint growing in the yard and to the blue sunny sky and the magnificent shaggy pines growing on the other side of the high stone wall.

"This," says Pedro, with a sweep of his arm, "is the real world!"

It's the morning and evening of the first spring and all around us, wherever there's a bit of earth and a ray of sun, life goes on. Even on these high stone prison walls, wherever shows a crack and a crevice grows a green shoot of tender grass, a small flower, a tiny tree.

Pedro's right, I believe. Only the given is real and true.

The rest we manufacture, we make-up.

Beethoven's Violin Concerto in D, Op. 61; Shakespeare's *Romeo & Juliet*; the great pyramids of Egypt and Central

America; the roads of ancient Rome and the freeways of L.A.; pick-up trucks and country music and tantra yoga; the authority of the Pope; the Holy Bible; the Koran; all the gods and goddesses; the poems of Sappho; the dwellings of Mesa Verde; the Bill of Rights; our technological civilization; our nuclear toys and race wars and canned soups and designer suits; the Nobel Peace prize; the shroud of Turin; the legend of Billie Holiday; the poems of Kabir; Marilyn Monroe and valentines and lacy black underwear; karma and Mecca and the Holy Grail; Navajo sand paintings; the poems of Tsvetaeva; Georgia O'Keefee's "Grey Line with Black, Blue and Yellow"; the Nocturnes of Chopin; Fellini's *Satyricon* and Alexander Jodorowsky's *El Topo* and rock 'n' roll; your grandmother's favorite recipe; Walt Whitman's "Song of Myself"; the lovely hymn "Amazing Grace"; the poems of Issa and all the poems that have ever been written; the Tao, sorcery; the Looking Glass Bookstore; the myths of dying and being born; the walls of this prison around me.

Dream upon dream.

Always chasing identity.

And the real world—this butterfly on Chuang Tzu's nose— perhaps this, too, we dream?

East, West, and Down Under
THE FIRST MAN
TO STOP THE HABIT

Freddy's from New Zealand and a book unto himself: *non-stop.* Freddy has the true storyteller's natural gift to embellish the world and enchant his listeners with Every Believable Detail in place, as he ensnares your imagination, and your willingness to believe, with outrageous tales of strange and unbelievable encounters. *The works: his body laid back: his mind spaced: his soul on a high;* such as the Ancient Mariner might dream, missing the Marriage Celebration within, because he's so stoned and strung-out on visions and omens and outlandish birds devouring his heart, that you never know, unless you look really close into his piercing, but, caged, blue eyes, just how down and out he might or might not be. He keeps the dark horses frothing the surface, riding the breakers in his mind, weathering the storms of his ups and downs without self-pity or bitterness, but with a sense of non-attachment and acceptance of his foolish ways, never stopping his mad pursuit of other worlds, but only pausing in the rain before night falls and the guards descend upon us, to ponder another avenue of escape, another adventure.

Freddy rubs his scrub chin. A tiny gold earring hangs from his left ear. "Is it possible to travel in time?" he wonders aloud. "Reincarnation, that's possible. Isn't it?"

Freddy's been in and out of jails all over the world. New Zealand, Australia, Thailand, India. In England he entered a rehabilitation center for users. The first day in, Freddy tells me, he scored some junk off the pretty, red-haired nurse who showed him the grounds. Later, Freddy pulled a few tricks and actually convinced the director that he'd kicked the habit. THE FIRST MAN TO STOP THE HABIT!!! The director got so excited over the success of his program that he almost wet his pants, and he missed every one of Freddy's tricks. Freddy stopped, *only,* as he explains the scoring procedure to me, so as to arrive in India without a habit. That way, he could build up a good one, a few rupees a day. Freddy ain't about to get off junk. You might as well stop the world.

He was on his way to India and I'm-repeating-myself-to-death-trip, when, half-an-hour in Athens, broke, and on the street, Freddy closed his eyes just long enough to deal a little of his personal stash.

Whamo, he and his woman got busted by a "ruffiano."

Without the *ruffiano*—the informer—would the Greek police ever catch a single person? A Greek pharmacist from another village, passing by Johan's house on the way to the beach, saw my ten scrawny plants and informed the police. This I found out at the trial. Even Andonai, so Johan told me, recognized the plants. Andonai just looked the other way. He considered me a friend and my business was my business. (I would have appreciated a kind word, though: "Hey, David, you're about to step on a dangerous snake!" I know…I know. The *I Ching* warned me.) Later on, at Nafplion, Angelina brought me a ripe "Sugar Baby" watermelon, a gift from Andonai's garden. Like Artemis, Andonai's a true saint. A saint in the sense of humbleness and gentleness and connectedness to the earth. May these two men never go broke or hungry or cold!

"YOU MOTHERFUCKERS!!! LET ME OUTTA HERE!!!"

Freddy's woman went crazy in jail, screaming at the guards night and day. The guards didn't understand English but I'll bet they understood her.

"YOU COCKSUCKERS!!! I'LL CUT YOUR BALLS OFF!!!"

Freddy didn't say a word.

Actually, he was ripped most of the time. An American, busted at the same time as Freddy, had two hundred window panes of acid on him. The guards don't seem to know about acid.

Freddy scratches his flyaway hair, his mind tossing in the wreckage of reason and imagination. "We can reason anything, given enough desperation and desire," he says to me. "Don't you think so?"

How am I to know what mad and reckless adventures—or the cautious and timid half-steps—that a soul must experience

177

in order to gain wisdom? Or what path of self-knowledge one must travel, though to me, and others, the path may seem to make little or no sense?

The last sign I see of Freddy is a message that he scrawled for a friend, on the wall of a little holding station, on his way to Athens and the work farm on Crete: IT WAS A DRAG AT THE GATE BUT TIME YOU READ THIS YOU'LL BE WELL ON THE WAY.

Oceanic birth

A way without language / A way through action

One time at sea Tom Sawyer almost jumped overboard. It wasn't suicide, he assures me, but an overwhelming urge to surrender to the ocean. It was all he could do to stop himself. "Good thing I wasn't stoned!" he muses. Why does Tom smoke dope? "Do I even want to?" he wonders aloud and frowns slightly at his dilemma. Tom comes from Mobile, Alabama. Like Freddy he works as a merchant seaman. On board ship Tom would smoke and listen to music. Harmless enough it seems. But the Divine plays in mysterious ways. At Piraeus the Greek police arrested Tom and took him off his ship. The police didn't bother to wait for an invitation from the ship's captain nor did they care that Tom had never set foot on shore. They only needed an accusation. While in Turkey he had picked up half a kilo of hashish. He gave some to a nineteen-year-old kid who worked on ship with him. The kid went ashore and got busted. The police wanted to know where he got the hashish. The kid, naive and scared, figured that he'd get off easier, or maybe go free, if he gave them Tom's name. It turned out that he still got one year, the minimum for possession; which is what he would have taken anyway. The police charged Tom with buying hashish *while in Turkey*. The court gave him three-and-a-half years.

"It wasn't even worth smoking, this hashish!" Tom shrugs. "But like a fool I hung onto it."

"I've always worked in Asia and the Far East. I've never even wanted to come to Europe. When I first took the ship I knew better. Something inside told me. But I let a buddy talk me into it. It's my own fault."

The funny thing is, Customs wouldn't allow Tom's clothes into the country. Not without a passport. Tom has no passport, only his seaman's papers. *Dhembirazi, dhembirazi.* "You can go to jail but not the clothes!" Six months go by before they allow him to change his Levis. Even then, only after he threatened to walk around the prison yard naked.

"THOSE MOTHERFUCKIN' CATS!!!
GET OUT OF HERE, YUH BASTARDS!!!"
Almost any night in spring you can hear this outraged oath and some prisoner banging on the bars of his cell door: BANG, BANG! "GET OUTTA HERE, GODDAMIT!"
"Fuckin' hell, man, those cats must be right out in the hall!"
But the very next day we're all out in the yard, crowding around, watching, and cheering their howling-scratching-hissing-courting ritual. There's only one female in the yard at Corfu this year and God knows how many males and she's giving them all a run for their money. Suddenly, one tom boldly pounces on her back, gripping her neck in his teeth with a death-like grip. Another tom jumps into the act, attempting to push his rival aside. Or perhaps he's trying to help, it's difficult to tell. But this pussy will not easily be won. They try again and again. By this time everyone's getting excited. "Eat your hearts out!" yells Freddy from across the yard.
Uh-oh. Here comes Ol' Bruiser.
Bruiser's the biggest, meanest, ugliest tom in the whole prison. His left eye has been torn out from a fight, his fur's dirty and matted, and his intentions, well, his intentions are pretty obvious.
Then...alas...there's Snurd.
Poor Snurd. Snurd's running around sniffing asses. He's so weirded-out he can't remember WHAT or even HOW. He looks game for either and they say that last year he did take it in the ass. Is that possible in the cat kingdom? I don't know. They say some Greeks gave him a full hit of acid and he hasn't been the same since.
Poor Snurd.
Dhembirazi, time passes and the other males have had their chances and now the lady wants Snurd. She's purring and twisting seductively and going crazy at his feet, but Snurd

looks puzzled, like some character in a Woody Allen film, as if he's trying to figure it out with his head. He's trying, God knows he's trying. But just when it seems Snurd might be getting his act together, a guard comes running through the gate with a tightass grin on his face, waving his arms in the air, and shouting.

At Corfu a single cell is a prized possession. When I first arrived in October our section had no empty cells and Tom Sawyer offered to share his with me. Later, I found out that Tom had waited two months for this cell. It had been promised to him by an English prisoner before he got transferred out. Tom had the cell to himself for less than a week before I showed up. At first Tom said very little to me. I thought perhaps he resented losing his privacy so soon. As I found out, words do not come easily for Tom. Only gradually did he reveal his thoughts to me. Unlike a lot of prisoners Tom never kept anything stashed under his bed; not even peanut butter, which the American consul from Athens would leave us, and which our friends from other countries considered a favorite treat, as were German chocolates to us. Tom would give his clothes away if he had anything that you wanted: a belt, a jacket, a pair of pants.

"It's a common thing with sailors," he explained.

For a while we had a cat in our cell. She came and went as she pleased through a vent beneath Tom's bed. He called her Mitzi and treated her as a queen. He spoiled her, played games with her, pampered her affections and afflictions, her greed and her boredom. On the days that we had small fish for lunch, instead of holding some back, Tom would feed Mitzi all the leftovers in a single meal, knowing that tomorrow we'd get thin rice soup with meatballs so god awful tasteless that even the cats would turn up their noses and refuse to eat them. That's the truth. The cats would walk away and leave the meatballs untouched.

On the other hand, Tom would totally ignore Mitzi for days. He would use her as a pastime and project his own boredom upon her and put her through circus routines that definitely aroused her displeasure. Beneath the fluff and purr, as you no doubt know, these pretentious, pint-sized house cousins of the leopard still remember their untamed origins and they can react with incredible swiftness of tooth and claw. I grew fond of Mitzi but kept my distance. Sooner or later cats and I always get into territorial disputes. As soon as the cat finds out what you don't want the cat goes crazy with determination to do that very thing. (I'm thinking of Magic, a young male cat that Angelina brought home with her, when we lived in Portland.) Now the cat's in control and you can't turn your back. Turn your back and he'll grab your breakfast right off the kitchen table. Unless you re-arrange your life around the cat's meow. Actually, I think cats just plug into your energy—wherever you put a lot of energy—your hands, your belly, your heart, your head, your house plants, your morning toast. Most cats just naturally want to be in the center of the action.

When Johan and Eva went back to Denmark, and left us their house, they left us a cat named Lady Hamilton and her litter of four kittens. Each September, when Johan returned to Monemvasia, Lady Hamilton would always show up at the house within a few days of his arrival. Apparently she knew Johan was back by the sound of the running generator. This last spring she and her wildcat lover had four kittens, which Johan and Eva promptly named Bubu, David, Angelina, and Barney.

The Greeks would probably just drown the little ones in the sea, they have enough cats. (I remember seeing a mama cat pacing back and forth on the shore, looking anxiously out into the water.) Johan would not come out and tell us to drown these kittens. He wouldn't and I wouldn't anyway. Just the same we didn't want to bother with these cats, keeping them in fish, which offended Sotiris the Greek merchant, who sold us the fish, when he discovered we were buying them for a mother cat and her kittens.

Angelina and I moved Lady Hamilton's kittens out of the house to a cool spot beneath the carob tree. Lady Hamilton didn't like the carob tree neighborhood, for she quickly moved them into the tall grasses. The kittens grew up wild and we couldn't even get close to them. They disappeared long before I got busted.

Mitzi never saw her first spring. She grew fat and lazy and bitchy. Then she came down with cat's flu or *Feline Enteritis*. For ten days she refused to eat anything. She seemed to recover only to plunge back into fever. We did manage to score a penicillin tablet from a German prisoner. Tom dissolved the tablet in a spoon and tried to force-feed her but she rejected everything. One morning we found her nearly drowned in a small cistern near the toilet at the end of the yard. The night before Mitzi died, Tom saw what he called "a dark angel of death" in our cell.

"The guide is only someone to blame in case you're misguided," Tom says with a slight chuckle. He shrugs off the entanglement of words, the mind trips, the prison gossip, the pretenses, the evasions of self-responsibility. "If all else fails blame it on destiny. Or blame it on karma. It was bound to happen!"

"There must be a way without language or thought. A way through action."

It's Christmas Eve. Tom and I have just taken some window pane acid. A friend of his sent the acid, concealing it under the postage stamp of a birthday card. Tom gazes out the window through the bars to a still night sky and an ocean of stars.

"And this action is love.

"It's simple, Dave. Get rid of the *I*."

On the backs of sea horses' eyes

(A journey of bridges)

What are we all looking for? I wondered, as Ben Abrams and I drifted through the smoke and small talk of the party's crowd of beer and wine drinkers. It was September 1966 and I was back at the University of Oregon for my second year of graduate work. A cluster of people had gathered around the piano. Like them I felt drawn to the music. I stood watching the piano player. When the music stopped the woman playing the piano glanced up at me. She held my gaze curiously for a moment, before lowering her eyes to the keys. Her face had a clear, sculptured beauty, softened by her curly blond hair and dreamy eyes. Her eyes seemed to be vaguely searching, as if she were standing on the Oregon coast looking out and remembering, or perhaps anticipating, some exquisite moment. I had seen her in Max's tavern a few times, always accompanied by her husband.

Her husband reminded me of a squirrel in a cage. Physically, he resembled me a little. We both had thin bodies and quick, nervous energy. Ed Deiters worked at the University as a teacher's assistance in History. A weird duck, for sure. One night he gave me a lift home from Max's. He took a roundabout route and stopped off at a big old two-story house that had been condemned to make way for a parking lot, across the street from the Sacred Heart Hospital. In fact, the year before, when I first came to Eugene, I had rented a room in this very same house. Now the house stood empty and condemned. Larry Czenkoszy had been the last renter to move out and Larry had expected the wrecker's iron ball to come swinging through his room at any time.

Ed wanted to throw rocks at the windows. He collected several stones from the ground and tossed them at the house. I watched, perplexed by the satisfaction that the man seemed to derive from throwing rocks at the empty house. He urged me to throw a rock. I shrugged my shoulders. Why not? The wrecking ball would soon smash the windows anyway. I threw a rock but missed. I threw another one. I felt nothing, no release of anger or frustration, nothing, except perhaps a little foolish.

Did Ed need to act out some childish defiance?

Did he need a witness? Did he need to be seen?

I couldn't decide. Perhaps the man just wanted to throw rocks at windows in condemned houses. It would take me years to fully realize the expense of energy in trying to figure out the reasons people did or did not do things. Human beings act upon a mixture of motives, and, in the end, as you respond to their actions, out of your own personal bias of needs and wants and cares, how can you really be sure of their private reasons, great or small? Or, for that matter, of your own?

...I looked
up
and saw your scarf
caught
on a twig
your robe
burning
in the tree
your slippers
flaming
in the branches
and I heard
the echo
of your voice
calling my name
so I climbed

Douglas Blazek
"Edible Fire"

I followed the piano player up the stairs through the smoky crowd of people. I waited for her outside the bathroom door. When Susan came out and saw me standing there she smiled softly and said hello. Without a word I took her in my arms and kissed her. To her own great surprise she kissed me back. I loved her crazily and she returned my love, meeting me whenever and wherever she could: at the Laundromat, on her way to work, going to her piano lessons, at parties, at taverns. I wrote her poems in letters and once her husband actually found one of my letters in their bed. I had written a note on a scrap of paper and it fell out of Susan's purse. Susan grabbed the note from her husband, telling him it was private. Ed didn't pursue the matter.

One Sunday I heard light footsteps coming up the stairs to my apartment. I knew at once those steps belonged to Susan. Too many times I had listened quietly, waiting for her soft knock on my door. This time, however, her husband and Larry Czenkoszy both were in the room with me. They had stopped by just to chat. I quickly said something to Larry, calling him by name. By the time I slowly reached the door to answer her knock Susan had already disappeared back down the steps. Just the same my heart almost stopped.

Susan had never lied to her husband before. She found herself amazed at how easily she could lie to him, without guilt or remorse. Their marriage had simply gone out the door and her husband hadn't even heard the door closing. At a history faculty party one Saturday night Ed actually forgot that Susan had come with him and he drove home by himself. He went to bed and fell asleep. Susan caught a ride home with a friend and then slipped into their house through an unlocked window. She found the keys to his VW. Ed never let Susan drive. She didn't even know how. But at four in the morning Susan drove over to my place and knocked softly on the door; and, smelling of brandy alexanders, she curled up in my arms and immediately fell asleep.

It was almost noon the next day before we ventured out into the wintry sunshine. The VW battery was dead. Susan had left the lights on. Later, she made up some story and Ed accepted it. I figured the man just didn't know what else to do.

We never talked about the future. We made no promises to each other. I never asked her to run away with me and Susan never spoke of expectations or even possibilities. "It is enough that I love you," she said.

In late spring, the spring that I left Eugene, Susan decided to stop seeing me. She wanted to make an earnest attempt to save her marriage. She felt obliged to try once more. I said nothing to stop her. I wanted her to have what she wanted. I could not wish in my heart for anything other than this.

Their marriage didn't last of course. Later, I heard that she got involved with another man. Ed found out and went looking for him with a gun. Then came the divorce and Susan moved to L. A.

∞

Ed could be found at Max's almost anytime he wasn't teaching. Usually he was playing war games with Larry Czenkoszy. Czenkoszy had been a graduate student in history until he became so disillusioned and cynical with the university system that he dropped out. Larry possessed an exceptional mind and from the very beginning I felt drawn to him. At the same time I felt intimidated by the other man's knowledge and his compressed, emotional intensity, and the power which emanated from him. Czenkoszy had all this personal power burning inside him, but he imploded this great power, and he nearly destroyed himself. Whenever I came across the beginning line of Allen Ginsberg's notorious poem *Howl*: "I saw the best minds of my generation destroyed by madness," I thought of Czenkoszy.

A second-generation Hungarian, Larry Czenkoszy came from a mining town in Minnesota, not far from the area where Bob Dylan had lived as a boy. At the University of Minnesota, Larry had taken an "Honesty Evaluation Test" and scored a hundred per cent. He scored *too* honest. They considered him abnormal. A man this honest might be unstable. For this reason the Peace Corps rejected him. Physically, Larry reminded me sometimes of an ancient Viking warrior, with his red curly hair and beard, and his strong, wiry body, his broad forehead. I first met him about the same time I first read the poetry of Charles Bukowski. These two men merged and overlapped in my mind, for both men seemed larger than life to me. And both men seemed bent on hurling one last flaming spear into the darkness, before the darkness could claim the fire within them as its own.

Larry lived wherever he could find a room, with the rent money usually months behind. How he managed to dodge landlords amazed me. Sometimes he lived with friends and sometimes he slept in garages, back alleys, the bed of a pick-up truck. He survived on what money he could bum or borrow or come up with by selling his books or classical records. Every once in a while his sister would send him a little money, which he usually blew on double rums.

Larry had just been thrown out of his room, being five or six months overdue in his rent. He started out drinking early in the day and then he ran into me that evening. The two of us went to Max's for a beer. About midnight we went back to my place. Larry immediately passed out on the sofa.

I lived just off High Street. I had a studio apartment with a tiny kitchen, a single bed, a sofa, a desk, a closet. I shared a toilet and shower in the outside hallway. I rented No. 3, right at the top of the stairs. The apartment was small and grungy, but inexpensive, and close to campus and closer still to Max's.

I woke up, startled by a noise. I saw Larry staggering on his feet with a knife in his hand, raging incoherently to himself, trying to undo his shirt to slash his chest with the knife. I jumped out of bed and wrestled the knife away from him. Larry collapsed on the couch and immediately passed out again.

When he drank too much, which happened at every chance possible, and for as long as possible, Larry crossed that thin, blurred line into madness. He carried deep scars on his chest from slashing himself in one of his deep-end, mad, drunken frenzies. As if he had wanted to cut out his own heart. As if he had wanted, out of some personal torment, to scatter his own bones under a juniper-tree to feed the hungry leopards of a god that he had long ago abandoned. It wasn't until I traveled to Greece did I again witness the wounds from this kind of blood-spilling, this form of self-destructive passion, born out of pain and despair.

One Saturday night, at the ending of a long party, after dancing to the Stones and the music of "Zorba the Greek," Larry, Doc Streeter and I made our way back to Doc's place for more wine and conversation. Doc was in his forties and worked for the railroad. He liked to hang out at Max's and drink beer and ride his bicycle to parties and to delve as deeply as his beliefs would allow him into spiritual matters. Doc put a record on the turntable, a classical piece, perhaps Kodaly's Lieutenant Kije Suite, or maybe Debussy's Violin Sonata, or something by Borodin. I watched in amazement as I saw these two men down on their knees on the floor, too drunk to stand, their arms around each other, both men weeping over the profound sadness of life. Never before had I seen grown men weep like this. Never before had I seen men display such passion and sorrow for this thing called life.

Larry didn't romanticize his pain or his madness or his dying. He once institutionalized himself in Damash, the state mental hospital near Salem, Oregon. No, Larry didn't romanticize his madness or his acts of self-destruction; nor did I admire his drunkenness or living homeless in garages and alleys and on the cutting edge of other people's handouts. I admired Larry's deep inner strength and wisdom, however distorted by doubt and confusion and self-pity and arrogance and speed and alcohol and God knows what else. I admired the man's intensity of expression and feeling and perception and the power that flowed through him; and I admired his capacity for suffering and his compassion for others, his intelligence, his kindness, and his endurance.

Larry eventually left Eugene and moved to Venice West. He got into wood carving and learned carpentry. Eventually he worked as a service rep for a national harp manufacturing company that had an outlet in L. A. Sometimes Larry traveled all over the country, repairing Classical and Celtic harps. He even went to Italy to study harp making. He married a good woman. He stopped drinking and joined AA. He quit smoking cigarettes and started running. When the harp company scaled back its operations, Larry and his wife left California and moved to Arizona, to a place where the air felt clean and wholesome. He began to practice Buddhist meditation and entered ever deeper into the process of healing his mind, body, and soul. His wood carvings begin to sell. He had a showing at a local gallery, with symbols of the world's major religions as the heart of his show. His was the most popular show the gallery had ever sponsored. To his amazement, suddenly he became more than a craftsman; suddenly he became an artist.

Blow out the candle

"Take that carnation out of your teeth," she said, standing breathlessly naked in a pool of images, jeweled rings, scented clothes, and crinkly, painted toes. "Put down that bottle of wine and blow out the candle."

I stood there with my long pants, and volumes of literature in my throat, and I could only repeat what she had once read to me from the *Diary Of Anaïs Nin*, 1931-1934, p.131. I quoted Henry's words: "Strange, how blindly I have lived until now."

During the course of our love affair Susan had urged me to go out with other women. She felt that I needed more attention than she could give me. At first, I rejected this idea. The thought of being sexual with another woman made me feel a bit uneasy. I didn't want to betray Susan. That old moon in Taurus I figured.

Then I met Allea Rose.

Allea Rose took acid and had visions and painted pictures, and she laughed so gaily when I pursued her, and then she entrapped me one day when I least expected it, in broad daylight, so to speak, and guided me into the elusive dream world of her wise and passionate gypsy body. Delicate and retreating in the presence of a stranger, in the presence of a trusted friend her vagina flowered like an outrageous, single-bloom orchid. Uncertainty reigned in other areas: in her sense of self-worth and expression, and she had a great need for approval from men, but Allea could always trust her womb to tell her the truth about the world around her. What did it say about me? I never had the courage to ask, but I knew that she allowed herself a freedom with me that she had not experienced with other men, a freedom that she would take with her when she left, even as I would take the sense of joyous abandonment that she had awakened within me.

We would smoke a little grass, if we had any, and she might put on the Jefferson Airplanes' *Surrealistic Pillow* album in the background, or something by Vivaldi or Saint-Saens, or some funky jug band music that I didn't recognize, and we would sweetly kiss, and she would tease me at first, and evade me, and hold me off until the moment I touched her between the legs, and then her body turned to fire and she went into an almost fit of twisting and soft moaning, and she would roll under and over me and turn and turn and sometimes it felt a little scary to me even, Allea so lost her pretenses, and her identity, and any sense of time and place. (I worried about her too for another good reason. Allea had a history of epilepsy and I feared that such ecstatic love making—and certainly acid—might trigger a seizure.) Once, in a heap of laughter, we did go tumbling off her bed onto the floor. Another time, she came up with the brilliant idea to put ice cubes on my testicles to delay my orgasm. And delay my orgasm it did. About seven years.

I met Allea McLain accidentally, so to speak. I had seen her around campus of course. Even in Eugene, in this most exotic of times, it would have been difficult not to have noticed a woman with her unique appearance. She had long dusty colored hair that she wore in a single thick braid down her back, or else she allowed it to fall free to her waist, and if the old Italian proverb is correct—that the beauty of the heavens is the stars and the beauty of a woman is her hair—then Allea Rose with her dusty blond hair hanging low would probably appear as one of the most beautiful sights that any lovesick Italian might imagine. When not wearing faded jeans and gypsy blouses and leather sandals that showed her barefooted painted toes, Allea Rose mostly dressed in long and loose-flowing skirts that came almost to the heels of her boots and that seemed to match the country of origin of her ear rings. One night at a party, sitting on the floor behind me, she playfully slipped my hand inside her skirt. To my delight I discovered that Allea Rose did not always wear what most women wore under their skirts.

On her pierced left ear Allea wore five dangling ear rings, each different and each coming from some faraway place like India or Nepal or Afghanistan. To go with these dangling ear rings she covered her slender, aesthetic looking fingers with a line of antique, jeweled rings. In hindsight I realized that these jeweled rings served as a clear intimation of Allea's strange and baffling emotional moods. For at times Allea felt as sunny and intimate and inexhaustible as a fountain of pure joy and energy. At other times she felt totally distant and withdrawn. She felt inaccessible and remote and self-absorbed, as if she wanted to hold, and even to hide, all her energy, her feelings and thoughts, and her power, inside her. When she went into her silent, withdrawn moods, I would just simply disappear. I couldn't deal with my own emotional hang-ups; what could I do with hers? So I watched with amazement and curiosity, as much as desire, that first time, as she stopped to take each of her jeweled rings off, all of them, until her fingers appeared as naked and sensual and vibrant with subtle energy as her whole shining, lyrical body, before she allowed me to enter her.

We first met at Max's one Saturday night. I saw her sitting in one of the booths having a beer with an artist friend of hers, a man I casually knew. I bought a pitcher of beer and walked over to their booth to say hello. They invited me to join them. I sat down next to Allea. While making introductions and small talk, Allea's friend mentioned a party that he knew about on the other side of campus. We all looked at each other and shrugged Why not? The three of us jumped into her friend's old car. For some reason Allea rode shotgun. At an intersection near the campus a car pulled out in front of us. Allea's friend hit the brakes but he also hit the other car. The impact threw open the passenger door and Allea Rose went sailing out onto the street. Fortunately, only her right arm and leg got bruised. But we didn't make it to the party. Her friend waited for the police to show and I walked Allea to the emergency clinic a few blocks away.

From then on we began to see each other.

Our accidental friendship soon grew into heated courtship, although Allea Rose had a boyfriend in the army, somewhere in Vietnam, who she would someday marry.

That first time, we had been drinking wine and talking most of the afternoon about art and the flower paintings of Georgia O'Keeffe, and God, and nature, and psychedelics, and the feminine revelations of Anaïs Nin, and right in the middle of one of my intense and animated monologues on the necessity of allowing the poetic self out of the mind's dark basement, not as some Frankenstein monster or some diseased and afflicted bird of Paradise, or some hairline scream between reality and madness, but as a fountain of clear sparkling water bubbling up from the earth, catching the light of the moon at night and the sun of a summer day and the frost on the bare trees of winter, and reflecting the inner light of all things so that the soul might drink from these life-flowing waters, Allea placed her fingers gently upon my lips, and without saying a word she walked over and put on some strange, soft, flute music, and began to dance, the little spangled mirrors on the walls reflecting her dusty beauty forever in my mind, as she allowed her clothes to spill gracefully into a pool of color on the bare wooden floor, and she danced for me and for the passion within her.

Allea lived by herself in a small white house not far from the Williams' Bakery, near the east end of campus. Faded roses and lilac blooms covered most of the interior walls, except for her studio room, which had been painted over in white. The bare wooden floors appeared well-worn and scuffed, and the small windows pinched the natural daylight and made the house a little dark, except for her studio space, which seemed to almost magically gather the daylight inside. The house gave Allea the privacy that she needed, and she paid the rent from stock investments that her grandmother had made for her years before. The house had a large backyard, with more crickets than the state of Georgia, and almost as many tiny spring crocuses and wild irises. A black walnut tree and a Queen Anne cherry took up most of the space. A wooden, unpainted side fence, which separated her yard from the neighbor's and their huge German shepherd dog that howled whenever he heard a siren going off, seemed just on the verge of collapse. A white picket fence bordered the tiny front yard and enclosed a rose bush and a lilac bush and an outrageous bed of tiger-spotted Chinese lilies. An English walnut tree grew in the strip of grass between the sidewalk and street and from this tree Allea had gathered a good winter's store of walnuts. Inside the picket fence and partly hanging over the sidewalk grew a mock orange, with a most wonderful scent, especially on those spring mornings when I left for my History of Chinese Landscape Painting class, after staying all night with Allea.

I remember one particular Saturday afternoon. Allea invited me over for an early dinner. She wanted to make her "famous spaghetti sauce." Famous, no doubt, because of the magic mushrooms simmering in the tomatoes and garlic and onions and spices—mushrooms that she herself had picked last fall in the hills outside Eugene, then carefully dried and stored.

No wonder her paintings felt like organic explosions. Her plants and flowers seemed to almost pulsate with sensual, biological intensity. Looking carefully within her smooth, sea-washed stones, her lush, overgrown plants, her gorgeous and voluptuous flowers, everywhere I could see subtle suggestions of bodies, faces, genitals. In one series of images she had painted naked bodies, sometimes male and female, sometimes all female, entwined as if they were ethereal, singing voices, or strands of consciousness weaving into sea horses dancing, or sensuous, clinging vines, spiraling upwards toward the light of a radiant sun. To Allea these organic forms expressed the nervous system of the planet. To her, the earth was literally the living child of the sun. She explained to me once how she perceived the light from the sun as streams of love pouring out from the sun's center to the center of all beings on the earth. To her, the sun represented the fusion of the Great Mother and the Great Father principles, alive with intelligence and purpose and love.

I helped Allea with the tossed salad. Then I opened a bottle of cheap red wine. I poured two glasses of wine as Allea dropped the brittle pasta into some boiling water. I went and sat cross-legged on the edge of her small bed, and, as she listened a few steps away in the kitchen, I read to her from a peculiarly odd book that I had just finished reading called *Jurgen* by James Branch Cabell.

I was in the middle of Jurgen's adventure in the garden, the day Jurgen traveled back into time with the magical centaur and encountered the girl that he had courted in his youth, the girl he most desired in his dreams and his imagination, after giving up writing verses and marrying Dame Lisa and becoming a respectable pawn broker, and growing old, and enduring Dame Lisa's constant nagging.

I heard Allea Rose leave the kitchen and walk toward me. I looked up from the book just as she stood over me, pushing me back onto the bed. Quickly she straddled my legs and undid my belt. By the time she had my pants down to my knees I had a full erection, and she grasped me tightly, stroking me with tight, quick strokes. I looked curiously into her wonderfully gray, mischievous eyes. Her hand slid up close to my balls and began swaying in a gentle, rhythmic motion. Suddenly I was coming. Allea laughed with delight and walked back into the kitchen. Damn, what was that all about? I lay back on the bed with my book closed. I could smell the magic mushrooms simmering in the kitchen.

Julie

Julie Kramer came by one day in the pouring rain to see me, just to tell me that she wasn't going to see me anymore. Later, this sweet girl shared her virginity with me, as we slept together one night in late spring, just before I left Eugene. Julie moved to Berkeley, then went to Mexico, and then to Poland and Czechoslovakia. I lost track of her somewhere in Europe. But she would always remember me, this I knew; and I would always remember her and the simple, instinctive, natural quality of her giving.

What was I doing with Julie Kramer?

My friends pondered this question but they had no answer. Julie was just a sophomore, demure and idealistic in her ways, pure of heart and soft spoken of voice, with clear hazel eyes and thick, shiny black hair; and I was an old reprobate, an uncouth poet, as liable to insult as not, especially when high on something-or-the-other, God knows what.

Julie seemed like such a rare flower, slowly coming to bloom, and our paths seemed in such vastly different directions. But the path for me, as for my sweet friend, would in time come together again and converge on a soul level, however distant our individual lives. This I realized, as I thought about these things in my prison cell in Greece. For Julie lived in the simple radiance of her heart. She admired my quick mind; but she loved me, not for my single-minded vision, but for the kindness that she felt in my eyes. I hid and protected this tenderness as much as possible with my mercurial and sometimes caustic wit, and my clownish defenses, and verbal contortions, but I couldn't deceive Julie Kramer when it came to matters of the heart.

On a political level, Julie's empathy for others and her heart-felt compassion caused great pain and confusion in her mind, for she wanted to take the hurts and injustices of the world, each and everyone of them, into her self and care for them, like lost, hungry children. When she discovered the impossibility of this she lost much of her innocence. In time, though, I knew that this false innocence would be replaced by a pure, distilled passion for life; a passion, that, once again, would circle my friend back into the wisdom of her heart and to that which can not be lost or corrupted by time or chance or seeming misfortune.

All night the river flows

November leaves rattle under
my feet, the street light
flashes WALK;
I cross, holding
these words to you
in my hands,
a flower
to my heart,
a flower
in the Buddha's
hand, true
as a red rose;
as you lie sleeping
in bed

next to your husband,
you dreaming me,
touching you,
my hands, an ache
to recognize you,
at last,
my hands, all
that I am,
a man in love,
a kindness in the dark;
your blond skin
a promise of light;
my hands, touching
you, moving
over the round,
lovely moons of your
breasts and pale
blue-sky veins
that flow
beneath your white
skin, and down
into the warm,
blond opening inside you,
your body a golden ring
into which
I slip my finger,
my mouth
kissing wet
circles
split by your
nipples,
blond hair between
my lips,
blond legs under
and over mine.

2
I'm walking and it's cold
I'm dreaming of dying
The leaves taste sweet
in my mouth They rattle
as I step

3
Drowning, I think,
must be a long way to walk

But none, not Julie, not even Allea Rose, could displace Susan from my heart. Susan came and went in all the freedom that she dared. I made no demands upon her; she made none upon me. "I was born and raised by the Columbia River," she told me, on a warm Saturday afternoon, several weeks after I had followed her up the smoky stairway at the party. Susan was twenty-four; I was about to turn twenty-five. After the party, we saw each other again, a week later in Max's. But we had little opportunity to talk. Then one day, our paths crossing by chance, I walked her home from school, after her piano lessons. Susan had a part-time job as secretary in a branch office of an insurance company. This particular Saturday she had worked until noon and on her way home she stopped by to visit me. "I want to see you naked," I told her suddenly, before I lost my courage. We were sitting on the bed together. It was the first time she had come to see me. "What's stopping you?" she asked, looking me in the face and smiling, her curly blond hair catching the afternoon sunlight through the small window that faced Pearl Street.

Later, I would remember the sunlight and the fragrance of her body on mine, and the heat that swept through my belly, just before I let go; and I would remember her blondness like a meadow of shining buttercups, just before the line of gravity that connected me to this solid world suddenly snapped; and I would remember the incredible sweetness of her kisses over and over, just before an unearthly cry tore from the center of my being and sent ribbons of light streaming through my brain and propelled me into pinpoints of stars that I knew were stars not from this earth, but from the origin of creation; and in that moment I knew without a doubt that I had come not from darkness and desolation and muddy indifference but from the same loving, more-than-human, intelligence that had created these stars.

In the days and nights to follow I wandered the worlds of my mind like a stranger, knowing that something of great import had occurred, that some great seal within me had opened and love had poured into my being, but I didn't have the concepts to understand these new feelings and memories, and in the broad daylight of the social and political world around me these feelings seemed so vague, tenuous and unreal. So I put my feelings on hold and spoke to no one, not even Susan, about what I had felt that night in the heaven of her arms and in the soul of my being.

I walked her home one winter night from a party. The wind was blowing strong and we stopped for a moment on the sidewalk of Willamette Street, under some huge fir trees, for Susan loved the wind. As she listened to the singing of the wind in the tall trees and felt its caresses on her cheeks, she took my hand and the two of us stood there together, lovers in a storm. This felt all so very romantic, but she gave me more than romance, more than pleasure, and more than a glimpse into the sweetness of my own soul. When Susan took me inside her, the marriage of heaven and earth flowed in the circle of our arms. She allowed a healing energy to enter into the wounded memories of my soul. She showed me a glimpse of love from the whole mind and heart, gracefully in the moment, gracefully forgiving. And then she left. But that felt all right too. As with her, it was enough that I had loved her, and that she came to me when I needed her, and that she touched my being forever with her crazy blond daring.

The letters of Jamie Brown

My angels are made of flame
not feathers
of incandescent light
not softness
they do not comfort me.
They are guardian angels
in that they bar the way
back to Eden,
the gates of paradise,
the paths to earthly happiness.

They stand around me
like sentinels,

they have not spoken.

If they reached out to touch me
I would be-white hot heat-
consumed in fire.

They sing sometimes
in high wordless incantations.

They have not spoken.
They do not comfort me.

They are like my father:
remote, alluring,
beautiful and forbidding.
He knew, if we ever

touched again,
we would both go up in flames.

Sometimes I see flames around
the heads of strangers.

In my most intimate encounters
there is the flaming sword
between us.

I used to think of it as passion
but now I know it is
exile.

Audy Davison,
"My Angels"

I left Melina Foster once, before our final break-up, to live briefly with this truly, deeply wounded woman. Indeed, at one point Jamie so lost her will and her sense of direction that she ended up in Bellevue. I first met Jamie Brown in the fall of 1966, in the beginning of my second year as a graduate student at the University of Oregon, only a few days before she left Eugene to go back to the East Coast. We saw each other briefly three or four times, and that last time, as we stood in her empty apartment, her suitcase packed and Jamie wearing an old faded shirt and dance leotards, she spoke to me of her love for dancing—she had taken years of ballet but not soon enough to become a professional dancer—and she spoke to me of her love for poetry and the arts, and for everything delicate and beautiful and harmonious. Her dark eyes burned brightly in her pixie face, her small body barely able to contain her intense, emotional spirit. I had met other crazies, their souls like spiders crumbled up in dark basement corners, their emotional wills twisted and enmeshed in confusion and bizarre door-slamming-in-the-face cries for help, like telephones that ring and ring and ring until you answer and then there's no one on the other end but a clicking sound. Neither Jamie nor my friend Czenkoszy belonged to this truly lost asylum. Jamie seemed to me just way too open and too vulnerable. I thought her delicate, emotional nature had simply been overwhelmed, thrown out of balance by her analytical, psychological mind. As if to serve some antique, sacrificial male god—some false, idealistic belief that she had accepted about the nature of herself as a woman—Jamie had created this great bleeding wound within her self: *"the scream inside, trapped as a bird in a bag"*—a rip in the energy field around her body; and, at some point, life, in all its immense disregard for the saviors and the martyrs we serve and for the false masks we wear like smoke passing before our eyes, had just come pell-mell pouring into her nervous system, blowing her mind like burnt toast. I thought of Rimbaud's *A Season In Hell.*

The dog directs the master of the hunt, she wrote....
It is over for me. They cut open my head. Two flowered dresses red blue, one backwards over a robe, one pall mall in pocket wheeeee....
A negro nurse dragging me down the hall.
FOLLOW THE NURSE!
FOLLOW THE NURSE!
Bring her to our spiritual meeting, say blue uniform guarding doors. Think! The other side! I was to go but through what door? In the tub room? Naked? What was I to do?
Later, I sit feet dangling form bed. Were you coming to get me?
I lie down, dream.

When I was seventeen, she wrote, I went to Boston, alone in a dirty green room. I fell in love with a homosexual. He lived across the hall. We walked along the Charles in autumn rain, crystalling orange burnt leaves against iron fence. La Jetee', will I ever forget that damn movie?
The pills, they do nothing.

I wanted to take the whole bottle but didn't. They would not kill me.

What do they do, David? These people dressed and perfect in appearance. How do they live? Where? Trees, the music says trees and air and birds and GARBAGE, purple pansies. I wonder who in the hell ever believed the music, writing it and making a bunch of fat old peasants sit in wonder and paying pennies?

Oh, David, I am so happy! I will read and be well one day.

I WON'T DIE BECAUSE I DON'T WANT TO!

There are kids who fish and throw away what they catch and what they aren't going to eat, but by Christ I believe, and if there were a fish jumping in the pail, and if he was still jumping after I walked six miles, I'd personally walk back and let him swim.

In Eugene, last spring, she wrote, I saw three birds, fallen while in midst of self-imposed hypnotic states. I knew them to be placed there for me, dressed in monks camel coat and off-white levis, hunched on corner bench in view of the fountain, blooming fuchsia flowers. Then later at the pot shop, "It really isn't very good, it has a hole in it and the glass is bubbly…" and the giant sized one with the funny whiskers, who in a photo wore a beret, and on the night I saw him: "You feel so Goddamn much. You bleed all over the street, I've seen you!" And I standing there, knowing nothing to be done.

The girls, she said, today the girls were tossing their kitten in a cheesecloth curtain given for some unreason by the landlady. My seeing them and as it is and what they did and them singing lullabies thinking it doesn't hurt and because its voice isn't very loud hanging the cat up as mistletoe in the form of a hummingbird's nest. "And never hurt a cat in anger," they said, while driving it insane, so it will never know the outside and be frightened to leave.

Oh, David, it is no use.

I have no strength, no mind.

They hurt me. They loved me so much, they wouldn't let me go. They killed me. And when I awoke there was a gray stone wall and I couldn't withstand it. I couldn't fight. I couldn't hit them. I can't hate, I can't. SHIT! I hate the word; there are worse. Vulgarity. Garbage nor worth the heave to the truck. Scream it.

SEND ME TIO THE SCREAMERS!!!!!

I wrote to Jamie and told her about my love for Susan. I told her about taking sugar cube acid with Ben Abrams, the Sunday morning that Doc Streeter had aroused Czenkoszy out of a dead-drunk sleep, got him dressed in a suit, and dragged him off to church. Sprawled out on the sofa, still half-drunk and still in his rumpled suit, The Owl watched the sparrow in humorous amazement as one of the lenses fell out of my glasses, just about the time the walls of the room came undone in a spasm of tumbling, electric laughter. Worlds later, Ben and I found ourselves in the sparkling sun in the tall fir trees in the low hills on the edge of town, listening to our friend Maggie, who wore several strings of long colorful beads around her neck, and flowers in her hair, and a worn, thin dress that barely covered her body, as she played her Gibson guitar and sang an old spiritual song: "You got to cross that lonesome valley, you got to cross it all by yourself; Nobody else can walk it for you, you got to cross it by yourself." Remembering my mother, who loved this song and wanted it sung at her funeral, the tears came flowing to my eyes, and I just let them flow and flow out of the fountain of my heart.

Living in San Francisco with Melina Foster, I wrote to Jamie about Melina's paintings; pictures that seemed to hover in my mind like intense mythical dreams that you remember just briefly, just before you awaken, just before you discover your dream dissolving and turning into this warm, sensual body, miraculously entwined with your own. I told Jamie about Douglas Blazek and his dynamite-in-the-ears little magazine "Ole!"; and about the strange, underwater poetry of Tom Kryss; and about the wild, smoke-filled, red mountain, Haight-Ashberry cockroach hotel adventures of long-haired, crazy Willie Bloomfield and his bottleneck "Silver Lady", with her intimate, sultry voice, sweet as fire singing in a whiskey-hoarse wind. I told her about meeting this wonderfully, oddball comic book cartoonist Robert Crumb, and about going to concerts at the Avalon Theater to see Janis Joplin sing, and to see Country Joe and The Fish, and how they had the music so loud I couldn't even hear the songs.

Sometimes I wrote Jamie these convoluted, episodic monologues that I had skillfully, (or not so skillfully), woven together out of my enthusiasm and exhilaration for life into a growing synthesis of praise and exaltation for the emergence of the poetic self: the dancing light within: the natural creative isness in every soul and in every cell of the body. For while I had no desire to support my friend's despondency and her self-indulgent destructive thought patterns, I wanted to honor the integrity and truth of her feelings and I wanted to honor her being as a woman; and always I wanted to inspirit and encourage.

About her own monologues Jamie wrote back: "It's something I've always done. As far back I can remember. My head bent as if studying my toes or wrinkles in the shoe leather. Or bordering the bed of the house to the tiny rock garden with daffodils or jonquils and making death set right in my mind by believing I'd be but a flower and thinking of the ground and water to find I'd be so disturbed because the flowers died so often in the cold and wilted and were eaten by the bugs; but then there was dormancy of seeds and that would get me back on a more settled track and I'd remember the cycle diagrams from some science book objectively the whole process explained. Then the morbid would grab hold again and I'd think of all those horrible graveyards that are so starkly present in suburbs of town. Then go squeamish inside. It didn't set right with me, these organized graves and splash of showy dead people that were after all insignificant when one considered it. Thoughts being the only thing carried on."

Now living in Hartford, Connecticut, Jamie found a job at a book store and art gallery called Brentano's. She studied yoga and read books on psychology and art and she seemed to be getting better. "If nothing else," she wrote, "I am cured of being Savior. But I still have not released myself from victimization which I plead for and turns to bite me. There is still hatred in my heart. Because one can not give to everyone."

Jamie worried about me taking acid, and she offered to send me money if I needed any. She told me of her love for Jay, who lived in Boston. She couldn't seem to get over this love affair that had happened years before between her and Jay, and that was quite finished, and, yet, was still going on.

She wrote of her great love and her despair with dancing. "The flying and leaping, following I know not what. The dance which was me. Me and all the things I was exposed to. All that was caught inside. Fleeing. I knew no exhaustion. As life dying and reliving an unending process. And then—then getting caught. And the time. And the age. The death and the pain. The loneliness so intense as to be almost inexpressible. The willful detachment."

Jamie sent me poems that she had written and she shared with me the confusion and pain and self-doubt that she felt as a woman, that she could not express or share with others. "Barry comes. We make love for the first time but he does not burn as we. It is pleasant. But the flames—he is missing."

Then disaster struck again.

The drapes of her room caught fire from an iron that she had left on; and she was burned out of home, losing her clothes and books and typewriter and all the letters and poems that I had sent her, everything. Her right hand got badly burned when she tired to put out the fire. Caught in a tail spin depression, Jamie went on self-destructive eating binges, sometimes eating candy bar after candy bar until she wanted to throw up, her stomach bulging and swollen. She smoked too many cigarettes and drank too much coffee.

She wrote: "I rise and look at the face I have destroyed. The body I wanted to have danced destroyed. The sweet simple person once contained-destroyed. All of it deteriorated, destroyed by my own will."

At times Jamie remembered wanting to be some man's delicate wife, to be taken care of and adored; but that probability had gone down a long time ago and she felt confronted and challenged by her aloneness.

"I the woman. So wanted to be a toy, an object or loveliness, a puppy to be petted and lapped. Yesterday I see Mia Farrow in LIFE Magazine. Little Fawn. I was once. But I have a mind. Disliking its own objectivity. Not being able to face the brutality of men. Yet containing the objectivity which refused its own independence."

I wanted to comfort Jamie with love and wisdom and understanding in her journey through this personal city of desolation—this wreckage of self-illusions—which she felt trapped in like a crazy dream, like being in a locked room where every time she found a key to unlock the door the lock would automatically change. I wanted to walk with her through this war torn city and say something like this to my friend: *"See, here, this is where the bombs fell. See, here, this is where the children died. See, here, this is where your natural instincts were sacrificed. And this is the place where you lost your natural beauty. And this is where you gave up your natural form, in order to hide, in order to please others, in order to confuse them. For this is the point where you began to realize that you were not being loved or healed or nurtured or fed or comforted, but you were being hurt over and over and over in the process.*

"But you didn't understand the beliefs you were operating from, nor did you remember that at a certain point in the history of your consciousness you took very deeply within yourself certain beliefs and ideas and held them above your natural instincts, and the natural processes of human expression, and you attempted to become more than you were and to sacrifice yourself. You accepted the belief that the female sexual energy had to be put under the control and the manipulation and the trust of the male energy, for the betterment of the world, so that man could begin to control nature, and could bring forth more fruitfulness, and could experience more enlightenment. And this, of course, was a lie, my friend. But you accepted this belief system into the core of your being, and therefore you didn't know it was there beyond a certain point. You acted upon it in all your life situations, and it caused you much pain and much frustration and

much difficulty and the cutting away of parts of yourself that were joyous, that were your natural instincts to lead you where you needed to go, and you cut into these ruthlessly in order to fulfill this ideal that you had, for you believed that it was right.

"To divide yourself this way, Jamie, is a very, very dangerous thing to do, and causes much difficulty and pain, for this is not the purpose of life. Any life that is being sacrificed is not in harmony with life, but is being cut off from life. But you didn't understand how to change your beliefs, or how to come to an understanding and to invite back those parts of yourself that had been banished. And so now you must walk through these deserted areas, these areas of destruction, and you must look upon these various places. You must see the bomb craters and the burned bodies of the children. You must see the scars where the trees have been crushed and will not grow and will not bloom. You must look at the barren soil and see that, rather than fruitfulness, you have created a burned and barren earth. You must recognize in full detail, and in great depth of understanding, how the process that you began as a great adventure, and with high hopes that it would bring much truth and much light and much wonderment to humankind, has, indeed, brought this desolation, and you must understand that it is a part of you now and accept it; and in that process the healing begins. Once you have done this then you can begin the renewal. But the beginning of the process is to walk into the ruins and to face them boldly and without compromise and without squeamishness.

"This is where you are right now, my friend, and why you feel so much stress within your body and your emotions and why you feel so desolate and pained. You need to stand here for a little while, until you take it all into you, and come to the fullest understanding of what is actually here for you, and to go back to those first thoughts and beliefs that brought you on this long road to stand in this burned and broken city that you have become, and to understand how this has taken place, and to retrace some of the steps that you have taken to get here."

But I didn't say any of this.

I didn't know how to encourage Jamie to love this period of her life, as painful and desolate and self-destructive as it seemed, nor did I understand how holy and valid and necessary it was for her to undergo this experience, in order for the self-healing to take place and in order for the renewal and the flowering of her spirit to come forth in the fullness of her being, like a desert flower that overnight will burst into lush appearance following a heavy rain after months or even years of harsh, burning dryness. I couldn't speak from the wholeness of my being; I didn't have the necessary awareness. I couldn't access that part of myself in the shadows of my damaged nervous system and the molecular codes of my brain, that part of myself that I denied through ignorance and fear and doubt and mistrust, that so much needed self-healing and self-love, that greater consciousness within me that longed to speak clearly and unequivocal to my friend.

In Jamie's letters, I watched, with some impatience, my own unexpressed feelings and my own beliefs being mirrored and acted out on the screen of her moodiness, her ambivalence and indecisiveness, her self-indulgence, her constant analysis of events and thoughts and emotions, as if she were adrift in a backwater and did not have the forcefulness and the purpose to break free.

I encouraged Jamie to flee her city of desolation. I urged her to come back to Oregon for God's sake, and the two of us would live together a life of romantic passion and write poems and be famous someday.

"I don't know, David," she wrote. "I am alone by choice. I must content myself my selection. I must be my own doll to care for and dress because there is no other suitable to me—so it must be."

Eventually, Jamie quit her job at Brentano's. She went on Welfare and became a case history. Emotionally this hit her like stepping out into a hard cold rain without an umbrella or even a raincoat. She found herself drenched in feelings of frustration and powerlessness and loss of hope. She went spinning sideways right back into the Funny Farm, (as she called it), and entered the St. Francis Psychiatric Clinic.

The medication they gave her seemed to help, however, and calmed her nervous system. Through the hospital she met a kind and gentle man, a dentist, who took her into his family and gave her a safe place to live and a place to heal. She worked as his office receptionist but soon the job got too boring and after a few months she quit. But she had gathered her strength and recovered some of her lost power and confidence. She started taking classes again and reading again and taking care of herself again. As she began to improve, the idea of coming back to Oregon and living with me lying in my arms all day on sunny days and rainy days too and allowing the love between us to take on flesh and blood grew from desire into a passion. Finally a letter came saying that she would be arriving on a Greyhound bus. "At sometime, as in Hesse's *Siddhartha*, one longs to return home. And I leave the world to war in its absurd way for I cannot believe in it. Private person, is that what we are?"

"What am I suppose to do?" Melina asked, her voice tight with anger.

I had no answer.

I stood there in the doorway, in the pain and shame of my betrayal; and yet I could not let go of this fantasy that I had nurtured for so long.

Our first night together, Jamie and I realized our mistake. She had been right all along. Our passion belonged only to our writings, our poems, our dialogues, and not to the flesh. I felt no chemistry, no spark, no attraction between our bodies. Worse, now we couldn't even talk to each other, as we had in our letters.

Two painful weeks we spent together, in a room in a big house on S. E. Belmont Street, with me all the while hoping beyond hope that a miracle would happen between us. Either that, or that God would magically lift me out of this incredible mess. But no miracle happened. And God don't do magic, I decided. No, I had to make a decision myself. Out of my own pain and my own power and my own integrity, and—to my surprise—out of my need and love for Melina. Besides, I muttered beneath my breath, what did I have to lose? So I

swallowed every ounce of my pride and went to Melina, to ask
her if I could come back.

Without saying a word she took me in.

There are so many little dyings

> Hello   Beautiful
> hand & eye & mouth
> & prick
> The day was a sea
> of YELLOW
> liquid in which i
> plunged, & sank
> & swam & drank.
> And when i reached
> the land, the
> field stretched
> from my feet to
> infinity & i was
> allowed to pick
> all the flowers
> my cunt would
> hold.

> Melina Foster,
> San Francisco '68

rachels mother bot the new DOORS the other day (& others).
man are they weird. rachel & i went to see them the other nite
here in long beach. jim morrison the lead singer is a psychopathic
sex freak. he jerks all over the stage like demented marionette
& jumps off the stage right into the audience, screams, slobbers.
looks like junkie. but their music is fantastic. the first surreal
rock band that i know of...dark, & ominous words. they are one

of the most creative musical groups in the world. i didnt close my jaw the whole time he was singing. rachel & i were on the floor in front of the stage. she was sitting between my legs & as i put my arms around her my hands fell quite comfortably on her snatch which i stroked in tune w/his gyrations & she loved it & my balls later ached like crazy. rachel is amazing. she is w/out sex hangups. im practically fingerfucking her in line as we wait to get in & she is moaning & people all around (i dont even know if they noticed) & she is totally unaware of them...never "oh my god what are we doing in Broad Daylight" kind of thing...she is always feeling me up when her parents are around, but you know just out of their sight xcept i dont figure how they dont notice it. then the other nite after they have gone to bed (they sleep in a room out in the garage) i am prepared to lick her vale of xstasy but im nervous abt her parents see, & so i suggest she go turn out her bedroom light so they will think she has gone to sleep & she says no i wdnt deceive them & my skull blows & thats right thats right... no games no deceptions no hiding...if we get caught we get caught...the thing is honest sex in the open.....(only i hope we dont get caught)...but if we do it'll be clearlight all the way. god bless young beautiful girls for they are real....

i was gonna apologize for the nite me n ray were by but i got to thinking that i shd really apologize to david & melina as by the time we got to their pad (we knocked on joel m deutschs door & he came in shorts sniveling abt 5:30 a.m. at the post office & i point my purple finger at ray who is holding the building up who also gets up at that time & joel m deutsch dont wanna hear it, goes back to bed or something) we were approaching incomprehension & ringing the doorbell brot david's landlady out & i remember she was either a nice old jewish lady or a nice old german lady. i kept waving the red mtn bottle in her face to describe arcs of necessity me-see-david-pendarus-me-from-long-beach-only-here-few-days, & she understood but was very firm abt not seeing davey pendarus & i shdnt lean against the doors & whatnot becuz cdnt i see the wet paint signs & to this day & forevermore i will have white paint streaks on my coat when FINALLY melina comes out and says OH WILLIE (little did she know that ray & i were drunk enuf she shda never come out EVEN!) & says come right in & very gently assures the landlady & her by now husband at the door...upstairs there are 2 other people and david & melina & we are talking & out comes (i believe 2) joints & more red mtn & soon ray & i are staring at each other while melina & the other 2 people are in another room & david is fretting behind me n ray who are staring at each other & i think we are so stoned we cant even giggle & david helps us down the stairs & from that point on from that point on from that point on::::

Willie Bloomfield
—from a letter to Doug Blazek, 1-04-69

Melina and I were living together in a clean, modest flat on Frederick Street in San Francisco, near the botanical gardens of Golden Gate Park. On nice sunny days the evening sun would stream into Melina's painting room, where we often ate our meals Japanese style on the floor near the white stone fireplace. In back of our flat a tiny wooden porch with a stairway led down to a garden of red tea roses and trimmed green grass. A neon whiskey sign flashed outside our bedroom window and trolley cars rounded the corner and clanged softly in our sleep.

Then came spring and the summer of '69.

In late June, over her protest, Melina returned to Portland, to help Marcus and Naomi open their Moon Palace Cafe. That was my big idea. Marcus and Naomi had persuaded me that, by helping them in their Moon Palace Café, we would escape the eight-to-five rat race. In the middle of hand printing *A Bone For The Dogs*, I intended to stay in San Francisco another month and then join Melina in Portland, and we would all run the café together. I must have had rocks in my head....

One night, getting ready for bed, I suddenly felt terrified. *Death! I felt death in the house!*
My mind raced to explain this fear.

A thief was in the house, waiting to kill me!

"Oh, don't be silly," I chided himself. "It's just your imagination." But how do you reason with a feeling that freezes your spine to a single unshakable thought? Cautiously, I went to lock the back door. Then another thought terrified me. *If there's a thief in the house, now he's locked in with me!* I checked behind all the doors and inside the closets. I even looked under the bed. I found no one. "Relax," I told myself. "It's all in your mind."

∞

When I was younger I thought of death as a constant shadow, like a brooding actor on the stage of life, hovering just at the edge of every scene, every action, every call. "There are so many little dyings," as the poet Kenneth Patchen had so succinctly put it. No matter how grand the part you played, or how fine your performance, death could upstage you with the slightest gesture, the softest whisper. Death spoke not in an arrogant and rowdy manner, not in a super heroic bravado, but, like the quiet, haunting voice of the great blues singer Blind Willie McTell, death sang to me in a voice as direct and familiar as my own.

> I die alone;
> I die with millions around me,
> each dying alone;
> with millions around them.
> In the crying arms of my true love
> I die,
> & in the lying heart of my enemy
> I die.
> I die alone,
> hearing your voice calling me,
> sweet as the lights of home,
> calling my name.

My friend Bobby wrote this poem when he was about twenty years old. Bobby Newman and I grew up together in Georgia. As boys we roamed the nearby woods and streams and built forts in the high kudzu fields and went camping and hunted squirrels and played baseball and joined the Boy Scouts. We had school boy crushes on the Williams twins JoAnne and Jeannette. Later, we both raised riding horses and we both had a secret lust for Wanda Jones. Bobby and I loved each other like brothers, though we never spoke to each other of this love. A year or so after high school Bobby got married to a passionate, hot-tempered, good-looking woman a few years older than him. Veneta had been on the verge of suicide when she met Bobby singing in a club in Atlanta. Their marriage lasted two years. Later, Bobby married again. This time he married Laura, a lovely sweetheart of a girl from Ohio. For the next year or so I lost track of Bobby. Then, the week-end after Thanksgiving, my first year in Oregon, I got a phone call from my sister Jenny. Bobby had died the night before. He had entered a hospital with an erupted appendix. The emergency operation had been successful but then an infection set in. The doctors could do nothing. Bobby knew that he was dying. His wife Laura couldn't even attend the funeral. She was in another hospital having their baby.

I didn't want to believe my sister. I felt stunned, bewildered. I didn't know what to do. I didn't know how to relieve the pain and loss that I felt. My friend Ben Abrams came by, saw my condition and, like a guardian angel, guided me to a tavern. I got good and drunk; and, as Ben listened without interrupting me, I spilled out my anger and frustration and grief at the doctors who had stood by helpless, and at fate and bitterness of Bobby's death—to die just before Laura gave birth to their child.

Winter passed and spring came.

Over spring vacation I went to San Francisco with some friends, my first time to visit this mythical city. When we returned from San Francisco I had a message to call Evie, my oldest sister. Stephen, our brother, had died. He had taken his own life. Stephen had closed the windows of his car and stuffed rags around the vents and then turned the motor on. I stoically accepted the loss. Right or wrong—I refused to judge—my brother had made a conscious decision to end his life. And that was that. Stephen and his wife Debbie had five children. But I knew that their marriage had been in trouble for a long time. My brother had a history of sexual affairs and I remembered one woman in particular, for Stephen had come that close to leaving Debbie and the kids. Would he have been any happier? I seriously doubted it. Why didn't Debbie just leave Stephen? All the usual reasons I supposed. In the end, her anger and resentment toward him probably turned into hatred. Then she had an affair with a friend of Stephen's and turned the tables on him. To make matters worse my brother had been plagued with financial and health problems. He never talked to me about his problems, however, and, being away at college, I hadn't seen the despondency and the feelings of hopelessness building up in his mind. My other brother, Jack, closer in age to myself, had, at the age of seventeen got into a horrific fight with our father and Jack left home that night, never to return. He joined the Marines and was over in Viet Nam; so Stephen must have felt terribly alone. A few nights later, after the news of Stephen's death, while at a party, I suddenly allowed myself to feel the loss of my brother. I broke away from the party. I went running outside into the night and cried.

I felt my unseen foe Death once again, the next evening, this time with such a presence and intensity that I dashed out the door in panic. I bounded down the stairs and out into the street. I walked nervously around the block, trying to clear my mind.

What is this death I feel?

I pondered this question, time and again, as I walked around the block. I kept thinking of Melina. I remembered the time we woke up in the middle of the night to find a stranger standing at the foot of our bed. The woman had let herself in with a key that her boyfriend—or someone—had given her months ago and she thought that he still lived in the flat she said. Strange as the story sounded the young woman seemed to be telling the truth. A nice looking woman too. I would have invited her to stay and smoke a joint with us but I knew Melina would have paled three shades of white at this idea. The next day Melina had the landlord change the lock on the door.

A few days after this a painter friend of Melina's showed up. He came barefooted, ragged, and hadn't had a bath in a week, not since he left the commune where he'd been living, somewhere in New Mexico. Her painter friend even had a little mongrel pup with him. Her friend and the pup stayed for a week and then left for Oregon. A few mornings later we woke up in a bed of fleas.

I thought about the night Crazy Willie and his sidekick Lightning Ray showed up with a bag full of Mexican weed that nearly knocked our socks off. And I remembered the gorgeous spring morning that Melina and I took acid together. Flinging our clothes off in a dance of warm light streaming through the window of her studio room, we thought about making love, but the idea of coupling in these physical bodies seemed so anti-climatic or something that we just starting laughing. Melina had a sister living in Sacramento. The two sisters seemed so close to each other that I sometimes mixed them up in my mind. The day that Melina and I took acid, I watched in amazement as I saw Melina shifting back and forth between herself and her sister Rebecca. At times she even took the face of her sister, her sister's face emerging from her own. Whenever Melina's sister came to visit I found himself drawn to her, and she to me, and for years we danced this odd, skittish dance around this furtive attraction, never speaking of it, yet always finding momentary chances to be alone, especially whenever Rebecca had a few gin and tonics; and so the dance we danced felt like a dance around a tree called the Forbidden Fruit. At first I thought that my attraction to Rebecca had to do with Melina, as if through Rebecca I would know the wholeness of Melina, as if I could never truly know Melina without entering into the irresistible mystery of her sister. Later, as I came to separate and differentiate the two sisters, as Melina's art grew more and more articulate and Rebecca completed law school and her daughter grew into a lovely woman, the affectionate bond between Rebecca and I did not fade but grew stronger, softer, sweeter. Did I play the role of a brother to Rebecca? Did she perhaps need a special friend, a man who loved flowers (as she did), who could speak to her from his being, who could talk to her about the Russian film *A Slave Of Love*, who praised her cooking, who found her desirable and yet respected her slightest nuance either yes or no? Rebecca would forever remain to me an irresistible mystery. Eventually, when I spoke to Melina of this attraction, Melina, who had been quietly observing this situation for years, did not seem to understand the attraction any better than I did.

Melina had such an immediate intensity about her, such a piercing glance in her blue eyes as she watched her thoughts, as a cat might patiently watch the undulating movements of tropical fish in a tank. She had a slender nimbleness in her body, a really fine balance between strength and tenderness, reminding me of a tai-chi warrior; and she had a thoughtful, seriousness about her, and a controlled tightness in her heart that mirrored my own need for freedom and expression and trust. My quick, passionate laughter attracted her, as did my spirit of celebration, and the poetic fire in my body. Sometimes the energy between us felt like the sweetness of honey amongst the smoke-drugged humming of bees; and sometimes like a narrow passage of dark heat that longed to open to deep, rhythmic joy, as the sun might break through rain clouds and barren, wintry trees into a field of golden light, the way people who have been through near-death experiences describe the light they see at the end of a long tunnel. Kindred spirits, we needed each other for emotional support and protection, and to nurture and expand our artistic and creative dimensions. Melina had a great love for astronomy, and, like ancient societies that saw a mythological theater in the constellations of the heavens, the first gallery showing of her paintings reminded me of a great weaving across the night sky, depicting the soul's journey through universal dreams, myths and symbols of human evolution. Across the void between the known and the unknown, between ignorance and self-knowledge, between density and transparency, she imprinted her archetypal images, her poetic truths, and in the act of acknowledging her dreams and the wholeness of her being, and embracing her identity with the natural world, and in giving voice to the Great Mother energy within her, Melina created and entered into a dynamic, sacred engagement with her own aliveness.

I pondered these memories as I walked the street.

Melina's energy, her enthusiasm and creativity, her fire, her aliveness, had given our apartment so much warmth and comfort, even as she had deeply touched and enriched my own life. Melina had left—.

I stopped in mid-thought. *Melina's spirit! That's it! Of course!*

Her presence—her energy and love—her memory—her ghost—her thoughts—her everyday life in our apartment, disappearing, leaving: this loss—this loss had created the feeling of death in the house.

Instantly I felt my mind relax.

I climbed the stairs and entered the apartment. The feeling of death had completely vanished. But now the rooms felt empty and colorless and cold, as if a comforting fire had suddenly gone out. I hurried to finish my book, working late into the nights, and a few days later I left San Francisco.

There's a bridge in each of us

How to begin the process of opening? To my mind, even the act of love seemed to bring with it a prediction of pain and loss, for I had a great fear that if I allowed myself to be truly sensitive and to enter into those realms of awareness which are not clearly formulated and thought directed and ego conscious that I would lose my identity as a man. It's as if I had been a king playing a king all this time, wearing a crown and caring about my robes and my staff and walking through the proper hallways and standing on the throne and decreeing ultimatums and yet never feeling that I was truly a king, for I did not know what indeed it was to be a king; and suddenly came the time to cease being the actor and to become the real king. And this thought filled me with terror. For I had become accustomed to the old ways, always thinking in terms of structure and control and specific forms of power; but this new spaciousness that now and then I could glimpse in the female essence was an awareness unlike the delineating consciousness of the male—unlike a clearly focused pen light or a spot light in the prison yard; but more like the moon or a star; or like the light of a foggy day where there is simply a sense of lightness everywhere. I felt as if I had been given a box but when I opened the box I found it empty; for I could not discuss or analyze or grasp or hold this new spaciousness in my mind with any sense of certainty. To take away the ego and the structure and the thought process and all the strategies I had used against the female to control and dominate her in my mind was to take away the role pattern I had come to equate with male consciousness. This made me feel extremely vulnerable. For I had spent much time polishing the hard shell of my image and there was no way at this point in time that I had the courage to confront inside myself the emptiness of the old male myths.

Still, I knew that I had to begin.

∞

Out of the blue came a letter from Jo. I had not seen or heard from Jo Myhra since the wedding of her good friend Mary three summers ago in '67. I went to Mary's wedding reception just to see Jo but I had caught only a glimpse of her and a flash of her warm smile. Actually, I knew very little about Jo Myhra. At the University I had been struck by her classic Madonna beauty—her dark eyes like deep, sparkling pools, and her rich, dark hair and her full lips, the gracious curves of her body, the softness of her voice. I had adored her from afar but Jo belonged to the undergraduate sorority crowd. I considered her out of my reach altogether. Besides, I was already into my last spring semester when I first met Jo. She was a friend of my cousin Yvette. Yvette, Jo and Mary. These three women seemed as inseparable as the Three Graces.

One Sunday afternoon, Larry Czenkoszy and a friend had stopped by my place, to cook up a hit of methadrine. I merely observed this ritual; I had no desire for crystal or speed or crank or smack or coke or anything that had to do with needles. Suddenly we heard the Three Graces singing in the hallway outside the door. My first impulse was to hide the drug outfit but Larry suggested that the rah-rah-sorority-let's-try-dope-for-fun might as well see the dark, ugly side of drugs too. I had smoked pot with Yvette and her two companions at my cousin's apartment, a few blocks away; but here, before their wondrous eyes, stood a bushy red-haired, red-bearded Hungarian with his left sleeve rolled up, a leather belt around his arm and a needle in his hand, and standing beside him was a tall black dude with a spoon and a lighted match. This was a little too much for the Three Graces.

Ah, but the Three Graces were a little much for me too.

The night before I left Eugene, Mary, with my cousin's help, craftily set out to seduce me. I rambled on in my mind for a long time about this one. It's not really what happened but how it happened. I had already moved out of my place on High Street and was planning to sleep this last night at my cousin's. My cousin and Mary shared the same apartment. Yvette had a final exam the next day and left early that night to study, she said, with a friend. I left Max's tavern around midnight, to find Mary alone at the apartment. We sat on the floor and talked and drank wine. Eugene had been the first place I could call home. I had never really felt at home in the South. Tomorrow, I'd be leaving Eugene. I'd be leaving my friends Larry Czenkoszy and Doc Streeter, and the secret trysting places that I'd shared with Susan, and the good times and the hard times I'd had with Allea Rose. Ben Abrams would be leaving too, going to Ann Arbor to teach creative writing at a small college, and his wife Karen had set her sights on a PHD in Political Science at the University of Michigan. Unlike Czenkoszy and me, who moved outside the mainstream, Ben was a communal man, a natural family man and a natural teacher. We all have our strengths and weaknesses but I will say nothing disparaging against Ben. He was a steady, reliable friend; a man comfortable with himself and who valued comfort; a man who had no alignment with hatred and bigotry and war and violence; a man who thoroughly enjoyed discussing poetry and the nature of reality and everything under the sun and who loved to go fishing and to sit quietly in nature and who loved to eat good food and drink good wine in small, intimate cafes in places like France and Italy and Spain. I would miss Ben and Karen and I might even miss—just a little—their Siamese cat Kerouac, who always tried to attack me when I came to visit. I had felt sad all day, my thoughts intense and inward. Sitting on the floor with Mary, this felt good to me, and comforting, and even a little cheerful.

Mary pulled out a bag of grass and I rolled a joint for us. The hour was getting late. I wondered about Yvette but Mary didn't seem concerned at all. I had never felt any electricity between Mary and me. I'd never even paid much attention to her. A few days ago her fiancé had come through Eugene from Stanford University. He had been on his way to his parent's home in Portland. I had talked to him briefly. He certainly seemed like a nice guy. Ordinary but nice. Like Mary. Mary planned on going up to Portland to meet him when she finished her exams. They were to be married in June.

As we finished the joint, suddenly I felt this sexual energy between us, as if Mary were drawing me towards her. This puzzled me. Was it the grass? Was I projecting this energy? I didn't know what to think. I didn't trust my perceptions. So I tried to ignore the feeling. But the desire grew more intense and unyielding. This woman, I thought, will not be ignored.

But what if I were wrong? Then I'd make an ass out of myself.
Well, in my book, there was only one way to find out. I reached
over and kissed Mary. She didn't let go. The next morning,
Mary smiled and told me it was just as she had imagined it
would be. Whatever that meant. But I vowed then and there
to begin trusting my secret senses. Yet, for all my avowed
intentions, it took me a long time—a very long time—and many
missteps—before I could truly begin to heal this place of self-
doubt and mistrust within me.

   After Mary's wedding I wrote a letter to Jo. I honestly wanted
to know her but I felt intimidated by her beauty and her social
grace. I stole an image from Douglas Blazek. I told her she was
"more beautiful than rice crispies on a Sunday morning." But
mostly in my letter I attacked her. The possibility of knowing
her seemed so hopeless anyway, that, out of my frustration and
pride and feelings of powerlessness, I insulted and belittled
her intelligence and mocked her "magazine clothes." I told her
that she was like a flower stuck in a "Better Homes & Gardens"
vase, that she saw only the package and gimmicks and toys of
this world, that she didn't understand anything at all. I really
wanted to provoke her, to challenge her, for if Jo were really
only what she seemed would I have bothered in the first place?
Would I have insulted her if I had not wanted to break through
her camouflage image, and reach inside her mind and gently
touch her true identity? I came on too strong and angry and
brash not to be sincere and Jo realized this at once.

   "What would you like for me to do?" she answered me
back. "Would you like for me to stamp my feet and hurl back
insults and forget about you so you can be rid of me? Or shall
I say, 'Yes, come' and allow you to beat away your frustrations
on my body? *What do you want?*" "Why do you magnify
the bad so much?" she wanted to know. "Look at the bad,
remedy or refute it, and concentrate on the good. That's why
I dislike religions and their philosophies which degrade and
stifle man."

   Jo wasn't a child, and she wasn't stupid by any means, as
I seemed to imply in my letters. (I never believed this for one

moment of course.) Until she was twelve and went to live with her step-father and his wife, Jo had grown up in a slum area in San Francisco. She had been illegitimate; her real mother had worked as a prostitute. Her step-father had given Jo a good home and everything she needed. The sorority, the honoraries, all these she saw as a way of paying them back, because to them these things meant respectability, recognition.

Two years passed.

Jo got married, become pregnant, had an abortion and then quickly rid herself of one very confused husband. She then moved to Portland and took a job in an advertising agency. Jo Myhra wanted to be a writer. She wanted to travel in Europe and become a bum. A migrant fry cook, that's what she had always wanted to be. Every so often she went through her journal and each time she re-read the three letters that I had written her in the summer of '67; and each time the letters appeared finer and what a young fool she must have seemed to me and why in the world had I bothered at all? Her friend Mary came down from Canada on a visit. Mary's husband had a teaching position in a Canadian university. My name came up. "What ever happened to Yvette's weird cousin?" Jo asked innocently enough, and, by God, Mary knew that I was working for a radio station in Portland. But Mary did warn her about me, Jo confessed one night as we lay in bed together. I shook my head in amazement. Why would Mary have done that? I suspected, though, that Mary's warning, rather than dampening Jo's enthusiasm, may even have excited her curiosity. What are you? What are you saying? What are you doing? *Where are you??!!*

After meeting each other for lunch, we retreated to our separate lives, perhaps feeling a little better, or perhaps a bit frustrated by the How-are-you-I-am-fine ritual of strangers. The old man made her nervous; he scared her. Did he still have those preconceptions about her? Jo could feel me sitting there playing Snoopy's Eagle, waiting to pounce on her, to rip her apart with my words. It's not fair! she cried in her imagination, stamping her feet. You're not *fair!* Ahhhhh...I

225

smiled. But, Ma'am, I have never tried to be fair. The old man made her smoke too much and write letters on company time. He wore Venetian blinds over his eyes and Jo hated that. He would let a chink of what's really there filter through, hiding most. Was he gentle when loving a woman? More important—*after* loving a woman? Was he ever frightened? Frightened because the Monkey Demon *really did* exist and man was really nothing but evil, and frightened because intelligence and love and acceptance had nothing to do with anything; they did not change the evil within man.

Did he like dogs? What happens when he walks alone on the beach and feels the sand and ocean and mist and gulls? Jo wanted to take his hand and shake it very gently. But maybe it wouldn't work. Maybe it's true they could never come together. Why try? Because warming oneself against a fire is nice for a time but how much nicer to curl against someone's mind. Because there are too many warm bodies around but when you press against the mind you're as cold as if you were alone. But why is it so hard? Is it worth it? It *was* when she saw (if only for a moment) his eyes widen and warm, the laugh or scowl lines deepen, the mouth (beautiful!) break through the bristly cover and curve into a smile. Why didn't he smile more often??!! Then—zip! went the blinds and the eyes frowned and the fantastic mouth disappeared and he was all angles and rough and the hands jangled keys and coffee cup.

Jo didn't trust me. I might just use the container without trying to shake it around a bit to see what's inside. If she were a man and saw some bright little container available it would be awfully easy just to go ahead and use it. Only dogs and curious people screw. Making love meant a commitment. At the very least you were committing your body. And—amazing!—hidden down under all her godawful cynicism and grime she still felt the ache of romanticism and Jo Myhra wanted everything perfect and good and clear. Everything at once when making love. Like cotton candy all wrapped up tight in a ball to be eaten and savored and enjoyed at one REALLY FINE TIME rather than pulled apart piece by piece.

The whole thing together Jo Myhra wanted; and I gave what I could but I failed miserably. Jo challenged me on many levels and I didn't have the courage to meet this challenge. Her beauty, which I found so ideal, challenged me to face the harsh and ungraceful beliefs I carried in my mind about my own physical body. Her gentleness, her kindness, her integrity and willingness to feel, her deep need for intimacy: how strange that I could accept these things in her (these things that whispered love to my soul) but not in myself; and so in the end I pushed her away.

Everything perfect and good and clear.

Everything at once when making love.

Her beliefs challenged and disturbed me and yet I couldn't admit to myself YES, I AM FRIGHTENED. I did not want to face the question of evil. I wanted to believe that all souls were Good. That all souls desired the Light. That the closer a soul came to the unlimited love within, the more this soul felt and witnessed the miracle and mystery in everyone and everything. But what if this were not true? Perhaps there were indeed souls who truly hated their own Source, as a child might hate its mother, as so many souls seem to hate this planet Earth and, almost with a vengeance, seek to destroy this planet with their anger and their greed and their disrespect. Did some souls willfully choose to turn away from the light and embrace the darkness, believing that indeed it was the right thing to do; souls who desired to enslave others in order to empower their tenuous positions and create some kind of credibility for themselves? Did these souls belong to another time, another universe, and somehow they had come to Earth, and, now, like a cancer that devours the host it lives upon, these souls were determined to destroy everything around them, including themselves? Truly, these were disturbing thoughts to me.

I wanted to be honest but I hedged with Jo. Melina Foster and I were on the verge of a final split, yet I had given Jo the impression that Melina had already moved out, and this was not true. Our time together as lovers had come to an end, but I still felt stubbornly loyal to Melina and to our history together. Nor did I have the will (perhaps remembering Jamie) or the understanding to end the relationship with Melina at once. In my fear of loss and my lack of trust, I lingered in the transition, hanging out in a kind of limbo, waiting for Melina to pull the curtain. By playing the coward I wronged not only two women but I wronged myself. And Jo could not put up with my game of hide-and-seek. She wanted to be uppermost in my mind, and who could blame her? When I couldn't bear the craziness any longer I stopped seeing Jo, and without ever giving her a why or what for.

If only the timing had been different I told myself.

Three years ago—or three months from now…. Yah, if frogs had wings.

I had come to this sweet woman like the seeker in the Zen story who approached the master, and, wanting to impress the master with his learning, talked on and on. The master responded by pouring the seeker a cup of tea. The master did not stop when the cup became full, but kept on pouring. Like the overflowing cup, the seeker had become filled with beliefs and opinions and judgments, and had no room for the Unknown to enter. Rather than intimately examining my beliefs, rather than feeling my loss and the emptiness inside, I swallowed my anger and my pain and the feelings of shame, and I denied the great need within me for this woman and for the sweet friendship that I had let slip between my fingers.

"Insensitive and stupid!" I yelled at myself.

"And I have other names, a thousand more names!"

I met Brenda Lake at a farewell party. Her astrology teacher was leaving for India to join the Theosophists. I felt comfortable with Brenda right away. She seemed so centered and at ease with herself. During the party we kept coming back to each other, the whole evening chatting about casual things as well as deep, serious things. When the party began to break up we made plans to meet again.

Just like that, we were in bed together.

Brenda looked absolutely luscious in bed. Slim of body and fair of skin, (so fair and delicate that she reminded me of the creamy white-petaled Alba rose that grew in my mother's garden), Brenda beckoned me with her dark, shining matter-of-fact eyes to waste not another word on astrology or metaphysics: her dark tumbling hair splashing over soft voluptuous breasts as white as her vanilla ice cream thighs; her yoni a potent, mythical flower of primal darkness and tender matter-of-fact flesh, sweet to the tongue, gorgeous, disarming. And years later I could still recall, if I let myself indulge in the remembrance of the chaos at this time, the slippery pale light I saw in the delicate, half-opened petals of Brenda's soul, a pale light almost overshadowed by the dark, damp, triangular feast of her womanhood, just before I lost her to the stars and a handful of worthless cards.

One thing for sure, Brenda Lake wasn't hung up on ideals of romance with a lousy poet. All Brenda wanted to do was sit around with her two friends and play cards. And recover from her recent divorce. At the time I didn't understand this need for slow healing. Nor did I have much to say to her two friends. Sam and Sara were constantly tormenting each other in their private little ways. Sara played the victim in a drama of betrayal and unfaithfulness but she loved the rotten son-of-a-bitch, (so she said), even if he did cheat on her and bang her on the jaw now and then. So the air around my new courtship felt highly charged with tension and intimations of doom. (As I nervously paced the room and glanced sideways at Brenda through a wall of cigarette smoke and growing resentment.) But it seemed such a game, this melodrama between Sam and Sara. Like their eternal card playing. "I can't believe it," I muttered beneath my breath. "Even when they smoke dope they play cards. What a waste of dope!" I had been so easily accepted by Brenda, and, now, gazing out the window of Sara's Northeast Portland home at the drizzling rain, with a sense of futility and growing rage in my belly, I felt just as easily rejected. The sudden connectedness, the urgency: where had it gone? Was desire just another mask we wear at the convenience of our biology? And beauty too? Or were they arches through which lay the most arduous of life lessons?

Georgette came to my mind.

I'd never understood that one either. Only she wasn't as pretty as Brenda. Or as easy to talk to. Our interests seemed worlds apart. And besides, at the time, just two months before I would graduate and leave Eugene, I hadn't really wanted a lasting relationship with Georgette. Georgette Denum was a friend of a friend and I had talked to her at parties but we didn't seem to have much to say to each other. She seemed a bit on the cool side and remote and somewhat distant or maybe she just didn't like me. Certainly we came from different social worlds. She was a graduate student in mathematics. Her father taught mathematics at some Eastern Ivy League college. I could still see Georgette in her favorite plaid shirt and tight faded jeans, sitting on the curb of University Avenue, eating raw green peas from the shell, her reddish hair blowing in the soft spring wind.

It was such a beautiful day; I had put away my books and stepped outside to take a walk. I stood there unable to decide which way to go. Just then Georgette came by. She stopped to say hello. She lived just around the corner and she was on her way to a friend's apartment to pick up a text book. We chatted about the warm weather and I decided to walk with her. As we walked together I could feel the energy quickening between us. I felt a sweet tingling around my body and a slight buzzing in my head. Or maybe it was just spring. Anyway, the next thing I knew, for some strange reason Georgette was down on her belly, crawling around on the floor of her friend's apartment, looking under the bed for the missing book, and looking so pretty in her plaid shirt and tight faded jeans with her sexy little tush in the air, that I couldn't resist, and the next moment we were rolling around on the floor like two cats in heat, hotly kissing.

Jesus, where did this come from?

I barely had time to wonder and Georgette didn't even question our sudden courtship. Then a worried look came into her eyes. "What if my friend should come back?" I agreed that it wouldn't be too good. "Let's go to your place," she suggested. I thought that perhaps she was just saying this; that once outside in the clear spring air Georgette would change her mind. But that was all right too. Certainly I had no desire to coerce her and this whole thing had surprised me as much as her.

But Georgette didn't change her mind.

She pulled off her shirt and jeans and everything else and lay back on my small bed and opened her arms to me. As I entered her I felt this incredible rush of heat between us. I had never felt such heat from a woman's body. Yet I moved patiently into her, for I sensed that she needed to feel safe and that she wanted to totally surrender to her passion, as if in some ancient ritual. "Where am I?" she asked me in an anxious whisper, as if she were dazed or on some drug. "You're right here," I answered gently, looking into her green eyes, smiling to assure her that I was a friend, that I meant her no harm, that I would stop if she asked. Later, we lay without speaking for a long time; our fevered bodies entwined and soaked with sweat, her yoni still holding me tightly inside her.

We made love several times after this, and each time, Oh, Sweet Jesus, Georgette went crazy, burning at a fevered pitch. She burned so hotly, a biological flame; but where did she really go in her rapture and her fevered trances? I had no idea. And I saw nothing that might hold us together. I felt no spiritual connection; no closeness of minds or hearts beating as one; only our two bodies entwined like a hot wind blowing through antique lace curtains in some strange, white room.

What if I hadn't pleased Brenda?

Actually, I felt god awful and dreadful and sad because I knew that I hadn't pleased her, I just knew it. I had been too anxious that first night; my lovemaking had been premature, too swift. I wanted to blame it on her beauty. I had been taken by surprise, almost stunned by her body. When I first met her at the party, naturally I saw that she was pretty. But she had been dressed casually, in jeans and a simple blouse, and I hadn't even thought about how she might look naked.

That first date night we went immediately to Sara's house. Sara soon disappeared with Sam into another part of the house and Brenda went into a bedroom and took her clothes off without saying a word to me. She beckoned me to come lie with her on the bed, and, with a lamplight glowing on her naked body, I might as well have been a kid with his first ice cream cone on a hot summer's day. I wanted to slowly lick her wonderful, sticky sweetness with the tip of my tongue but Brenda soon urged me to enter her. "Now!" she cried. I barely got inside her before I came rushing into her. I felt embarrassed. I felt humiliated and cheated. I mumbled an apology, not knowing what else to say, and no matter what she said, I knew that I had failed.

I wanted a second chance. I wanted to show Brenda that I could love her sweetly and forever. I wanted this woman to hold me in her heart and mind as the mother holds a child in her arms. I wanted her to embrace me and give me life. But I didn't understand the need to heal the wounded self within. I didn't understand what kept me stuck in the old ways of the chase and hunger and lust and craziness. Nor did I understand the hidden truth in the myth of Beauty and the Beast. I would have to learn the hard way that behind the doors which seem to promise the sweetest and surest path to Paradise there often await one's most feared and terrifying secrets; while behind the doors that seem guarded by these very same monsters, the doors that you wish to avoid at all costs, that, once you face these terrible fears and the self-doubts and self-hatred within you, once you embrace the beast within you, once you allow love into the dark and secret places of your being, these terrible guardians lose their power over you and you can pass through their pitiful kingdoms, pure of heart, into the great mystery called creation, into the great unknown called life.

As I watched Brenda through the haze of her cigarette smoke and through the warp of my own feelings of disgrace, I knew that I would not get a second chance, and the remembrance of her body only made my feelings of loss and separation seem even more intense and painful. Had I been blinded by her beauty, as they say you can be blinded by a field of pure snow? Transfixed, I longed to behold her gorgeous dark center. I longed to drink from her feminine nectar and to fill myself with her exotic scent. Her dark beauty in a field of whiteness held my mind like a bindu to a single thought: the thought of love, the thought of surrender, the thought of life. And now, like the terrifying Goddess Kali, she looks the other way, as I, her devotee and lover, cry out for more.

Any fool might have known, I told myself later, but it never entered my mind that Hank would rather have sex with men than women. The two of us went drinking together, right after my swift break-up with Brenda, and, in my exaggerated suffering and sentimentality, I opened himself up emotionally to the other man. We got pretty drunk bar hopping all evening. Around midnight we decided to go to my place with a bottle of cheap wine. I was still living in the house that Melina and I had rented together, two years before. When we broke up this last time, she moved out into the country, with her frightful dreams, and her paintings, and her two cats.

In the back bedroom of our house Melina had left some large pencil sketches of a nude dark-skinned man, sketches which she would later use in one of her oil paintings. Hank knew nothing about Melina. He spied the drawings, and, because Hank was black, I suppose, he made certain assumptions about the pictures that were totally without foundations except in his mind. I decided that Hank, like me, centaur-born, probably more than once had confused his unspoken thoughts and fantasies with the unspoken thoughts and feelings of others; and being human, Hank had his personal reasons for his assumptions.

I made a fire in the fireplace and the two of us sat on the floor and smoked a joint. Out of the blue Hank started asking for "some dick" and he wanted to kiss me on the mouth. I had been in some strange situations before but never in a situation like this. I had the whirlies from the booze and smoke and now I experienced a rush of conflicting beliefs and unexpected curiosity. I loved women, I loved them dearly. Yet here I was on the floor with Hank, loaded to the gills and horny as hell. I let Hank kiss me. "Now, that wasn't so bad, was it?" Hank asked Actually, it was not what I had expected. Hank had full, soft lips and I had not felt repulsed by the kiss. I now had a huge hard-on, despite the total bizarreness of the seduction and despite my disbelief in what was happening. Hank unzipped my pants and easily brushed aside my feeble protests as he bent down to have his way with me.

Alone in the city, after Melina had left San Francisco to help Marcus and Naomi open their Moon Palace Café in Portland, I rode the bus across town one night to smoke grass with Alice, a friend that I knew from work. That night I met Alice's sister, a student at San Francisco State College. Kathy slipped into my mind almost unnoticed, but for her princess-like prettiness. During the evening, making small talk, she mentioned that she was Sagittarius. Later that night, unable to sleep, I could not get her out of my thoughts. My desire for her felt almost incestuous, like a current of energy turning in upon itself. I remembered a Tibetan Tantric painting that I had seen of a serpent eating its own tail. I pondered the meaning of this image. The serpent represented the Kundalini Sakti, the Inner Woman. But what did this have to do with Kathy?

What could this mean—if anything—this astrological connection—this planetary energy? Why did this archaic system of knowledge even interest me? The time of astrology, as a form of real knowledge, had passed. Astrology—real astrology; not newspaper astrology—could serve as a useful tool, to give us insights, like any personality system, I believed, but mostly it seemed to serve as a kind of mathematical screen through which we perceive the self or the other, rather than taking the care, the energy, the attention, that it takes to really see, to really listen, to really know the self or the other with as little distortion as possible. Besides, the earth had changed; the heavens had changed; consciousness had changed. Our perceptions of the stars and planets had changed and yet the mystery of attraction and the desire to know our starry connection to the universe and to each other, would that ever change? Would my restlessness ever come to rest? Would I ever feel whole? As a ray of sunlight belongs to the sun did I not belong to a greater whole? So why did I not feel this wholeness? Why did I feel so adrift? And why did this young woman that I didn't even know, and who meant nothing to me, show up at this hour of the night to disturb my sleep?

I walked into the bathroom and Kathy didn't seem at all surprised to see me. She lay naked in the tub, splashing her belly with small waves, her pale blond hair pinned back into a ponytail. She laughed a kind of horselaugh when I knelt and scooped some water up in my hands to drink, as if she were holy or something. I felt embarrassed by her horselaugh. How indelicate! Then I felt a deep shame for my thoughts and I turned away.

I watched Kathy dancing barefooted on a grassy knoll in Golden Gate Park. Other people came and went but they didn't seem to notice her. How strange, I thought. She had on a flimsy, sleeveless dress the color of summer flowers. A golden necklace in the shape of a serpent circled her throat. She saw me standing there and made a teasing face at me. She swayed her hips suggestively. Her summer dress fell to the ground like a rain of bright petals. I stared astonished as the colors turned into images of a man that I knew was her father. Her golden necklace lay at my feet. I reached down and picked up the golden snake. Kathy laughed her loud funny horselaugh and ran up and embraced me, entwining her sensuous body around mine. I then saw myself alone in a pool of golden light.

I curled my body into a circle and took my throbbing penis into my mouth.

I never saw Kathy again. I didn't understand my strange dream or the Tantric snake vision; and Hank and I never spoke of what happened between us. Hank had been married when he lived in L. A. He had fathered two children but Hank despised women, as I found out later. I couldn't understand this hatred and bitterness that I saw in the other man's soul. There's a bridge in each of us that connects the soul and mind to the body, to each other and to other worlds, other dimensions, other beings. But if you've filled your heart with fear and shame, with anger and bitterness and blame and self-hate, you may well swear that this bridge seems only a cruel illusion, a deception, a cross; and never realize that this bridge you travel is your own original consciousness, your own self in motion.

The only rational thing to do

At this point I made a decision. I did the only rational thing I could do. I stopped trying. I stopped kicking and screaming at the universe. I stopped beating my head against the wall. I stopped courting craziness and death of the ego and I gave up expecting enlightenment to perform cartwheels before my eyes. I gave up looking for love at every corner and twist of fate. I just let things happen of their own accord. In short, I stopped taking myself so seriously. I didn't see this decision as either an act of heroism or desperation. Nor as something spiritual. Or magical. If anything, this letting go of outcome, this exhaustion of effort, came as a sheer act of mercy toward myself. A moment of rest, a moment of grace.

Then an amazing thing happened.

I met Angelina.

Angelina wore a sweet summery dress and wild flowers in her hair. She flashed an impish smile when I first called her by her true name; and she waited for me outside the print shop door and then I kissed her. She longed for a winged stallion to ride her upon the winds of consciousness, dreaming, ever-dreaming, herself new identities. Without plot or manipulation or design I knew precisely the necessary action I must take, regardless of outcome.

I just let it happen.

I went on a 4th of July week-end fishing trip to eastern Oregon with Angie and her husband and a friend of theirs. We had all planned to take acid together. Inside their small camping tent I dropped the acid Merry Prankster style into some orange juice. At the last moment her husband John decided not to try the acid and so did his friend Rick. Angie had never taken acid before but she gulped down the orange juice with me.

John rolled a joint of Thai weed and passed it around. Then another one. We listened to a tape of Jimi Hendrix and his band of Gypsies singing "Are You Experienced?" The crowded tent soon felt like the Starship *Enterprise* about to enter warp factor seven. I crawled outside the tent and Angie followed me. We decided to take a walk in the old growth forest that surrounded the lake. John and Rick decided to go fishing.

For a long time Angelina and I walked together in silence. We both knew that this was a sacred journey we walked. The earth felt magical and alive. We sensed a deep connectedness in our souls and bodies to each other and to this wonderful being our Great Mother. Angelina wanted to take in the beauty and the quietness that surrounded us. She yearned to honor this relationship and this deep communion that she felt with the earth, and to honor herself for being female, and for being such a lovely expression of earth. She knew that the earth had a desire to merge with her, that earth had reached out and given her these cells that made up her very sensual and soft and feminine body, to use in her own way, and that Our Mother does not force us or direct us or control us but that she offers freely the substance of herself to be a part of who we are, and Angelina wished to honor the earth for this.

For the very first time Angelina felt recognized. She knew that I acknowledged the woman within her. She felt that I understood the stream and storm of thoughts that flowed continually through her mind. If I looked upon life as a search for identity, she thought of life as a finding of one's self. Stop searching; start being. Stop sleeping; start remembering. Life is a journey; not a destination. A sparkling, clear intense light danced around her. I looked upon her presence and her woman's body with love and wonder and friendship. Angelina felt my eyes and reached out to take my hand. Lightly we kissed.

Angelina dreamed of going to Europe. She wanted to go before the kids came, before the mortgage was paid off, before she grew old. I considered the idea. I wanted to publish my second book of poems but then—? Yes, why not? I loved her and I loved her vision. We decided to tell John as soon as we returned to Portland.

Scared to death, she told her husband.

A few days later, Angelina got cold feet. She came to me with the idea that maybe the three of us could live together in the house that she and John had recently bought. I didn't say much but suggested that we go see John and tell him what she had on her mind. John threatened to throw me off the balcony of their third floor apartment into the swimming pool below. So I quietly left. The next day Angelina packed her clothes. That night she and I made love to each other for the first time.

THE DAYS COME
AND GO

"Look inside your heart, Amur.
There in your heart God is, even as I am."
Naomi, in a past life

Beyond Dreaming and the Stream of Time, Linda Neufer, 1970, oil on canvas, 134 cm x 114 cm

Transformation, Linda Neufer, 1972, pastel, 35 cm X 43 cm

On the work farm

A new-born calf kicks up its heels
& in the distance, across the sea,
past ancient olive trees, I gaze
upon the home of the ancient gods,
snow-capped Mt. Olympus.
A clam blue sea laps the fires
Of Ithaca.
Bravo,
there's only ONE truck to unload!
We're spitting dust, stacking
bales of hay high into the barn
—a barn made of concrete,
encircled by guards in towers
& loaded guns; hills,
bright with golden wheat,
rippling to the water's edge.

2
I drag my body to an apple tree
& wipe the sun from my forehead.
Is this the Tree of Life,
of Knowledge, of Good and Evil?
This isn't the tree of my dreams;
this isn't the farm I had in mind!

"Let's go! Let's go!"
barks an impatient guard.
I dig a circle around the tree;
only three thousand more to go....

Chopping corn

War!

We grab our choppers and run.
"Inside, inside!" the two-striper shouts.
They lock all doors; confiscate radios.
The guards wait: ON ALERT.

A storm blows in off the sea.
Even the elements agree:
Clear the air! Revolution is here!

2
Cyprus, her cities bombed
by Turkish fighters,
portends doom for the Greek junta;
and rumors, faster than war planes,
fly inside these prison walls.
In Athens, the army falls
to the people in the streets;
and the old Prime Minister
they recall.

THIS IS OUR CHANCE.
THE KING WILL RETURN AND SET US FREE.
(FOR SURE!)

3
The days come and go.
We go back
To chopping corn.

4
Black crows in a wheat field,
White moon in a blue sky.
On the hill, a circle of goats;
and on the sea a blazing sun.

When a devil gets inside you

For some reason Gobba picked me out to be his friend. Perhaps because I truly enjoyed listening to his stories. Gobba talked incessantly. Mostly he talked of home, his travels, God, and smoking dope. God and dope—Gobba could praise these till Doomsday. In Gambia, the African country of his origin, he told me that marijuana is known as the "leaf of knowledge." He claimed to be a Moslem and believed only in God. Gobba was convinced without a doubt that he belonged to the Chosen Ones. He would hide behind a mischievous grin and roll his black eyes and I could catch a fleeting glimpse of the very devil that he warned me against. "When a devil gets inside you," he would say, "you swell up like a pregnant woman!"

"The devil inside you is very hungry and you must feed this devil. If you don't get the devil out, you'll die!"

"Don't talk so much, Gobba!" I'd tell him. "The devil is your own mind."

Gobba would babble continuously to me about his oppression.

What could I do?

"I can't help you, Gobba. I'm in jail, too."

"But you're always in high spirits!" he would argue. "You can take this prison. But not me. I'm different. I don't belong in jail!"

Gobba would tell me about the times his Mama used to point out the prison gangs to him when he was small. She would warn him: "You stay away from those people! They'll kill you!"

Gobba chuckles. "And now I'm one of them."

Before leaving Gambia, Gobba was given a magical talisman. The talisman would protect him from harm he was told; but he would lose the charm just when he most needed its protection. (Fine protection that is...I thought to myself.) Gobba wore the charm on a leather thong about his neck. Over time the warning slipped from his mind. Then, one day on the streets in Athens, a Greek woman hustled him for fifty drachmas. Gobba stayed with the woman all night. When he left the next morning he left his talisman on the table beside the bed. A few days later he got busted. The court gave him three years and four months for six grams of hashish that belonged to another man. Gobba knew about the hashish of course. He and the other guy had smoked together. But the other man went free. Then, a year later, the court notified Gobba that they were dropping the four months off his time. They had discovered that he was given the wrong sentence.

To Gobba's imagination the word spirit meant ghosts, demons. At Corfu he was convinced spirits were coming into his room at night. He thought they were after his ass. He spread olive oil on the floor in order to catch their footprints. When Latif, a mischievous little devil from Pakistan, suggested that he should put sugar under his mattress to keep away the spirits, Gobba did so straightaway. Gobba even rigged up his door so that it would open with a loud clanging noise and awaken him. And everyone else, too, so I hear.

One day the old defrocked priest at Corfu did make a grab for Gobba. This was after the priest went to Gobba's cell with little gifts of candy, pretending to be a friend. When the old priest clearly revealed his intentions Gobba reported him to the head guard. The guards immediately moved the old man to another compound.

On the work farm at Kassandra Gobba was living in a section with mostly Arabs. Then he moved in with us because he claimed the Arabs wanted to fuck him. (Now who would want to fuck a six-foot-three muscular African dude who didn't want to be fucked?) Inside our compound Gobba kept to himself. He hardly said a word, even to me. He slept most of the time and on TV nights he sat in front of the tube watching Greek and sometimes American movies. He had learned to speak English in school—it's the official language of Gambia—but he couldn't read or write English, which means he couldn't read the books we had. Keith Guellow and I even had to write his letters home. (Arabic, Chinese, tribal languages, the Ministry of Justice will not translate.)

One night Gobba leaps out of bed. He's swearing and mumbling to himself and accusing three of the guys of trying to take his pants off.

"Come on, Gobba, you're dreaming! Go back to sleep!"

The next day Gobba brings in the head guard, or the "four-striper" as we call him, meaning that he has four stripes or bars of rank on his uniform. Alex Demianenko translates Gobba's accusation to the head guard. With an astounded look on his face, Alex turns to us.

"Do you know what he's saying? He's saying that we tried to fuck him!"

Obviously the head guard finds this difficult to believe.

Gobba defends himself in broken Greek.

"It's true!" he cries. "I'm not dreaming! Three of them—"

The prison officials take no action, but Gobba has painfully isolated himself from us. There's nothing I can say to him to cut through his paranoia. In fact, I'm one of the first he accuses.

It happened one day when we were chopping water trenches around some olive trees. Out of the clear blue Gobba hints that I've been after his ass while he's asleep during afternoon lock-up. Exactly what I've been doing he won't say. I can only guess but I'm in no mood for his bullshit games. Whenever Gobba ran out of genuine tales he usually came up with the most outlandish stories. I suppose he was just passing time as we traveled from one unending row of corn to another. I tell Gobba straight out that it's a lie and walk away to join another group of choppers.

From then on Gobba sleeps in his pants and with a sheet wrapped tightly around him. He's careful when he takes his showers. When we have hot water in the showers by the kitchen—the only hot water at Kassandra—Gobba won't go because of the other men.

When Gobba first came to the work farm there were only twelve of us and we had plenty of space. As more transfers arrived from Corfu the beds got shoved closer together. Each day I watched Gobba grow more and more tense. Still, I thought it'd be okay since Keith had just arrived from Corfu and moved next to him. Keith had been his friend on Corfu.

It's late one night. Keith is just putting his book away, and crawling sleepily down into his covers, when he hears Gobba mutter threateningly: "I'm gonna kill you!"

Keith is a friend. That's the only reason, Gobba explains, that he's giving him a warning instead of crashing his head in with a boot. Keith's arms are trapped inside his blankets but he's edging fast out of the bed.

"You don't need to worry about me, Gobba. I'm moving."

Keith grabs his blankets and mattress, dragging them to the other end of the room. Gobba runs to the big window and yells for the guards. He backs up against the wall. "I ain't dreaming! I ain't dreaming!"

A guard comes up to the control window. Gobba sticks his face to the window and tells the guard that Keith tried to fuck him. Keith is standing nearby and Gobba sweeps his long arm angrily around and catches Keith in the eye. I hear the slapping sound and then I see a blur of three guys leaping and pounding on Gobba. I grab my glasses as quickly as possible to see what's going on. I see Terry, the petty thief from London, viciously cursing and hitting Gobba. Charley, a German smuggler, and Fabio, an Italian, are trying to hold Gobba down. It's a mad scramble over beds and bodies and before the guards can stop the fight Gobba has a bloody nose and he's howling like a trapped animal for his life. The guards hustle Gobba off to the infirmary. Next morning, the three who jumped him are called in to see the head guard. Three days later Gobba is on his way back to Corfu.

A horse of another color

When I left Corfu for the work farm I was startled to see the police stop at a holding station to pick up two gypsy girls. The girls were being transferred to the women's prison in Athens. They had been busted for filching cigarettes off tourists. These girls couldn't have been more than thirteen or fourteen years old. (And very pretty girls too.) As far as I can tell age doesn't matter in Greece. At Nafplion I met one high school kid who got eight months for patting a woman on the butt. True, the lady whose temptation he couldn't resist, as he sped past on his motor scooter, turned out to be the wife of a high ranking army officer. After three months he appealed the decision. The appeal court set him free.

The political prisoners they keep at a special prison. I've never talked to any of them, unless you want to count the old man who made a derogatory remark about Popodalophous. The police pulled him out of the taverna and gave him a month in jail. This happened just a few days after the junta's new "democracy" had been established.

The Greek prisoners that I've met have been peasants and farmers from the villages. To find a Greek who hasn't been in jail—I think that's the exception! They seem to accept prison as the normal way of life. Any time under five years they laugh off as just a visit. A few are in for hashish; some for petty thievery, such as stealing money from the church boxes in the shrines along the road; or more seriously, for stealing their neighbor's goats or sheep. One gypsy stole a horse and actually painted it another color.

Mostly, though, I hear about their weird sex crimes. Like the young peasant who got his mother pregnant. When the old man discovered this incestuous deed, his wife and son butchered him. The police caught them just as they were throwing his last remains into the sea. Then I heard about the man who was baby sitting his three-year-old niece. They were watching TV together. He was holding the little girl on his lap and got an erection. He became so excited that he penetrated the girl's vagina and she died. In the prison at Nafplion I met three gypsies who were in for raping a nine year old girl. In Greece, the younger the better, I've been told. By age eighteen they're over the hill. But it seems that girls take second place to little boys. It's called the "Greek Way." Perhaps boys are simply more accessible than girls. Perhaps, as one gypsy on the work farm put it: "I like to ball women, sure. But if a man's good-looking, I'll fuck him too!"

Is this a practice left over from Turkish invaders, like retsina and dusty coffee? They busted one English bloke with twelve kilos at the Turkish border. The border guards really scared him with their talk of prison. Ten, twelve years, maybe. But... if he would drop his pants. Ten guards lined up in the back room....

At Corfu there's an old defrocked priest who's in for murdering his young lover by throwing him in an oven. (The same defrocked priest who tried to chum Gobba with his gifts of candy.) The old man killed his young lover in a fit of jealous rage when he discovered the boy was planning to get married.

On a sunny day at Corfu it's like a zoo, with the foreigners sunbathing in the exercise yard, or playing volley ball in ragged cutoffs, and Greek prisoners lining up outside the gate like a bunch of goggle-eyed tourists.

Perhaps we just appear strange to them.

At Nafplion the prison barber strikes me as a man who might easily slit your throat, though he grins slyly and says he is my friend. One day, so Nick tells me, the barber went out hunting on his land and he came across his sister and a man together. The barber blasted away with his shotgun, killing both his sister and her lover. "Every Greek must marry a virgin!" Nick explains. "Of course, it's irrational," he admits; but even he would not have married his wife—she's Greek-Canadian--had she not been a virgin. Nick owned a restaurant in Bowling Green, Kentucky, and a pizza parlor that catered to the college crowd. Because of the long hours he put in Nick kept a bed in the back room, (he smiles as he tells me this), and a stereo and Scotch whiskey. Nick would often have a lot of money on him after closing hours, so he carried a pistol for protection. One night he came home and discovered his wife with a friend. In a jealous rage Nick shot and wounded his wife. Then he panicked and fled back to Greece.

What can be said that hasn't been said a thousand times over?

You and I don't see Greece. We see Ancient Greece.

(Or Kazantzakis, who brought back the dead.)

We carry with us a nebulous collection of museum pieces, sunken cities, ruins; people who idolized their illusions; the continuous Greek drama. We see centuries of plundered warriors; women cloistered in black, eternal black; and children devoured, the atrocious Turk licking his lips and a sword. We think of austere Byzantine monks, heaping their skulls beneath a golden Icon. At the crossroads, peasants, on donkey back, wave, perfecting our gentle image. All the pretensions of the past we carry with us and the pretensions of our own self-illusions. The Greek Way is to whitewash the walls, stick a candle in the door, and turn the road into a shrine.

The days come and go

In the orchards Greek prisoners gather shiny red apples into big piles and haul them off to feed the pigs. We stuff our pockets full as we pass the apple trees on our way to the corn fields, the guards turning their heads and pretending not to see. It's October and the days clear and warm with mellow sunlight. After we harvest the corn—the scrawniest, wormiest bunch of ears I've ever seen—the prison cows munch their way haphazardly through the rows. We follow the cows with our choppers, knocking over the dead stalks and piling them into huge stacks and then burning the fields. The good ears that we find, we roast in the burning coals. Coming back inside each day we plunder the pear trees growing near our path, robbing them of their low-hanging fruit, as the guards swear and shout at us that these pears are no good. One day I realize that the two black-and-white storks have gone. Each spring they return to the farm, to mate in a large nest they built one year on the roof of the supply barn. I smile, remembering their graceful flights across the valley.

The nights turn cold. A small wood burner is all that we have for heat in the room, and before winter is out we won't be able to go near the damn thing, it'll be smoking so badly. The guards allow us one sack of firewood each day and an armful of corn cobs for kindling. Last winter, a big snow fell on Kassandra, a peninsula on the Aegean Sea, not far from Thessaloniki in the northern district of Macedonia. It got so cold on the work farm that the foreigners broke up their bed boards and threw the pieces into the stove, along with bars of olive oil prison soap, books, anything that would burn. It's forbidden to cook on the wood stove. But, as soon as the guards lock the doors in the evening, we cook everything from brown rice to Italian spaghetti with savory sauce to English puddings.

On Thanksgiving, the American consul in Thessaloniki shows up with a roasted turkey and stuffings, gravy, cranberry sauce and pumpkin pie. There are six of us Americans at

Kassandra. I share some turkey and a piece of pie with Alex Demianenko. Alex was born in Montreal, just a few weeks after his parents arrived in Canada from the Ukraine during the War years. Still, it seems a bit strange, eating Thanksgiving dinner in a room with "foreigners."

We pick olives in the crisp, early mornings of November and in the drizzling December rains, and we snack on wild blackberries growing in the hills among the oldest olive trees near the sea. One guard tries to warn us that these berries are poisonous. (Even as he's telling us this, in the distance we see the gun guard stuffing berries into his mouth.) *Dhembirazi*, we go to great lengths to smuggle the poison blackberries inside so that we can eat them with yogurt or milk.

The early morning sky never ceases to amaze me with its breathtaking changes, as the sun breaks over the curtain of clouds above the valley. On a clear day I can even catch a glimpse of Mt. Olympus—that old snow-capped rascal—just across the sea. We take a short break from picking olives and I gaze without pity or regret upon this blue Aegean Sea, knowing that I shall probably never see this beautiful land again. Already this country seems like a memory to me.

Deception on all sides

It's August and the room is swarming with flies. Or should I say flies are swarming the room? Whatever, no matter how many we swat, every afternoon it's the same as yesterday and the day before. "If you think this is bad," Keith tells me, "you should work in the stables!" Keith gets up before dawn every morning to milk the cows. "Actually," he says, "it's not a bad job." Come rain or shine he works seven days a week. That's a good deal since each day that a prisoner works counts as two days off his time. The better jobs, such as working in the bakery or kitchen, or taking care of the animals, or harvesting the fruit, usually go to the Greeks. The foreigners get stuck with the grunt work: chopping and breaking ground for spring planting; baling hay; unloading grain trucks at harvest; picking olives.

Each day I grow more nervous and edgy. For two months now I've been waiting to hear about my anostoli—the suspension of the last one-third of my sentence. I've even stopped going out with the chopper team. Instead, each day I stay inside to sweep and clean our barracks room and, before afternoon lock-up, I go to the bakery and pick up our daily bread. On Saturdays I flood the room with water and scrub the floor with a broom. Easy work; but cleaning the room only counts as one-and-a-half days, not two days like chopping weeds.

I rob fifty straws from a nearly-new broom.

With my back to the South I consult the Book of Changes. RELEASE.

A favorable wind blows my way but not the wind that brings the nourishing rain. A moving line warns me of misfortune. The best course of action lies in the Passive Principle. Ah, but hope is a one-eyed beggar. Already I'm getting a head start on a new beard for the outside. "Tomorrow, tomorrow!" I assure the guards, when they mention the barber.

Last January the *I Ching* foretold the approval of my work farm application and even the "undeserved blessings" that would come my way. The Superior Man is hardworking; he has a goal which he sets out to accomplish; modesty brings success (in accordance with the terrestrial forces). The symbol of this hexagram: a tree growing out of the earth. Well, I knew where I'd be spending my summer!

A few days later I received the letter from George—the lawyer in Athens—asking if he could help me in any way. He made out an application to the work farm; the application arrived at Corfu; I signed it and sent the form to the Ministry of Justice. The Ministry of Justice approved the application and in early April I was on my way to Kassandra.

When the Turkish-Greek conflict broke out in Cyprus, Russ Whitmore and I immediately threw the *I Ching*. FU:RETURN; with six for the top place. Armies will go to marching. The ruler will suffer a great defeat and not for ten years will things be set right.

The very next day the military junta fell and the Greek government recalled their old Prime Minister from Paris. As for foreign prisoners, the *I Ching* indicated hard times.

September comes.

The wind blows like crazy for days but the nourishing rains do not fall. My anostoli comes back NO. The District Prosecutor has decided that I'm "not ready" for the future.

The Greek law requires a prisoner to serve a probationary period after anostoli. But the law requires foreigners in for drugs to leave the country immediately upon release. So how can we serve a probationary period? (Catch-22 it's called in the USA.) The Greek police have no way to control our behavior if they grant us anostoli. In the past this has been overlooked. But things have changed. Therefore, the District Prosecutor at Poligirous, who has the final say on anostoli for prisoners at Kassandra, decides there will be no more anostoli for foreigners. "Absolutely not one hour of anostoli will I give you!" he shouts in a fit of tempter on one of his visits to the work farm. Our only hope lies in making an appeal to the new Ministry of Justice.

The prison director catches wind of our discontent and calls Alex Demianenko into his office. The director wants to help us he tells Alex. (That is, he wants to keep our protest under thumb.) The director has personally written a letter to the Ministry concerning the Prosecutor's actions. He urges us to write letters and suggests points of attack. (He wants to make sure that we criticize just the District Prosecutor—and not the director of the work farm.)

This director once promised us that we could have credit for taking lessons in Greek language, on rainy days when there was no work in the fields. But after a few rainy days and several lessons taught to us by a Greek schoolteacher inmate who could speak German, the four-striper tells us: "No, we can't give you credit for these lessons!" When Dietrich confronts the director with this news the director tells him with a straight face: "*Dhembirazi*, we'll all be home by Christmas!"

Alex Demianenko and I compose a letter to the Ministry of Justice. We deplore the action of the District Prosecutor under the old military junta. We appeal for mercy and understanding from the new Ministry. They allow Greek prisoners anostoli but they deny this privilege to us because we're foreigners. We miss our homes and many of us are students. Is this Greek justice? Is not our imprisonment in a foreign country harsh enough punishment? Why deny us anostoli? (I'm told the Greeks don't have a word for bullshit. So what could we lose?) Whitmore writes a letter. Then Fabio. And, in another section, the Germans.

The Inspector of Agriculture—a person of considerable power within the penal system—gives us a grand speech on his next visit. He promises us that he will do whatever he can to help. Meanwhile, he says, we must continue to work everyday.

Two months go by.

At last a letter from the Ministry of Justice arrives for Demianenko. The Ministry informs Alex that the District Prosecutor will be glad to come to the work farm and personally explain to him why his anostoli has been denied.

So that's the end of our protest.

The earth keeps turning

Can you think of anything more valueless to a dying woman on her bed than, "Gee, you have nice legs!"
       Naomi

I stare at the letter and the color photographs. What wonderful pictures! There's Melina Foster, smiling into the camera and waving. She's standing next to "Howdy," her VW bug. It must be early spring, she's wearing a maroon colored wool sweater and a gray wool cap pulled down over her ears. Naomi probably took the picture. The letter and the photographs came from her. She didn't really know what to say, I can tell. But it doesn't matters. Instantly I fell in love with her letter and the pictures.

"Dear Amur" her letter beings.

I shake my head in amazement. Naomi has such a strange sense of humor. Just before leaving America we had a long talk together, one of the few times we've ever spoken to each other without pretending we were talking about something else. She told me about a dream she had. In her dream she and I—only she called me Amur—were living with our people in a tribe on the edge of some Middle Eastern desert. We were living as husband and wife and had a small son and another child on the way. I tended animals and worked with her father. We were so much in love with each other she told me. Our minds and feelings were so closely connected they seemed to be one, and although I was a quiet man and spoke little she seemed to always know what I was thinking in my heart. Naomi saw the second child being born but something went wrong, there was some difficulty, and she felt all this pain in her body, and suddenly she was no longer in her body.

She saw me walking in the desert, alone, and weeping.

She had never seen me weep before. I seemed to be looking for something. "Amur, my beloved," she called, "why are you so sad? What are you seeking?"

As if I could hear her voice I answered: "Naomi is gone."

We sat for a long time in silence and she watched me, not fully understanding my meaning. Suddenly I spoke again. Without taking my eyes from the desert I said: "I come seeking God. I come to the desert to call upon this God of Our Fathers. This God was the breath between Amur and Naomi. Only she understood Amur. Only she could see into his heart. Now I come seeking HIM."

"Amur, Amur, my beloved," she murmured and reached out to touch me with her hands; her small, warm hands that I had loved so well. "Do not seek Our God in this barren land, my beloved!" she cried. "Look inside to your heart. There in your heart God is, even as I am." I swiftly lifted my eyes from the ground, as if hearing a sudden sound in the still desert air.

In the spring of '73 Marcus and Naomi moved to a rural community about thirty miles from Portland. They bought an old farm house on five acres of land with a small running creek and a grove of pine trees and a backyard field overrun with tall weeds and blackberries and wildflowers. In her letter to me Naomi enclosed colored photos of their house in the country. In one picture, taken from their front yard, I could see snow-capped Mt. Hood in the far distance. My friends in jail wanted to ooh and ahh the pictures. There's Marcus, beaming so proudly, as he holds in his arms their new adopted son, less than a month old. There's a close up shot of Jim Carpenter, playing old-time fiddle music on his new fiddle. Jim Carpenter had just returned from a tequila-glazed trip into Mexico, when he and I first met, the summer that I went back to Florida. We liked each other immediately and I introduced him to Lisa. After I went back to Oregon, Jim and Lisa fell in love with each other and got married. Jim decided to come out to Eugene, to go through the graduate creative writing program at the University of Oregon. Years later, Jim would remind me of a certain conversation that had taken place between us that summer that had deeply affected him, as we drank our ice coffees and listened to folk music in a popular, trendy coffee house. "What *do* you believe in?" Jim asked me, after I had eliminated most of the things that the people Jim knew believed in or pretended to believe in. Without any hesitation I answered, "I believe in awareness."

In another picture, Jim's horsing around with their small son Ben, with Ben riding on Jim's shoulders. Lisa's in the background with Zorba, their German shepherd. Someone, probably Marcus, took a picture of Naomi and her sister Tammy at the Eugene Saturday Market. Another photograph shows Naomi making breakfast at a camp site, and in the next picture she's sitting on a rock in the middle of a swift flowing river and smiling at the camera. She's wearing a plaid shirt and faded blue jeans rolled to her knees. Back at the homestead, Naomi's feeding a handful of grass over the fence to a horse in the neighboring pasture. In another picture she's holding a large smooth river rock in her hands as she crouches by the rock wall of a flower bed that she's building in front of her house. Her long curly hair hides some of her face but her short burgundy skirt reveals her nice looking legs. On the back of the picture she scribbled this comment: Can you think of anything more valueless to say to a dying woman on her bed than, "Gee, you have nice legs!"

How odd, I'm thinking. All these pictures of Naomi and she hates to have her picture taken. Oh, well. Then, there's a slightly out-of-focus group picture of Naomi holding their new baby, and Lisa holding Ben; and Jim, smiling for the camera, sits squeezed on the sofa between Lisa and, to my surprise, Angelina.

That night in San Francisco

It was the summer of '68. One week-end in late June, on the spur of the moment, Marcus and Naomi drove down from Portland to visit me in San Francisco. They had never been to San Francisco before. They wanted to see this mythical city and they wanted to encourage me to move back to Oregon as soon as possible. They wanted me to help them run a restaurant they had recently bought in the industrial section of Northwest Portland.

Melina and I were living together at the time. Melina and I had first met two summers ago in Portland, the year I finished graduate school. Melina had just graduated from the Oregon School of Arts and Crafts. She had received a grant from the Brooklyn Museum School of Art and that September she flew to New York. A few weeks later I took off hitchhiking to San Francisco. Melina didn't like Brooklyn. That following spring she took a train to San Francisco. We moved into a quiet, sunny flat above a small real estate office on Irving Street near Golden Gate Park. When Marcus and Naomi came down, Melina had already left for Portland, to help them open The Moon Palace Café.

"Crab and shrimp, shrimp and crab.

Take a trip, blow your mind!"

I took them to Fisherman's Wharf for lunch. As we strolled by the restaurants and the hawkers of sea food on the Wharf, one hawker, a man probably in his sixties, kept shouting this pitch like a mantra:

"Crab and shrimp, shrimp and crab.

Take a trip, blow your mind!"

That night, back at my place, Naomi wanted to hear the Beatles' *Sgt. Pepper* album. Marcus kept trying to sell me on the restaurant. He saw the Moon Palace Café as a way to get out of the 8-to-5 rat race. Yeah, right, like I said before, I must have had rocks in my head…. I had seen the long hours and hard work that my brother Stephen had put into his drive-in restaurant, back when I was in high school. But what the hell. Maybe, as a writer, I wouldn't starve.

After the Beatles I put on an album called *Holy Music* by Malachi.

I opened a bottle of wine and we smoked some grass.

In fact, we smoked some of the same cannabis that I had sent to Naomi last May for her twenty-first birthday. I had rolled two joints and put them in a birthday card. It was dynamite stuff; but I didn't mention this to her in my card. That was a mistake. Naomi had never smoked much pot. She collapsed on the bathroom floor, crawling dizzily in circles, swearing that I had poisoned them. I had scored the grass from Crazy Willie. Melina had smoked it only two or three times. The stuff really scared her. She felt out of control and had strange visions and past life recollections, like living in fourteenth century Russia and being raped and left for dead by a group of nomadic warriors.

Around midnight, on the second side of *East Meets West*, Marcus stretched out on my bed and fell asleep. I crawled into a sleeping bag on the living room floor and Naomi took a bag and went to the other side of the room near the fire place. But no way could I sleep. A thousand times I wanted to cross the darkness and find Naomi's small hands reaching for mine. And a thousand and one times I stopped myself. What if I were just imagining all this? What if it were just me? Or the grass? Back and forth I went, tangled up in a field of energy as maddening and as insistent as the flutter of moth wings against a screen on a summer night. I knew that if I crossed the darkness and she rebuffed me that I would feel absolutely awful. On the other hand, I knew that if I went to her and we did make love it would be even more disastrous. I could not and would not cross the line of friendship that I felt for Marcus. Friendship meant a lot to me.

Marcus and I grew up together in Georgia. Indirectly, he was one of the reasons I had moved to Oregon. In August of '62, after quitting my summer job, I had two weeks left before taking off to college in Florida. Marcus had already joined the Air Force and he was stationed in Billings, Montana. I decided to hitchhike across the country and make Montana my destination. From Atlanta I caught a ride with a truck driver that took me almost to Chicago. Outside Chicago I caught a ride with a sailor going all the way to Santa Rosa, California. From there I hitched to Seattle, traveling the scenic route up 101, to visit the World's Fair, and Oregon so impressed me with its natural beauty that I vowed someday to return. Three years later, when I applied to several graduate schools around the country, including the UO, Oregon sent me a one-page application while the other schools wanted me to fill out a four-page questionnaire about my life and what I wanted to do with it. I knew right away that Oregon was my kind of place. When I returned to Florida that summer to set up house with Lisa I went home to see my folks. My sister Jenny had been in a car wreck and I planned to visit her in the hospital. My folks took one look at my beard and we got into an argument. They were too humiliated to be seen with me, even to go with me to the hospital. "You're not too old for a whippin'!" my father said to me. I looked at the man like he was crazy. But I said nothing. I gathered my things together and called Marcus to come pick me up. I stayed at his house the few days of my stop-over. Marcus was married to Charlotte and she was pregnant; but all he could talk about was this woman that he had recently met and that worked for him at the pizza place he managed in Atlanta. That's when I met Naomi for the first time. The following spring Marcus and Naomi drove out to Oregon and they stopped in Eugene to see me. They were headed for Seattle when their old yellow T-Bird broke down in Portland. They decided to stay in Portland.

From the beginning, when I first met Naomi, I felt this disturbing energy between us. Sometimes as a subtle, playful spark. Sometimes as a kind of recognition; a seed of knowingness. Sometimes, when we came near each other, I felt as if we were entering into a ring of power, primordial, volatile. Deep within an ancient forest we approached each other, cautiously, warily, temporarily lost and uncertain, each seeking a way out of the dark woods but neither one fully trusting the other.

As the years passed, this feeling never diminished.

Looking back, I realized that I had a great desire and curiosity to know this woman, for I sensed from the beginning that she carried within her a profound knowledge. This was not, I realized, a kind of showy knowledge, like bright feathers that male birds often display. She carried this knowledge silently, intimately, as a woman carries a child. Her knowledge possessed a kind of calmness, a kind of sweetness, like the river washed stones and like the form of a path that has been worn by many feet and the smoothness of the pillar that has been touched by many hands. Yet she seemed totally unaware of this knowledge. She would always turn the other way anytime that I would even hint to her that the world might be more and something greater than the shallow dramas she saw on her TV screen, or read about in her throw-away novels, and more splendid even than the dreams and fantasies which she seemed to be creating in and around her life and marriage like an invisible wall.

I didn't know how to reach out to her. I didn't know how to communicate with her about this crazy wall and about the beauty and the uniqueness within her that she so desired and yet that she denied herself. I suspected that anything I might do would feel like a violation of her privacy and her marriage, as if I were throwing rocks at her or storming those castle walls. I didn't realize that the bridge between us felt so awkward and painful exactly because Naomi acted as a great mirror and teacher for me of the many ways in which I protected myself. Her dreams and fantasies, her silent withdrawals, her feelings of shame, her skepticism and mistrust, these were some of the very defenses that I used to distance myself from my own fear of loss. I did not understand this mirroring nor did I know that someday I would come face to face with these shadow images in the unblinking mirror of her eyes. At the time, she seemed so remote and so set in her beliefs and so different from me that I finally decided I could really do nothing, that she would have to dismantle the wall for herself.

All those years

Naomi sipped on her lukewarm coffee. A half-smoked cigarette lay burning in the ash tray. Earlier, she had turned the radio on to her favorite country music station but now she hardly heard the words to the song. Willie Nelson singing about blue eyes crying in the rain. Did she know anyone with blue eyes? Oh, yes, Melina Foster. She and Melina didn't get along very well. Naomi had tried to be friends with her. At first, Naomi had wanted Melina to be her friend. A best friend, like a sister. But they never did anything together. Never went anywhere together. Not even to a movie. Melina would call when she wanted help with her hair. It was always when she needed something. Never just to chit-chat. Never just to be friends. Melina reminded Naomi of her mother. They were both wiry, sensitive, nervy women with sharp edges. They both had a flair for drama. Her mother getting into a drunken rage at Clyde and throwing the dishes across the room and smashing them. Not the good ones of course. The good dishes she kept in the china cabinet.

It had been so different with her real dad. Her real dad had died when she was just eight years old. They were living in Idaho then. He got caught out in his truck in a blizzard snowstorm. He tried to keep warm using the truck heater. They say he died of carbon monoxide.

Her real dad had been a preacher. His name was Virgil. He had a kind heart and played the guitar. She'd sit on his knees and he'd sing to her "You Are My Sunshine". He'd tell her stories. He wrote poetry too. They had been best buddies until he died. She felt betrayed. She felt angry at him for leaving her. Her mother had tried to explain that it wasn't her fault that he had died but no matter what her mother told her she still felt guilty, as if she had done something wrong. As if he went away because of her. The child inside her clutched this feeling tightly to her heart, as if, somehow, if she carried this feeling around long enough, her dad would come back and everything would be all right again.

But things only got worse.

She hated her step-dad. He was not at all like her real dad. Clyde worked hard long hours at his job and he drank a lot. When he drank he and mom almost always got into a fight.

Clyde had his own construction company but he had no social skills. He built restaurants for a fast food franchise. They would send him to Colorado for two years. Then to Georgia. Then to California. They were always moving. Clyde made good money but he had a tight-fisted heart. He acted as if he were doing the kids all a big favor, taking care of them.

Her mom had been sixteen when she married Virgil. She was ignorant. She didn't know anything. But Naomi remembered only good things about Virgil. Even if she couldn't believe in his God. There had been other men in her mom's life, after Virgil's death. They drove motorcycles and didn't have jobs. Here Norma had five kids. What was she thinking?

Then there was Jules. Jules seemed safe at first and kind-hearted. He befriended her mom and for a brief time they were lovers. But for some reason he had to go out of town and that's when her mom met Clyde. Later, Jules came back to visit them, pretending to be an old friend.

Naomi was fourteen then.

For some reason Jules felt that Norma had betrayed him. Naomi didn't understand his reasons at the time. All she knew was that one night, when her mom and Clyde were out for the evening, Jules came to her room. Jules warned her not to tell anyone about what happened between them that night. Naomi kept quiet. She never spoke of this to her mom, ever. She felt sure than Norma would blame her. Jules came to her room many times after that first night. He taught her ways of pleasing a man. She liked Jules. He paid attention to her. He didn't treat her like a stupid teenager. At times, the idea of having sex with her mother's old boy friend had excited her. At other times, she felt guilty and scared. When Jules left for California he told her how she could get in touch with him, if ever she needed help. She never told anyone about Jules, not even Marcus. The whole thing left her feeling weird. Men didn't feel safe anymore. No matter how much you loved them, they betrayed you, they used you, they left you.

Marcus had helped her out of a jam. He gave her a job in the pizza place that he was managing in Atlanta and he never said anything out of line to her. He thought she was a virgin when they met. That was almost eight years ago. The summer of '66. Slowly, those old feelings of trust and friendship that she had felt with her real dad began to re-surface. She knew she could trust Marcus. He wouldn't hurt her. They shared a real bond of love and friendship. She knew, however, that it had been the wrong thing for her to marry him. She didn't really want to but she couldn't come up with any real reason not to. After all, they were living together. He certainly loved her. What else do you do?

At least Marcus wasn't an alcoholic. He would never hit her and he wouldn't cheat on her. He was a good provider and he felt a deep responsibility to their marriage, after his first two failures. But...and this next thought terrified her...she felt no passion between them. What romance she had felt in the beginning, even that was gone now. There was just a feeling of deadness there. Even the little extra things that she used to do, like hanging stockings at Christmas, she had just stopped. Marcus didn't know what to do. He would never ask for help or go to a marriage counselor. Our problems were our private business, he said. She knew that he knew about her feelings for David. She had wanted to go with David and Melina Foster to the Vortex rock festival at McIver State Park. This was the famous rock festival sponsored by the State of Oregon in order to diffuse the potential street violence they feared might erupt in Portland between war protesters and the national convention of the American Legion. Governor Tom McCall had officially ordered the state police to stay out of the park during the three festival days. She pleaded with Marcus to let her go but he wouldn't budge. He had no desire to go and he didn't want her there. He knew her real reason for going was not to smoke pot and mud wrestle or walk around naked in front of thirty thousand people or drop acid and dance all night inside a womb-like circus tent to a rock group playing "Love Is Just A Kiss Away". She wanted to go because of David. She wanted to be near him in the wild uncertainty of what might happen at that festival. And who knows what might have happened between them...inside that womb-like tent? But Marcus didn't want to deal with her feelings for David. Just like he didn't want to deal with the deadness in their marriage. He would agree to talk about it later. Later would come and nothing would be said. This happened again and again. He believed that if you just didn't talk about a problem that somehow it would go away. Or fix itself. But it wasn't going away. David was going away. But not the problem. God, David had said they might even stay in Europe.

She left the kitchen and walked into her bedroom. She started to make the bed and then remembered she was alone in the house. Marcus was working overtime this Saturday till noon. Such an awful job, welding. It hurt his back, his eyes. She would be glad when he found another job.

The bed was unmade. The house was unmade. Her whole fucking life was unmade. She thought of painting the outside of their house green. From the road it would blend right in with the grove of pine trees. Maybe then she would feel safe. The world would just pass her by. She longed for a child. A female child. A friend, a sister. Years of taking fertility pills hadn't helped. Marcus certainly wasn't to blame. Something was always wrong with her system. First her mucus was hostile to his sperm. And then...

Now they were talking about adopting a baby.

She lay down on the bed. She still had her nightgown on, the blue one that Marcus had given her for Christmas two years ago.

Her thoughts drifted to David.

She felt a sudden panic inside her. What if he should stay in Europe? This idea terrified her. She wanted to be near him, even if he were married to Angie. That would be okay. She smiled, thinking of the last time they were together. The four of them were taking a Sunday drive along the Columbia River Gorge. They were all riding in the front seat of Marcus' old pick-up. She and David were sitting in the middle, their legs pressing together, ever so tightly. It felt so intense she thought for sure EVERYONE knew. She stared straight ahead, afraid of looking at him.

"How can you hide something THAT BIG?" she wanted to tease him.

Suddenly, her whole body got hot. She lifted her nightgown and pushed down her panties before they melted. She thought of David as she closed her eyes. She thought of the times he would make love to her while she slept peacefully in his arms. He would touch her so very lightly and carefully with his finger until the moisture came, then he would slowly enter her, so as not to fully awaken her. The next morning she would linger in bed, wondering. Had she only dreamed he had come? Touching herself, she would find his seed inside her. She prayed they would make a baby together.

A post card from Paris arrived and a card from Rome. Then a card from someplace in Greece called Monemvasia. The card had a picture of a little fishing village on the Aegean Sea. With a pen David had circled a red-tiled house near the harbor. On the message side of the card he wrote that he and Angie had rented this house from an old sea captain and his wife. Naomi studied the card, thinking of him and thinking of his modesty and those ragged cut-offs he wore sometimes and no underwear and she was about to go up the walls, that bastard.

Months passed and summer came again.

She and Marcus sold their house in Portland and bought a house and five acres in the country. They put their names on a list at an adoption agency.

Then came the telegram from Angie.

David had been arrested for growing marijuana plants.

To be in jail in a foreign country, Naomi's imagination was filled with dreadful images of what it must be like. She knew about the military *junta* in Greece. She knew the ruler of Greece was a petty tyrant. David had written to them about how the police had thrown some German guy in jail for playing a forbidden song. What would they do to someone for growing ten marijuana plants? The court wouldn't even let David post bail. Angie said the judge was afraid that David might skip the country. "Of course he would skip the country!" Marcus said. Marcus talked about going to Greece and breaking David out of prison. "If necessary," he said.

What was he doing now? Naomi wondered.

She thought about his last visit. Just before taking off for Europe he and Angelina had gone to a party a stone's throw from her house. David had taken a break from the party and walked over to say hello to Marcus. Naomi had answered the door; she was half-asleep.

"I was napping," she said.

Marcus wasn't home.

David quickly walked back to the party.

A few days later David stopped by to drop off some financial papers. Marcus was at work. Naomi poured David a cup of coffee. They got to talking. She told him that when he knocked on her door that evening he woke up from a dream. In her dream they were about to make love in the back seat of a car. Then Marcus showed up in her dream and interrupted them. This happened all the time in her dreams she said.

David didn't know how to take this news. So he asked her about that night in San Francisco. No, his feelings had not lied to him. She had wanted him just as much as he had wanted her. Naomi asked him about the night that he and Marcus got so smashed and drank everything in the house and then swore that she had hidden the last joint and wouldn't tell them. She had to drive David home in his VW with Marcus following them. David had put his head in her lap and wouldn't leave her alone and he wanted to kiss her *there*. Naomi couldn't say the word. She blushed even as she told him this much.

Oh, yes, David remembered that night quite well.

He remembered the other nights, too, the nights that he had gotten stoned and tried to touch her. Naomi studied him carefully but she said nothing more. For her, this new information changed everything. All those years she had thought that he was just between women when he made those passes at her. She never dreamed even when she lay in her bed almost unable to breathe her body so hot thinking of him that David could really desire her. She allowed herself now to imagine David wanting her. He wanted her so much he couldn't keep his hands off her and she loved every moment of it. She wanted him in the mornings before crawling out of bed to go to work at the bank and she wanted him at lunch time in her car at the Mary S. Young State Park (if she thought no one would see them). Even with other cars in the parking lot his large hands would slip under her dress and inside her panties and she would get so damn wet with excitement. He would teasingly lick the sticky wetness from his fingers, as she watched, and looking into her eyes he would smile so sweetly and tell her that he loved her.

"Strawberries," she said, touching his lips with her fingers.

"Your kisses taste like strawberries. Like ripe strawberries in the sun."

She saw that her words pleased him. That made her happy.

All those years she had thought that he was too romantic, impractical, a dreamer. How could any woman live with him? He was too idealistic. Don Quixote dashing here and there with a sword in his pants and a rose between his teeth. All those years wanting him. Maybe prison would change him. Maybe he wouldn't want her anymore. Thank God she was pregnant. That would give her at least another nine months to keep her feelings out of sight. When Angelina flew back from Denmark over the Christmas holidays and talked so proudly about their free style of living in Copenhagen and all that stuff about free love and then she went off with Eden Maldek, Naomi felt all kinds of weird feelings. How could Angelina do that? David was still in Greece in jail.

And then came the miscarriage; her second one.

Rushing to the Emergency at three in the morning. All that blood and disappointment and loss. To lose the baby really hurt. It scared Naomi too. She knew now that she had to do something about her marriage. She couldn't stay much longer. No matter what. But what would she do? What would David do? What if he stayed over in Europe? The thought of not being with him felt like a dead weight in the middle of her heart.

They had such a big house. David and Angie could live with them. They could have the downstairs bedroom next to the kitchen. David could put in a vegetable garden and he could dig out the blackberry vines that were taking over the grove of pine trees in the front yard. Naomi wanted to look at him now. She could see his face so close to hers, but his kisses felt so delicious and warm and kind on her skin that she couldn't keep her eyes open. As she lay in bed with him for the first time, her heart pounding and her hands covering her vagina, ashamed that he would find her ugly, he gently took her small hands into his large ones, calling her beautiful and beloved and kissing her with his soft, sensual lips. His kisses lingered on her crushed mouth and on her throat and nipples as he searched out secret places. Places never kissed before. Places that caused her to burn with both shame and excitement. She almost giggled. He had such soft animal noises as he hovered over her. She had never felt so looked at. Or so appreciated. She felt like some strange flower. She pictured him as a hummingbird, the delicate tip of his tongue darting inside her, tasting her, sucking her, as if her whole body were nectar. She shivered suddenly. She wanted to speak but couldn't. She wanted him inside her. Now. Oh, please. She reached out instinctively. She found him and wouldn't let go. Later, she expected him to turn away from her and fall asleep. Or go make tea. Or read the morning paper. But he surprised her. He didn't leave. Instead, he wanted to talk, he wanted to hold her, he wanted to kiss her.

"I eat crackers in bed," she told him.

"So?" he said.

"And I wear socks in the winter time."

By now he suspected she was teasing him.

(Although she did have awfully cold feet.)

"My boobs are too small," she protested.

"But that's not true!" David assured her.

He meant it too. Naomi had lovely, exquisite breasts, and he was astonished at her admiration for bigness.

"And my legs are funny. You said so yourself."

"Aw, I was only teasing you, Naomi. I know how sensitive you are."

But did he really?

Being away in Greece, David would have no idea how much things had changed in her marriage. Now, she almost never undressed with Marcus in the same room. She even went into the closet, closing the door, to change her clothes. She hated wearing a bra but she never went outside the house without one. She knew that Marcus wouldn't approve. Marcus even thought that she was frigid.

"The space between us feels like home," she murmured.

David smiled knowingly. "Your body is my home."

"More," she whispered in his ear. "Oh, please, please."

This time she didn't cover herself.

Are we all not one?

My love,

I'm in Boston. Dusty's sister and husband are housing me. They have a grand old house outside of the city. Trees, earth, birds, squirrels, and a dog plus two cats. I share the cost of food and help around the house. Michael goes to school and works and Susan works. I planted some bushes, chopped down some young sapling trees, pruned branches, cut grapes, and my biggest project is Susan's studio. Stripping off wallpaper, about five layers. House vintage 1886. Then white paint. She plans to open an etching studio before Christmas at home.

My first few days in America. Wow, culture shock. There really is such a thing! Business, a mess of papers, photographs and the Danish Consulate. I mail everything to New York and pray for sunshine. Over a week now and no news. I asked them to hurry. That's like pissing in the wind. Meeting people, selling a friend's jewelry at Howard Square, looking at stores. Half of America is junk. Called my aunt and Melina called me. We had so much to say trying to speak it all in 3 minutes. Frustrating. Afterwards we sat down and wrote to each other. She's still thinking about coming to us in Denmark. I do hope I make it home for Christmas. And a second coming when you arrive. Wear warm clothes!

Angelina had returned to America for a short visit. Something about going to Boston to see the Danish Consulate. She wanted to get a student visa so that she could remain in Denmark. She and her Danish friend Lily had cooked this scheme up. Angie would take ceramic lessons from Lily and the pots they made together would be sold in the store-front window of Lily's flat. Lily had studied ceramics in Japan. There she met Jun, a Japanese ceramics student. Jun fell in love with her. They married and he returned to Copenhagen with her and enrolled in the Royal Academy of Arts in Copenhagen, or whatever it's called. The details I got through Angie's letters seemed a little sketchy. Last spring she wrote me a long letter, telling me about Lily. In this letter, among other things, she wrote:

I have just moved in with Lily and Jun. They lived around the corner. I'm sleeping in the kitchen temporarily till my room is finished. I pay no board but cook and clean and create and inspire and generally just be myself. A little later a system for collecting fun and pocket money will work itself out. Everything does come along, good old Barney! To describe Lily, I can only say I wanted a relationship like this one all the time we've been in Europe, because Melina and I were just beginning ours. It took 3 visits, Lily coming over to see me and the third time we were together there was no space between us. We understood and felt and communicated so deeply we could only look at each other and in the end say "I love you." It's so beautiful a thing, so mentally alive and so *deep*. We will all be together one day and you will feel the same and will then, if not already, understand my clumsy writing.

David, these last 7 months have been such a learning time. I really needed it all and hope to see and fit and complete the puzzle. When I feel good or should I say my heart is calm (or just the opposite), I can write letters. I know you accept my silence. It must still worry you, but please know you are with me 24 hours a day. I write so many things to you in my head. A million mind messages and one paper letter. And, you know, I feel you really know what I think to you with my head. Some day I will fully realize just how much you know me and will see more than just brief glimpses of your depth. The days pass and I think of our time when it began. Your gentle and beautiful way of guiding and teaching. The expanse of your vision still stops my mind. If I strayed too far off the path you gently placed me in the center and let me walk again until I needed guidance back. The path never left your sight and you never let me get lost or stuck too long in one place. My last lesson, or, should I say, the difference between Passion and Compassion, was what I was trying to work out. I now have felt Compassion; and it is Love.

Lily has an idea for an experiment. To spend a week or two weeks without sight and speech. To be away from any interference from people. Preferably in a cabin she knows in Sweden in the forest by a pond. We would wear those sleeping masks. Our only communication with each other will be through touch. To totally experience thought without the subtle interferences of sight and speech. Uninterrupted thought. The experiment can only be complete with sex. As sex is involved in our total being and let's say the whole test has to be a complete unit of life. To sharpen our dormant or dull senses, expand and move beyond limited sensual observations and conditioning. I feel it can be such a good thing. We will stop to think on it for a while and then discuss it later....

And the two-eyed devil is pride. What a monster I have with me. We were discussing it last night and Lily was helping me to look at myself and how I used my pride to control other people and how worthless it is. I never thought I had pride or that it was a problem I needed to work out. Naturally I didn't. Whammo, right on the old proud chin. My next work is dissolving the myth that a Gemini is a jack of all trades and master of none. The number of things I'm able to do, naturally is unimportant; but my ability to complete it as well as possible (on all levels; in all directions) most definitely will not sleep while I'm in command. Onward Angelina. My hands are showing me many things, even the ability to become a palmist. Ironic?

Shucks no. I'm just an old sod kicker at heart. Somedays I'm fire—somedays I'm earth—but always ready to move as wind; not to avoid but move over the unnecessary. Fire engulfs—earth maintains stability. And water, of course—penetration—absorbing—fluidity—reflection—sure am water too. Just an all around sort of A. girl B. woman C. being D. existence E. God F. take your pick, it's all the same.

And you know what, I'm SKINNY too! La-da-da-dah

> Ain't she sweet
> Joker Joker
> Jester
> Queen of Hearts
> Madwoman
> Witch and
> Elf-luna-tic
> tak-toe

This silk screen is from Lily. There were five and I wanted the one that was closest to you. But, again, is it me? Are we all not one and the same? Isn't there something so fine, so subtle, in all of us that is the same? Something so deep and simple. What it is I can't seem to touch with words. My mind runs into an empty space when I tried to discuss it with Lily. If I chase it, it runs faster and always just out of reach. It must come of itself. Do you know it's essence? My god, it's 4 in the morning and we've been sitting here writing since 12. I lost all time. I do that every day. I haven't known the date for a month....

The only thing I have to give anyone is Love.

I am alright and always will be. I think I'm un-sinkable. My problems work themselves out and show me many things. I am learning to live and especially to live with people, and how to quiet myself in the middle of a storm.

I had mixed feelings about going to Denmark and about the whole situation. Whatever the situation might be. I didn't ask Angie many questions and I had an uneasy feeling about Lily. Everything seemed pre-arranged and set-up and controlled. They hadn't even asked about my feelings. What if I didn't want to live in Denmark? I pondered this for a long time. Finally, I decided to consult the *I Ching*. Using fifty broom straws as divining sticks I threw hexagram 12: P'I: STAGNATION, OBSTRUCTION.

Hmmmm.

I decided to ask the *I Ching* about our relationship. A funny question to ask maybe, but why not? I phrased the question carefully. "What is the necessary action that Angelina must work out with me and I with her? Why are we here together?"

I threw hexagram 31: HSIEN /ATTRACTION, SENSATION.

That made sense. But the hexagram showed movement in the second place, indicating possible misfortune, with the resulting hexagram 28: TA KUO /EXCESS.

Too much of a good thing maybe? Perhaps I shouldn't have asked!

On the work farm I move in a day-to-day routine, working in the fields, and, after lunch, sitting quietly, sometimes writing and sometimes doing nothing. I don't play cards with the others or even read much. At night before going to sleep I sit quietly in meditation. Some nights I watch the whole room turn to light. Are my eyes going bad? I can't decide. Finally I mention this to Whitmore. He gives me a funny look. He says maybe I'm on to something. I sleep long hours and dream a lot. I decide to think about Denmark later. I have no urgency to do anything about that right now. Nothing I can do anyway.

Aspirations of a poet,
Or,
A minor urge to explain myself

I want to steal your poems.
I want to carry them off
To a secret den
In the undergrowth
Of a deep forest.
Devour them
Like a fox
One by one.
Like berries of summer
Like rain water
Like salt

I want to carry them upstairs
To my bed
Press them into my dreams
Like flowers
Like seeds

I want to spread them all
Over the kitchen table
Eat fresh tomato
Sandwiches
And honey and bread and tea
All over them until
They are covered, stained
And spotted with food

I want to roll your sensual
Phrases into bread dough
Dip wing tips
In my tea

I want to throw your words
Into my bathtub like suds,
To immerse myself
Soak them in
Absorb them through
My skin.

I want to carry them back
To my childhood, back to
The secret places
Where I hungered, where I
Starved for soul food.
Seal them in jars like fruit
Hoard them.
Hide them in a cupboard.

I want to steal you muse
Sleep with her
All night
Naked in tangled sheets

I want to call your poems
Out my window
On those grey, desolate mornings
When there have been no stars
No sunrise for months

Call them out
Over the prosaic street
Which is also
The enchanted street
Of my dreams

I want to rob you, beg
You, lay myself at your
Feet

Oh beautiful one,
Grey eyed, rose faced,
Muse faced gypsy.
Innocent.
Sensual, red lipped enchantress.
Changeling
Dancer
Image spinner
Sister of words
And water

I want to smear your poems
All over my body
I want to press my body
Against the pages
Until I push through
Push through
Into magic

Audy Davison,
"Asha's Poems"

∞

At first the poet bends the world to his desire. He distorts appearances. The poet nourishes upon his great emptiness. Greed swells his eyes and clutters his bowels. Envy obscures his vision. To hurry forces him to invent. He loses touch, he stalls and over-exposes himself. He plays the Fool, the Beast, the Chosen One. (The ego is a master of disguises, have you not noticed? And, please, I use the male pronoun only for convenience. Man, woman: we're both in the same leaky boat.) The poet reminds us how he sees the world in a "special way." (Through his nose, up against the mirror.) He's terribly sensitive, this poet; and you're on thin ice. He craves attention; he's jealous of power and always staring into the light, which causes him to squint perpetually. His words possess secret intimations; clues to his astral whereabouts. (He's usually in the bedroom, second only to God, and out on a limb.) Life turns on him at every corner. He suffers out of neglect and false pride. (It is not yet his time.) But, here and there, the great poet catches with his verses a single, shining moment; a glimmer of truth and his individuality, and the oneness of all life, and the continuous stream of creativity which flows through each of us. He's horrified, delighted, ecstatic. Which is real: this world of appearances or the mind? and is there a difference? and how do we know? (How do we know anything?) How will the poet escape self-deception? *What he is is what he sees.*

∞

"Transformations,
diabolical urges &
divine inspiration"

Three months out of the university with a Masters in Fine Arts and the job scene in the Northwest is a bust. I'm lucky to be picking beans and cucumbers, and polishing used cars, and landscaping gardens on the ritzy west slopes of Puddle City in the pouring down rain. What the fuck am I doing *here???* My friend Michael Ruby's laughing so hard he can't find the chords to his guitar. "You mean, my friend," he says and quotes one of his own songs: "This ain't the dream I dreamed?" Michael grabs his 12-string and a handful of acid, leaves out the back door of the old Avatar Tavern on 23rd and NW Burnside, and takes a merchant ship to Alaska. Melina says good-bye and goes off to New York City on a scholarship. Flaky Joe (the handsome one) gets some girl pregnant and hightails back to Florida. And I cut south to San Francisco.

But sooner or later we all come back.

(Except Flaky Joe.)

I'm living on the edge and evening of Haight-Ashbury, with riots and revolution in the streets, and five days a week and over-time, too, I'm punching a clock, and eating raw brown rice and seaweed and arrowroot. I'm smoking paregoric and Mexican dynamite and going through knot holes, and dreaming of back alleys in Eugene, Oregon, and thinking of a Mad Hungarian from Minnesota with knife slashes on his chest, and remembering a married woman I once loved and who loved me.

What the fuck am I doing *here???*

To get out of the 40-hour-a-week-rat-race, as my friend Marcus Holmes enthusiastically explains to me, (as Naomi bribes me with her dark, burning eyes), I'm going in at six a.m. to short order hot cakes at the Moon Palace Cafe for the factory gang on NW 14th and Warehouse Avenue in Portland, and living on cheap wine and poetry. The Health Inspector shows up and tells me the beard has to go. Remember this is '69, and I do mind, but the guy looks dead serious. We're living just off 19th and NW Lovejoy and Melina's paying the rent, but she's all nerves, and terrified of the dark, and can't make sense of her dreams...and I don't know what to say to her or anyone after Bob Dylan and ten thousand pages into Carl Jung.

The Moon Palace Café goes bust.

I get a job for one year as Director of Continuity for a top 40 station in Portland. The programmers of official morality, decency and respectability, they were, if you believed what you heard on the radio. "You say *fuck* on our stage,"—this to Canned Heat, a hot rock group the radio station had sponsored at the Coliseum—"and we'll not play your songs over the air." ("You bastards!" underneath their breath).

I watched them, these programmers of official morality. Any-and-everything to make a buck and to buy themselves a little protection in the world, a little respectability. And ME—who wanted to achieve satori and live in TRUTH—what the fuck am I doing *here???* What could I say to my friends? What excuse could I give? How could I explain? *This isn't the real me!* "Well," self nags self endlessly, "why dontcha walk out? Are you here for a reason? or lack of imagination? or for the money? Secret irons in the fire? (Meaning Jo Myhra.) There are other jobs. You're not proud, *remember?"*

"Heaven's own, ringed servants
& dust in his fiery hair,
& his spirit wrapped in blue"

In this world it seems power is the answer. But that implies a question and I want to know WHO asked the original question. Life is a quest for identity, I believe, not power. This burning question WHO AM I? has long ago, since the beginning of time, set my mind and heart on a course toward a timeless returning home: through visions: through dreams and countless deaths: through travels to different lands: through sadness and unbearable pain and the most exquisite pleasures: through magical stones, postures and mathematics, has this course remained as true as the remembrance of light. Never veering, never disowning the Source. In spite of my mind and the errors of my thinking. In spite of my romance with magical powers. In spite of drugs and prison. In spite of books. In spite of my circular efforts and my two steps forward and one step backwards. In spite of fear and desire and the arrogance of my pride. You see, I like to set the stage, and the director within me would control every line, gesture, and movement. The moon and stars and Creation too. All this, when, the truth be known, I don't even control my own unruly thoughts. I identify myself with the Magician; yet I see all magic as illusion. The greatest magician, I believe, is not the one who creates illusions but the one who sees through the illusions of the world. But what do I know about the world and illusions? What do I know about anything? Still, I believe that in the realm of dreaming all is possible. If you have the power. Yet I have refused to court power. Perhaps the Fool, rather than the Magician, would more aptly reflect back the inner image

out of my mind's mirrored tarot. The child in the golden dawn
reaching for a rose on the tree of life, protected by a lone wolf
on a leash. A beautiful, natural child, pure in the manifestation
of his new-born heart. Or perhaps the foolish, colorful Jester.
Yes, the happy-go-lucky Jester, unaware that he's about to step
off a dangerous cliff, totally trusting in the universe to take
care of him.

And why not? It always does.

(Once you remember.)

Come, I would say to truth

To speak directly to your heart, (there's only one way), I must
write from the heart. When the words come through the heart,
try as I may, I cannot force the image. I start out to say "I love
you" and end up in a cosmological fire. One day, at Nafplion,
I found a tiny, bright yellow flower in the prison yard. How
this tiny flower escaped from being crushed by all the men
walking back and forth I know not. But there it was.

I've always been somewhat passive when it came to
"choosing" events which ultimately shaped the current of
my life, believing, like Don Quixote before the Windmills,
that Fortune directs my Destiny better than I ever will. So
sometimes I find myself in the oddest places. What I thought
to be Windmills turn out to be Giants; and these Giants wear
uniforms with a dull metallic eye over their foreheads, so that
I won't be deceived.

What would I be doing if not in this Greek prison?

Is this karma or destiny? Or just a twist in the stream?

Often I've wondered how San Juan de la Cruz could have
written such cheerful and luminous songs of the Spirit while
imprisoned in a castle dungeon.

My question seems meaningless.

I am here.

In other words, *Am I not the stream?*

∞

As a man and a poet, I would tell you the truth and nothing but the truth. I would show you my deep, heartbeating love for the mystery, the beauty, the stillness, the wonder, the vibrancy, believing this to be my purpose and the purpose of all poetry. But I still live as if truth is something Out There. Something that fits all, like a pair of stretch socks. Something that can be put into words and theories like the speed of light, or the cure for the common cold, or the number of angels on the petal of a medieval rose. I still live in the past, in ancient imprints—memories that limit and tighten my mind like a surgical ecraseur; or like the Chinese cloth bindings that were once used on the feet of female babies, in order to keep their feet small.

There are moments...there are moments.

But fear gets in my way.

"Come!" I would say to truth. I would face my fears. I would drop all my pretenses. But they go too deep, too close to my heart. Deeper than my meditations; deeper than my realizations. I still love the drama more than stillness. I love the excitement more than silence. Even enlightenment is something you do, something you achieve. Even Now is something you experience and hold on to in your mind. Something you control. I live in fear but I will not acknowledge this. That would be unmanly. I need safety but that does not fit into my image of a poet. Within me abides a great power: the power of tenderness and kindness and honesty, and the power of letting others be. But I will not acknowledge this. This power lies in wait behind the images that I fear so greatly. The images of separateness and death, pain and loss. I feel caught in a drama and I do not recognize the actor I play. I see the dreaming of the world but do not know the dreamer.

Angelina and I are walking together by a stream in a quiet woods. We're holding hands and laughing. Suddenly a deer appears before us. A lovely, magical deer. This magical deer will answer any question we desire to ask. We must ask quickly, without a moment's hesitation. I know exactly what I want to know. "What is the meaning of my life?" Instantly there appears before me two open hands, large hands like my own, filled with ashes.

I wake up. I'm in my bed in a Greek prison.

I feel alive, happy. The handful of ashes does not sadden me. They do not intimate my death or loss or annihilation. I understand this image represents a process of purification, of cleansing; the refinement of gross experience. Like Rumi, I have entered the divine fire. Like Ramprasad, I can say: "I have offered my gift." I have harvested the wisdom of my human experience. I have increased my knowledge (and the knowledge of all beings) and now I'm going home.

The whole room turns to light

You came to me
through a handful of light,
a mere cluster of stars.
You called to me
and I answered your call;
or was it I
who called to you?

I remember a desert,
a great burning distance,
a caravan of illusions
passing like rain between us;
and I remember mountains, bitter
as the betrayal of a brother,
not knowing if I would ever see you
or if I were simply dreaming;
and I remember walking
in the ruins of great cities,

down streets diseased, overrun

with neglect and the crying

of children.

And they say I went crazy,

that I cursed the Mother

Of All Living Things;

that I tore out my heart

and made war on the Earth.

And they say that you built a great wall

out of fear, out of anger and jealousy,
high as a cathedral around you,
and that you never came out,
a long time ago.

*It was such a cold winter I remember. At times
the chill numbed me to its destructiveness; mostly
though, it caused pain, sharp and biting. I lost
several fingers to frostbite, and a toe as well.
And the storm froze one dear one to death.*

*Even now it brings me pain and fear, the memory
does. No way would I ever choose to live through,
or even try to survive, such a lonesome freeze ever
again.*

*But you remind me that these are memories,
real enough to grip my bones and make me shiver.
Yet merely memories, nonetheless.*

*To tell my story, though, helps me, my brother.
The elders know this. Their storytelling is for
instruction, a passing on of wisdom. However it is
also so clearly a means to validate their experiences
and try to make sense of the pain.*

*Those fierce and unpredictable winds burned my
face and rubbed my soul raw. The winter was real
with a vengeance.*

*And now here, by the fire with you, the telling
of my tale softens the sorrow, begins to heal
the cold knifelike pain that lingers within me.*

∞

But most of all,
I remember how you turned to me,
in a garden called Choice,
the light dancing around us,
and not even the meadow grasses
in fields of white clouds,
or even the thoughts of angels,
could know such tenderness as the love
we felt between us,
our hearts one with all that is,
and we made this covenant,
each to each—
before the beginning,
before sorrow and pain and self-doubt;
before our journey into loss and separation—
a sacred pledge
that we would never forget,
that not even ten thousand deaths
or all the darkness in the world
could overshadow: this
moment:
this love:
this something-in-movement
that calls me to you.

∞

Alex Demianenko quietly paints a picture of a prisoner in his stonewall cell, as the prisoner meditates on a book. A shaft of light streams through the bars of the prisoner's small window. He could almost be a monk in some monastery cell. As Demianenko quietly paints, Keith Guellow writes a letter to his friends in Amsterdam. Across from us, on the other side of the room, four men gamble with cards—handmade cards that the ever-watchful guards missed in their last search. The guards also missed the camera smuggled in by Whitmore, when his sister came to visit him. (That's me in the center, wearing a tattered straw hat, next to Australian Mike and the old fellow from Pakistan.) At the moment I'm sitting cross-legged on my bed. A few minutes ago I took a shower. A rare shower, you can bet, because the only water we have is so incredibly cold. Yet my body feels warm, comfortable, quiet. All day I've been pondering the words of the Russian writer Solzhenitzyn in *Gulag Archipelago.* "Every human being has a point of view—Every human being is the Center of the Universe."

Suddenly, my thoughts stop.

Just like that.

The whole room becomes instantly, totally luminous. Not like other nights, when I've experienced the room as a gradual, brightening glow. Tonight it's like an explosion or a cosmic dance. It's like nothing I've ever known before. It's like the heavens opened up, if you can imagine that. The brightness fills the whole room, everyone and everything, and everyone and everything seems translucent, everything appears radiant, clear, and I am filled with this tremendous, superloving energy, this unlimited joy. Everything around me contains this energy. I am not in a trance. My mind has not gone blank. Yet the few thoughts that come and go seem like strands or wisps of thin clouds across an empty sky. How long this illumination lasts I do not know. A moment. Ten minutes. Perhaps twenty. The light seems to go on and on and I have no sense of time or fatigue or incompleteness. I feel so alive and joyful, humming with love.

FREE

"Now is a time of healing. Allow yourself to plunge into this time as into deep water, to immerse yourself. Do not fear. Do not judge. For judgments do not make sense. You do not even need to ask forgiveness. You only need to forgive yourself."
Darshalana

A cold day in hell

A giant cement cross towers high above us in the cold December sky. Inside the church, tiny blue-and-white triangular flags hang on strings that crisscross the nave; a deathlike drone praises all that is Holy; and a priest, dressed in golden robes and swinging a smoky jingle-jangle incense burner on a small brass chain, appears before us. The priest solemnly blesses the congregation with the sign of the Cross and then disappears back into the transept. We take our seats and the monotonous drone rolls on.

Today it's raining and there's no work in the fields. The two-striper has promised the foreigners that we'll all be given an extra half-day credit if we attend church services along with the Greeks. (It's a promise that won't be kept; but what the hell, I'm curious.)

A woman with a small child enters the church. The woman lights a candle and crosses herself three times before an icon of St. George and the Dragon. The woman lifts her little girl so that the girl may kiss the image of their patron saint. An uptight guard dashes across the aisle to warn a prisoner that it's forbidden to sit cross-legged in church. The priest returns and blesses a basketful of loaves.

(On the way out I help myself to a piece of their holy bread, hoping that it'll be sweet. But it's the same prison bread we eat everyday.)

I hear the jingle-jangle again.

In a cloud of smoke the attendant to the priest emerges from the back room. The attendant carries a long white candle that's burning. The priest follows him. The priest holds a large golden Holy Book in his hands. I can almost hear the "Ahhhs" and "Ohhhs" as we hop from our seats, our wondrous eyes spellbound upon this large golden book.

The somber chant continues. The priest returns once more. This time he brings two brass goblets covered in purple velvet. One goblet contains the symbolic blood of Jesus the Christ; the other, the bread that represents the body of Jesus. The priest speaks some words and goes through a routine with four of the little choir boys. By now, though, I'm bored with this priest and his mumbo jumbo, his rituals, his religion, and his God Almighty self-importance. The only warmth I feel in this church comes from the burning candles and the body heat from other prisoners. The day is cold, as cold as this church and cement cross feel to my heart.

They release me

It's New Year's Day. A guard comes in and tells me that I'm leaving. I hurriedly gather my few belongings. I dismantle my bed and return the mattress and frame. I check in my prison clothes. Last April, when I first arrived at the work farm, the guards put my personal clothes and belongings in storage. They issued me grey woolen work clothes. The pants were so large I had to run a drawstring through the belt loops just to keep them up. As for shoes, a guard pointed to a small room with a big pile of used boots on the floor. Naturally the boots I picked didn't match. Later, I saw the head guard and requested some of my personal clothes, which he gave me, and I asked him for a new pair of boots. Before I could even wear these new boots I had to visit the cobbler. The tacks in the soles of the shoes kept sticking through the leather into my feet. Actually, the same thing happened when I first came to Greece. I bought a pair of boots in Monemvasia and the nails nearly killed my feet before I could get to a cobbler. For sure, these people are NOT the Greeks who designed the Parthenon.

I'm missing a pair of winter trousers. Someone stole the pants when I hung them out to dry on the fence, I explain to the prison official. I bid fond farewell to my tattered straw hat. I say good-bye to Keith Guellow, to Alex and to Whitmore, to Fabio, to Charly, to Alan and John, to Mike, to Dominique.

Houssaine, an Egyptian, is also being released.

We hop into the back of the transport truck. First they drive us to a little police station about an hour's drive away. We stand around for another hour or so while they stamp and process our papers. Then we wait in the darkness on the side of the highway with two policemen for a public bus to Thessaloniki. In the cold, clear night sky a full moon shines over the Aegean Sea, only a few steps away. I can hear the sea's calm waves rushing in to the shore, just as they've done for thousands of years. What an incredible night to be alive and to be outside among the stars.

For the next two days the police keep us in the holding jail at Thessaloniki. On the wall between our cell and the guard desk a prisoner with a sense of humor, but not enough escape velocity, has scratched this message in large capital letters:

I TRIED TO ESCAPE BUT IT WAS THE WRONG WALL!

On the third day the police take me to the office of the American consul. Here I pick up traveling money and my back pack. Looking inside my pack I'm delighted to see that Angelina has stashed a small cloth bag with some of the marble stones that we gathered from the sea. These marble stones and my tiny white coffee cup from prison are the only souvenirs I'm carrying out of Greece.

Later, the police take Houssaine and me to the train station. They check to make sure we have sufficient money to leave Greece. I have enough money for a train to Denmark but Houssaine has just enough money to get across the border into Yugoslavia. That won't do the police say. So they take us both back to jail.

The next day the police tell Houssaine they're transferring him to Athens until his embassy can be notified. Since it's a holiday, however, a transport won't be leaving Thessaloniki for another two days. Houssaine goes into a screaming rage. He threatens to beat his head on the cell wall. There's not much I can do. The police hustle me out of the cell and back down to the train station. I ask for a ticket to Copenhagen. The man behind the counter tells me I can only buy a ticket to Belgrade. Once in Belgrade, he explains, then I can buy a ticket to Copenhagen.

A detective escorts me to the border. I have a ticket to Belgrade in my pocket. A customs official clears my passport. I'm surprised that he doesn't stamp my passport EXILED or BANISHED. The customs official smiles and jokes with me when he sees that I'm from America. I overhear a young woman in the next room trying to get in touch with a hotel in Athens. She's from England and she left her passport in the hotel room. Silently I wish her good luck. I look around and the detective who escorted me to the border station has disappeared. I'm standing on the station platform wondering what the hell I'm supposed to do now. Suddenly the train begins to move. In a panic I run to the nearest car and jump on.

That's when it hits me. I'm in Yugoslavia. I'm free!

On a train going north

I stare out the train window onto the bleak, dreary Yugoslavian landscape. Thick snow covers the ground and dead corn stalks stand bent and twisted in the fields. The gray sky feels leaden and oppressive. The train to Belgrade was crowded with soldiers and I had to find a side seat for the night in the aisle of the second class car. The soldiers look so young and their drab olive green uniforms so depressing. I think of the Yugoslavian folk painter Ivan Generalic. He's one of my favorites. Generalic's magical trees, his red bulls, his farmyard dances, his sunflowers that seem to touch the sky, his gypsies with their strange mysteries, his fairy tale winters—how could Generalic paint such wonder and beauty living in this harsh country? *Dhembirazi.* I'm here and I'm free.

The Belgrade train station feels like a genuine mad house. I mean, sheer craziness. A half-hour goes by in a jostling, rude crowd of ticket buyers before I finally arrive at the ticket window. The woman behind the ticket window informs me that I do not have enough dinars to buy a ticket to Denmark.

"How much more do I need?"

The woman tells me and I rush back to the currency exchange line. I have no idea when the train for Denmark will leave. Perhaps already! Where will I stay overnight if I've missed the train? I'm low on money. Angelina's waiting. I feel panic setting in. Carefully I exchange just the right amount of drachmas. I fight my way back to the ticket line. This time I decide to get in the other line because it looks shorter. Now, the woman behind this window tells me that I don't have enough dinars. Shit, can't they even agree on fares? I persist. Finally the woman agrees to accept three American dollars in place of the missing dinars, and I leave with my ticket.

In the crowd I see a man about my own age and he's obviously a foreigner like me, and he's obviously coming straight toward me. He's an English traveler on his way to Munich, back from India. "Belgrade is worse than any place I've seen in the East!" he swears. He tells me that it's too late for us to reserve second class seats. Hell, I didn't even know you could reserve second class seats. The train is scheduled to leave in two hours. We find the train and it's jam packed with workers on their way back to Austria and Germany, after the Christmas and New Year's holidays.

We have to stand all night, all the way to Munich.

To sleep is impossible. Just as I'm about to doze off, my head on my folded arms, leaning against the train window, my back arched across the aisle, along comes a happy second-class ticket holder, a drunk on his way to the toilet. This goes on most of the night. Perhaps, I muse, this is ALL part of the Greek's vendetta. Even my release is a wooden horse.

In the early light of dawn appears the graceful, picturesque beauty of Austria. As we cross the border into Germany, however, the customs police act totally impersonal, cold, and even rude. Our train finally pulls into Munich about ten. My traveling companion and I part company and he disappears into the crowd. At once I'm struck by the sense of order and comfortable familiarity of Munich. Standing on the loading platform I leisurely roll my head across my shoulders a few times, relaxing my body, stretching my arms and legs and rib cage like a cat. I go into a little restaurant and order a cup of black tea. What a simple pleasure, to enjoy a cup of tea without ANY GUARDS at my side. Without any uniformed guards, at least.

I remember an incident right after my arrest. Two policemen were transferring me from the holding station at Sparta to the regular prison at Nafplion. While waiting for a public bus we went into a small cafe for coffee. The police took the cuffs off my hands and we were sitting at a table drinking our coffee. A young Greek at another table gave me a salute. He walked over and paid for my coffee. The gesture of comradeship touched me.

I finish my tea and send a telegram to Angelina, giving her my exact time of arrival in Copenhagen. That leaves me with two American dollars in my pocket. I eat a piece of cheese from my pack and then go find a seat on the train. I'm almost—by two minutes—on the way to Berlin. I dash off the crowded Berlin train and down the length of the platform, looking for Hamburg.

On the Hamburg train I fall asleep almost immediately.

When we reach Hamburg they load the train car for Denmark onto a boat. We cross the Baltic Sea during the night. With only two dollars in my pocket I'm worried that Danish Customs might not allow me into Denmark. But they never even ask to see my passport.

It's almost dawn when I leave the train car and go aboard the transport boat to the restroom. I look at myself in the mirror. My beard's growing out again and my flyaway hair looks as dry as straw. My body's still thin and angular as ever (will that ever change?) and my shoulders look tight, but my eyes shine warm and bright and I certainly feel happy.

I take my time on the john. Then I wash my face and brush my teeth. I dry my hands and walk back to the train car.

BUT THERE'S NO TRAIN.

I can't believe my eyes. I turn around madly to check my directions. Yes, I came this way. See, here's the train track. BUT THERE'S NO TRAIN. I've got my passport with me, and my writings, but everything else I left on the train.

BUT THERE'S NO TRAIN.

I race down the track. In the distance I see lights and a station platform. I break into a desperate run. I catch up to the parked train and hurry to find my seat again. Sitting across from me, an old Swedish couple breaks into a smile of relief and understanding. I grin back at them. I take a quick, curious glance at the young, pretty, Swedish blond who's sitting beside them, but she's totally enclosed in her own private thoughts. (All night long we crossed the Baltic Sea together, how could I not wonder about her?)

Five minutes later the train pulls out for Copenhagen.

Sweet Jesus, there she is!

Enter the dark stranger

(What goes around comes around.)

That first night in Copenhagen, Angelina told me of the lovers that she had taken while I was in prison. Funny, in prison I had watched one marriage after another dissolving. Relationships that had lasted for years on the outside fell apart after two or three years of a man's life in prison in a foreign country. A man facing five, seven, maybe twelve or fifteen years for smuggling hashish, what could he expect? I watched strange things happen to prisoners who attempted to continue their lives on the outside. Many seemed bound to repeat themselves forever. Some, like Joseph, felt betrayed and turned bitter and took vows of vengeance. Others, like John, a drafting engineer from London, disappeared into makebelieve. John told fascinating tales of his life on the outside. But, then, later on, you or someone else remembered the movie or the book that his story came from. My own desire and intention had been to center myself firmly in the everyday life of chopping weeds and in my daily meditations and writings. (Were my meditations—and all meditations—just another form of self-centeredness? destined to keep me spinning at the wheel? Certainly I had to consider this.)

I refused to indulge myself in thoughts about Angelina's life on the outside. I read her letters—letters that told me very little about what was going on—but I neither encouraged nor discouraged her plans for living in Denmark after my release. There's a wonderful poem by the Turkish poet Nazim Hikmet, a poem called "Some Advice to Those Who Will Serve Time in Prison." Hikmet was thrown in jail and sentenced to thirty-five years. The Turkish authorities convicted him of influencing students with Communists beliefs. Due to international protest, Hikmet was released early in 1951. So if you're ever in prison, say for ten or fifteen years, and you want advice on how to keep your sanity, how to hold fast, try and find a copy of his poem. Memorize it if you will.

Angelina left Greece to go to Denmark not long after my trial. The body was still warm as they say. She traveled to Copenhagen with a Danish man named Freddie. Freddie was married to—but not living with—a successful high-fashion model. He had a little export-import business. I met Freddie one day in Copenhagen when he dropped by to say hello. I did not care for him. He reminded me of Angie's first husband. He had a certain false bravado in his personality. I saw him as smooth, handsome, evasive and weak of character.

Angelina soon grew tired of Freddie. Alone and depressed, she met Lily one evening in a laundry mat. Lily offered her a smoke of hashish. The two women talked and Lily invited Angie to come stay with her and her husband, Jun, a young Japanese sculptor. Lily first met Jun when she lived in Japan. In Japan she studied under a master potter for two years. Jun was six years younger than Lily. Lily was about my own age.

In one of her letters Angelina had talked of coming to Greece for the summer, with Lily and Jun, the three of them to visit. This I did not encourage or even mention when I answered her. I had watched other prisoners, after visits from wives and lovers, go half-crazy with feelings of powerlessness.

(Angie did come to Greece that summer. This I found out in Copenhagen. She had even acted as a tour guide for a group of tourists.)

Lily and Jun lived in a basement apartment in the Osterboro district of Copenhagen. They sold pottery out of their street-level window. Actually, the apartment had been classified as a shop. This meant Lily received a price break on electricity and other utilities. This also meant that she wasn't supposed to be living in the apartment. Angie went back to America to extend her visa by claiming to be a student under Lily's training.

Jun went to the Royal Academy for the Arts in Copenhagen. He worked in stone and marble. He had a short, stout body, and strong, manual hands that expressed tenderness and sensitivity and sensuality in both his touch and his sculptures. That first night in Copenhagen, before Angie had a chance to really talk to me, Jun took me to a sauna in their district. He gave me a brief back massage. I liked his strong, healing touch. In the hot, steamy sauna I was able to relax and release the tension from the three-day train trip. I felt clean, resurrected.

Jun cooked dinner for all of us that evening. He prepared a delicious meal of fish and brown rice and vegetables stir-fried together. As I watched the two women ordering Jun to do this and do that, I saw the strange power trip that Lily and Angelina were running on him. They treated him almost as if he were a house boy. I had a hard time believing my eyes. But I said nothing. I simply watched.

Angie liked Jun, that seemed obvious. Jun and Lily certainly were not in love with each other. At one time they had been attracted to each other, Jun told me, but the first time they took acid together he realized clearly that he did not love Lily, even before coming to Denmark.

For awhile, Angelina told me, Lily had shared Jun with her. The two women even made love to each other, to find out how they felt. Both agreed they preferred men to women. Pretty soon Jun moved out of Lily's bedroom into Angie's. I saw a letter Jun had written to Angie, the time she went back to the States to take care of legal procedures for staying in Denmark. Jun really had been in love with her. And he still was. I couldn't fault him for that. I liked Jun. I respected his feelings. It had been Lily's idea that we live together in Copenhagen. Perhaps she had imagined that we all might be lovers.

In Lily's heart, however, there seemed to be little love for anyone, not even herself, although she read J. Krishnamurti and prided herself on her "consciousness." For Lily, any action seemed permissible, even the humiliation of the other person, because she had "awareness" of what she was doing. Or so she claimed. I had never before seen such misuse of the teachings of J. Krishnamurti, as far as I understood them. And, as far as I could see, Lily did not come from a place of loving awareness but from a place of control and manipulation.

Lily was superb in the game of controlling others. She instantly seized your most vulnerable spot, in the guise of kindness. She opened her protecting arms to shelter you from the storm, then she moved in for the kill. As she did with Jun. Lily nearly emasculated him psychologically. As she did with Angelina. Every thought of Angelina's was subject to Lily's analysis for approval or disapproval. As she attempted to do with me. Almost at once Lily set in on me, using Angie's love affairs as the sticky, interrogative threads to catch me in her web. She prodded and poked to get me to tell her my innermost thoughts and feelings, under the guise of "being open."

I sat on the floor in Angelina's room as Lily attacked me for hiding behind my wall of silence. As best I could tell, she wanted to intimidate me with her spiritual motivations, and to prod me with feelings of guilt, so that she might gain entrance to my soul and bring me under her power, as she had done with others in her life. I did not trust her. So I drew a circle around myself. I visualized a line of protective light. Lily could not cross this line; nor could she entice me out, to catch me in her treacherous web. I simply would not engage her in strategic dialogue; nor would I confront her. I knew that I could not confront her, for Angelina would interpret any confrontation as an act of ego and would surely defend Lily. I would have to wait for the precise moment to break the spell that Lily had over her. I realized once again, as I had realized when Angelina and I first met, that knowing when not to act was perhaps even more essential than acting.

Just how far Lily might take her logic, I didn't know. But one thing I did know: inside her soul there existed a place of great emptiness and great loneliness. Perhaps she saw herself as some kind of spiritual guru or high priestess. I could certainly relate to that. "I want to be enlightened, not imprisoned!" I remember screaming inside myself as I paced in a rage in a holding cell in Greece. To look around and see yourself *as just another prisoner;* to scream and rage at the walls inside you; to want to tear out your heart with your own hands; to shake your fist at God, your whole body trembling in rage and fear, because you have denied love for so long and you want love so much, and because love terrifies you more than anything, more even than prison and more than death; to want to be free and not know how; to be frightened to be free; to doubt your soul and everything that means anything at all to you; and then to see yourself in the midst of this storm as a teacher of peace, and in the midst of these dreams as someone awake, and in the midst of this journey as a traveler really going someplace; yes, I understood that. Perhaps Lily should go to India, to Poona. I had heard good stories about Bhagwan Shree Rajneesh. She could become one of his sannyasins. With her reddish hair she'd look good in orange.

We do not heal others. We do not change others. We can provide a safe, loving environment where they may dare to allow spirit within to heal. We can give others the space and understanding and support so that they may allow grace, they may allow love, they may allow spirit, and they may allow healing. We can love spirit in them, we can honor spirit in them, and we can recognize spirit in them. That's all.

When I learned of Angelina's affairs I let the pain pass through me like a dark cloud drifting across the sky. Angelina had done what she needed to do and I accepted that. Yet, something still felt unsettled. I felt a distance between us, a dark wedge, and I felt troubled. For the first time with Angelina I felt that I had one foot in the bedroom and the other in the street.

When I finally questioned her about this dark matter between us, this was the moment she had been waiting for. She then told me about Eden Maldek, and she showed me the love letters that he had written her.

Back in Oregon over the Christmas holidays, Angie had gone to visit Eden. She went out of pride and curiosity, I suppose, and perhaps even with the idea of conquest or conversion. She spent the night with him.

Now I remembered. The fortune teller—the woman who told us that we would be wanderers for three years and that something would happen to me on this journey that would change my life—she had seen "a dark stranger" in Angelina's future. As I read Eden's letters, I knew without a doubt that he was this dark stranger. I knew that, of all her lovers, Eden

Maldek was the only one who could be a proper rival. But I did not want to battle with my friend. Besides, how do you battle over love and win?

Like Tweedledum and Dweedledee?

I pondered once again her affair with Eric. Now, almost two years later, I found myself involved in another struggle of power, with Angelina as the prize and treasure.

Or so it seemed.

Angelina had gone through inner changes and trials of her own. As far as I could see, she had acted with integrity and self-respect. I could not judge her right or wrong nor had I any desire to. I could not know her destiny or the life-lessons hidden within her choices. She would not intentionally lie to me; nor would she betray or deceive me, though it might appear that this indeed had taken place. The fact is, Angelina could not, and would not, ever betray anyone, herself or me. "Follow your heart," I had always told her. That's how we came together. That's how I live. You don't just stop. For this heart is love. Understand me, I speak of the heart that we call the center of our being. This heart connects us singularly to the web of life. This heart belongs to you and to the universe. It is the flame within that lights us the way to our destiny; a single flame that lights the universe.

Angelina had no desire to live alone and yet this situation constantly challenged her. She had lived alone for the most part of her first marriage, while her young husband did soldiering in Vietnam. Then, less than a year after our marriage, I went to prison for hashish in a foreign country. Angelina needed someone—or something—to merge with. She needed some great discipline, some higher order, something to give her young and restless energy spiritual structure. She needed to join the other, and she needed to inspire, and to motivate. Like a chameleon she could merge with her surroundings. This had happened between her and Lily. Angelina's mind had mirrored my own so perfectly—or so I thought—that it never dawned on me that perhaps she was doing the same thing in our marriage. I wanted to believe that she was my double, my twin, my soul mate. But now the game had changed. I had been a safety handrail for her. By loving and accepting her spirit, I had encouraged her to open herself fully to the wind. Now she wanted to fly. She wanted to soar.

Still, I was not caught altogether off balance. In prison I had centered myself in my solitude and in my aloneness and in my love for spirit. After my trial, I had wept a river of tears. I did not know if I would ever see Angelina again. In my own way I had already said good-bye to our marriage. My destiny called me in a different direction, even as I wanted to hold on to the sweetness and the light that Angie and I shared together.

My destiny carried a great promise; a promise that would not go away. Like Odysseus, an untravelled world lay before me. I remembered Naomi and her dreams and her eyes like luminous moth wings. I remembered the kind messages that Alora had sent to me in prison. I remembered a child chasing butterflies in his mother's garden. I remembered a boy playing Tarzan, swinging half-naked in Southern woods on long muscadine vines. I remembered a young man writing his first love poem. And I remembered Johan's simple and beautiful words: *"In the beginning there was you; then there was light and I saw you."* In time, I would cross the bridge to remember my own source and individuality—a luminous bridge that connects each and every one of us to all that's true and free and whole. I had no desire to lose Angelina. Still, I did not dread nor fear loss as I once had. Could I really lose what never was mine?

Now is the time of healing and of love

With thoughts of Dweedledum and Dweedelee, and losing Angelina, and Naomi with her luminous eyes and her dreams, and the words of Johann running through my mind, I drifted off to sleep that night; and in the night I had a most remarkable dream. In my dream Johann appeared, wearing his leather cowboy hat and denim jacket, bouncing all these colorful balloons into the air, and smiling that great, warm smile of his. As I watched him my heart overflowed with love, for I knew that somehow we were brothers. Suddenly Johan morphed into this tall majestic figure wearing a kind of Roman toga. The figure radiated a light of such sweetness and joy that I immediately felt safe and protected, but I felt so overwhelmed by feelings of love that I was unable to speak. The light being smiled and raised a hand in a gesture of peace and spoke to me in a voice as sweet and as strong as I had ever heard.

"My name is Darshalana. I wish to come to you for I have a great love of this woman you call Angelina, and I wish to speak a few words of encouragement to you at this time. For this is a very special time, and I am indeed honored to be a part of your experience at this time. There was an epic of separation on your planet, and the male energy particularly was caught within this pattern with a particular force and power. And each male who has come through this period has been imprinted with this in some way and feels it within himself. This is not a judgment. You were part of an epic. You played your part. You felt and saw and heard and absorbed into yourself and acted upon what was there for you to act and know and feel.

"Within time there are difficulties. There are hard times; there are painful times. Any soul who has lived upon this earth knows that. There is no judgment. You have come into a time when healing is possible, and all those individuals who find themselves within this time period upon this planet will be experiencing this energy. And they will be able to use it as they see fit.

"My friend, in this time and age of betrayal you acted certainly no worse and definitely much better than most. Do you know that? There was within you at that time a great revolt against this difficulty, this hardness, this betrayal and separation. Great anguish within you. And yet you lived in those times and you were committed to this planet. And you carried yourself through those times. Not in order to do damage. Not out of arrogance. But out of love. Indeed, the Mother has never turned away from you, and the female has never rejected you. Nor have you ever become unacceptable. The time of reuniting is here. It is beginning. It is occurring.

"The life you presently live is like a shadow to what you really seek. This is important. Remember this. You are meant to inherit the light, and you are meant to inherit all space and all wisdom and all movement that you desire. Understand this deeply within your being. Allow yourself to know that this is your natural realm, that you are not a prisoner illicitly seeking freedom, that you are not a monk who is trying to run away from his obligations. You are not the role. You are the spirit inside which lives naturally and is destined to inherit those places you covet. There is no need to grovel like a slave wanting jewels. This is your natural habitat.

"Now is a time of healing. Allow yourself to plunge into this time as into deep water, to immerse yourself. Do not fear. For fear is a part of that time and a part of that consciousness and experience. Do not judge. For judgments do not make sense. You do not even need to ask forgiveness. You only need to forgive yourself.

"The coming age is one of balance and equality. The female essence will not be more than you. It will not be there to overwhelm—but to be in balance with you. To do a delicate dance of equality, of evenness, of sharing, of touching. Of being as one and yet different. It is a time of honoring and a time of love. Allow yourself to feel these emotions. There is so much that you have to offer. You are greatly honored and loved. There is no desire to keep you distant but a great desire to embrace you and to feel again your power manifest in a way that resonates with the feminine essence, so that the female can again experience you in the fullness of your being. For indeed that is her joy. It is not that she has ever judged you, but only that she has missed you greatly. And also missed herself. For how can she experience herself if she does not experience you? Know that you are necessary. Know that your power is necessary. Know that you are an essential part of this process. Know that you are a motivating force of life. Know that without you there is desolation, loneliness, loss, emptiness, despair, sadness, remorse. Know that as you come into your fullness that you bring joy and life and renewal of all things.

"I am greatly attached and connected with this one you call Angelina. She is a great light; as be I. I am part of a network of light and points of light that stretch throughout this whole solar system, and each point of light is a point of love and wholeness and joy and creativity and acceptance and manifestation, and all of these points of light collectively sustain all of these systems and maintain a level of life, joy and abundance that even your greatest fears and severest limitations cannot effect in a serious way. I am a healer of mind sets. And I allow entities to see the restrictions and the limitations that they place upon themselves. And I help entities to shatter the limitations. Then it is up to the entity to choose to fly away out of their cocoon if they desire. Some entities have their cocoon shattered and yet do not choose to fly away. Some entities fly away to be free. In the days to come many entities will come, and I will assist them grandly as will this one.

"Follow your heart and all that you desire in your heart will manifest for you. But you will need to do what is called 'take action'. You will need to put it into motion. When it is put into motion you will have assistance. Follow it. You do this because it fills you heart with joy. It does not matter what another does. You can not save another. If you honor the god within you, you will honor all god in all beings. Know that. This is the difference between the old and the new. It is time now for you to save yourself.

"Love yourself. Do not turn away from yourself.

"Do not turn away from the male power and the male energy. Love it and embrace it—it is you. It is needed. It is desired. It is hungered for. Bring it forth with joy.

"This is a time of healing and of love."

Epilogue

That night of stars

Let me remember THAT NIGHT
OF STARS over the Aegean Sea,
& the Scorpions (those awful
Scorpions!) that slept
Beneath the rocks in our garden,
& let me remember (this one
time only)
Before we are swept away into
Eternity after eternity,
Just how your arms enCircled me,
& the air was quiet THAT NIGHT
OF STARS over the Aegean Sea